# Chapter One



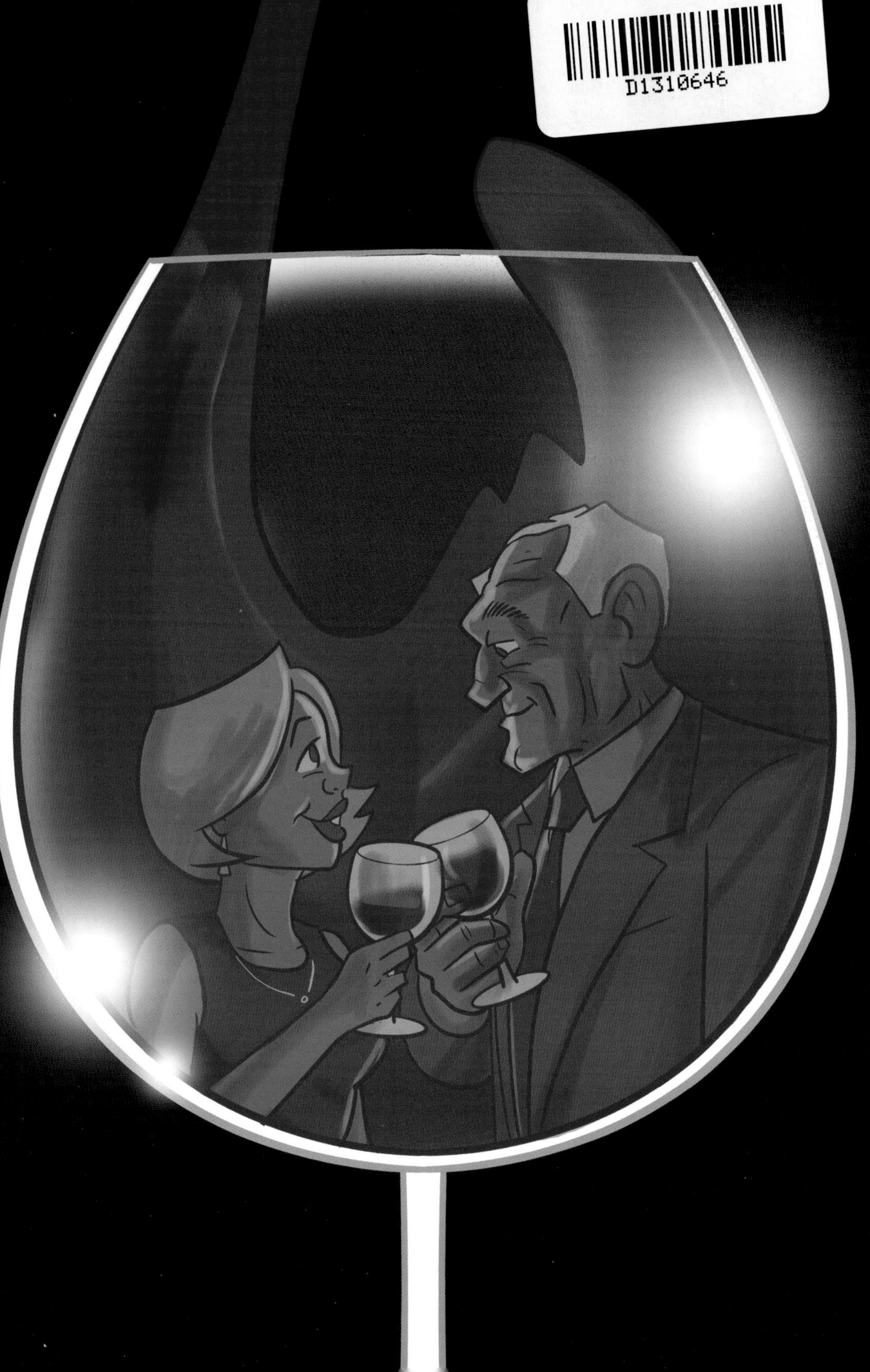

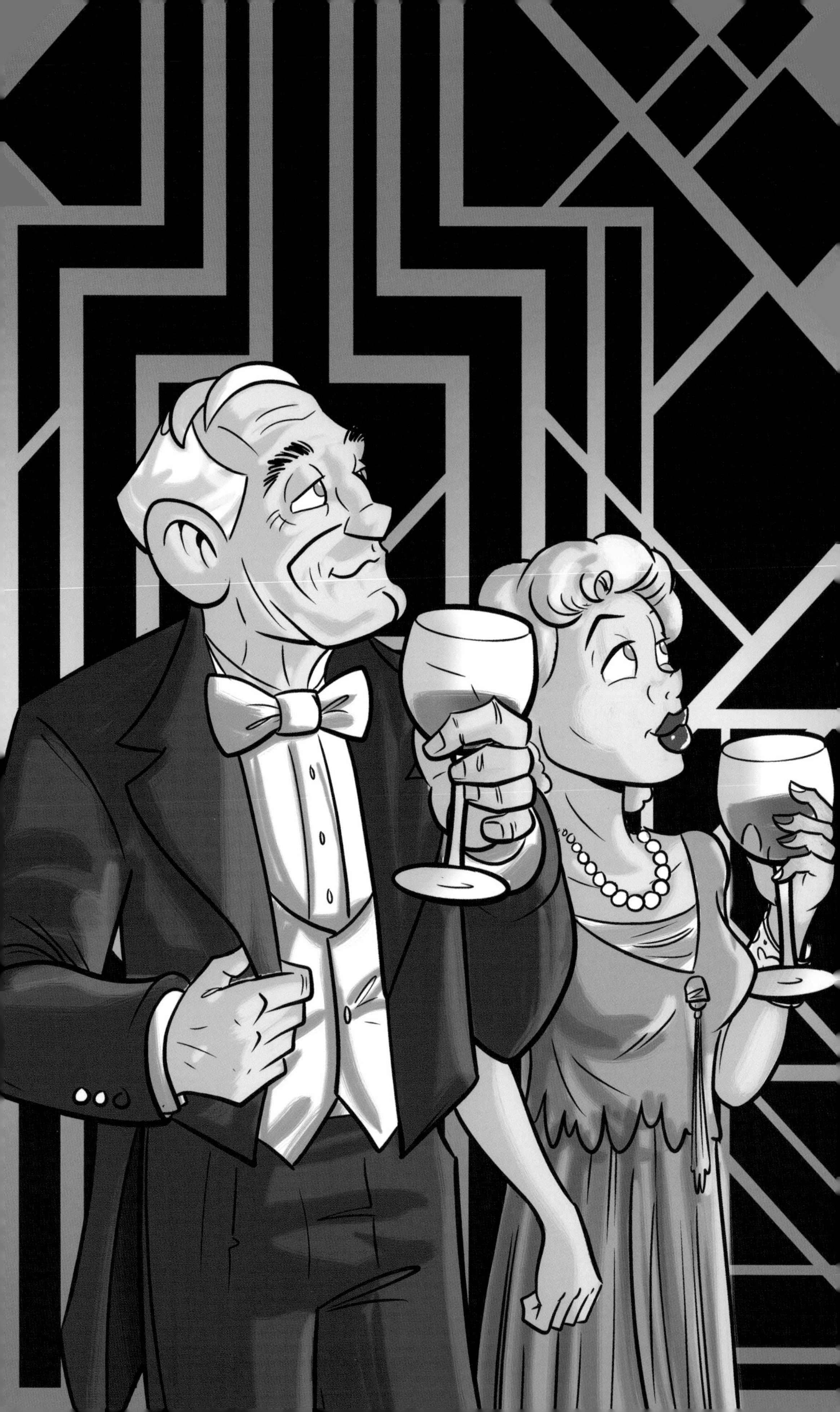

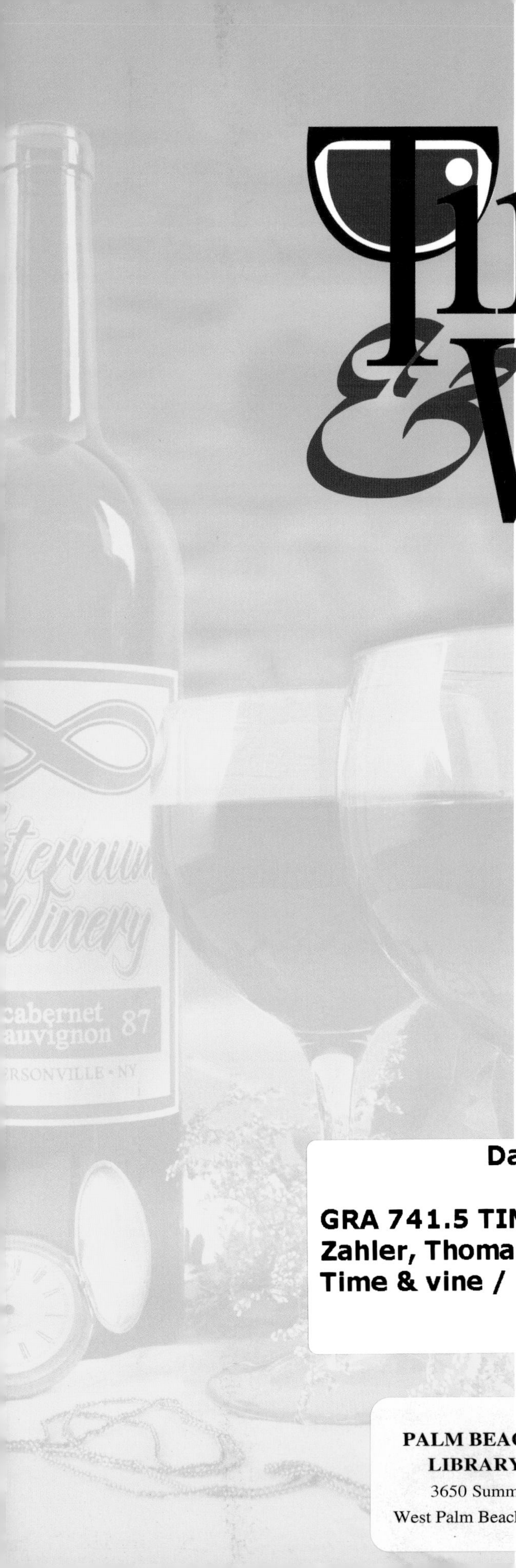
cabernet
87

# Time & Vine

story and art
Thomas F. Zahler

colors
Luigi Anderson

edits
David Hedgecock

*Collection Edits by*
## Justin Eisinger & Alonzo Simon

*Production by*
## Neil Uyetake

ISBN: 978-1-68405-036-9   21 20 19 18   1 2 3 4

Become our fan on Facebook **facebook.com/idwpublishing**
Follow us on Twitter **@idwpublishing**
Subscribe to us on YouTube **youtube.com/idwpublishing**
See what's new on Tumblr **tumblr.idwpublishing.com**
Check us out on Instagram **instagram.com/idwpublishing**

Ted Adams, CEO & Publisher
Greg Goldstein, President & COO
Robbie Robbins, EVP/Sr. Graphic Artist
Chris Ryall, Chief Creative Officer
David Hedgecock, Editor-in-Chief
Laurie Windrow, Senior VP of Sales & Marketing
Matthew Ruzicka, CPA, Chief Financial Officer
Lorelei Bunjes, VP of Digital Services
Jerry Bennington, VP of New Product Development

For international rights, please contact
licensing@idwpublishing.com

# So in the interest of topicality

I had two glasses of wine before I wrote this. I have never written the Intro to a book before so bear with me. ("Bear with me" makes it sound like there is a bear standing next to me reading the book, that is not the case. There's a cat with me… but no bears.)

*Time and Vine* is a magical time travel comic about wine and relationships. Really. I mean, who does that? Thom Zahler does that. It's such a unique concept and he's really put together something that is an incredibly fun and interesting read. It's engaging and weird in the best kind of way.

Megan and Jack's journey through this series is very emotional… and, like wine, meant to be shared. It's full of touching moments that really pull at the ol' heartstrings. Thom has given us something really unique with *Time and Vine* and I hope you enjoy it as much as I did.

## Katie Cook

*Katie Cook draws comics and has a lot of cats.*

for Mom and Dad...

...who showed me what
forever was for

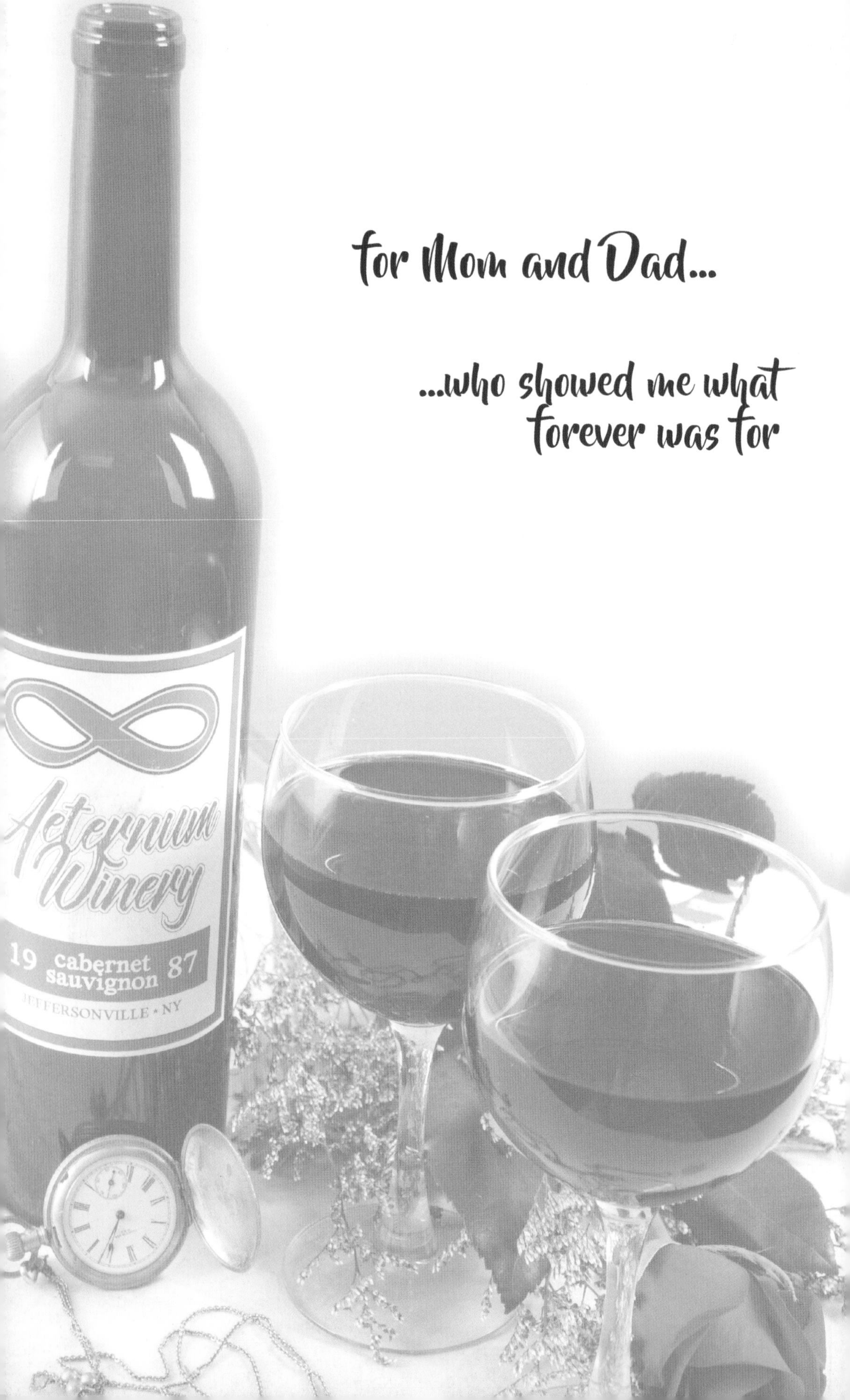
Aeternum
Winery
19 cabernet sauvignon 87
JEFFERSONVILLE • NY

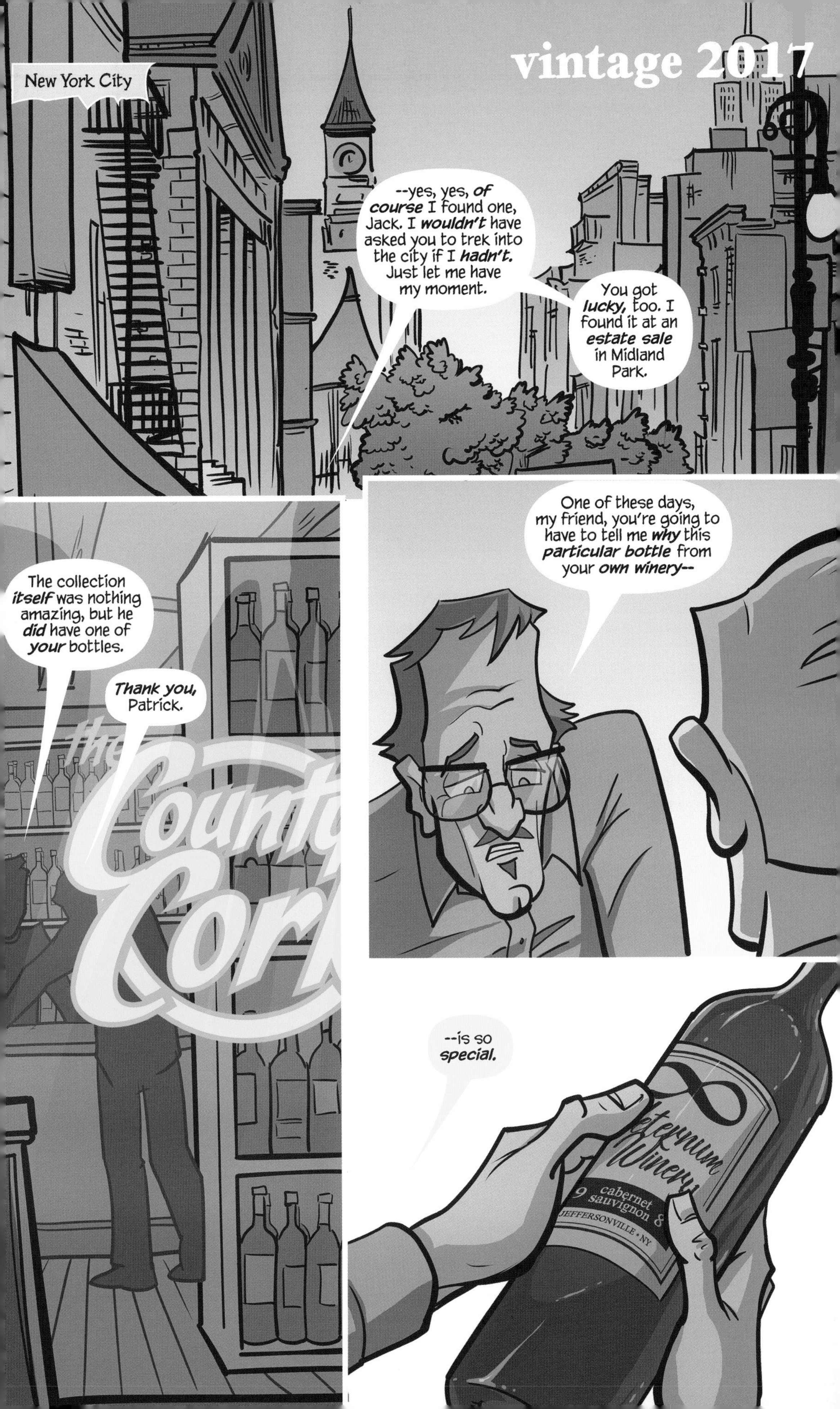

vintage 2017
New York City
--yes, yes, of course I found one, Jack. I wouldn't have asked you to trek into the city if I hadn't. Just let me have my moment.
You got lucky, too. I found it at an estate sale in Midland Park.
The collection itself was nothing amazing, but he did have one of your bottles.
Thank you, Patrick.
the County Cork
One of these days, my friend, you're going to have to tell me why this particular bottle from your own winery--
--is so special.
Aeternum Winery
9 cabernet sauvignon 8
JEFFERSONVILLE • NY

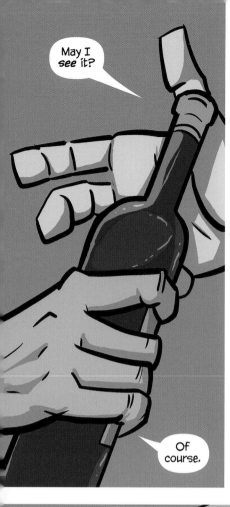

May I *see* it?

Of course.

I remember *bottling this.* The rains *weren't good* that year, and we had a much smaller crop. I had no idea *how precious* it would become.

What do I *owe* you?

You owe me *nothing*, Jack. Except an *explanation.*

*Someday*, Patrick, I promise--

--just not *today.*

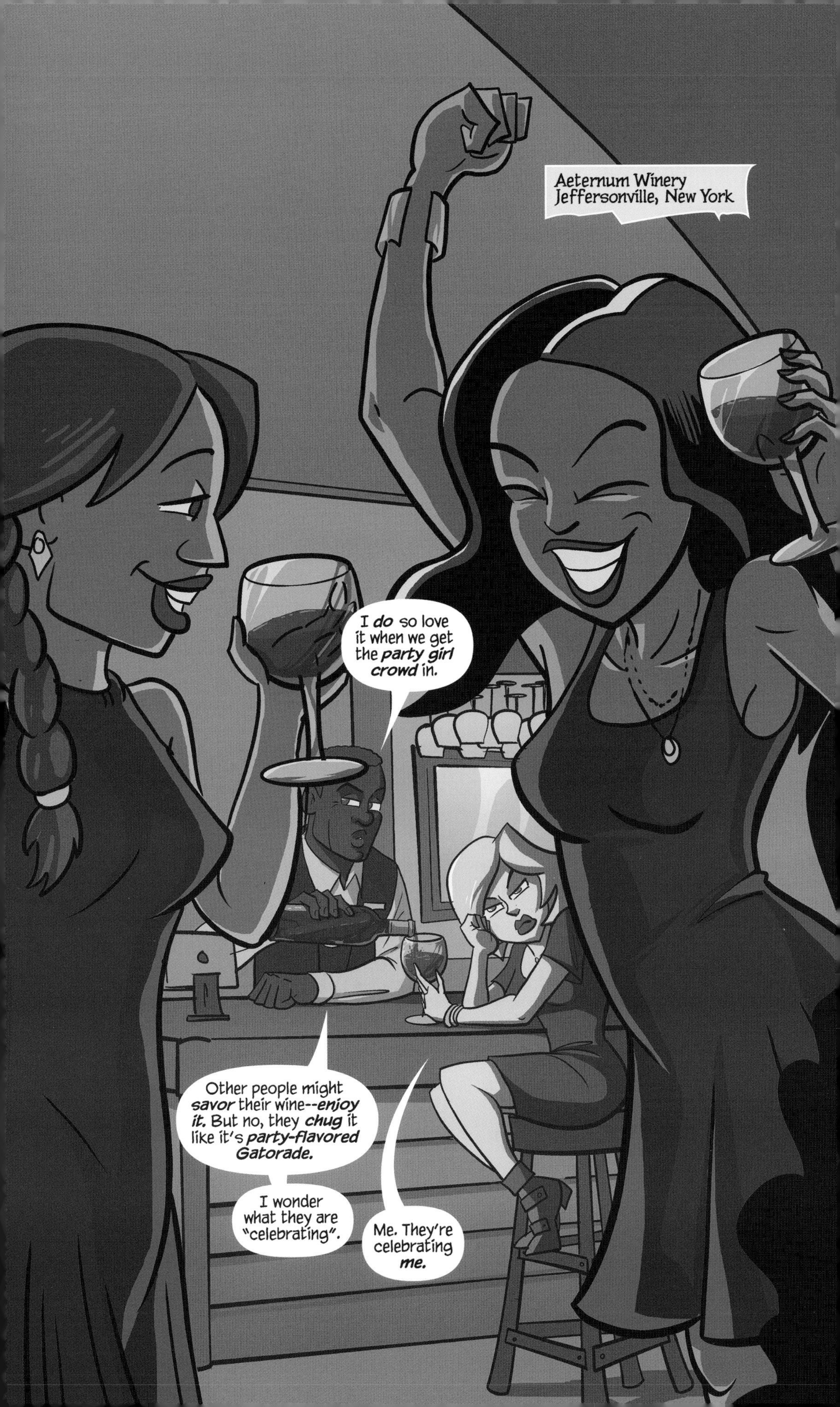
Aeternum Winery
Jeffersonville, New York
I *do* so love it when we get the ***party girl crowd*** in.
Other people might ***savor*** their wine--***enjoy it.*** But no, they ***chug*** it like it's ***party-flavored Gatorade.***
I wonder what they are "celebrating".
Me. They're celebrating ***me.***

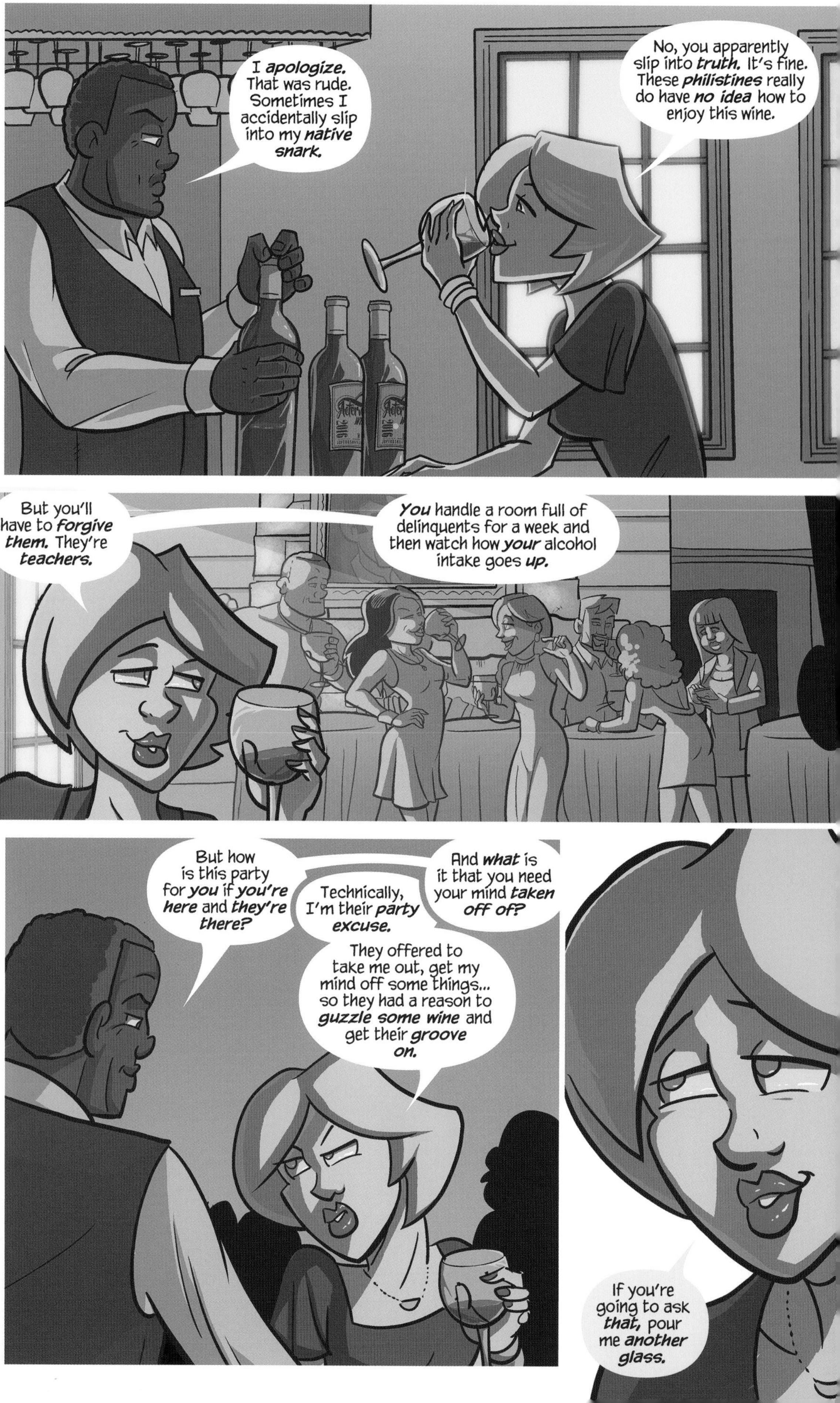
I apologize. That was rude. Sometimes I accidentally slip into my native snark.
No, you apparently slip into truth. It's fine. These philistines really do have no idea how to enjoy this wine.
But you'll have to forgive them. They're teachers.
You handle a room full of delinquents for a week and then watch how your alcohol intake goes up.
But how is this party for you if you're here and they're there?
Technically, I'm their party excuse.
They offered to take me out, get my mind off some things... so they had a reason to guzzle some wine and get their groove on.
And what is it that you need your mind taken off of?
If you're going to ask that, pour me another glass.

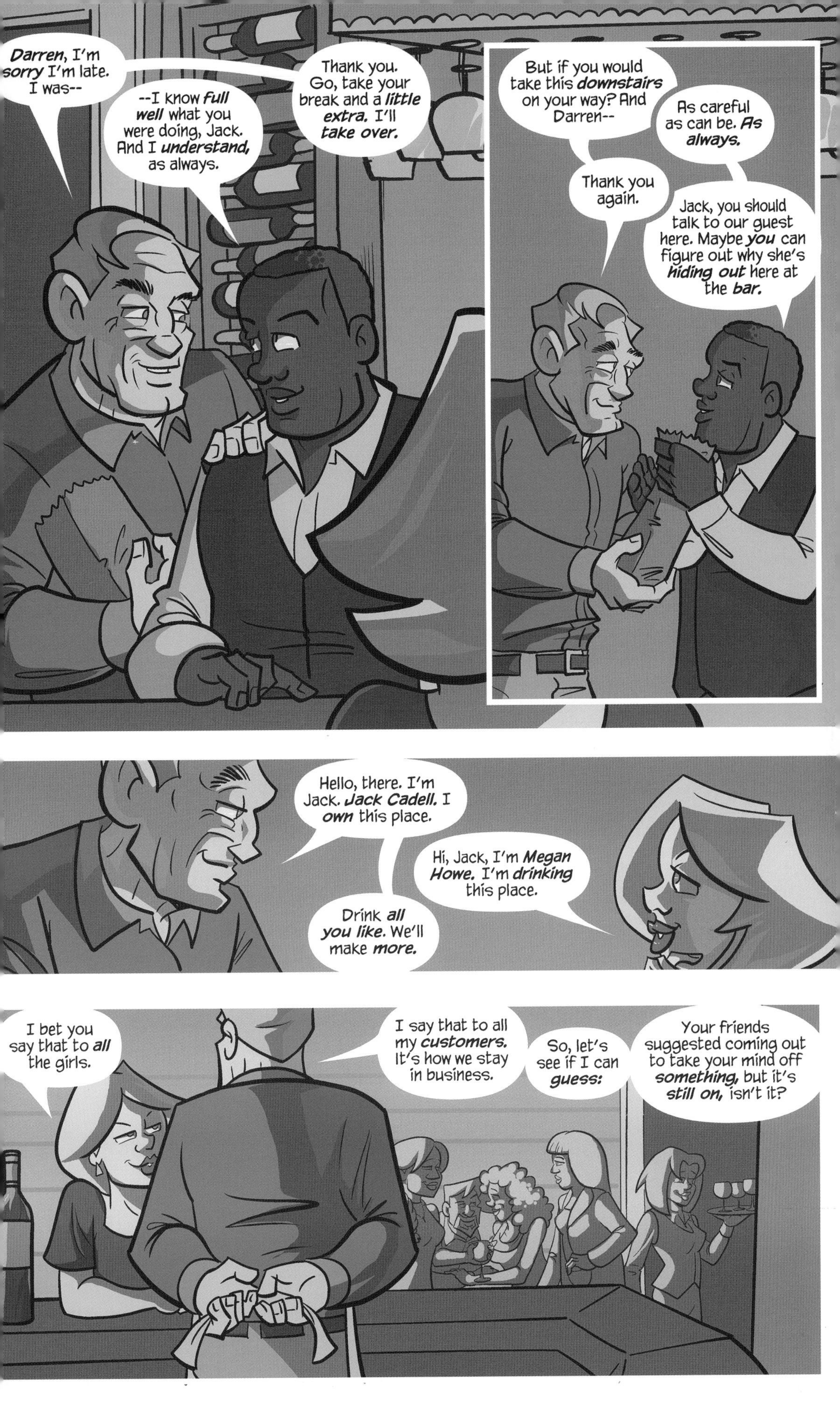

Darren, I'm sorry I'm late. I was--
--I know full well what you were doing, Jack. And I understand, as always.
Thank you. Go, take your break and a little extra. I'll take over.
But if you would take this downstairs on your way? And Darren--
Thank you again.
As careful as can be. As always.
Jack, you should talk to our guest here. Maybe you can figure out why she's hiding out here at the bar.
Hello, there. I'm Jack. Jack Cadell. I own this place.
Hi, Jack, I'm Megan Howe. I'm drinking this place.
Drink all you like. We'll make more.
I bet you say that to all the girls.
I say that to all my customers. It's how we stay in business.
So, let's see if I can guess:
Your friends suggested coming out to take your mind off something, but it's still on, isn't it?

Wow, you're *pretty perceptive.*

Well, I've owned this place for a *while* now. Yours is *not* the first case of this I've encountered.

So what is it?

→Sigh.← Why not? You're a *bartender.* Let's go *full stereotype.*

It's-- it's my *mother.* She used to teach *science.* She was *great* at it and *brilliant* to boot.

The last few years she's been a little *scattered.* But after *Dad died,* she had a *lot more* to keep track of, too. It seemed *natural.*

Then one day she called me from our *old house* wondering why there were *other people living in it.*

A house we *moved out of* in 1997.

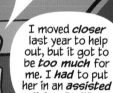

Oh, *no.* I'm *sorry.*

I moved *closer* last year to help out, but it got to be *too much* for me. I *had* to put her in an *assisted living facility.*

So that's what's on *my mind*: what's *left* of *hers.*

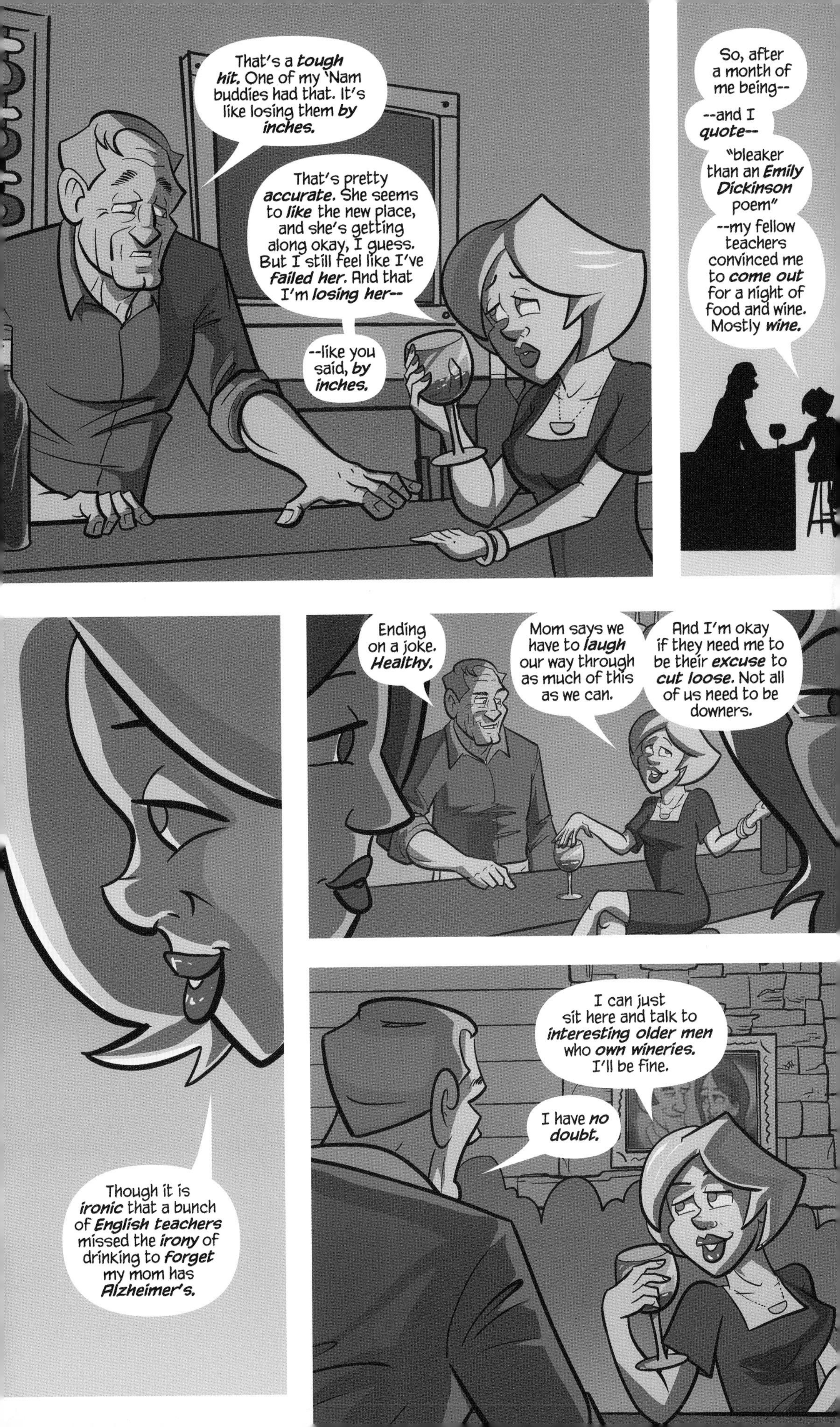
That's a ***tough hit.*** One of my 'Nam buddies had that. It's like losing them ***by inches.***
That's pretty ***accurate.*** She seems to ***like*** the new place, and she's getting along okay, I guess. But I still feel like I've ***failed her.*** And that I'm ***losing her--***
--like you said, ***by inches.***
So, after a month of me being--
--and I ***quote--***
"bleaker than an ***Emily Dickinson*** poem"
--my fellow teachers convinced me to ***come out*** for a night of food and wine. Mostly ***wine.***
Though it is ***ironic*** that a bunch of ***English teachers*** missed the ***irony*** of drinking to ***forget*** my mom has ***Alzheimer's.***
Ending on a joke. ***Healthy.***
Mom says we have to ***laugh*** our way through as much of this as we can.
And I'm okay if they need me to be their ***excuse*** to ***cut loose.*** Not all of us need to be downers.
I can just sit here and talk to ***interesting older men*** who ***own wineries.*** I'll be fine.
I have ***no doubt.***

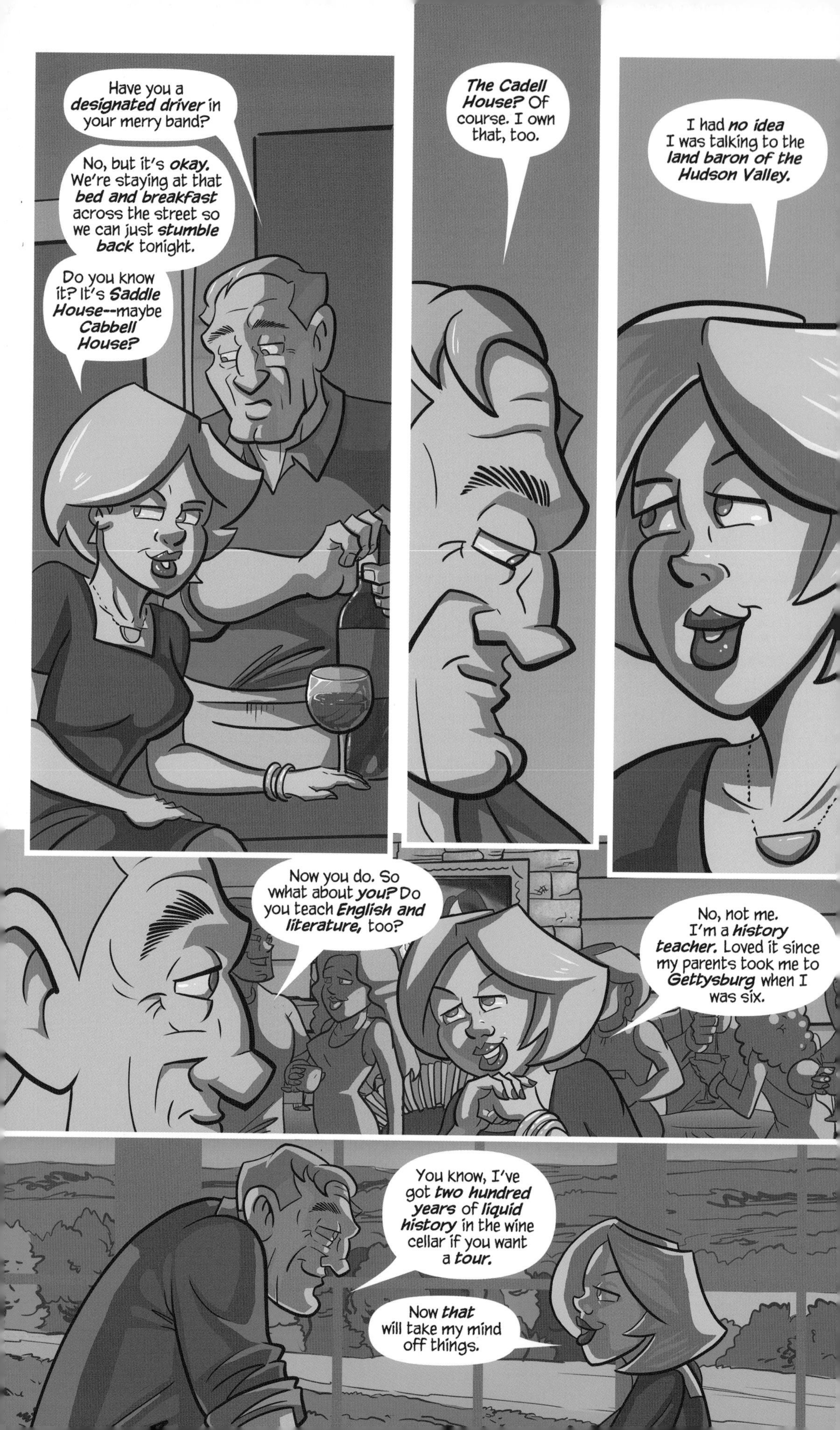
Have you a designated driver in your merry band?
No, but it's okay. We're staying at that bed and breakfast across the street so we can just stumble back tonight.
Do you know it? It's Saddle House--maybe Cabbell House?
The Cadell House? Of course. I own that, too.
I had no idea I was talking to the land baron of the Hudson Valley.
Now you do. So what about you? Do you teach English and literature, too?
No, not me. I'm a history teacher. Loved it since my parents took me to Gettysburg when I was six.
You know, I've got two hundred years of liquid history in the wine cellar if you want a tour.
Now that will take my mind off things.

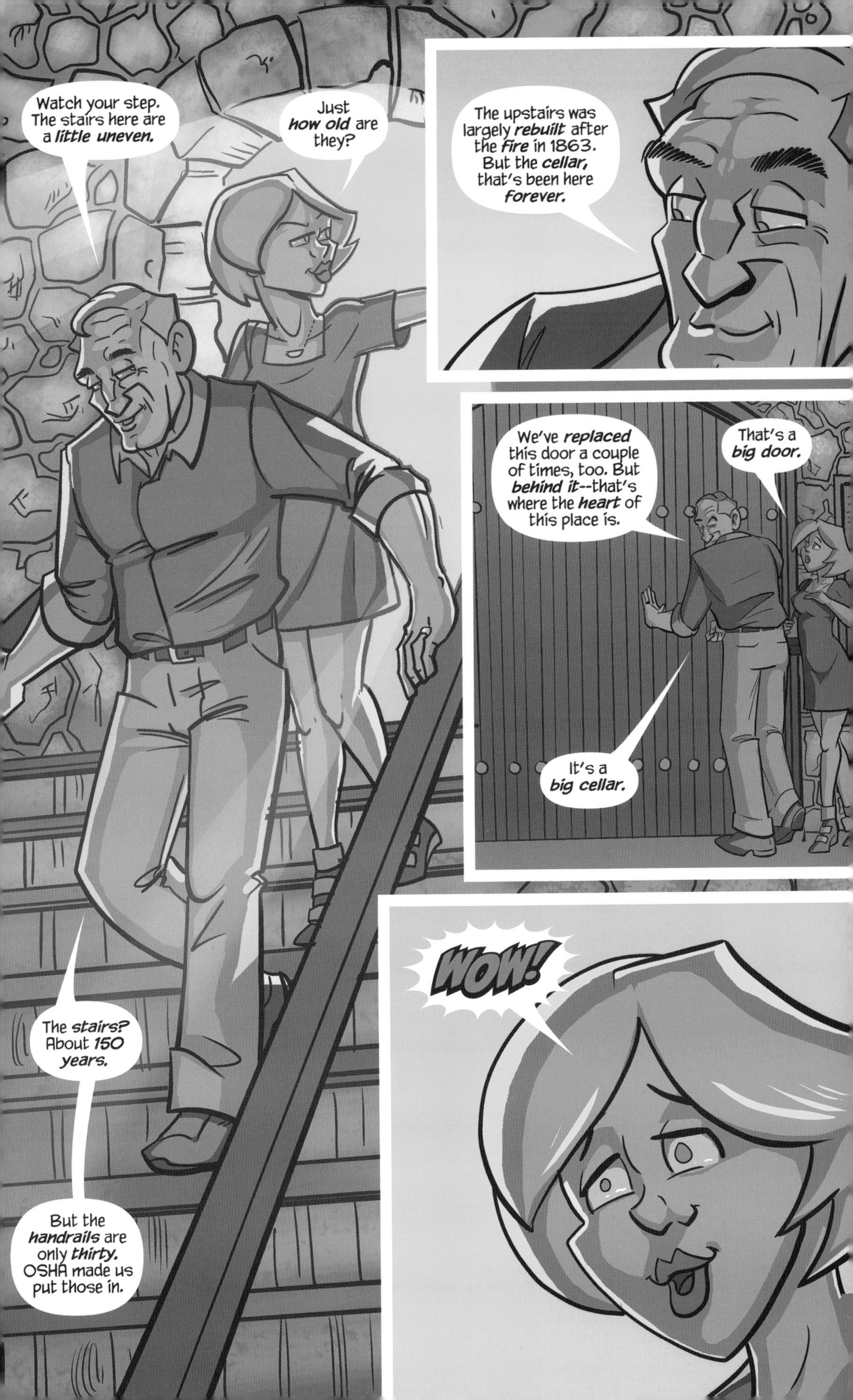

Watch your step. The stairs here are a *little uneven.*
Just *how old* are they?
The *stairs?* About *150 years.*
But the *handrails* are only *thirty.* OSHA made us put those in.
The upstairs was largely *rebuilt* after the *fire* in 1863. But the *cellar,* that's been here *forever.*
We've *replaced* this door a couple of times, too. But *behind it*--that's where the *heart* of this place is.
That's a *big door.*
It's a *big cellar.*
WOW!

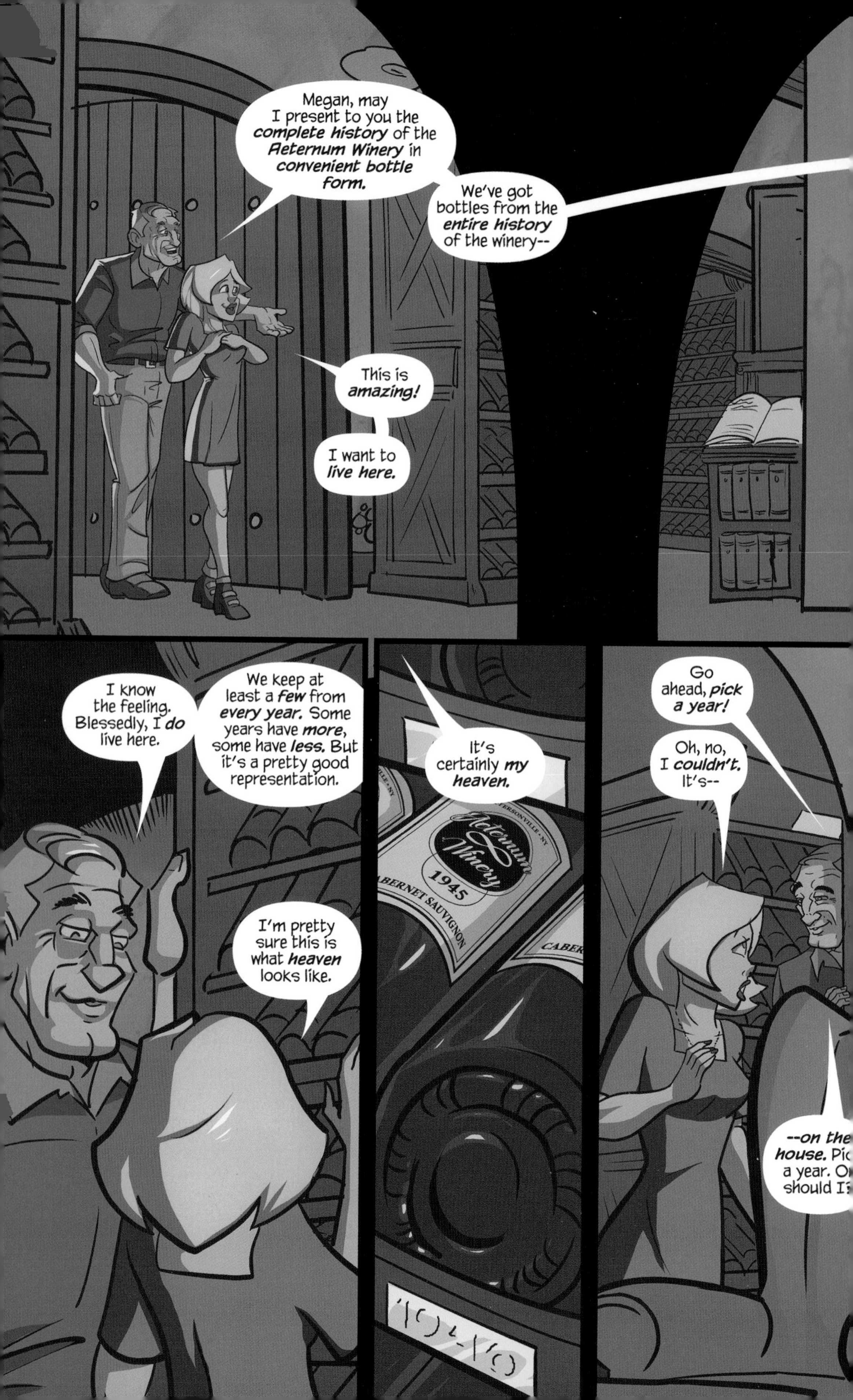
Megan, may I present to you the *complete history* of the *Aeternum Winery* in *convenient bottle form.*
We've got bottles from the *entire history* of the winery--
This is *amazing!*
I want to *live here.*
I know the feeling. Blessedly, I *do* live here.
We keep at least a *few* from *every year.* Some years have *more,* some have *less.* But it's a pretty good representation.
I'm pretty sure this is what *heaven* looks like.
It's certainly *my heaven.*
Aeternum Winery
1945
CABERNET SAUVIGNON
Go ahead, *pick a year!*
Oh, no, I *couldn't.* It's--
*--on the house.* Pic a year. O should I?

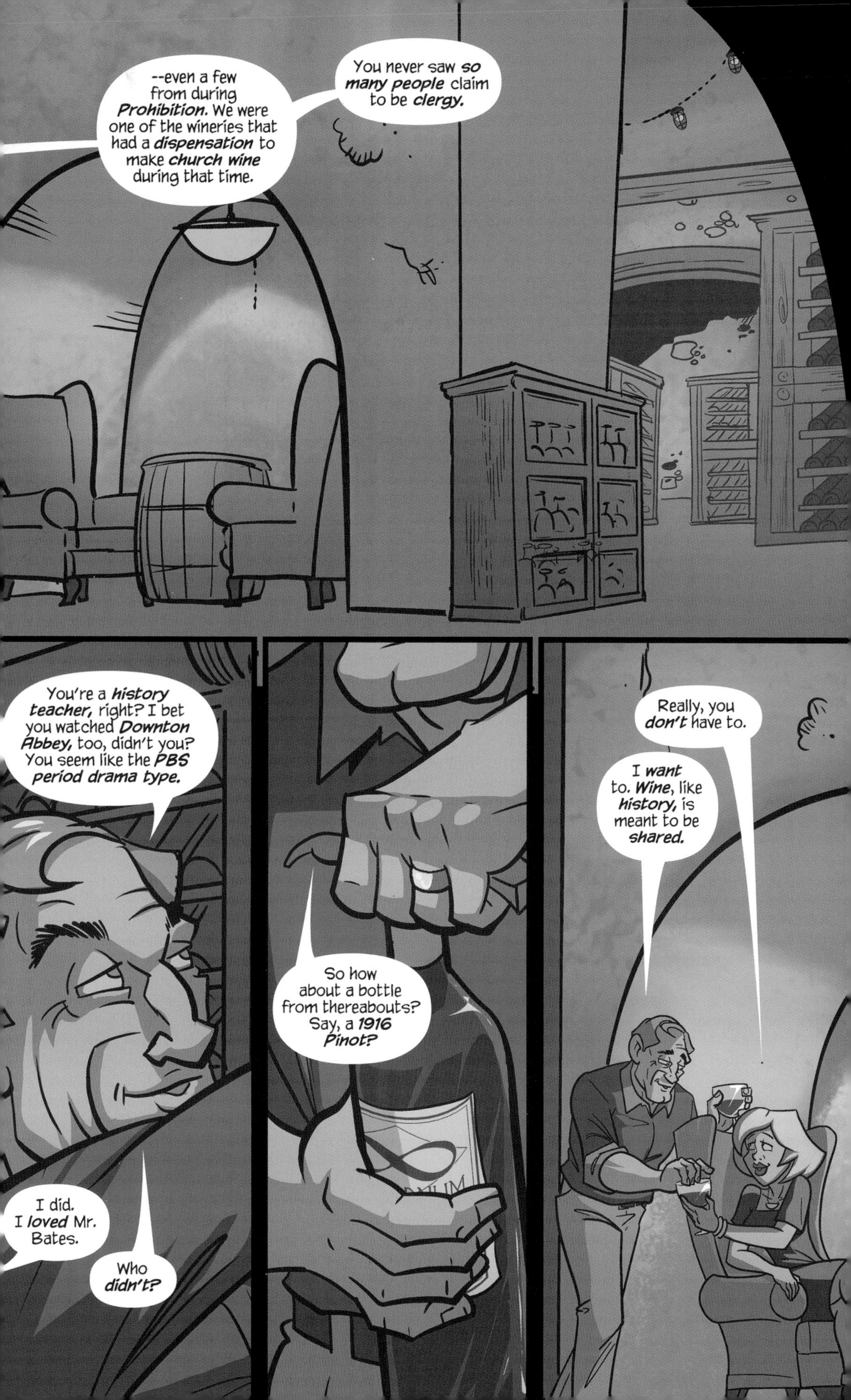
--even a few from during *Prohibition.* We were one of the wineries that had a *dispensation* to make *church wine* during that time.
You never saw *so many people* claim to be *clergy.*
You're a *history teacher,* right? I bet you watched *Downton Abbey,* too, didn't you? You seem like the *PBS period drama type.*
I did. I *loved* Mr. Bates.
Who *didn't?*
So how about a bottle from thereabouts? Say, a *1916 Pinot?*
Really, you *don't* have to.
I *want* to. *Wine,* like *history,* is meant to be *shared.*

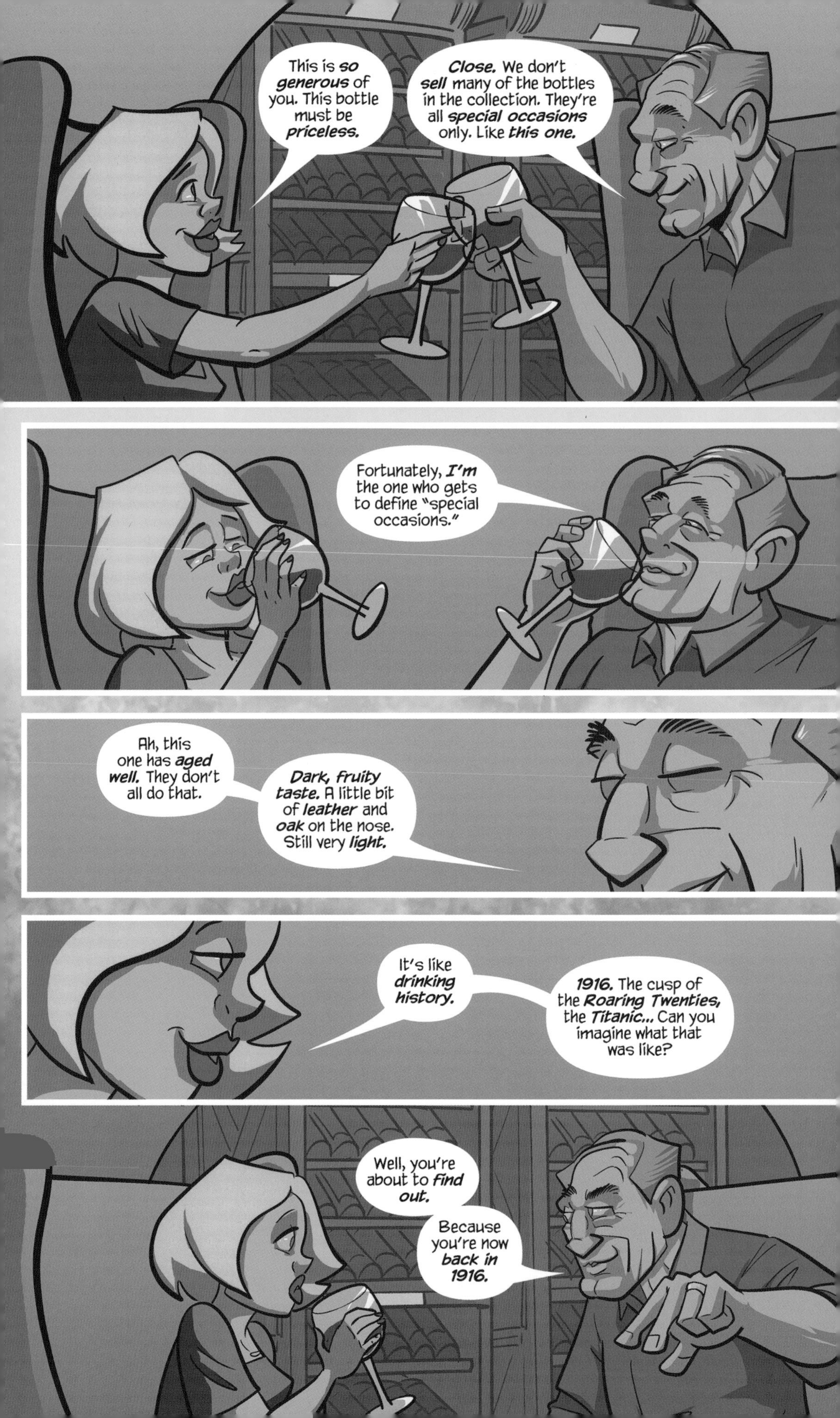
This is so generous of you. This bottle must be priceless.
Close. We don't sell many of the bottles in the collection. They're all special occasions only. Like this one.
Fortunately, I'm the one who gets to define "special occasions."
Ah, this one has aged well. They don't all do that.
Dark, fruity taste. A little bit of leather and oak on the nose. Still very light.
It's like drinking history.
1916. The cusp of the Roaring Twenties, the Titanic... Can you imagine what that was like?
Well, you're about to find out.
Because you're now back in 1916.

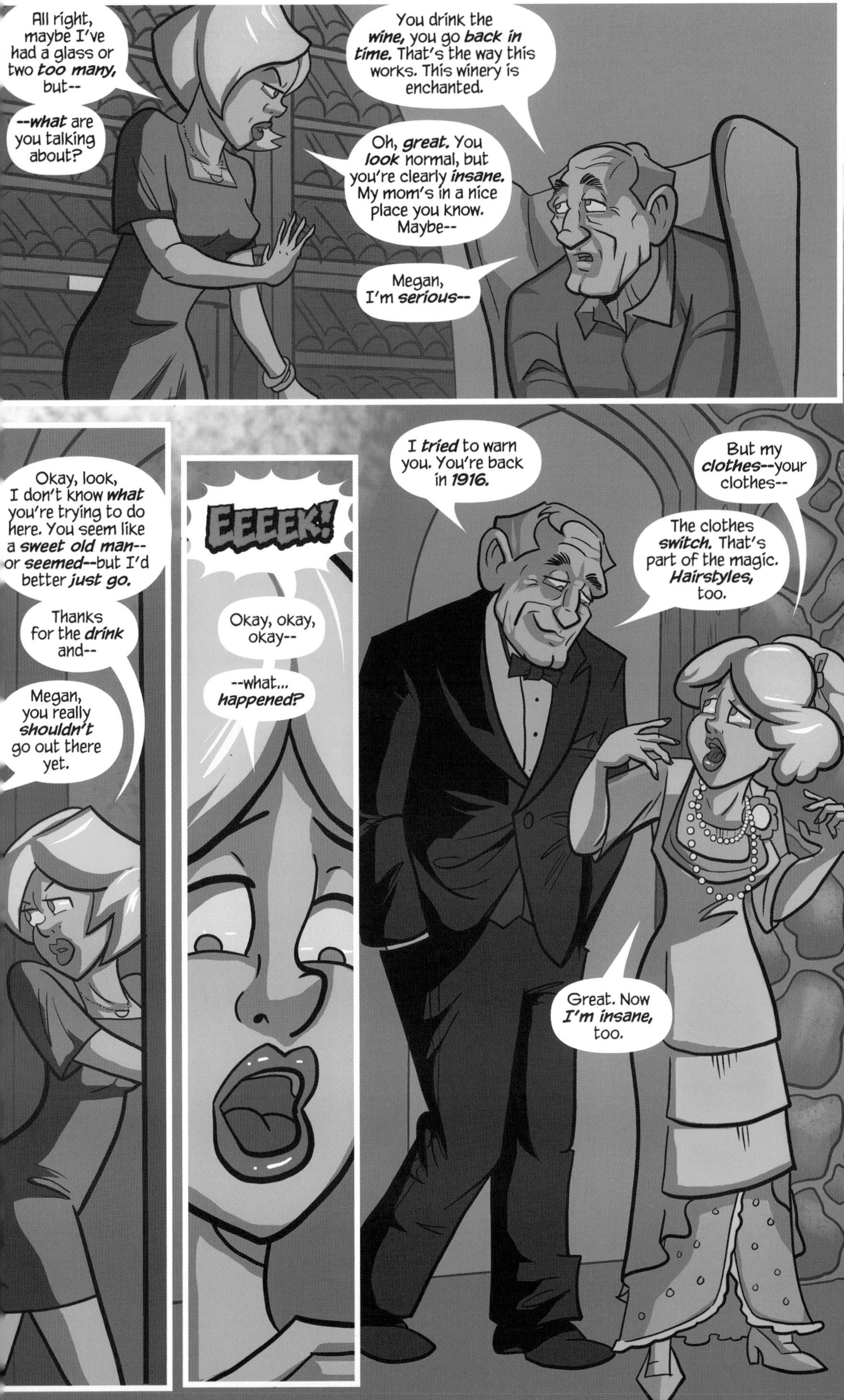
All right, maybe I've had a glass or two *too many,* but--
--*what* are you talking about?
You drink the *wine,* you go *back in time.* That's the way this works. This winery is enchanted.
Oh, *great.* You *look* normal, but you're clearly *insane.* My mom's in a nice place you know. Maybe--
Megan, I'm *serious--*
Okay, look, I don't know *what* you're trying to do here. You seem like a *sweet old man--* or *seemed--*but I'd better *just go.*
Thanks for the *drink* and--
Megan, you really *shouldn't* go out there yet.
EEEEK!
Okay, okay, okay--
--what... *happened?*
I *tried* to warn you. You're back in *1916.*
But my *clothes--*your clothes--
The clothes *switch.* That's part of the magic. *Hairstyles,* too.
Great. Now *I'm insane,* too.

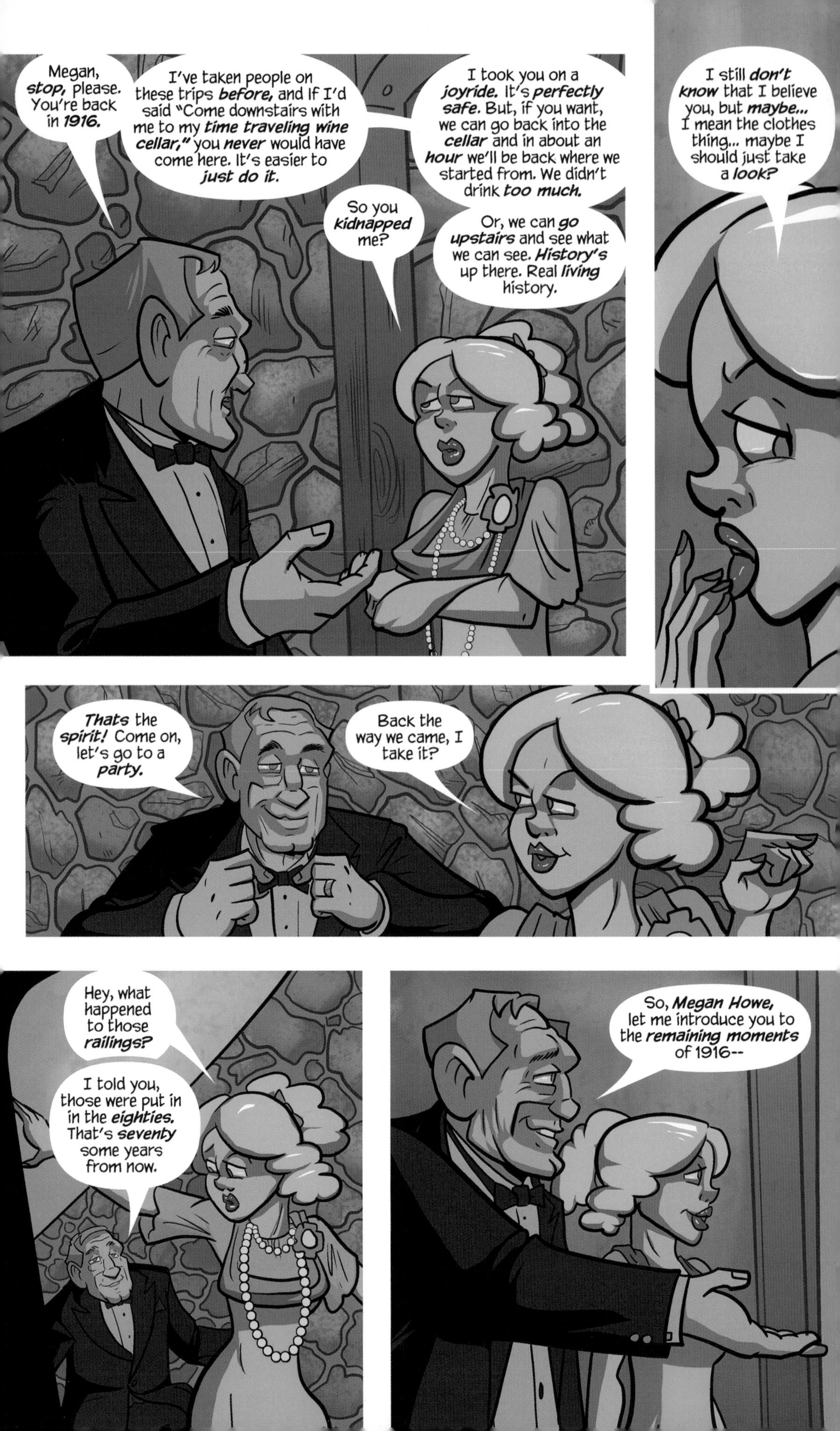
Megan, stop, please. You're back in 1916.
I've taken people on these trips before, and if I'd said "Come downstairs with me to my time traveling wine cellar," you never would have come here. It's easier to just do it.
So you kidnapped me?
I took you on a joyride. It's perfectly safe. But, if you want, we can go back into the cellar and in about an hour we'll be back where we started from. We didn't drink too much.
Or, we can go upstairs and see what we can see. History's up there. Real living history.
I still don't know that I believe you, but maybe... I mean the clothes thing... maybe I should just take a look?
Thats the spirit! Come on, let's go to a party.
Back the way we came, I take it?
Hey, what happened to those railings?
I told you, those were put in in the eighties. That's seventy some years from now.
So, Megan Howe, let me introduce you to the remaining moments of 1916--

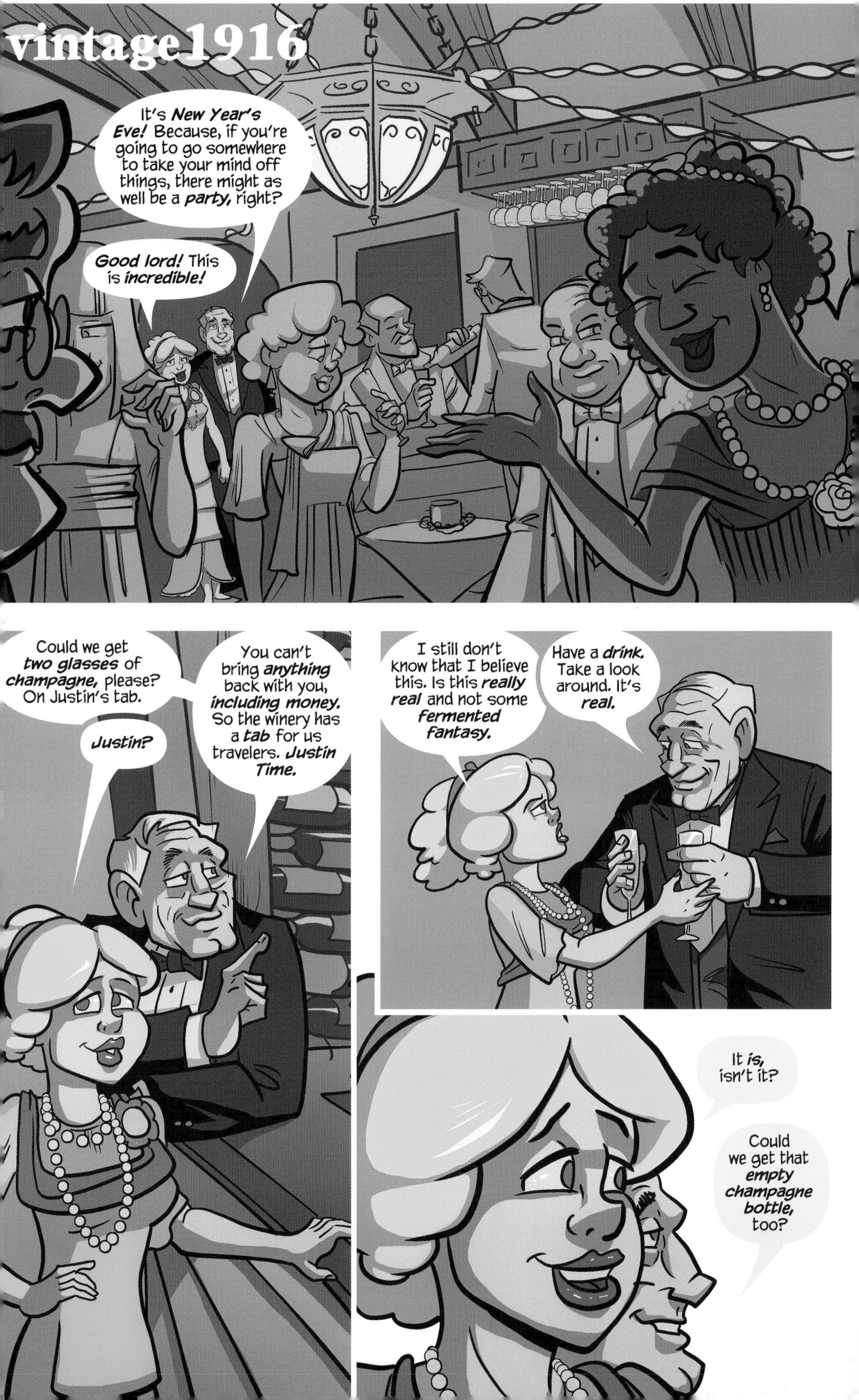
vintage1916
It's *New Year's Eve!* Because, if you're going to go somewhere to take your mind off things, there might as well be a *party,* right?
*Good lord!* This is *incredible!*
Could we get *two glasses* of *champagne,* please? On Justin's tab.
*Justin?*
You can't bring *anything* back with you, *including money.* So the winery has a *tab* for us travelers. *Justin Time.*
I still don't know that I believe this. Is this *really real* and not some *fermented fantasy.*
Have a *drink.* Take a look around. It's *real.*
It *is,* isn't it?
Could we get that *empty champagne bottle,* too?

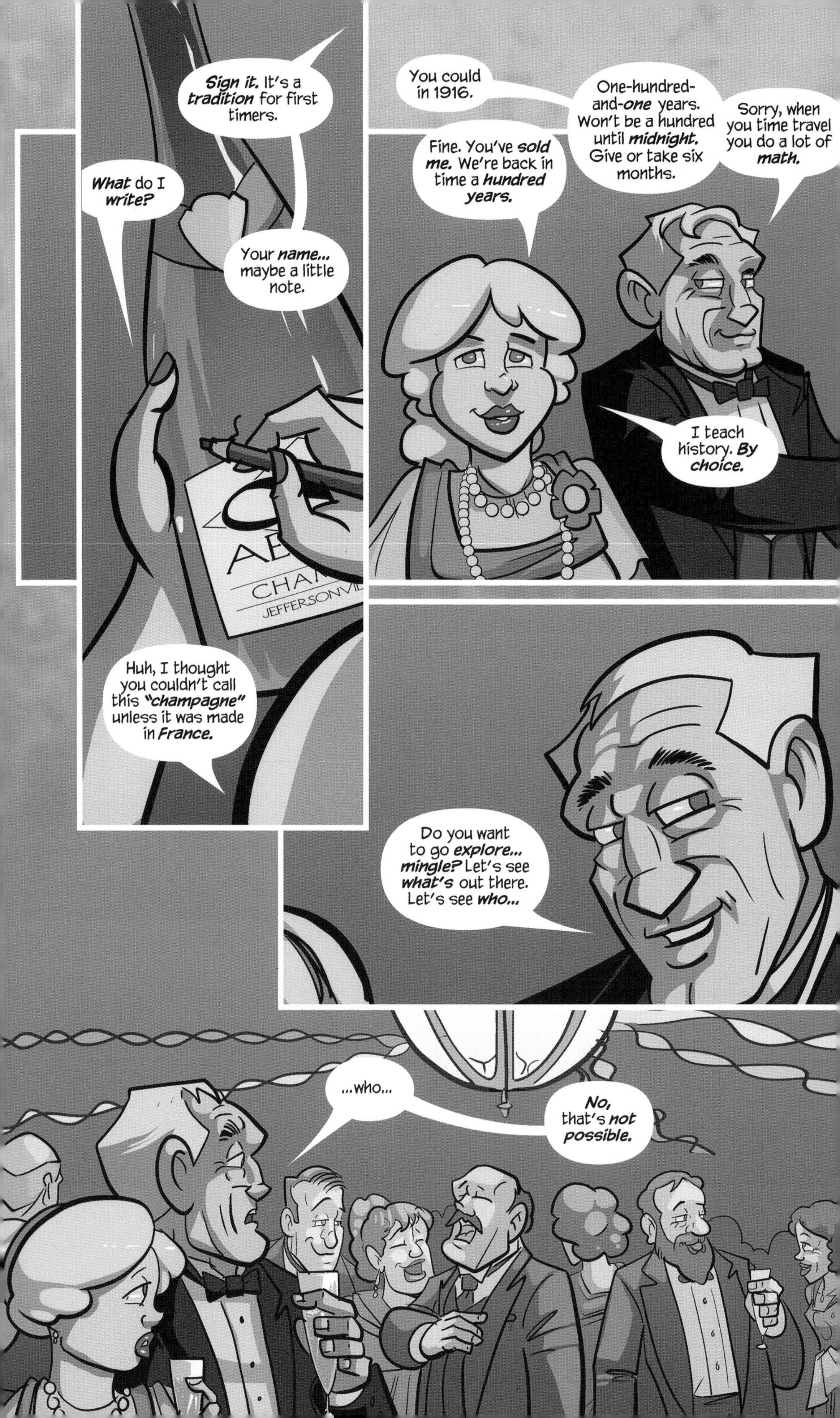

Sign it. It's a tradition for first timers.
What do I write?
Your name... maybe a little note.
ABE
CHAM
JEFFERSONVI
Huh, I thought you couldn't call this "champagne" unless it was made in France.
You could in 1916.
Fine. You've sold me. We're back in time a hundred years.
One-hundred-and-one years. Won't be a hundred until midnight. Give or take six months.
Sorry, when you time travel you do a lot of math.
I teach history. By choice.
Do you want to go explore... mingle? Let's see what's out there. Let's see who...
...who...
No, that's not possible.

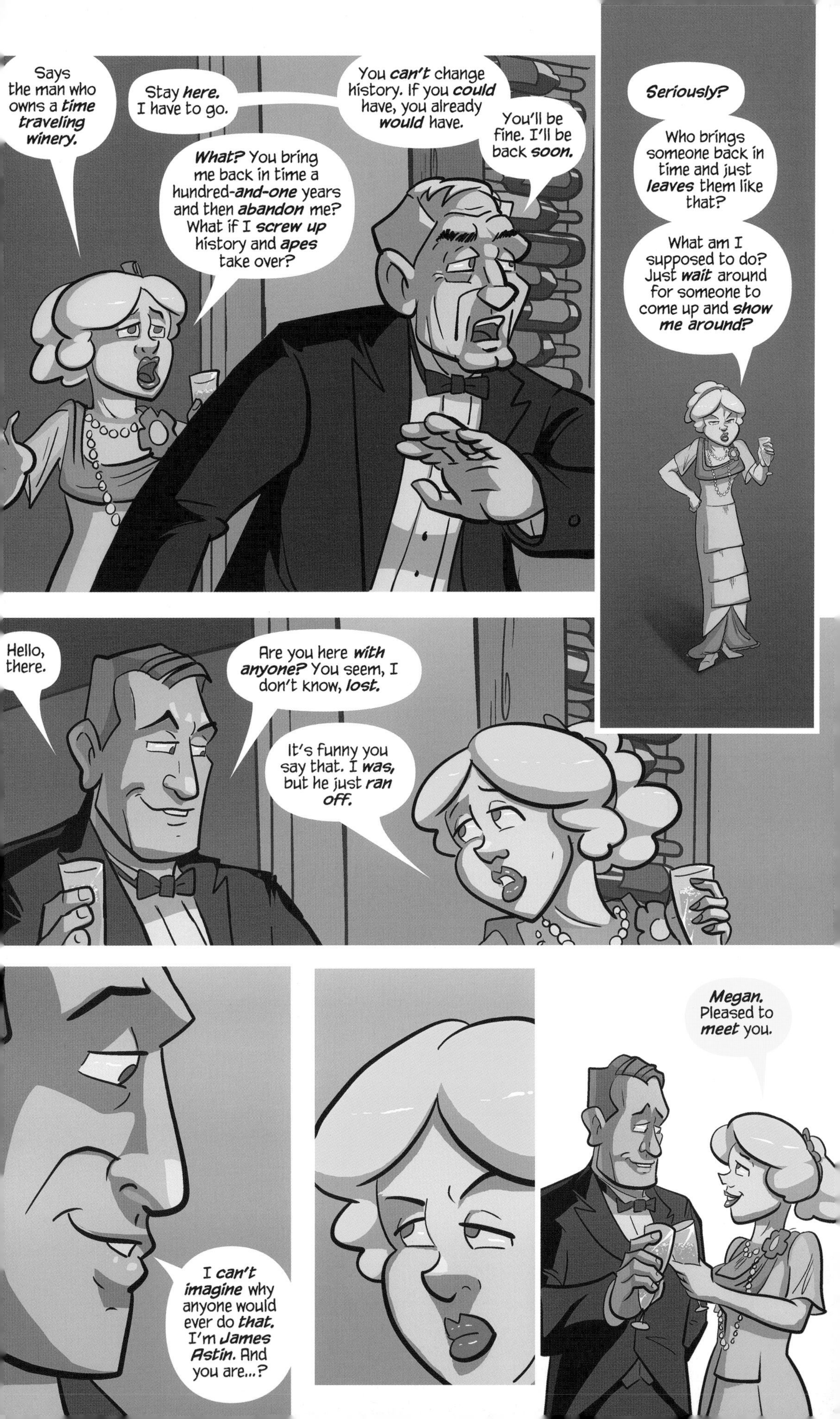

Stay *here.* I have to go.
Says the man who owns a *time traveling winery.*
You *can't* change history. If you *could* have, you already *would* have.
*What?* You bring me back in time a hundred-*and-one* years and then *abandon* me? What if I *screw up* history and *apes* take over?
You'll be fine. I'll be back *soon.*
*Seriously?*
Who brings someone back in time and just *leaves* them like that?
What am I supposed to do? Just *wait* around for someone to come up and *show me around?*
Hello, there.
Are you here *with anyone?* You seem, I don't know, *lost.*
It's funny you say that. I *was,* but he just *ran off.*
I *can't imagine* why anyone would ever do *that.* I'm *James Astin.* And you are...?
*Megan.* Pleased to *meet* you.

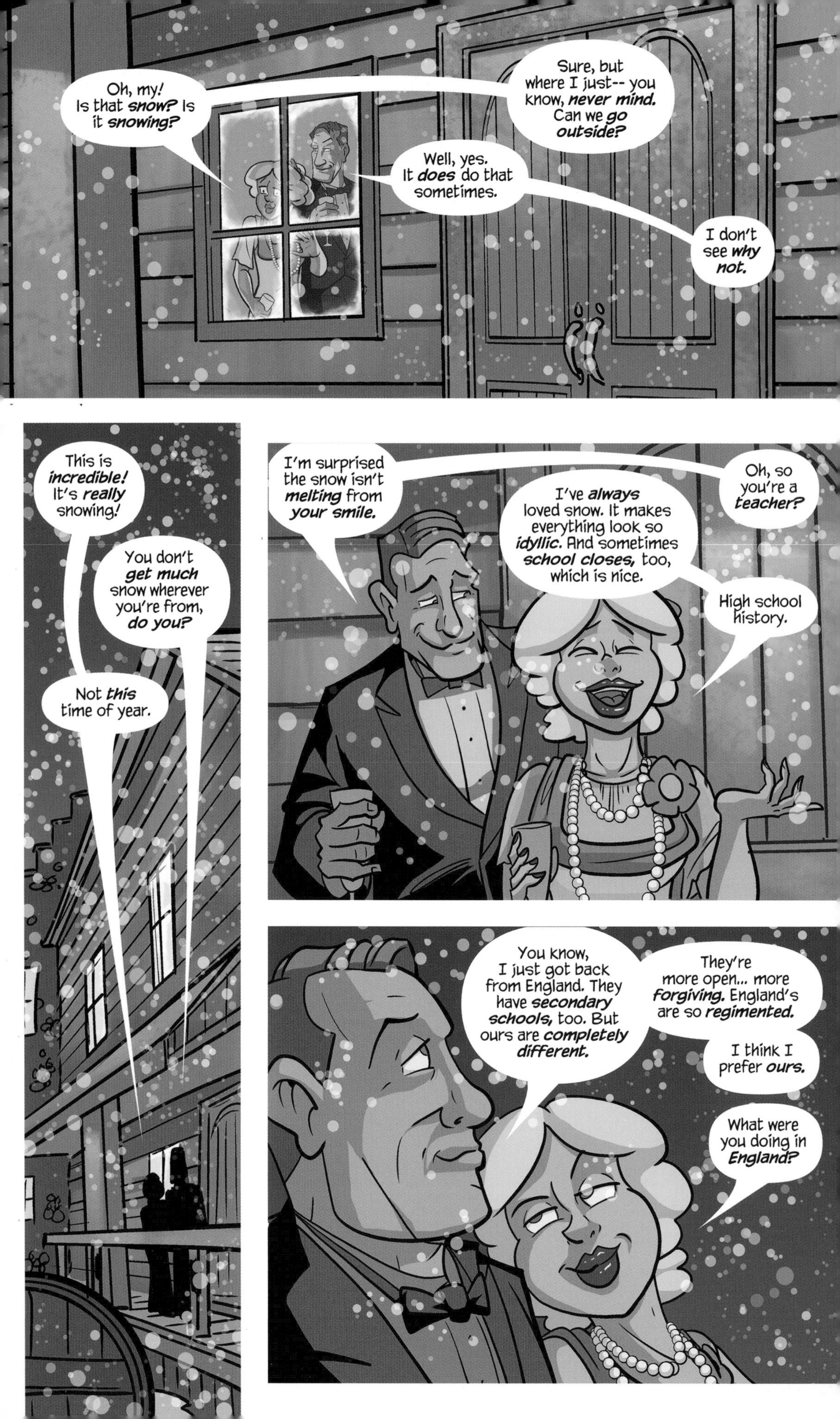

Oh, my! Is that *snow?* Is it *snowing?*
Well, yes. It *does* do that sometimes.
Sure, but where I just-- you know, *never mind.* Can we *go outside?*
I don't see *why not.*
This is *incredible!* It's *really* snowing!
You don't *get much* snow wherever you're from, *do you?*
Not *this* time of year.
I'm surprised the snow isn't *melting* from *your smile.*
I've *always* loved snow. It makes everything look so *idyllic.* And sometimes *school closes,* too, which is nice.
Oh, so you're a *teacher?*
High school history.
You know, I just got back from England. They have *secondary schools,* too. But ours are *completely different.*
They're more open... more *forgiving.* England's are so *regimented.*
I think I prefer *ours.*
What were you doing in *England?*

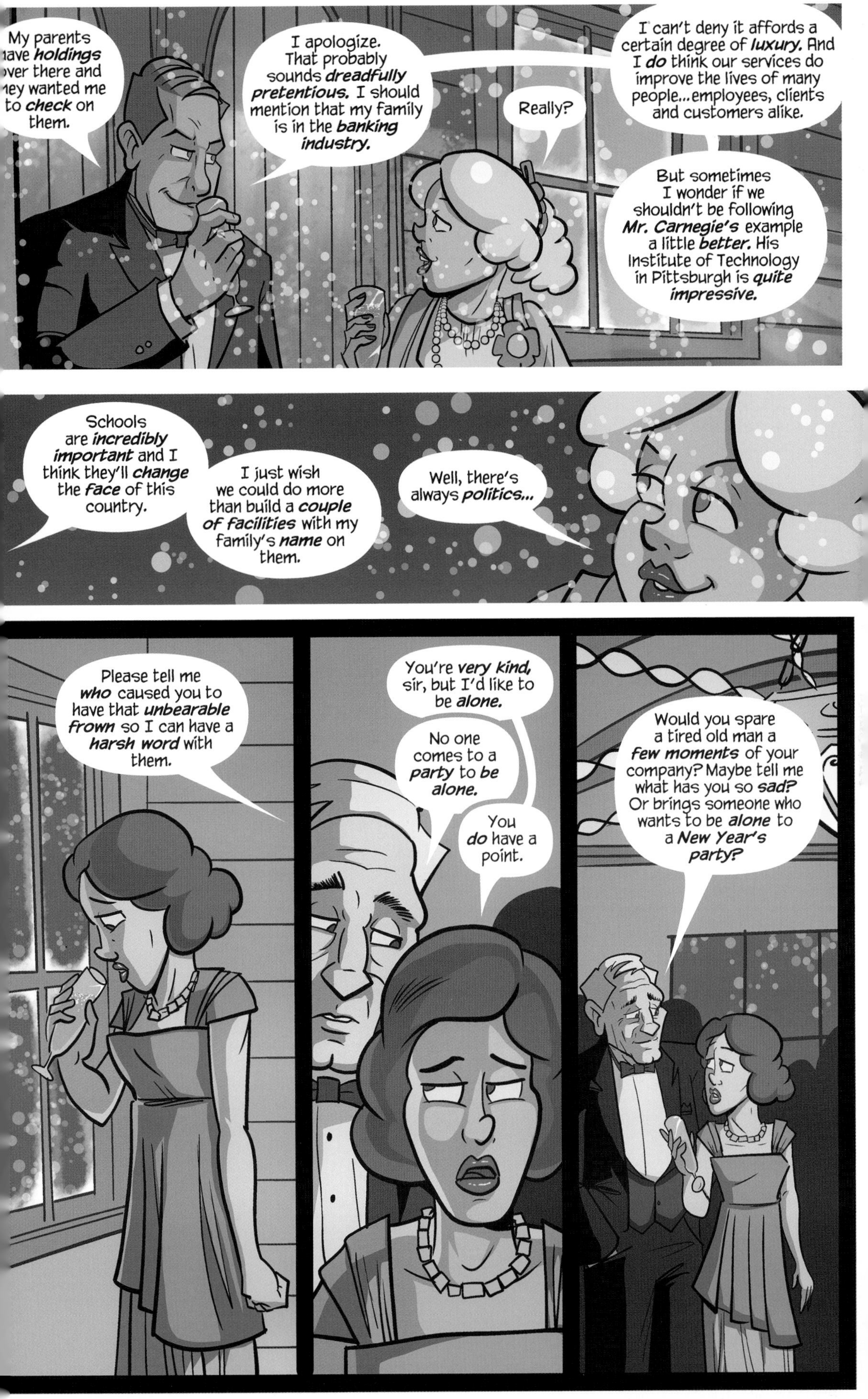
My parents
ave holdings
ver there and
ey wanted me
to check on
them.
I apologize. That probably sounds dreadfully pretentious. I should mention that my family is in the banking industry.
Really?
I can't deny it affords a certain degree of luxury. And I do think our services do improve the lives of many people...employees, clients and customers alike.
But sometimes I wonder if we shouldn't be following Mr. Carnegie's example a little better. His Institute of Technology in Pittsburgh is quite impressive.
Schools are incredibly important and I think they'll change the face of this country.
I just wish we could do more than build a couple of facilities with my family's name on them.
Well, there's always politics...
Please tell me who caused you to have that unbearable frown so I can have a harsh word with them.
You're very kind, sir, but I'd like to be alone.
No one comes to a party to be alone.
You do have a point.
Would you spare a tired old man a few moments of your company? Maybe tell me what has you so sad? Or brings someone who wants to be alone to a New Year's party?

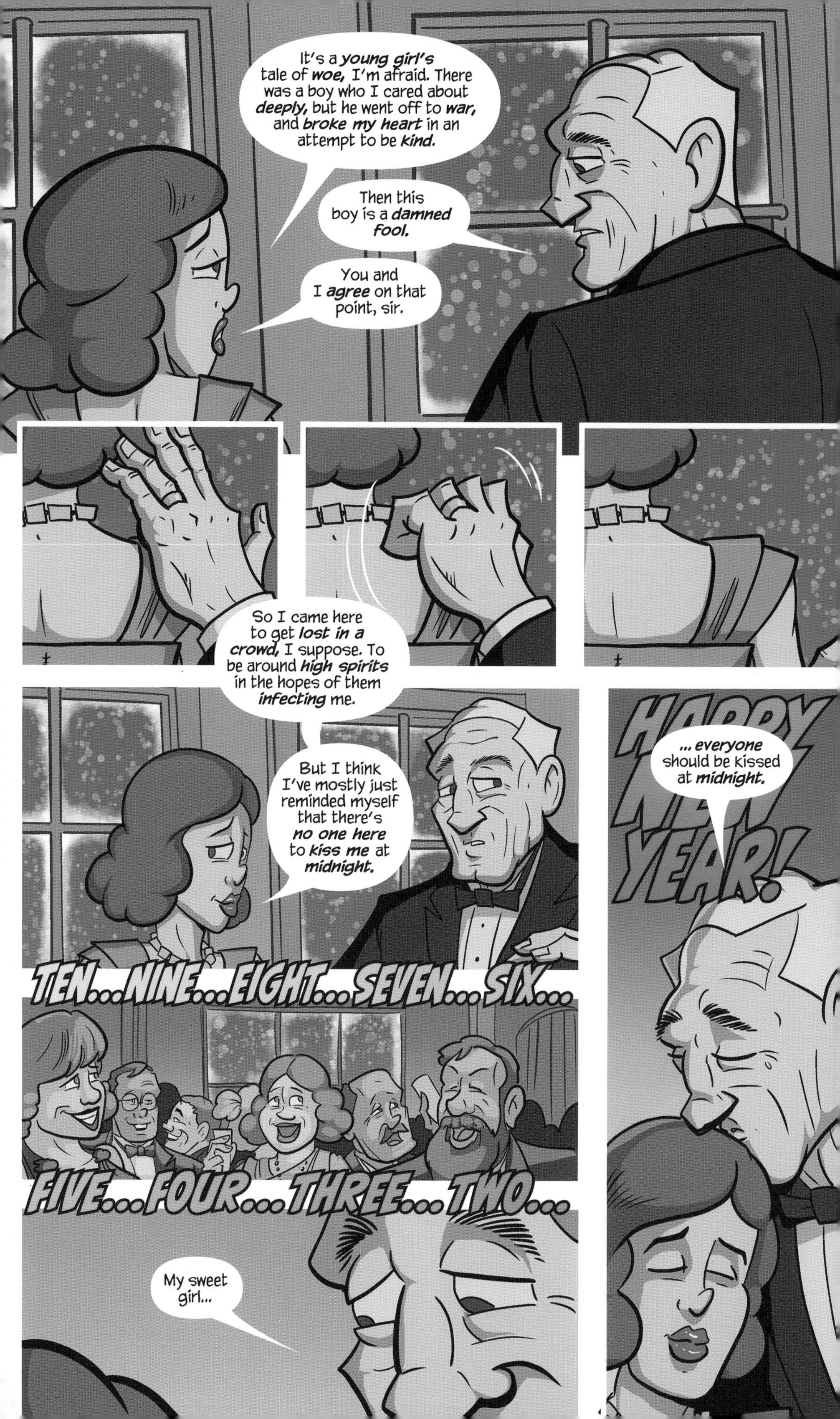
It's a *young girl's* tale of *woe,* I'm afraid. There was a boy who I cared about *deeply,* but he went off to *war,* and *broke my heart* in an attempt to be *kind.*
Then this boy is a *damned fool.*
You and I *agree* on that point, sir.
So I came here to get *lost in a crowd,* I suppose. To be around *high spirits* in the hopes of them *infecting* me.
But I think I've mostly just reminded myself that there's *no one here* to *kiss me* at *midnight.*
TEN...NINE...EIGHT...SEVEN...SIX...
FIVE...FOUR...THREE...TWO...
My sweet girl...
HAPPY NEW YEAR!
...*everyone* should be kissed at *midnight.*

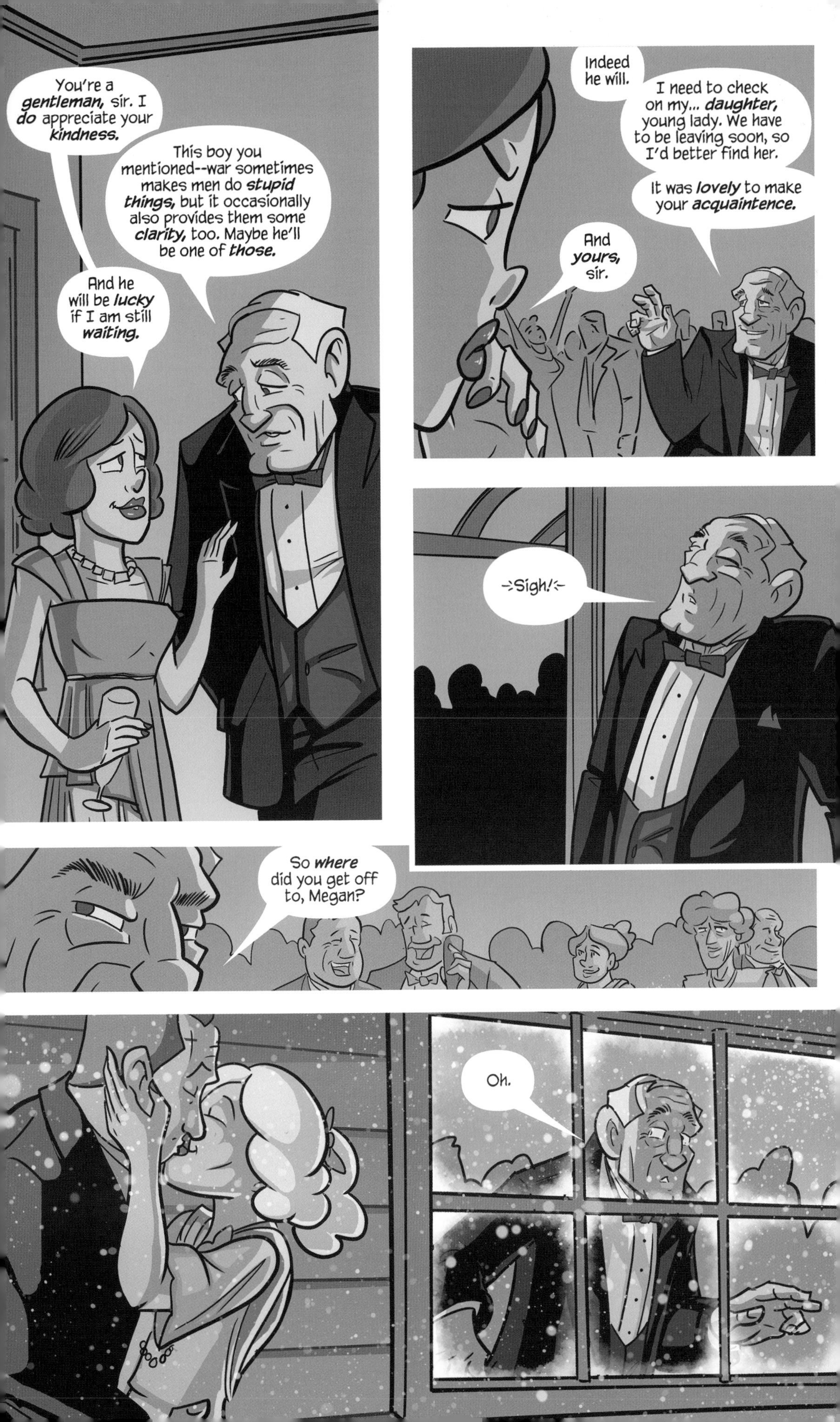
You're a gentleman, sir. I do appreciate your kindness.
This boy you mentioned--war sometimes makes men do stupid things, but it occasionally also provides them some clarity, too. Maybe he'll be one of those.
And he will be lucky if I am still waiting.
Indeed he will.
I need to check on my... daughter, young lady. We have to be leaving soon, so I'd better find her.
It was lovely to make your acquaintence.
And yours, sir.
-Sigh!-
So where did you get off to, Megan?
Oh.

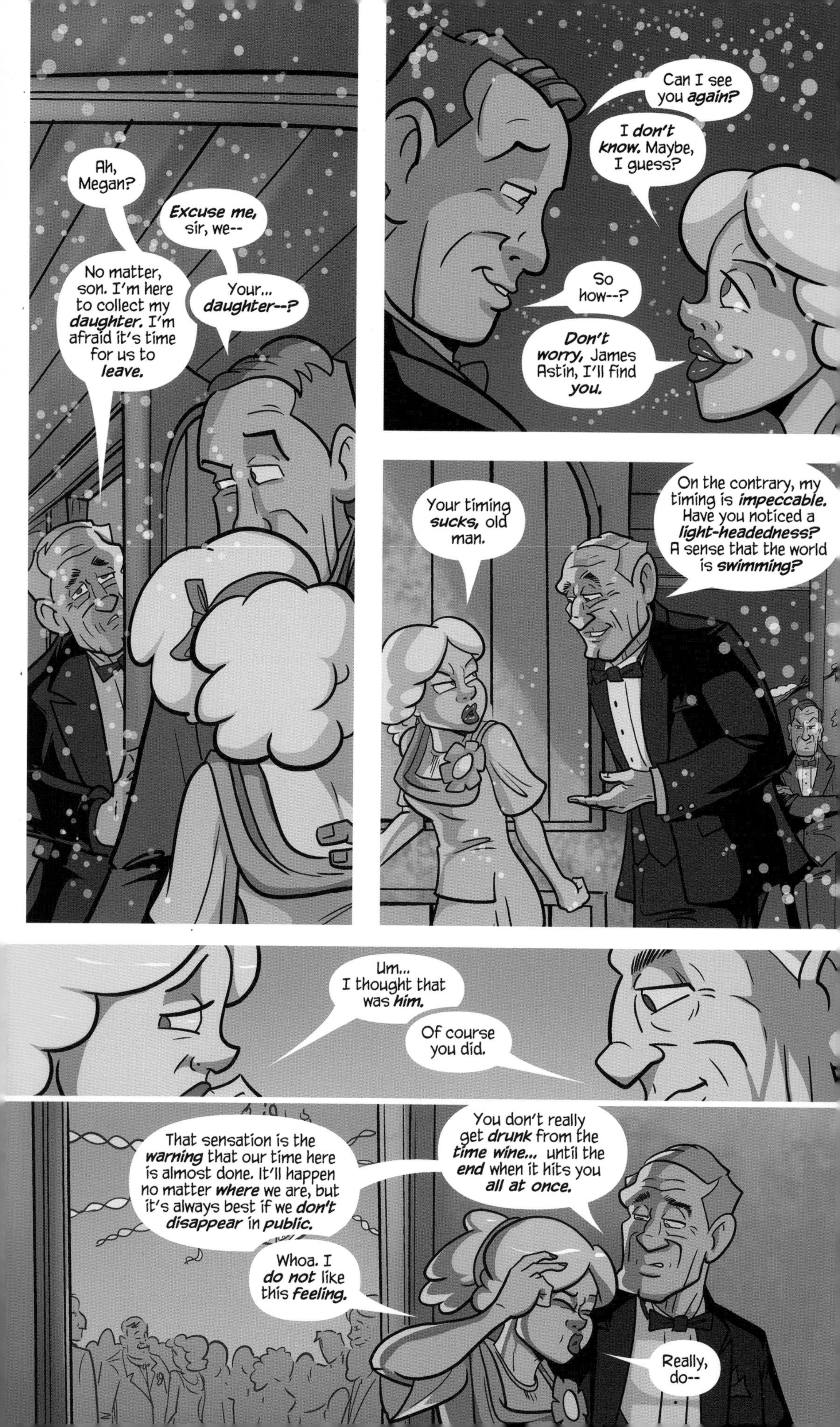
Ah, Megan?
Excuse me, sir, we--
No matter, son. I'm here to collect my daughter. I'm afraid it's time for us to leave.
Your... daughter--?
Can I see you again?
I don't know. Maybe, I guess?
So how--?
Don't worry, James Astin, I'll find you.
Your timing sucks, old man.
On the contrary, my timing is impeccable. Have you noticed a light-headedness? A sense that the world is swimming?
Um... I thought that was him.
Of course you did.
That sensation is the warning that our time here is almost done. It'll happen no matter where we are, but it's always best if we don't disappear in public.
You don't really get drunk from the time wine... until the end when it hits you all at once.
Whoa. I do not like this feeling.
Really, do--

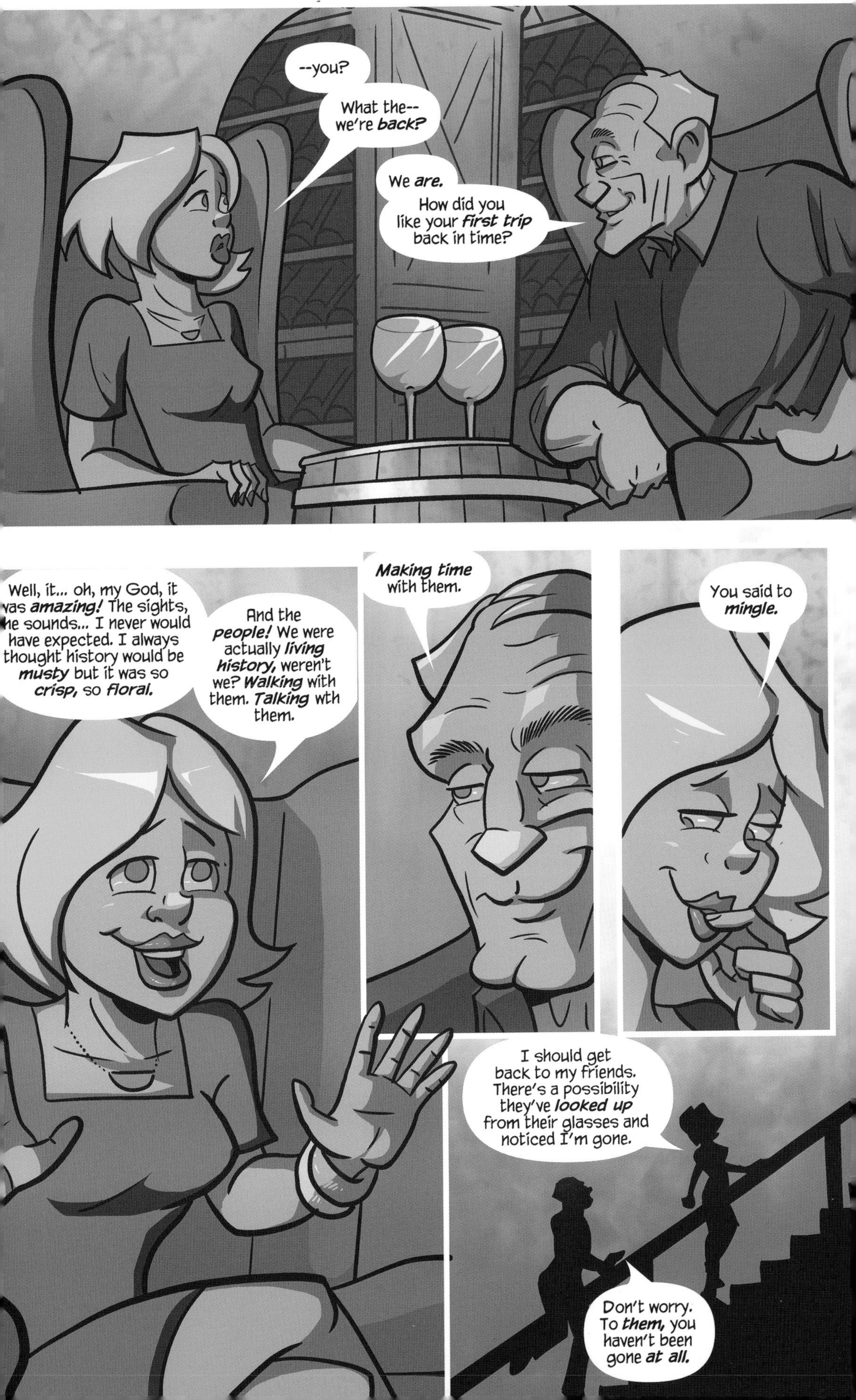
--you?
What the-- we're *back?*
We *are.*
How did you like your *first trip* back in time?
Well, it... oh, my God, it vas *amazing!* The sights, he sounds... I never would have expected. I always thought history would be *musty* but it was so *crisp,* so *floral.*
And the *people!* We were actually *living history,* weren't we? *Walking* with them. *Talking* wth them.
*Making time* with them.
You said to *mingle.*
I should get back to my friends. There's a possibility they've *looked up* from their glasses and noticed I'm gone.
Don't worry. To *them,* you haven't been gone *at all.*

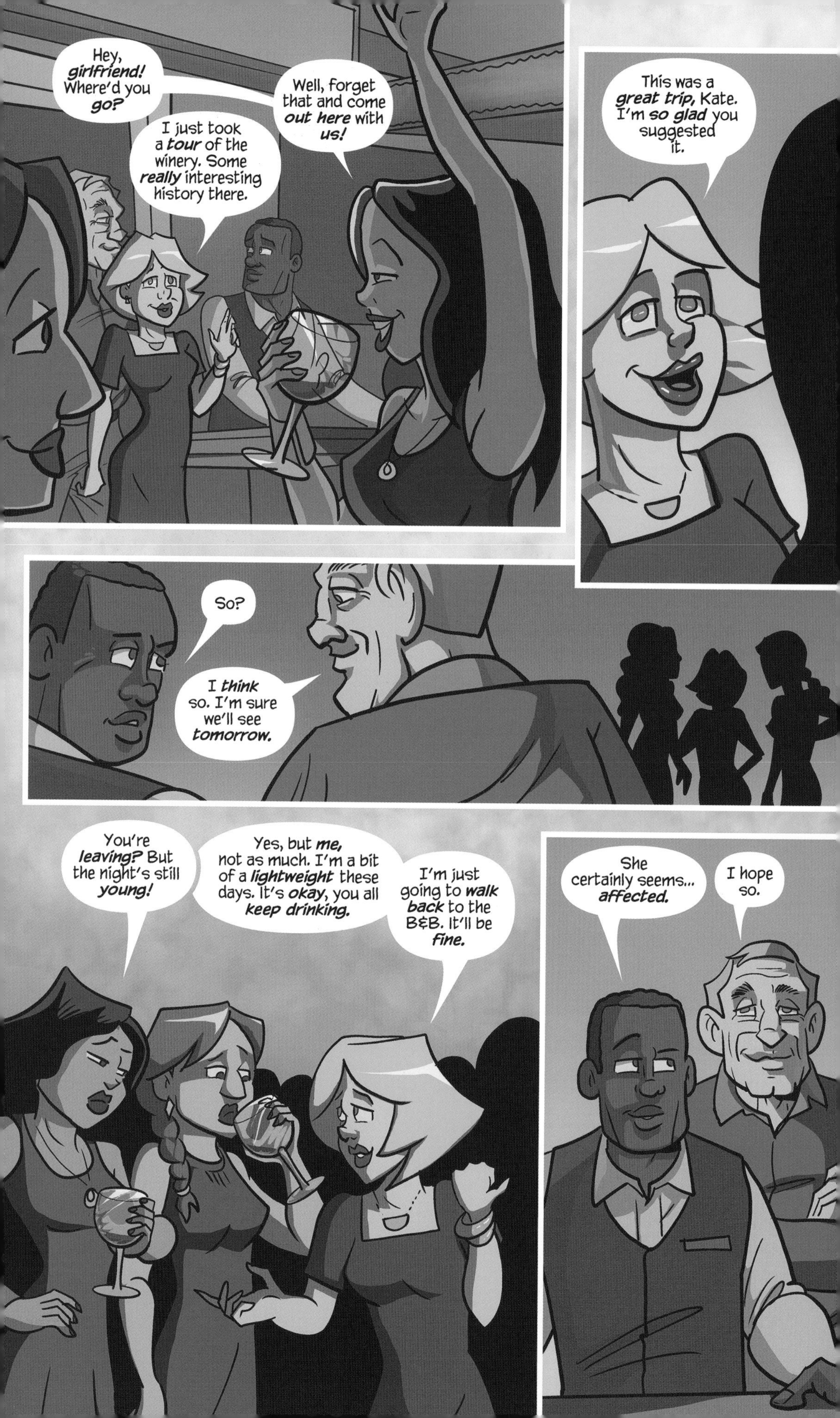
Hey, *girlfriend!* Where'd you *go?*
I just took a *tour* of the winery. Some *really* interesting history there.
Well, forget that and come *out here* with *us!*
This was a *great trip,* Kate. I'm *so glad* you suggested it.
So?
I *think* so. I'm sure we'll see *tomorrow.*
You're *leaving?* But the night's still *young!*
Yes, but *me,* not as much. I'm a bit of a *lightweight* these days. It's *okay,* you all *keep drinking.*
I'm just going to *walk back* to the B&B. It'll be *fine.*
She certainly seems... *affected.*
I hope so.

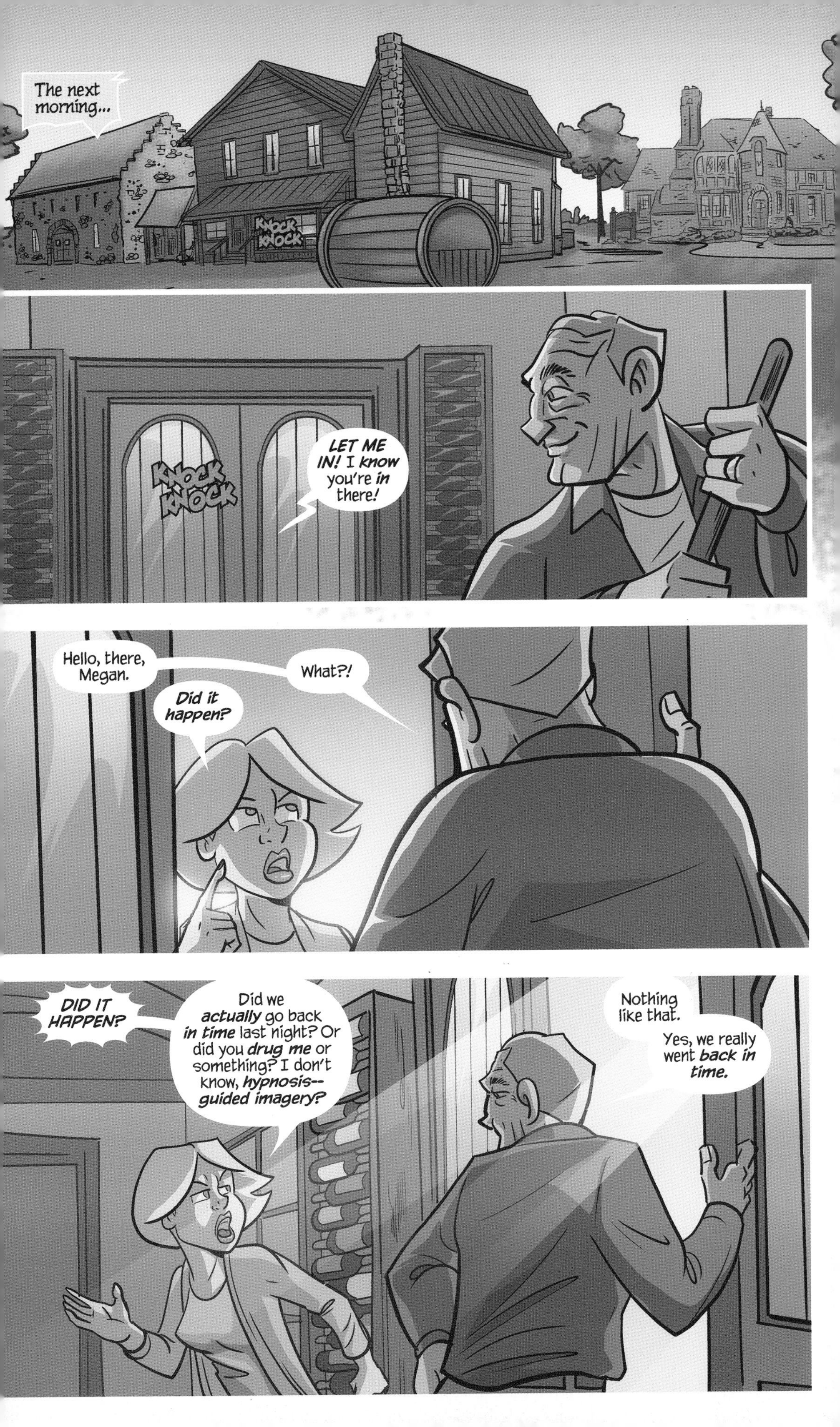

The next morning...
KNOCK KNOCK
KNOCK KNOCK
LET ME IN! I know you're in there!
Hello, there, Megan.
What?!
Did it happen?
DID IT HAPPEN?
Did we actually go back in time last night? Or did you drug me or something? I don't know, hypnosis-- guided imagery?
Nothing like that.
Yes, we really went back in time.

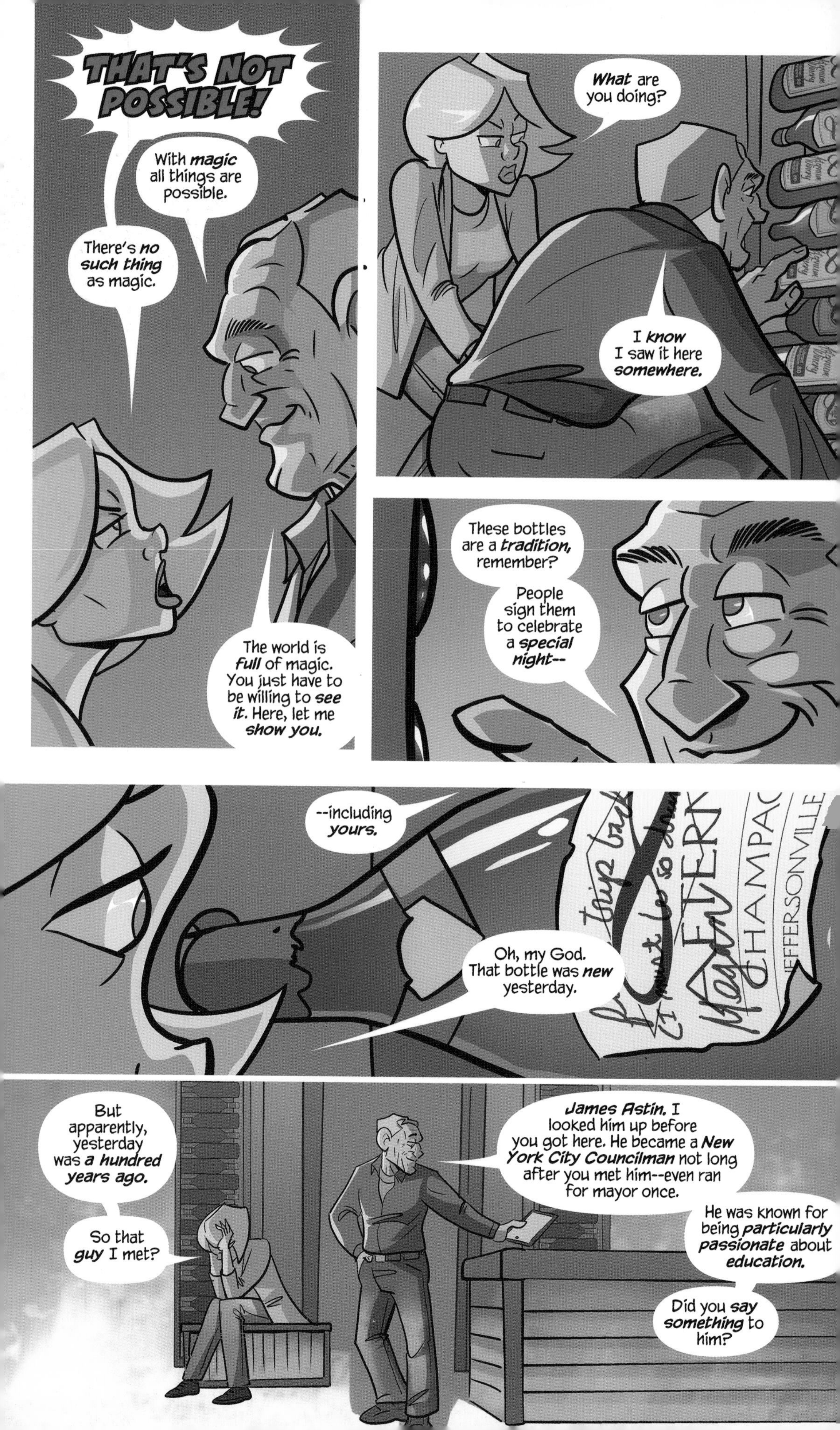
THAT'S NOT POSSIBLE!
With magic all things are possible.
There's no such thing as magic.
The world is full of magic. You just have to be willing to see it. Here, let me show you.
What are you doing?
I know I saw it here somewhere.
These bottles are a tradition, remember?
People sign them to celebrate a special night--
--including yours.
Oh, my God. That bottle was new yesterday.
CHAMPAG
JEFFERSONVILLE
But apparently, yesterday was a hundred years ago.
So that guy I met?
James Astin. I looked him up before you got here. He became a New York City Councilman not long after you met him--even ran for mayor once.
He was known for being particularly passionate about education.
Did you say something to him?

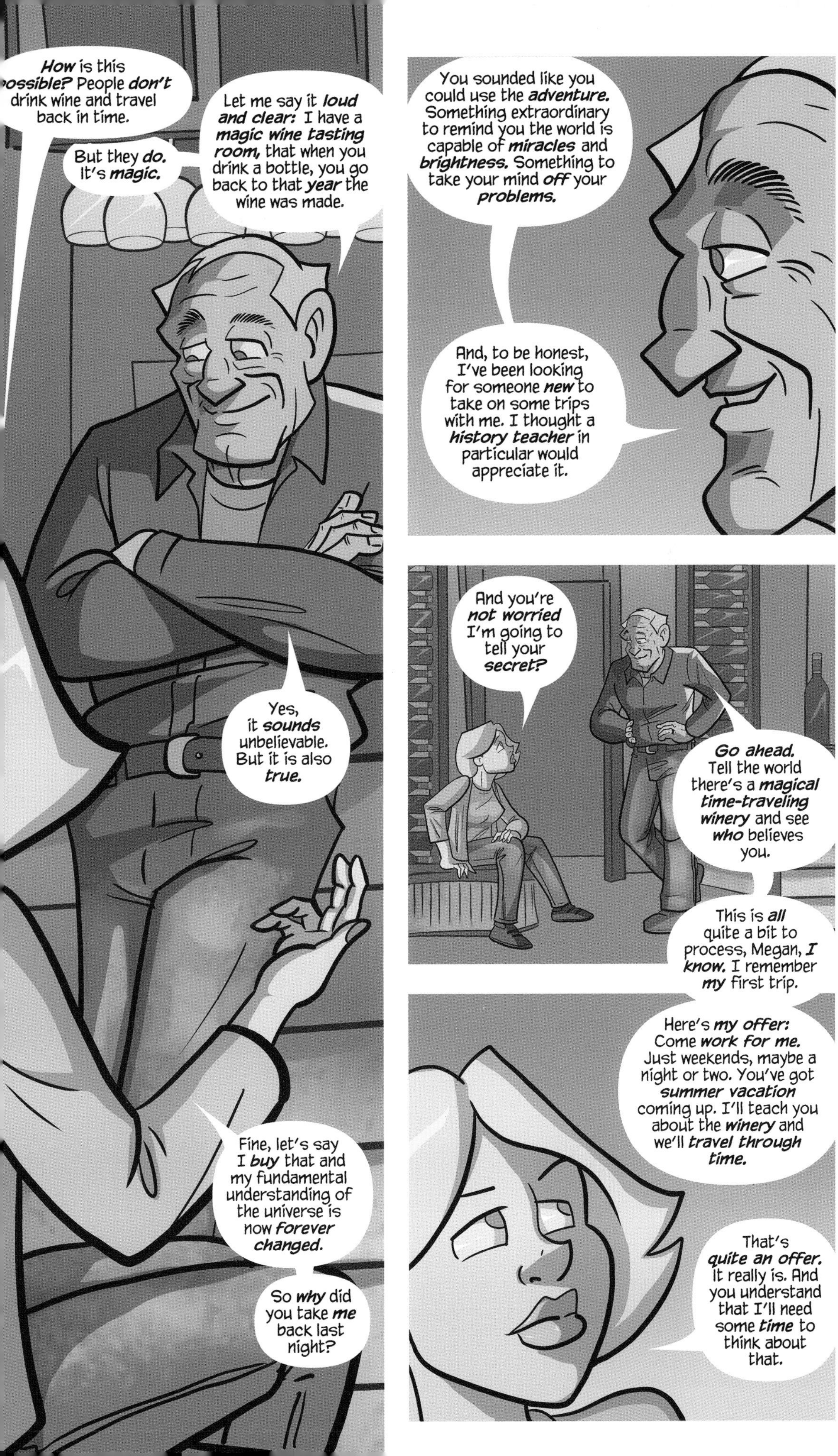
How is this ossible? People don't drink wine and travel back in time.
But they do. It's magic.
Let me say it loud and clear: I have a magic wine tasting room, that when you drink a bottle, you go back to that year the wine was made.
Yes, it sounds unbelievable. But it is also true.
Fine, let's say I buy that and my fundamental understanding of the universe is now forever changed.
So why did you take me back last night?
You sounded like you could use the adventure. Something extraordinary to remind you the world is capable of miracles and brightness. Something to take your mind off your problems.
And, to be honest, I've been looking for someone new to take on some trips with me. I thought a history teacher in particular would appreciate it.
And you're not worried I'm going to tell your secret?
Go ahead. Tell the world there's a magical time-traveling winery and see who believes you.
This is all quite a bit to process, Megan, I know. I remember my first trip.
Here's my offer: Come work for me. Just weekends, maybe a night or two. You've got summer vacation coming up. I'll teach you about the winery and we'll travel through time.
That's quite an offer. It really is. And you understand that I'll need some time to think about that.

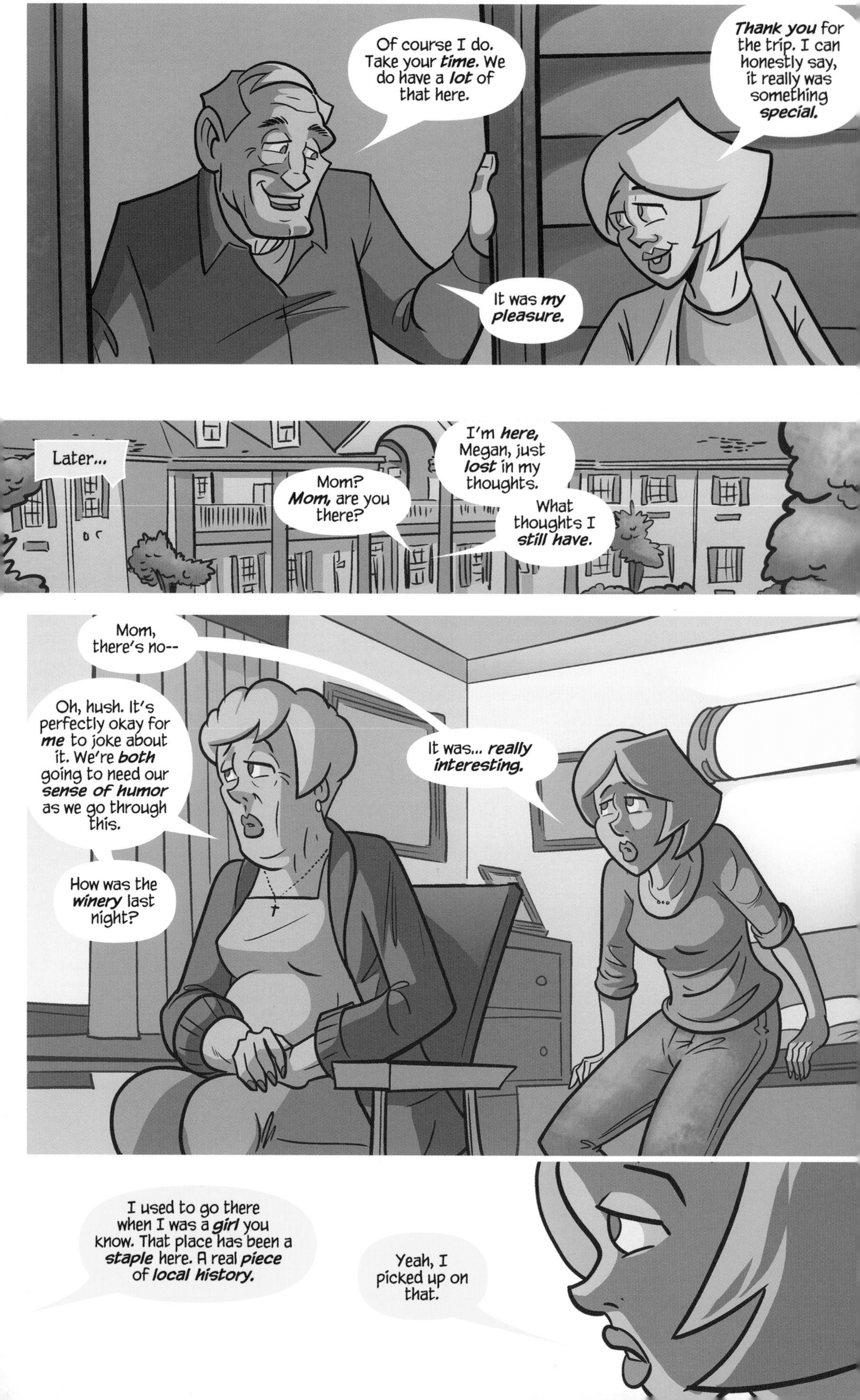
Of course I do. Take your *time.* We do have a *lot* of that here.
*Thank you* for the trip. I can honestly say, it really was something *special.*
It was *my pleasure.*
Later...
Mom? *Mom,* are you there?
I'm *here,* Megan, just *lost* in my thoughts.
What thoughts I *still have.*
Mom, there's no--
Oh, hush. It's perfectly okay for *me* to joke about it. We're *both* going to need our *sense of humor* as we go through this.
How was the *winery* last night?
It was... *really interesting.*
I used to go there when I was a *girl* you know. That place has been a *staple* here. A real *piece* of *local history.*
Yeah, I picked up on that.

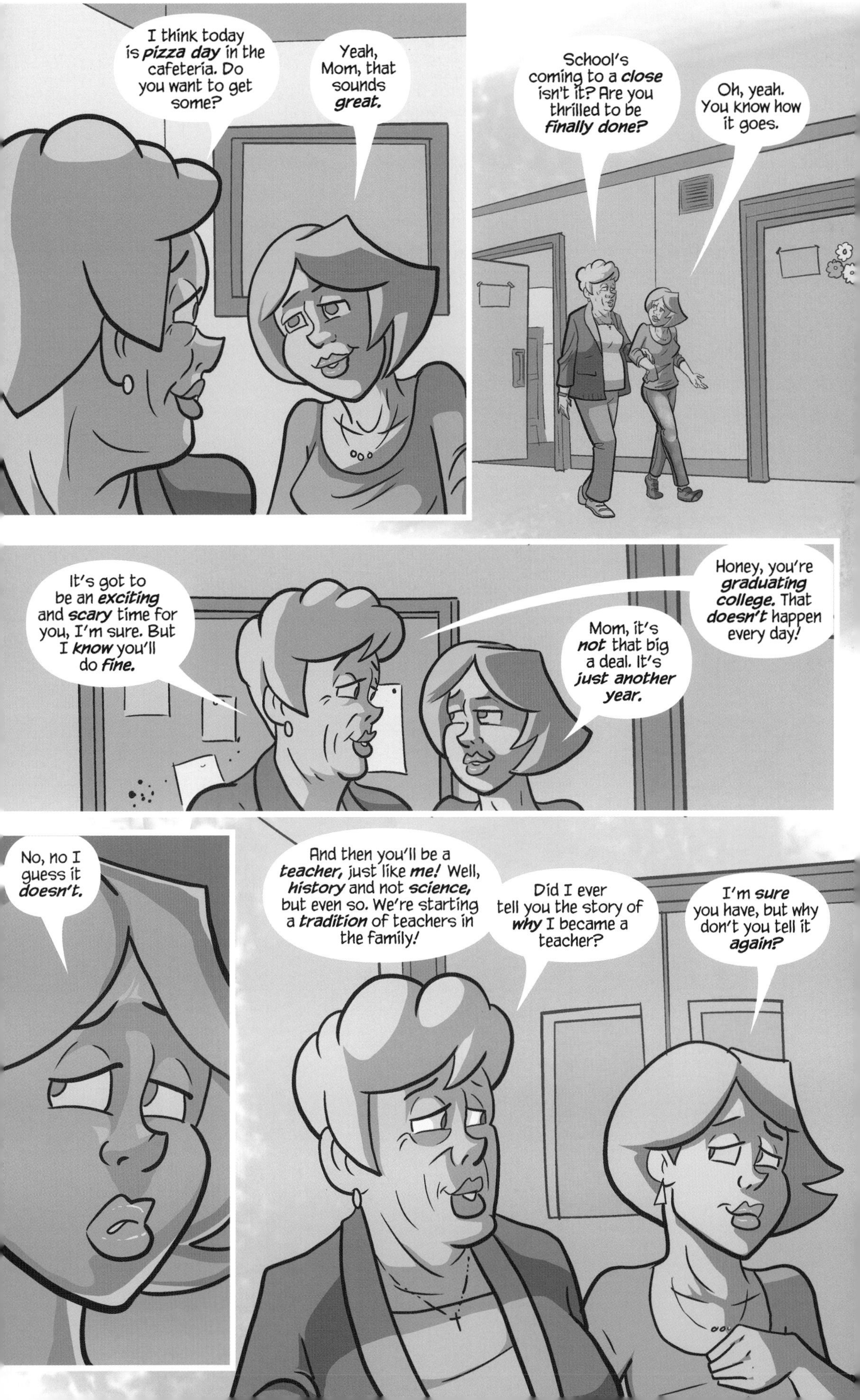
I think today is *pizza day* in the cafeteria. Do you want to get some?
Yeah, Mom, that sounds *great.*
School's coming to a *close* isn't it? Are you thrilled to be *finally done?*
Oh, yeah. You know how it goes.
It's got to be an *exciting* and *scary* time for you, I'm sure. But I *know* you'll do *fine.*
Mom, it's *not* that big a deal. It's *just another year.*
Honey, you're *graduating college.* That *doesn't* happen every day!
No, no I guess it *doesn't.*
And then you'll be a *teacher,* just like *me!* Well, *history* and not *science,* but even so. We're starting a *tradition* of teachers in the family!
Did I ever tell you the story of *why* I became a teacher?
I'm *sure* you have, but why don't you tell it *again?*

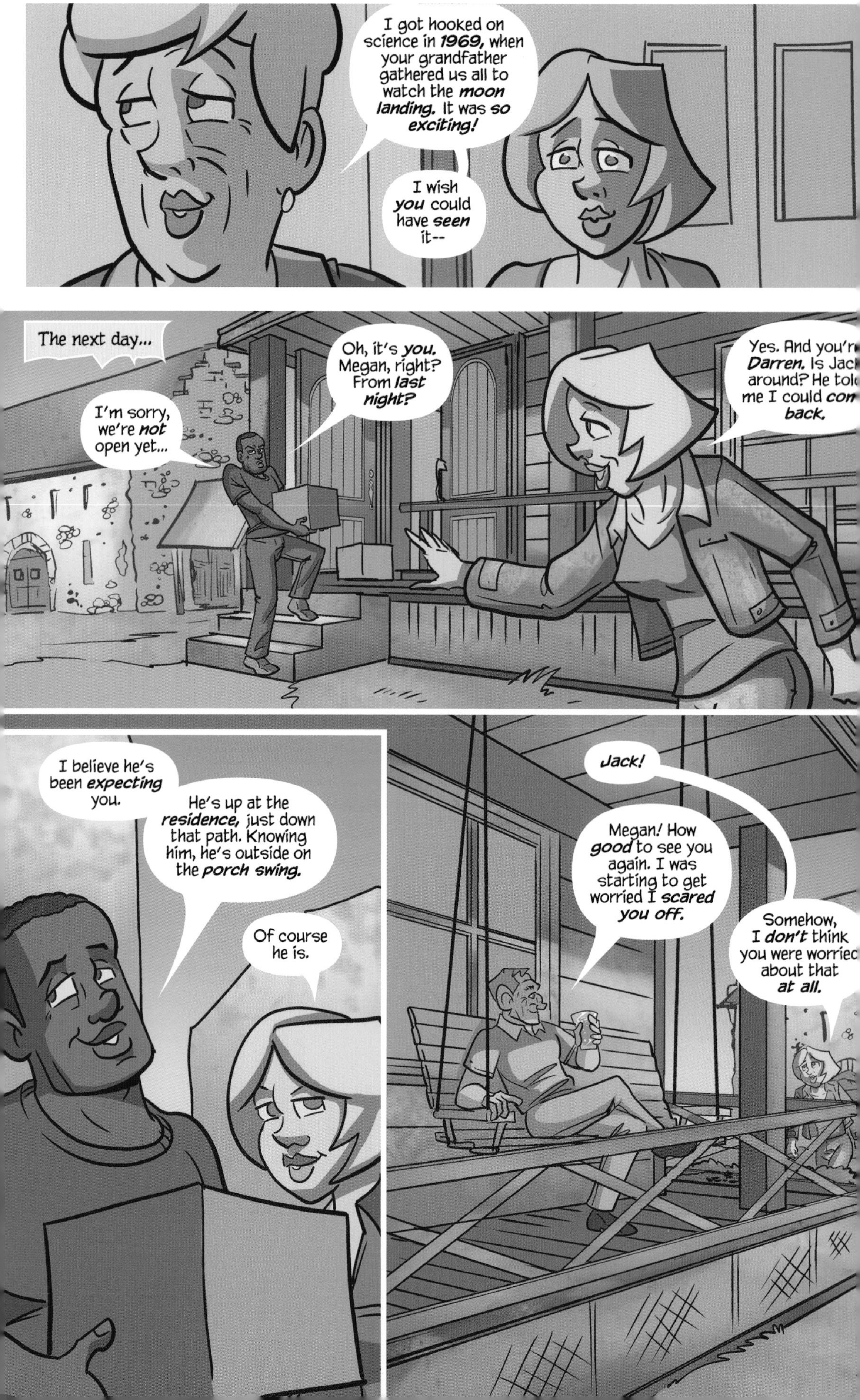

I got hooked on science in *1969,* when your grandfather gathered us all to watch the *moon landing.* It was *so exciting!*
I wish *you* could have *seen* it--
The next day...
I'm sorry, we're *not* open yet...
Oh, it's *you.* Megan, right? From *last night?*
Yes. And you'r *Darren.* Is Jac around? He tol me I could *con back.*
I believe he's been *expecting* you.
He's up at the *residence,* just down that path. Knowing him, he's outside on the *porch swing.*
Of course he is.
*Jack!*
Megan! How *good* to see you again. I was starting to get worried I *scared you off.*
Somehow, I *don't* think you were worriec about that *at all.*

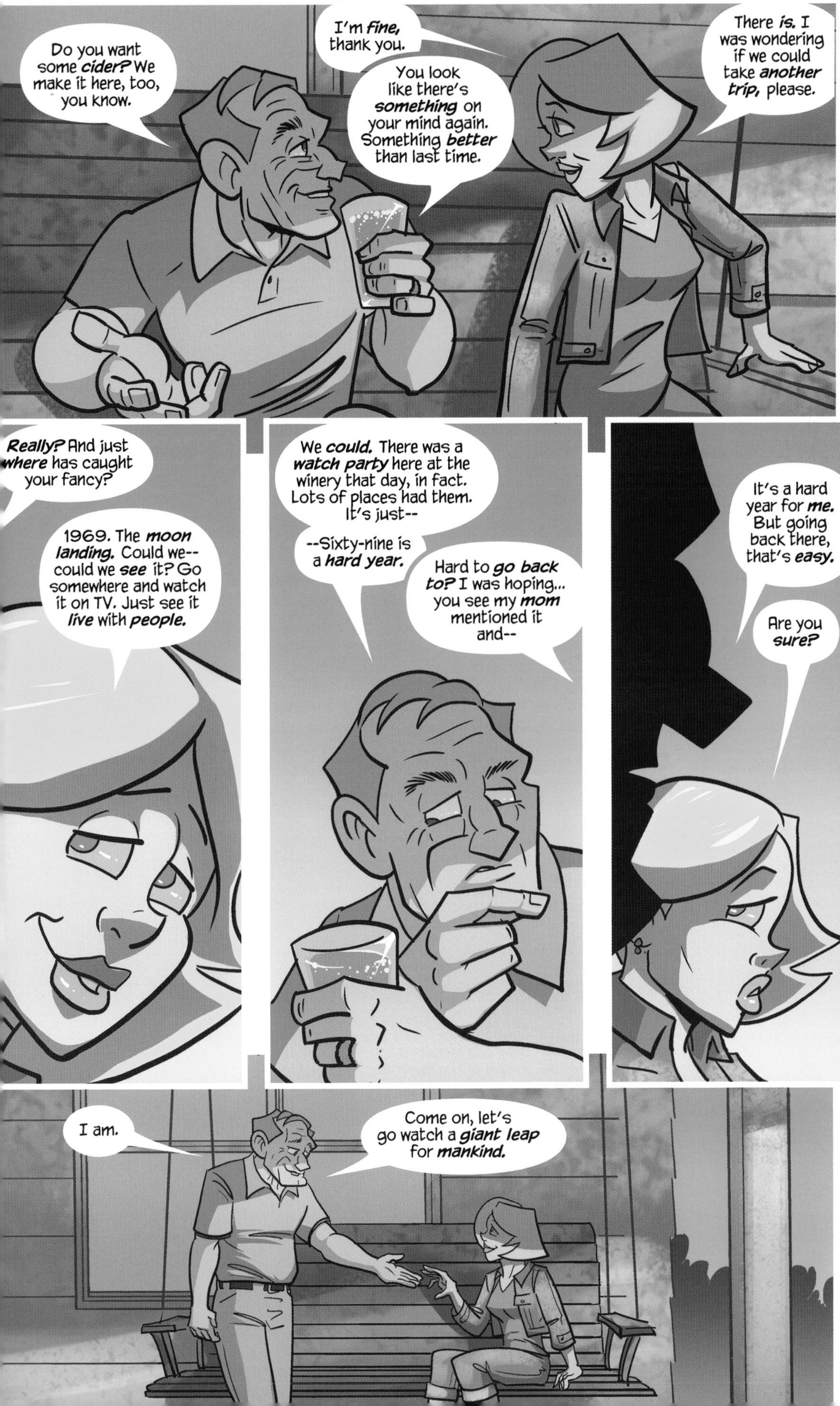
Do you want some *cider?* We make it here, too, you know.
I'm *fine,* thank you.
You look like there's *something* on your mind again. Something *better* than last time.
There *is.* I was wondering if we could take *another trip,* please.
*Really?* And just *where* has caught your fancy?
1969. The *moon landing.* Could we--could we *see* it? Go somewhere and watch it on TV. Just see it *live* with *people.*
We *could.* There was a *watch party* here at the winery that day, in fact. Lots of places had them. It's just--
--Sixty-nine is a *hard year.*
Hard to *go back to?* I was hoping... you see my *mom* mentioned it and--
It's a hard year for *me.* But going back there, that's *easy.*
Are you *sure?*
I am.
Come on, let's go watch a *giant leap* for *mankind.*

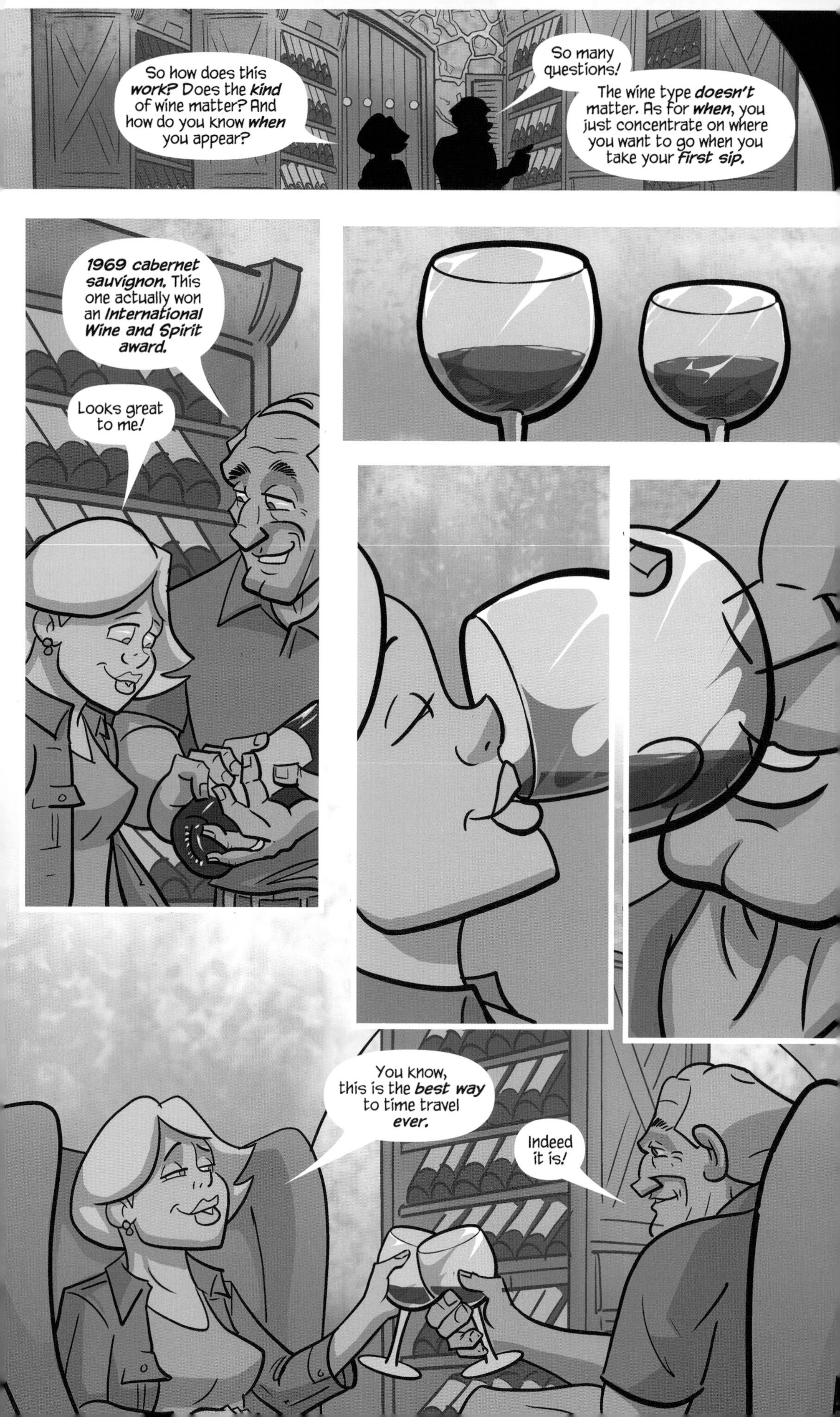
So how does this work? Does the kind of wine matter? And how do you know when you appear?
So many questions!
The wine type doesn't matter. As for when, you just concentrate on where you want to go when you take your first sip.
1969 cabernet sauvignon. This one actually won an International Wine and Spirit award.
Looks great to me!
You know, this is the best way to time travel ever.
Indeed it is!

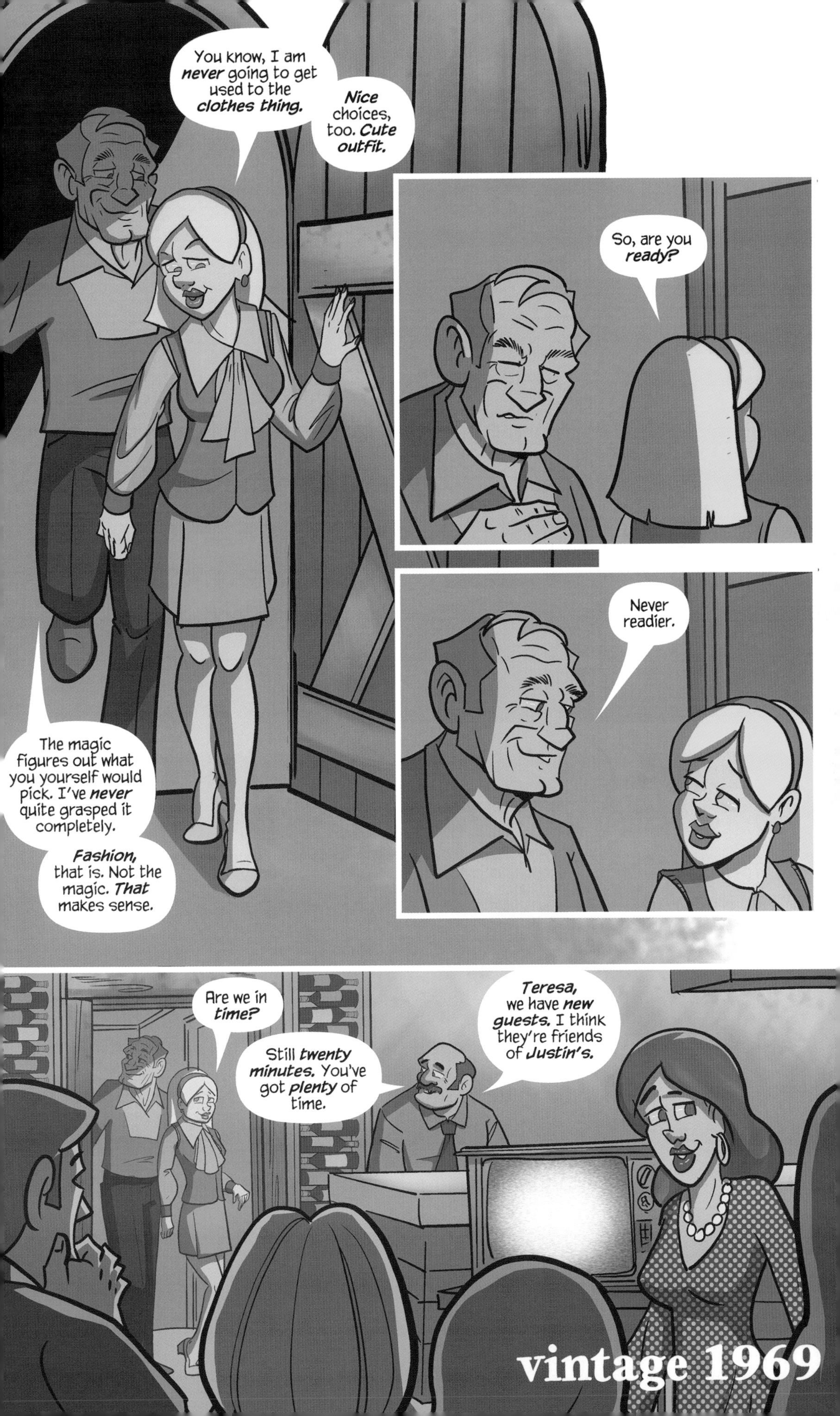
You know, I am never going to get used to the clothes thing.
Nice choices, too. Cute outfit.
The magic figures out what you yourself would pick. I've never quite grasped it completely.
Fashion, that is. Not the magic. That makes sense.
So, are you ready?
Never readier.
Are we in time?
Still twenty minutes. You've got plenty of time.
Teresa, we have new guests. I think they're friends of Justin's.
vintage 1969

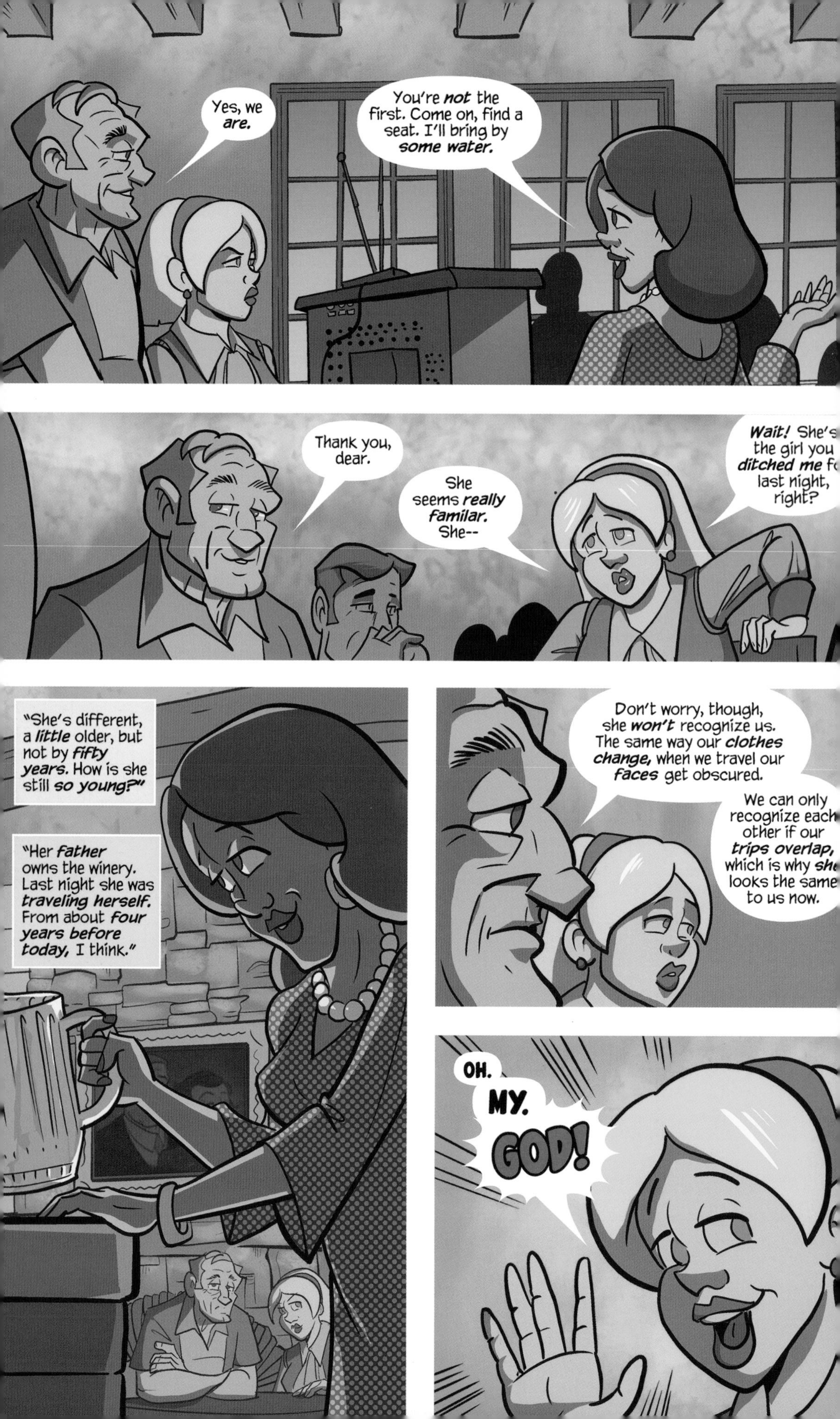

Yes, we *are.*
You're *not* the first. Come on, find a seat. I'll bring by *some water.*
Thank you, dear.
She seems *really familar.* She--
*Wait!* She's the girl you *ditched me* f last night, right?
"She's different, a *little* older, but not by *fifty years.* How is she still *so young?*"
"Her *father* owns the winery. Last night she was *traveling herself.* From about *four years before today,* I think."
Don't worry, though, she *won't* recognize us. The same way our *clothes change,* when we travel our *faces* get obscured.
We can only recognize each other if our *trips overlap,* which is why sh… looks the same to us now.
OH.
MY.
GOD!

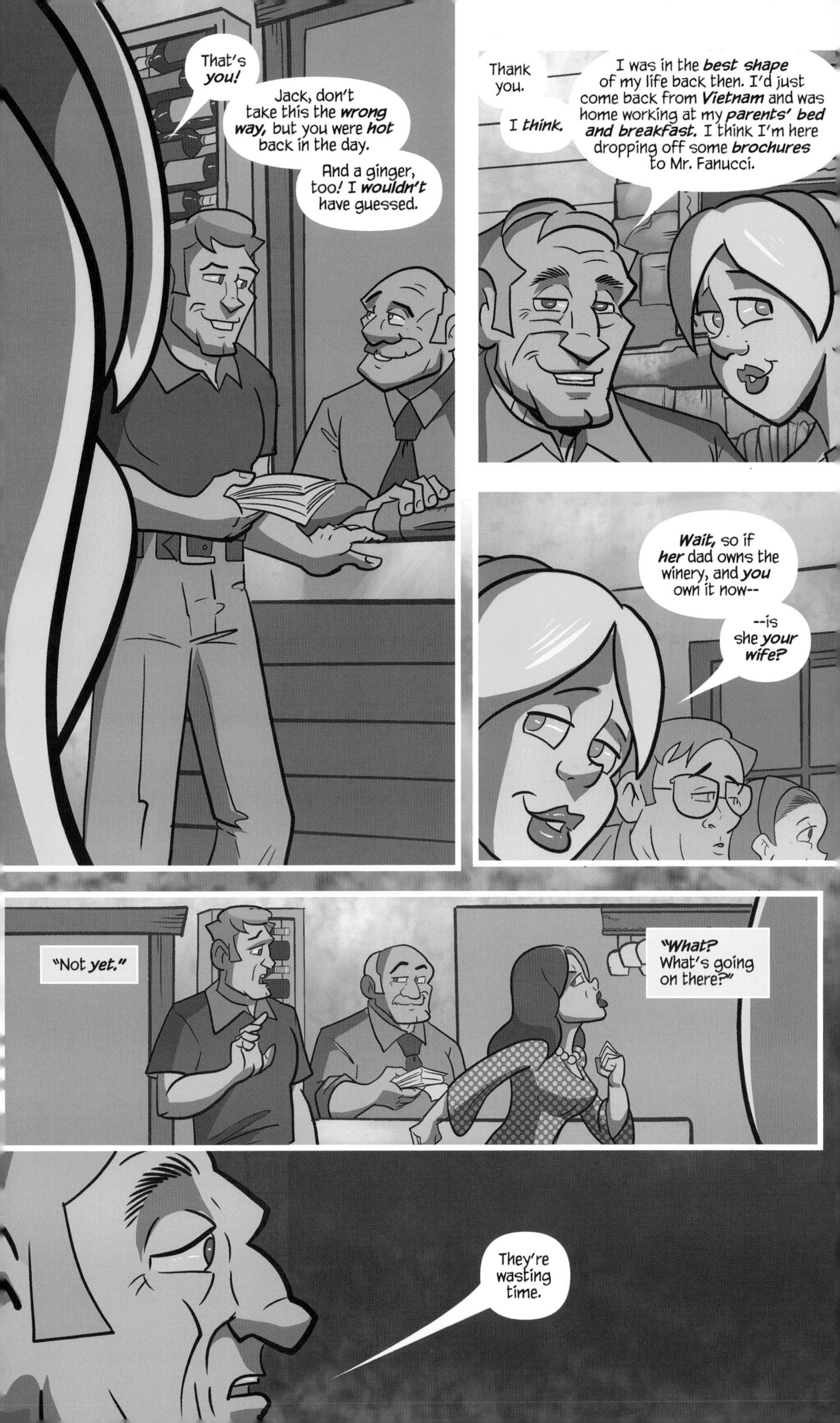

That's *you!*
Jack, don't take this the *wrong way,* but you were *hot* back in the day.
And a ginger, too! I *wouldn't* have guessed.
Thank you.
I *think.*
I was in the *best shape* of my life back then. I'd just come back from *Vietnam* and was home working at my *parents' bed and breakfast.* I think I'm here dropping off some *brochures* to Mr. Fanucci.
*Wait,* so if *her* dad owns the winery, and *you* own it now--
--is she *your wife?*
"Not *yet.*"
"*What?* What's going on there?"
They're wasting time.

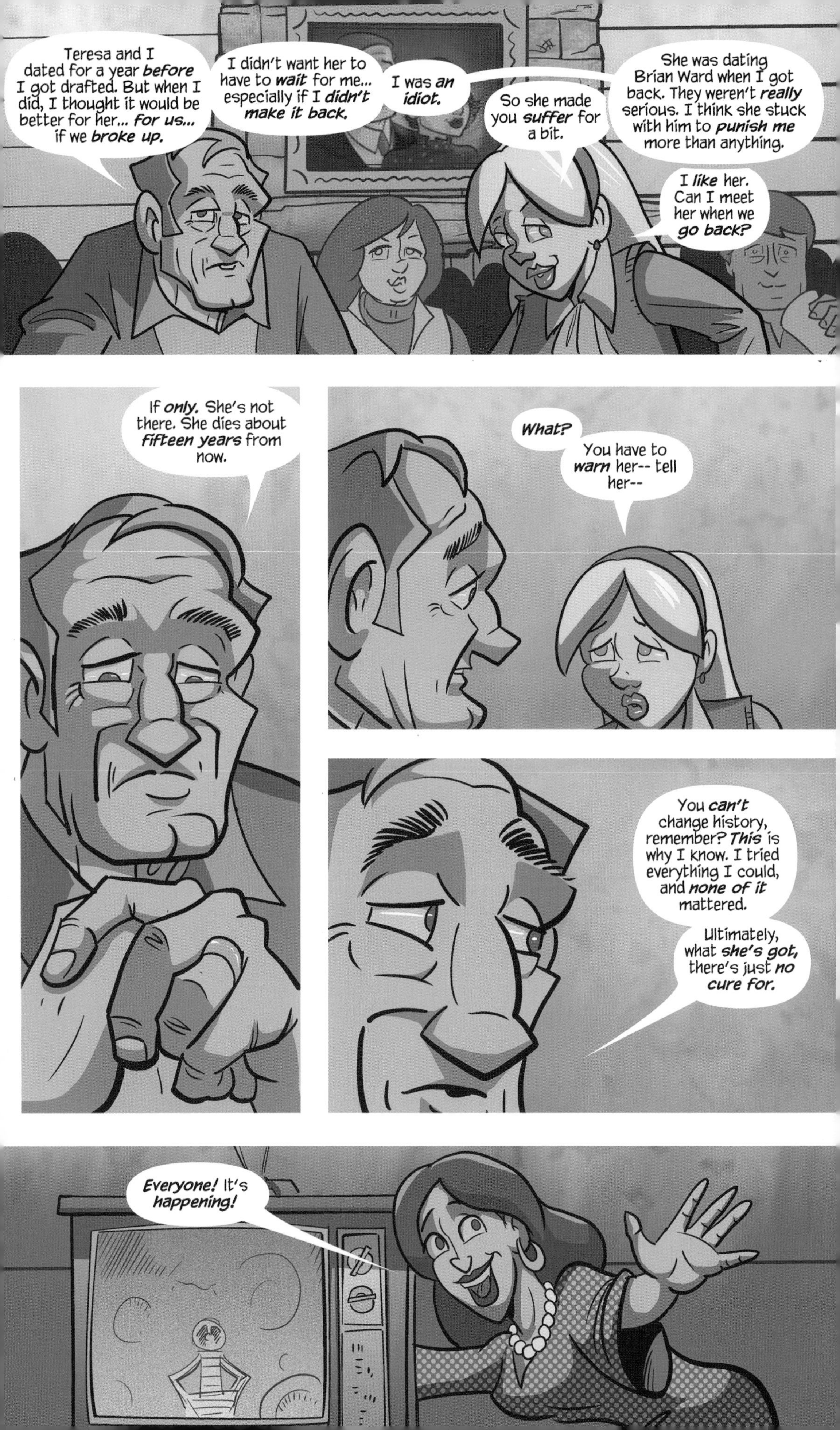
Teresa and I dated for a year before I got drafted. But when I did, I thought it would be better for her... for us... if we broke up.
I didn't want her to have to wait for me... especially if I didn't make it back.
I was an idiot.
So she made you suffer for a bit.
She was dating Brian Ward when I got back. They weren't really serious. I think she stuck with him to punish me more than anything.
I like her. Can I meet her when we go back?
If only. She's not there. She dies about fifteen years from now.
What?
You have to warn her-- tell her--
You can't change history, remember? This is why I know. I tried everything I could, and none of it mattered.
Ultimately, what she's got, there's just no cure for.
Everyone! It's happening!

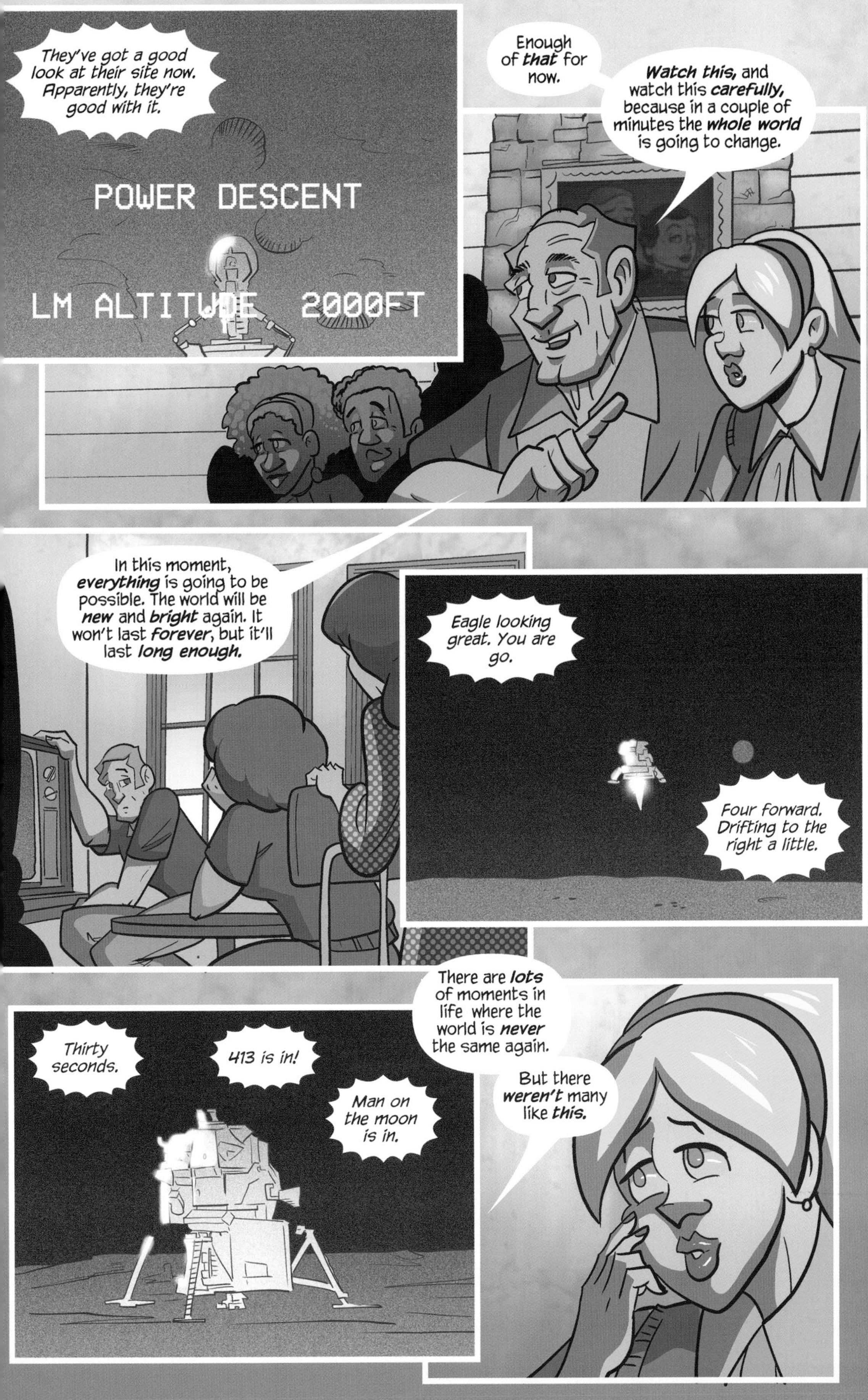
They've got a good look at their site now. Apparently, they're good with it.
POWER DESCENT
LM ALTITUDE 2000FT
Enough of *that* for now.
***Watch this,*** and watch this ***carefully,*** because in a couple of minutes the ***whole world*** is going to change.
In this moment, ***everything*** is going to be possible. The world will be ***new*** and ***bright*** again. It won't last ***forever***, but it'll last ***long enough.***
Eagle looking great. You are go.
Four forward. Drifting to the right a little.
Thirty seconds.
413 is in!
Man on the moon is in.
There are ***lots*** of moments in life where the world is ***never*** the same again.
But there ***weren't*** many like ***this.***

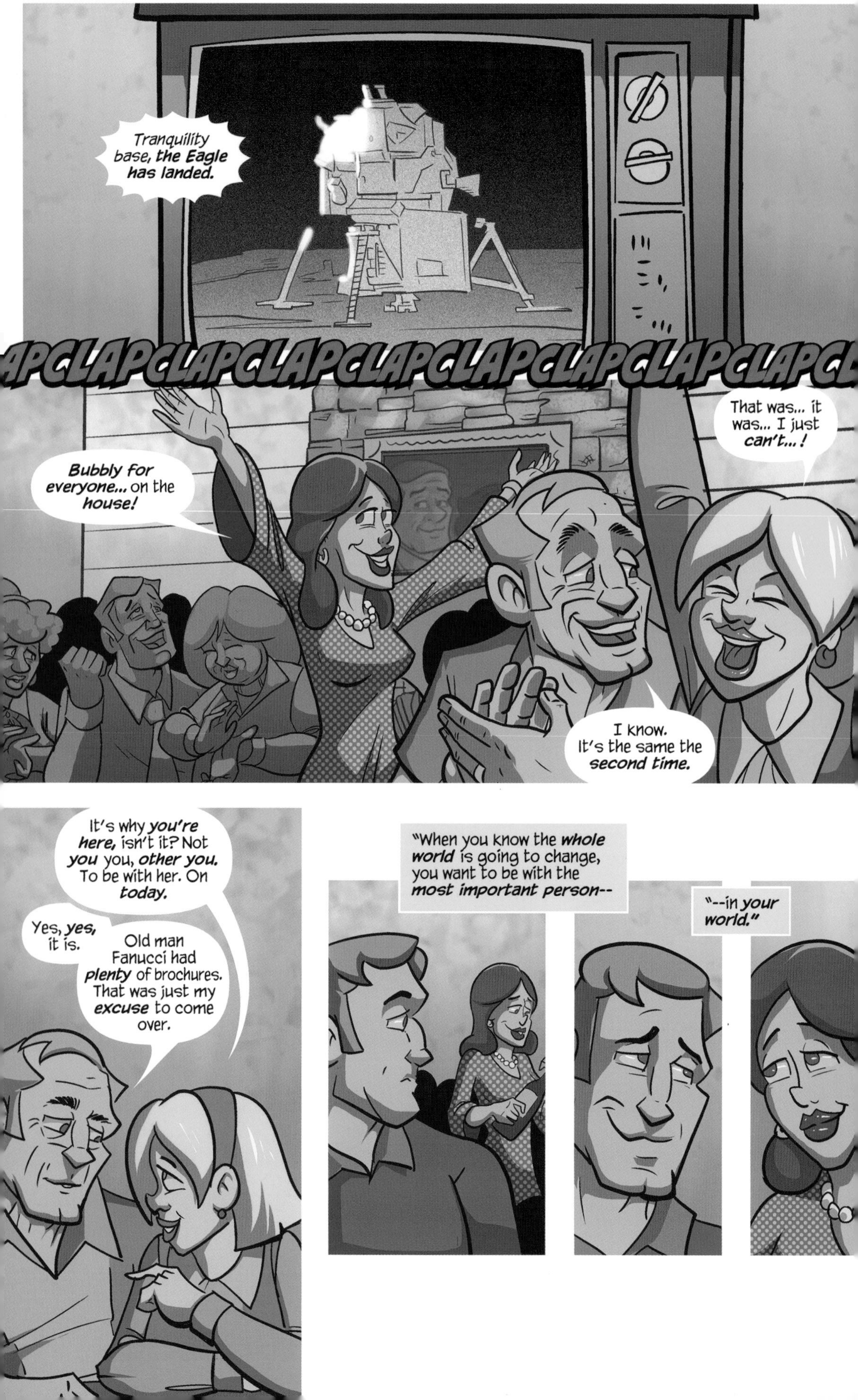
Tranquility base, the Eagle has landed.
APCLAPCLAPCLAPCLAPCLAPCLAPCLAPCLAPCL
Bubbly for everyone... on the house!
That was... it was... I just can't...!
I know. It's the same the second time.
It's why you're here, isn't it? Not you you, other you. To be with her. On today.
Yes, yes, it is.
Old man Fanucci had plenty of brochures. That was just my excuse to come over.
"When you know the whole world is going to change, you want to be with the most important person--
"--in your world."

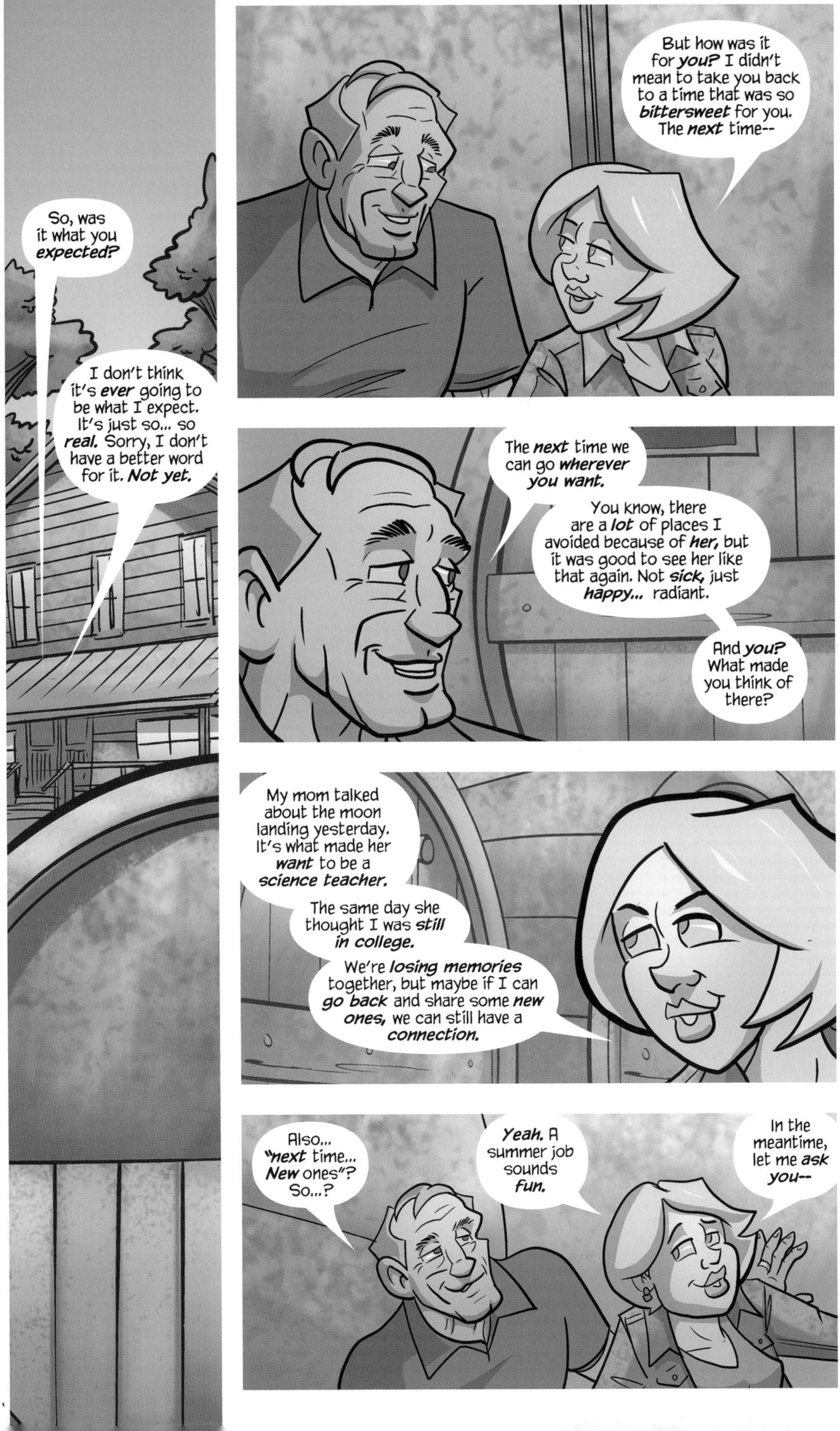
So, was it what you *expected?*
I don't think it's *ever* going to be what I expect. It's just so... so *real.* Sorry, I don't have a better word for it. *Not yet.*
But how was it for *you?* I didn't mean to take you back to a time that was so *bittersweet* for you. The *next* time--
The *next* time we can go *wherever you want.*
You know, there are a *lot* of places I avoided because of *her,* but it was good to see her like that again. Not *sick,* just *happy...* radiant.
And *you?* What made you think of there?
My mom talked about the moon landing yesterday. It's what made her *want* to be a *science teacher.*
The same day she thought I was *still in college.*
We're *losing memories* together, but maybe if I can *go back* and share some *new ones,* we can still have a *connection.*
Also... *"next* time... *New* ones"? So...?
*Yeah.* A summer job sounds *fun.*
In the meantime, let me *ask you--*

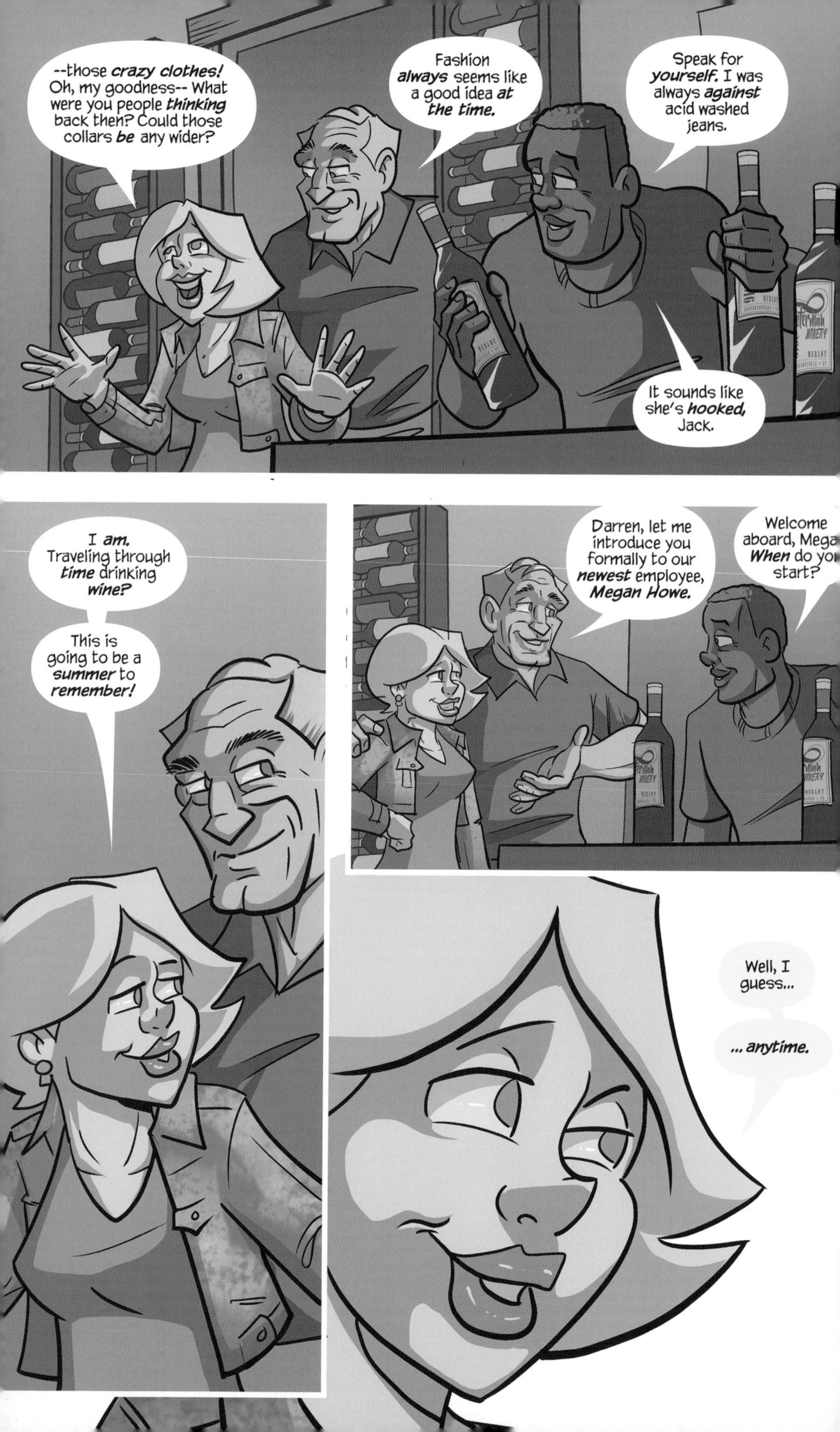
--those *crazy clothes!* Oh, my goodness-- What were you people *thinking* back then? Could those collars *be* any wider?
Fashion *always* seems like a good idea *at the time.*
Speak for *yourself.* I was always *against* acid washed jeans.
It sounds like she's *hooked,* Jack.
I *am.* Traveling through *time* drinking *wine?*
This is going to be a *summer* to *remember!*
Darren, let me introduce you formally to our *newest* employee, *Megan Howe.*
Welcome aboard, Mega *When* do yo start?
Well, I guess...
*...anytime.*

# Chapter Two

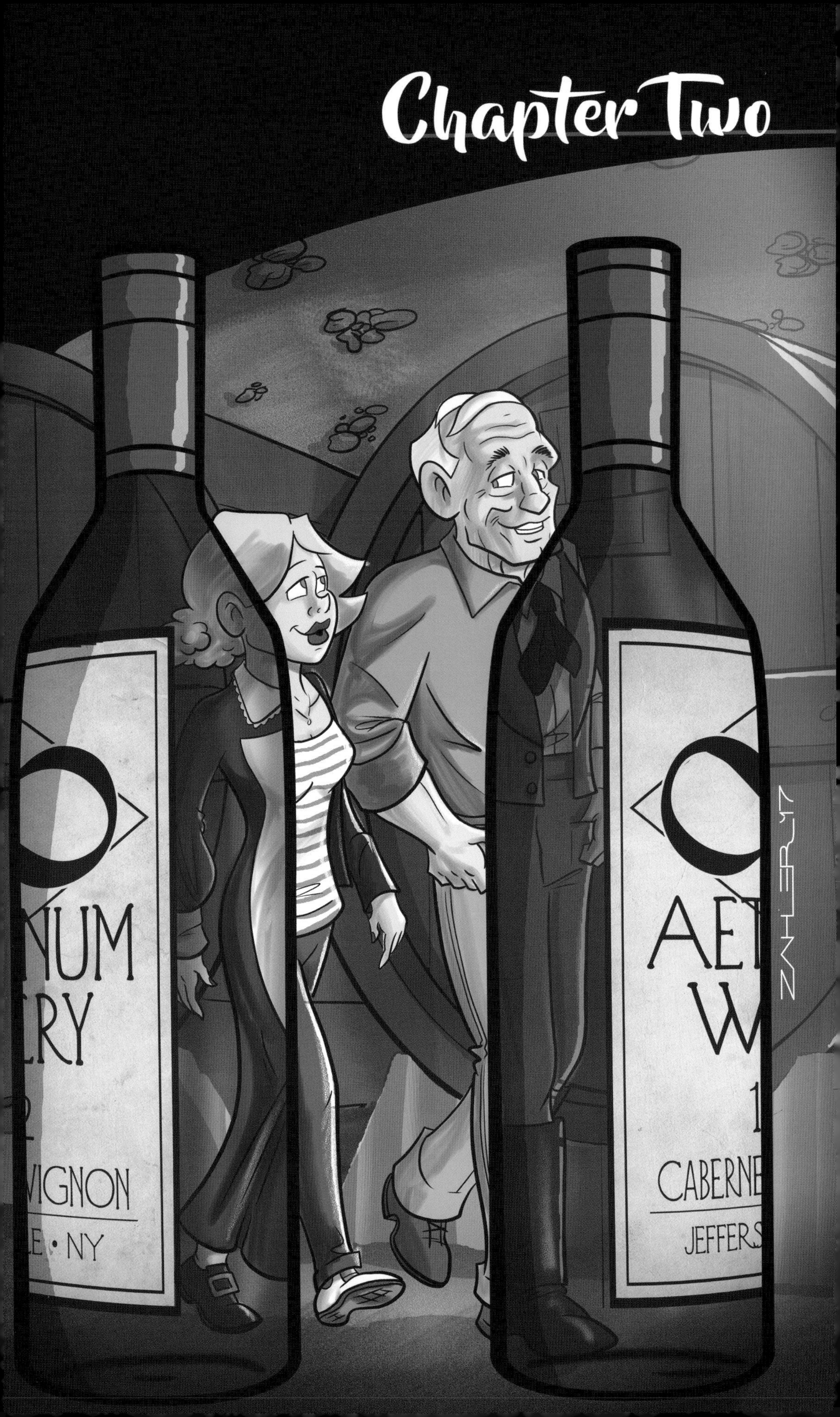
NUM
ERY
VIGNON
LE • NY
AET
W
CABERNE
JEFFERS

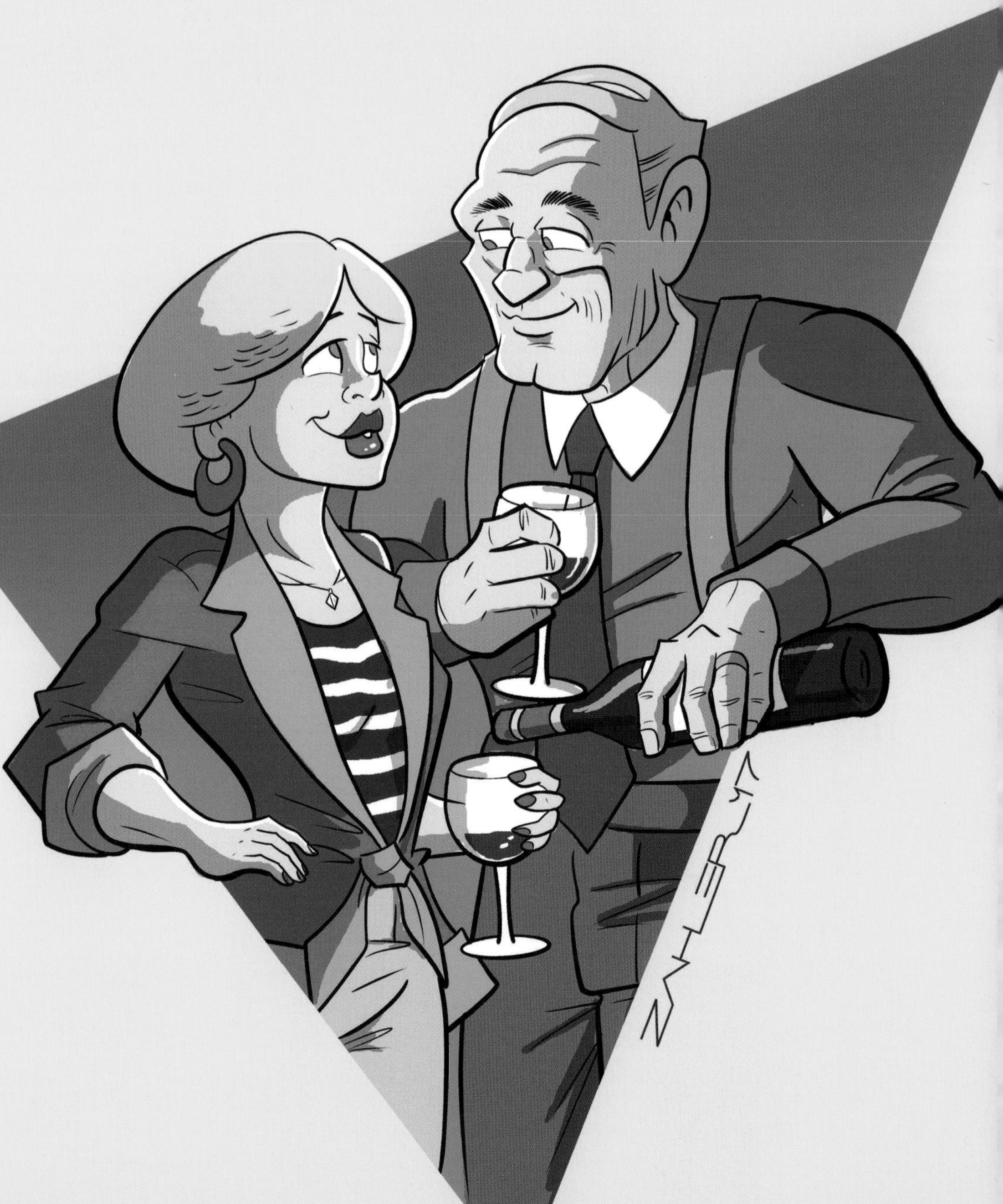
ZAHLER '17

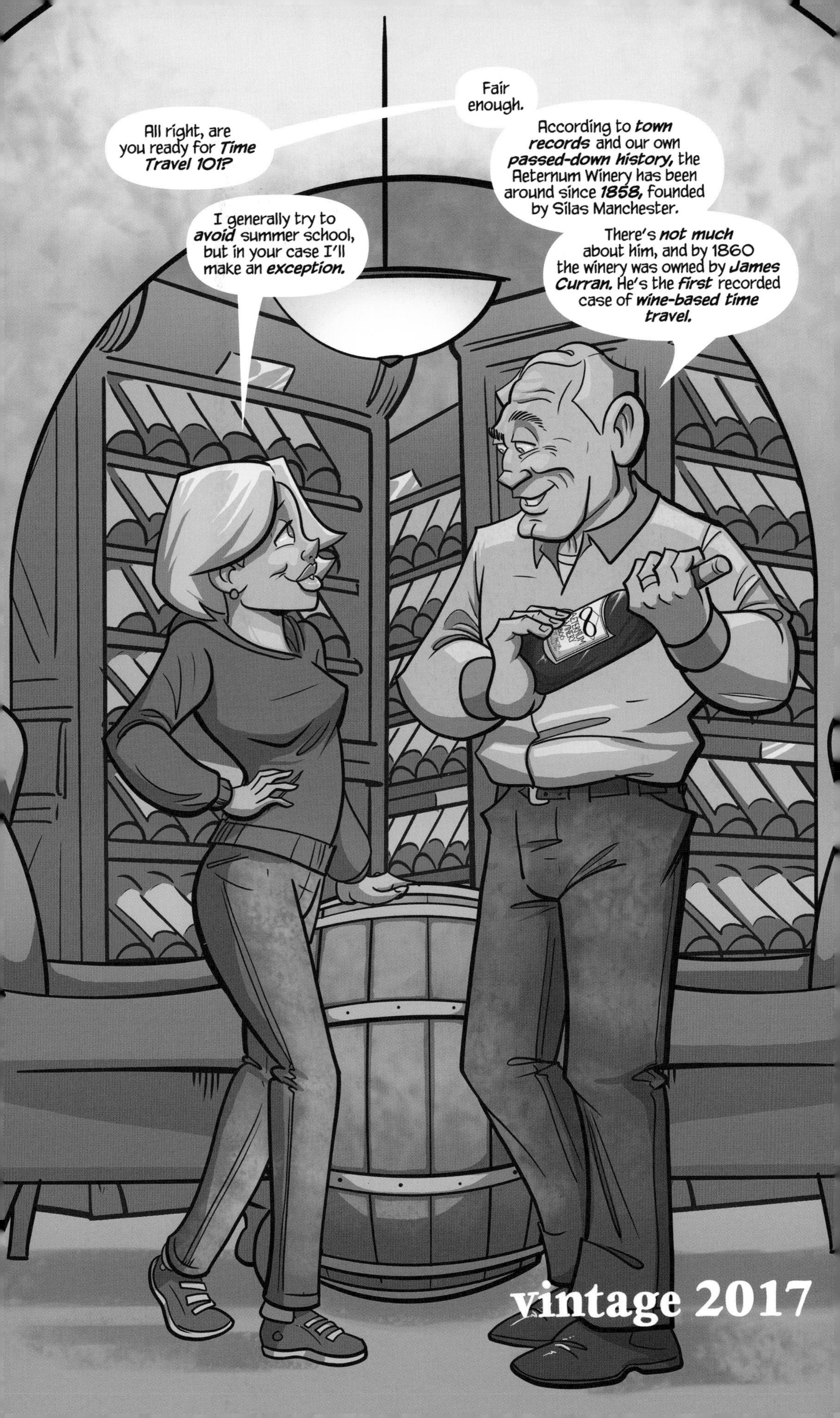

All right, are you ready for Time Travel 101?
I generally try to avoid summer school, but in your case I'll make an exception.
Fair enough.
According to town records and our own passed-down history, the Aeternum Winery has been around since 1858, founded by Silas Manchester.
There's not much about him, and by 1860 the winery was owned by James Curran. He's the first recorded case of wine-based time travel.
vintage 2017

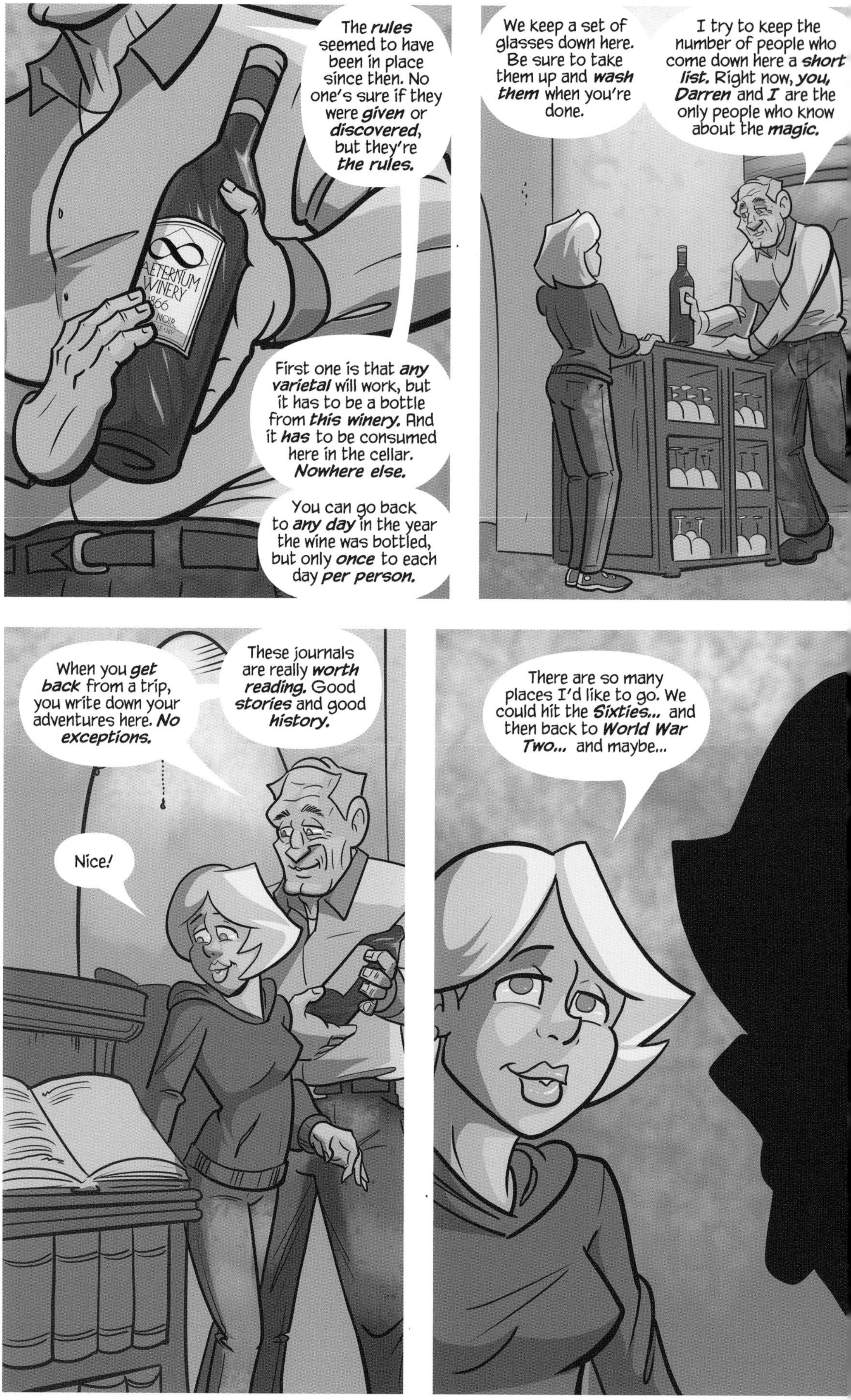

The ***rules*** seemed to have been in place since then. No one's sure if they were ***given*** or ***discovered***, but they're ***the rules.***
AETERNUM WINERY
First one is that ***any varietal*** will work, but it has to be a bottle from ***this winery.*** And it ***has*** to be consumed here in the cellar. ***Nowhere else.***
You can go back to ***any day*** in the year the wine was bottled, but only ***once*** to each day ***per person.***
We keep a set of glasses down here. Be sure to take them up and ***wash them*** when you're done.
I try to keep the number of people who come down here a ***short list.*** Right now, ***you, Darren*** and ***I*** are the only people who know about the ***magic.***
When you ***get back*** from a trip, you write down your adventures here. ***No exceptions.***
These journals are really ***worth reading.*** Good ***stories*** and good ***history.***
Nice!
There are so many places I'd like to go. We could hit the ***Sixties...*** and then back to ***World War Two...*** and maybe...

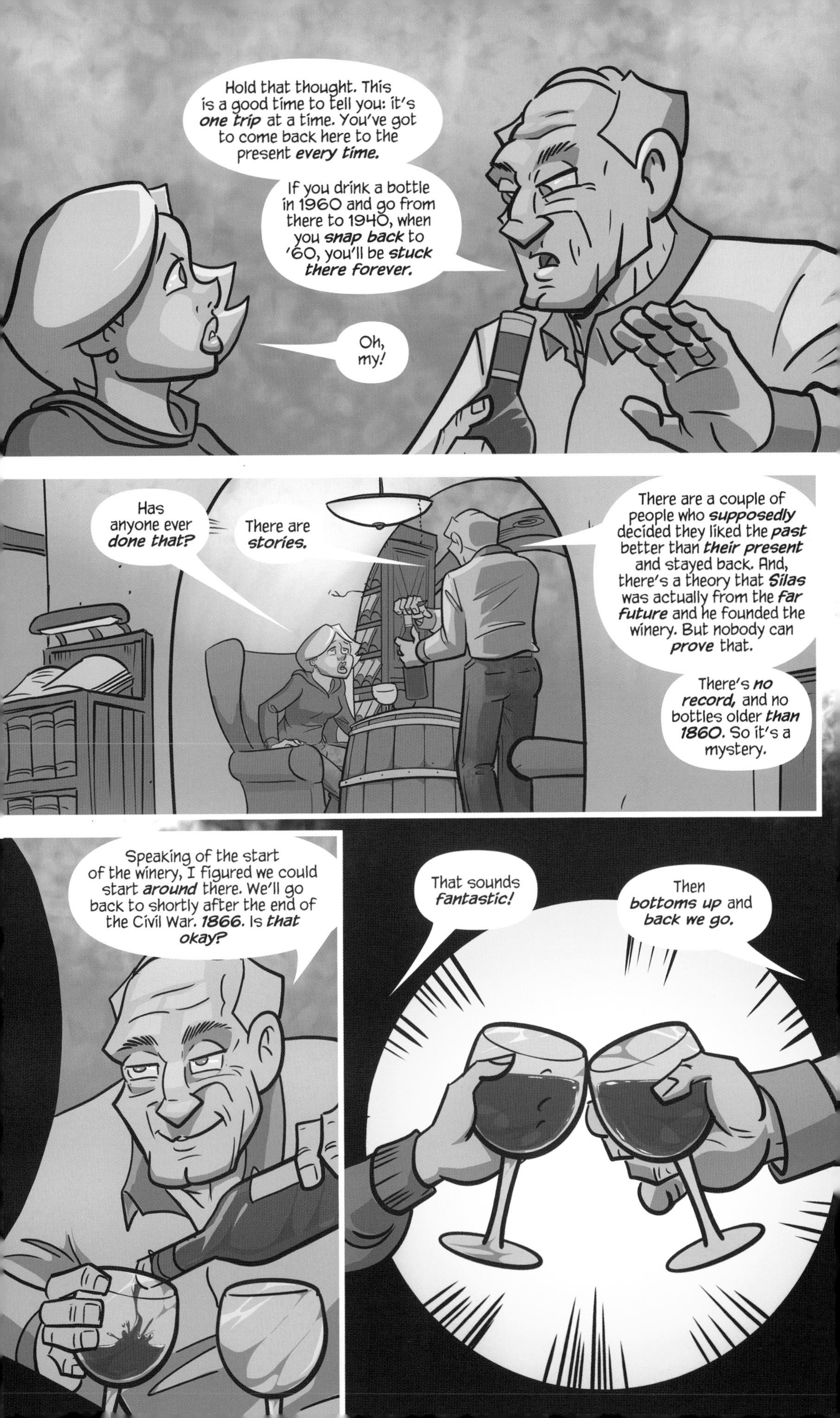
Hold that thought. This is a good time to tell you: it's *one trip* at a time. You've got to come back here to the present *every time.*
If you drink a bottle in 1960 and go from there to 1940, when you *snap back* to '60, you'll be *stuck there forever.*
Oh, my!
Has anyone ever *done that?*
There are *stories.*
There are a couple of people who *supposedly* decided they liked the *past* better than *their present* and stayed back. And, there's a theory that *Silas* was actually from the *far future* and he founded the winery. But nobody can *prove* that.
There's *no record,* and no bottles older *than 1860.* So it's a mystery.
Speaking of the start of the winery, I figured we could start *around* there. We'll go back to shortly after the end of the Civil War. *1866*. Is *that okay?*
That sounds *fantastic!*
Then *bottoms up* and *back we go.*

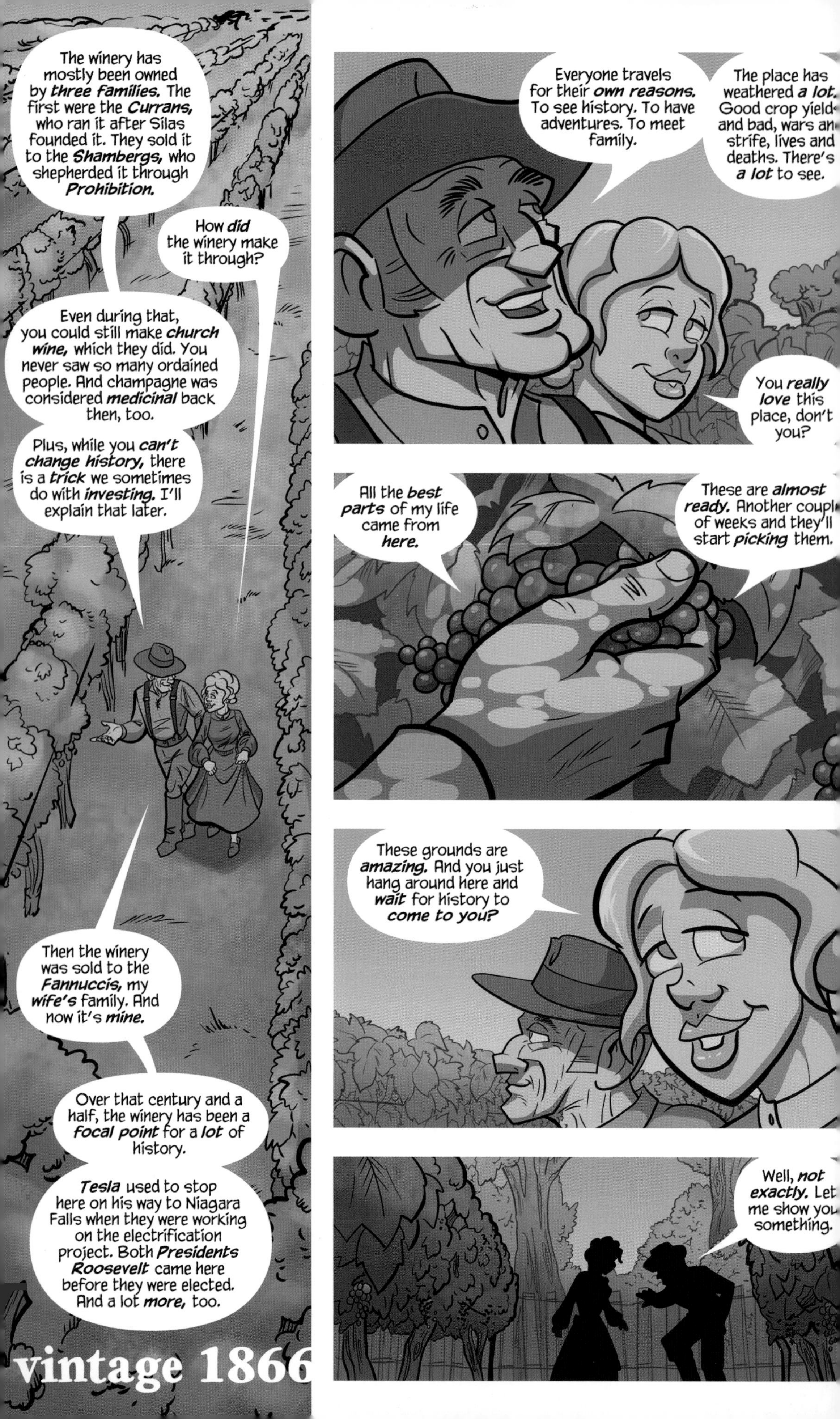
The winery has mostly been owned by *three families.* The first were the *Currans,* who ran it after Silas founded it. They sold it to the *Shambergs,* who shepherded it through *Prohibition.*
How *did* the winery make it through?
Even during that, you could still make *church wine,* which they did. You never saw so many ordained people. And champagne was considered *medicinal* back then, too.
Plus, while you *can't change history,* there is a *trick* we sometimes do with *investing.* I'll explain that later.
Then the winery was sold to the *Fannuccis,* my *wife's* family. And now it's *mine.*
Over that century and a half, the winery has been a *focal point* for a *lot* of history.
*Tesla* used to stop here on his way to Niagara Falls when they were working on the electrification project. Both *Presidents Roosevelt* came here before they were elected. And a lot *more,* too.
vintage 1866
Everyone travels for their *own reasons.* To see history. To have adventures. To meet family.
The place has weathered *a lot.* Good crop yield and bad, wars an strife, lives and deaths. There's *a lot* to see.
You *really love* this place, don't you?
All the *best parts* of my life came from *here.*
These are *almost ready.* Another coupl of weeks and they'll start *picking* them.
These grounds are *amazing.* And you just hang around here and *wait* for history to *come to you?*
Well, *not exactly.* Let me show you something.

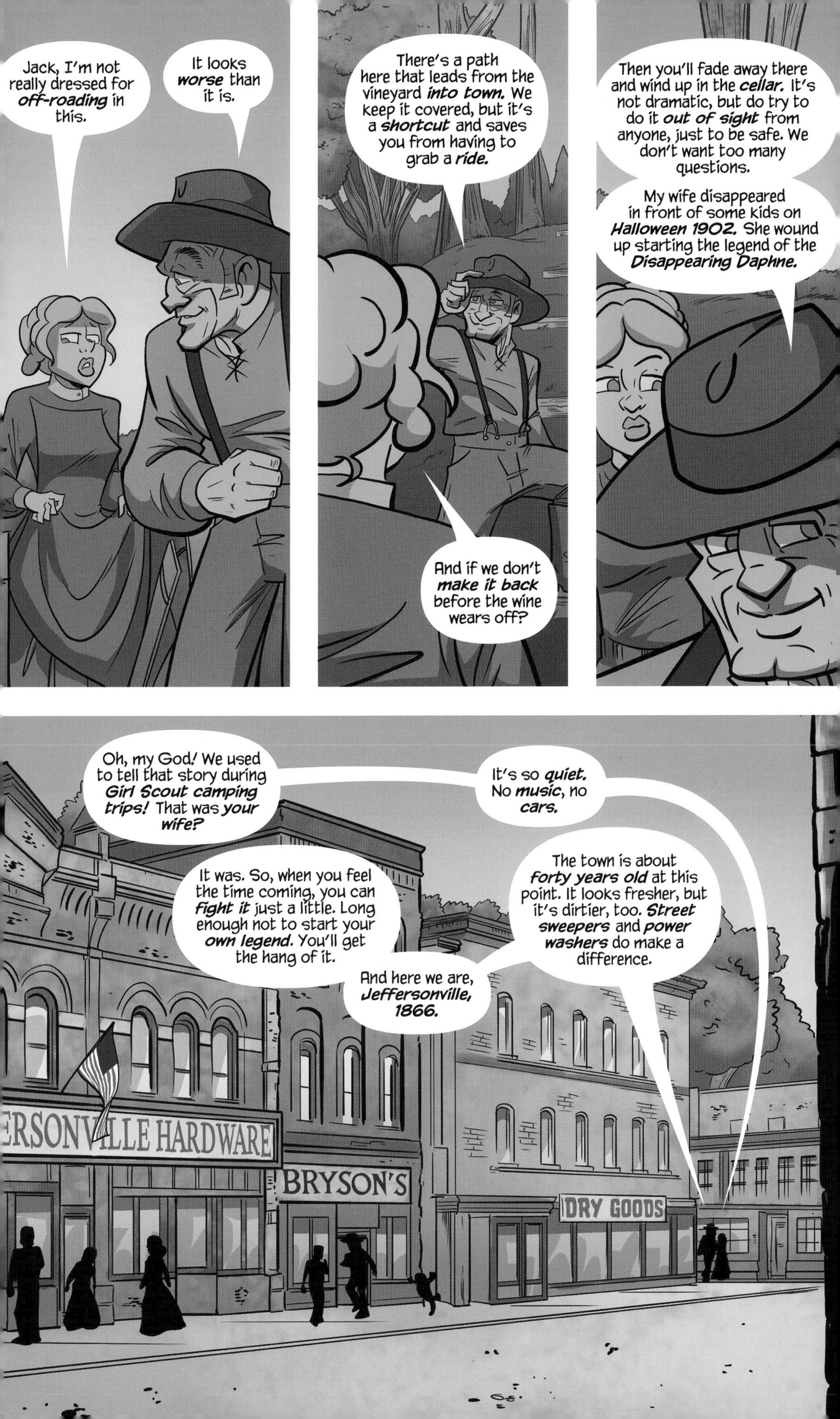
Jack, I'm not really dressed for *off-roading* in this.
It looks *worse* than it is.
There's a path here that leads from the vineyard *into town.* We keep it covered, but it's a *shortcut* and saves you from having to grab a *ride.*
And if we don't *make it back* before the wine wears off?
Then you'll fade away there and wind up in the *cellar.* It's not dramatic, but do try to do it *out of sight* from anyone, just to be safe. We don't want too many questions.
My wife disappeared in front of some kids on *Halloween 1902.* She wound up starting the legend of the *Disappearing Daphne.*
Oh, my God! We used to tell that story during *Girl Scout camping trips!* That was *your wife?*
It was. So, when you feel the time coming, you can *fight it* just a little. Long enough not to start your *own legend.* You'll get the hang of it.
And here we are, *Jeffersonville, 1866.*
It's so *quiet.* No *music*, no *cars.*
The town is about *forty years old* at this point. It looks fresher, but it's dirtier, too. *Street sweepers* and *power washers* do make a difference.
ERSONVILLE HARDWARE
BRYSON'S
DRY GOODS

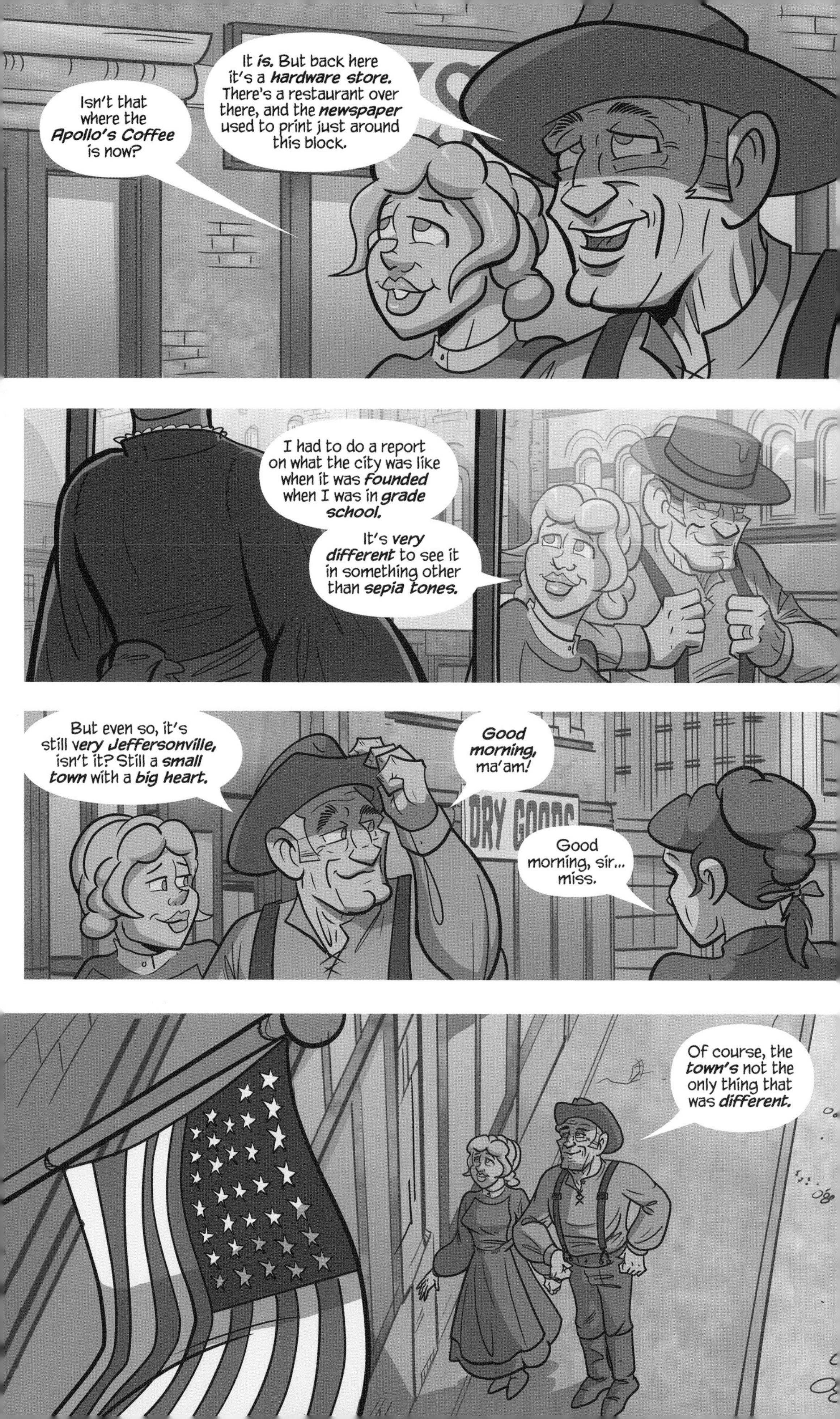
Isn't that where the Apollo's Coffee is now?
It is. But back here it's a hardware store. There's a restaurant over there, and the newspaper used to print just around this block.
I had to do a report on what the city was like when it was founded when I was in grade school.
It's very different to see it in something other than sepia tones.
But even so, it's still very Jeffersonville, isn't it? Still a small town with a big heart.
Good morning, ma'am!
DRY GOODS
Good morning, sir... miss.
Of course, the town's not the only thing that was different.

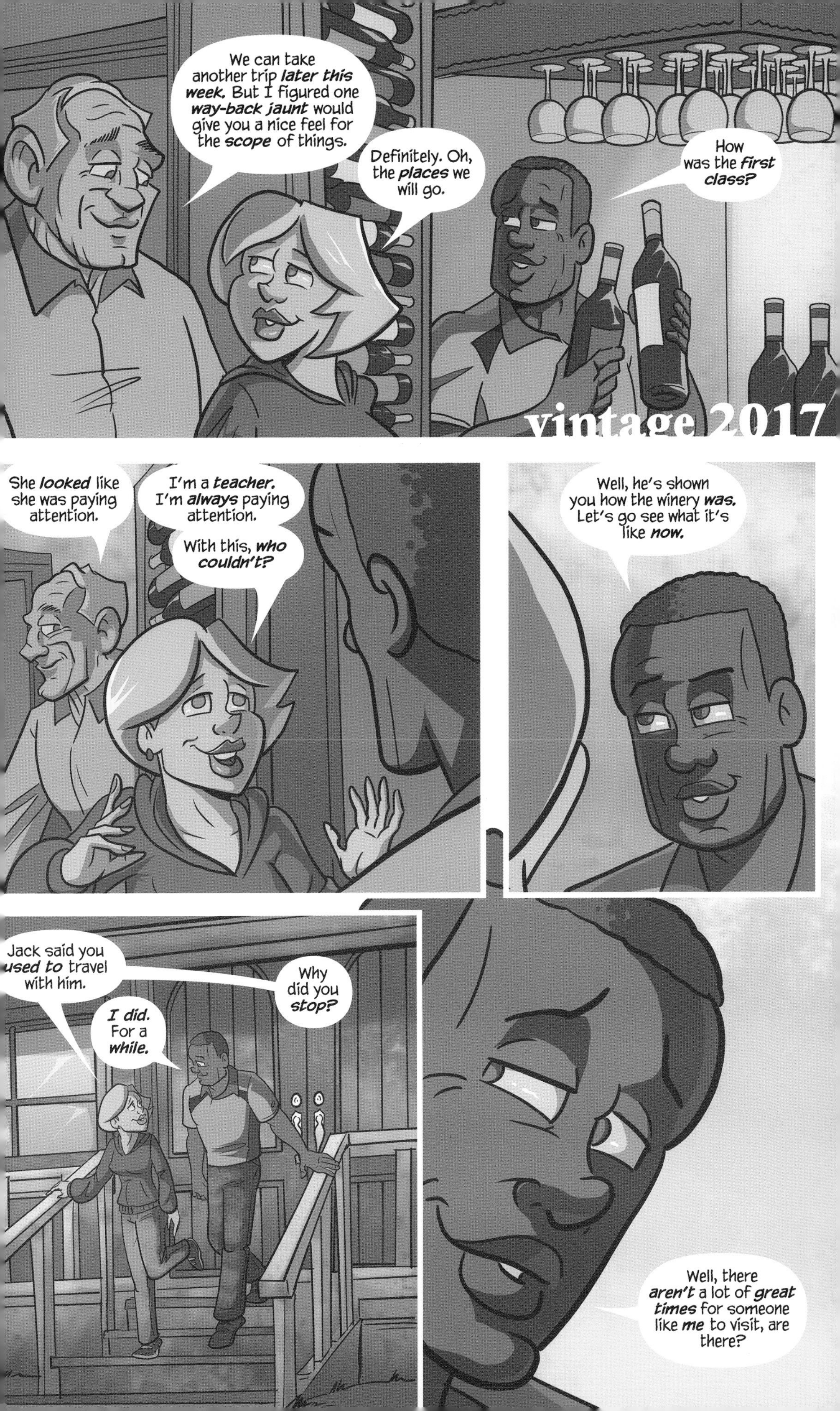
We can take another trip later this week. But I figured one way-back jaunt would give you a nice feel for the scope of things.
Definitely. Oh, the places we will go.
How was the first class?
vintage 2017
She looked like she was paying attention.
I'm a teacher. I'm always paying attention.
With this, who couldn't?
Well, he's shown you how the winery was. Let's go see what it's like now.
Jack said you used to travel with him.
I did. For a while.
Why did you stop?
Well, there aren't a lot of great times for someone like me to visit, are there?

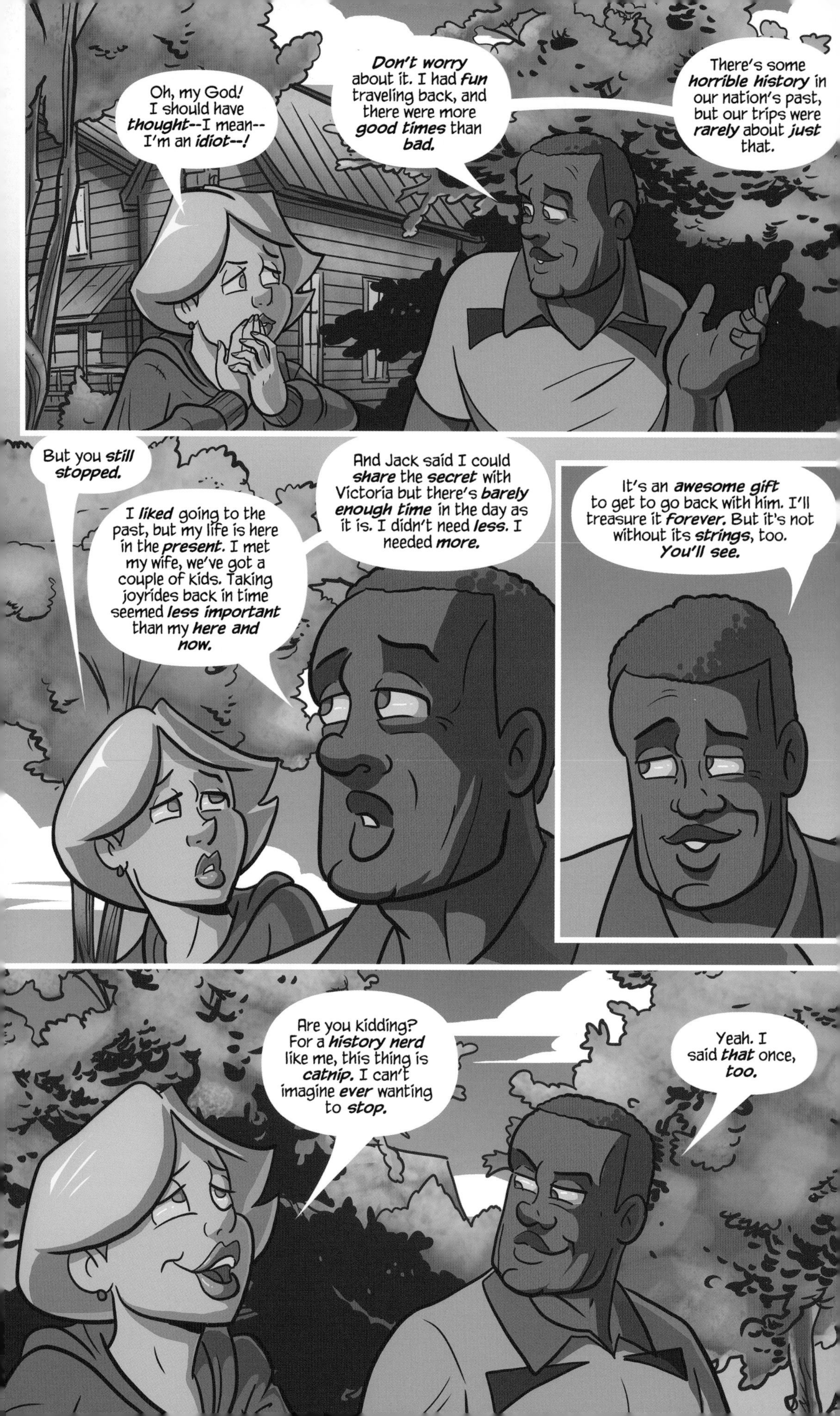
Oh, my God! I should have thought--I mean-- I'm an idiot--!
Don't worry about it. I had fun traveling back, and there were more good times than bad.
There's some horrible history in our nation's past, but our trips were rarely about just that.
But you still stopped.
I liked going to the past, but my life is here in the present. I met my wife, we've got a couple of kids. Taking joyrides back in time seemed less important than my here and now.
And Jack said I could share the secret with Victoria but there's barely enough time in the day as it is. I didn't need less. I needed more.
It's an awesome gift to get to go back with him. I'll treasure it forever. But it's not without its strings, too. You'll see.
Are you kidding? For a history nerd like me, this thing is catnip. I can't imagine ever wanting to stop.
Yeah. I said that once, too.

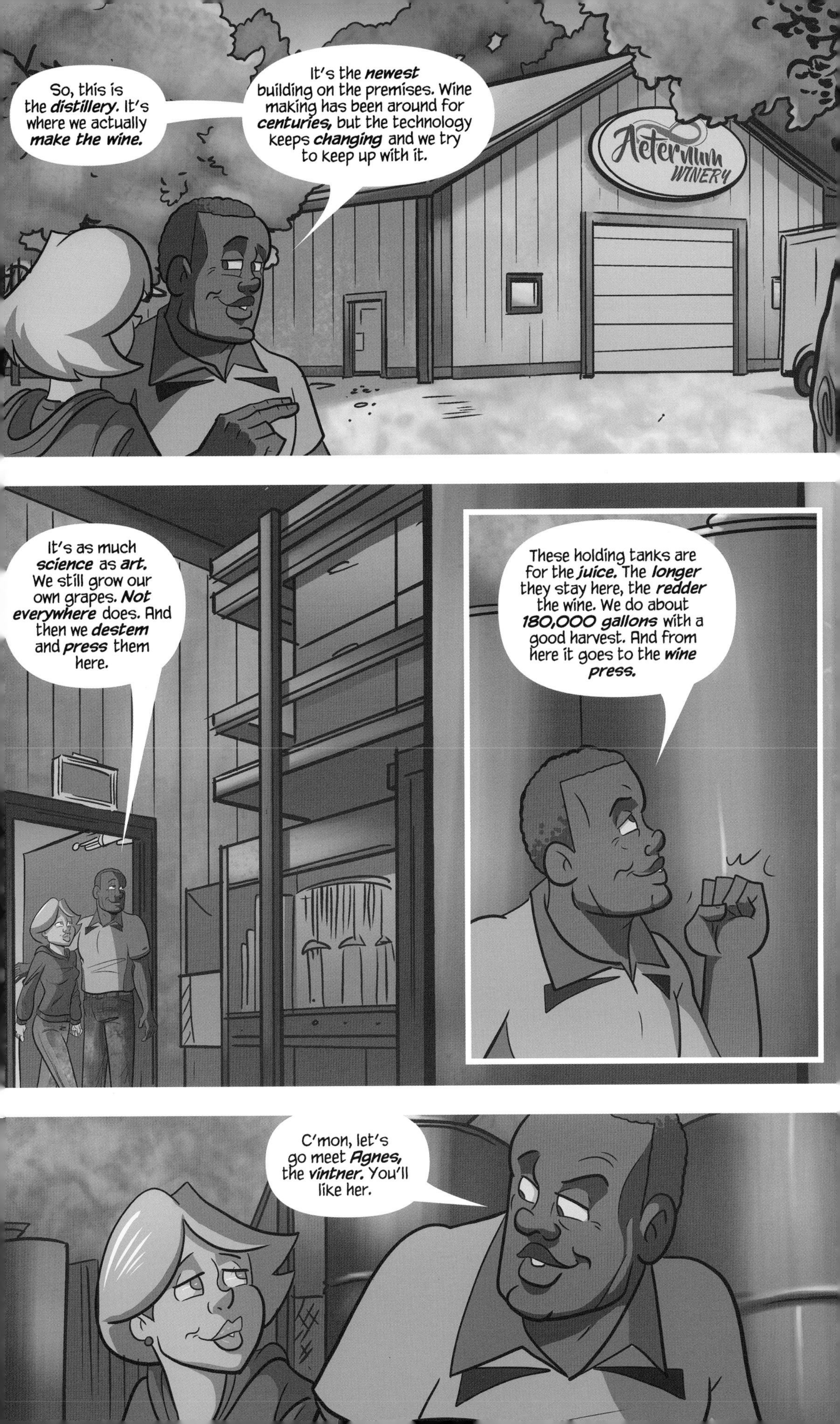
So, this is the distillery. It's where we actually make the wine.
It's the newest building on the premises. Wine making has been around for centuries, but the technology keeps changing and we try to keep up with it.
Aeternum WINERY
It's as much science as art. We still grow our own grapes. Not everywhere does. And then we destem and press them here.
These holding tanks are for the juice. The longer they stay here, the redder the wine. We do about 180,000 gallons with a good harvest. And from here it goes to the wine press.
C'mon, let's go meet Agnes, the vintner. You'll like her.

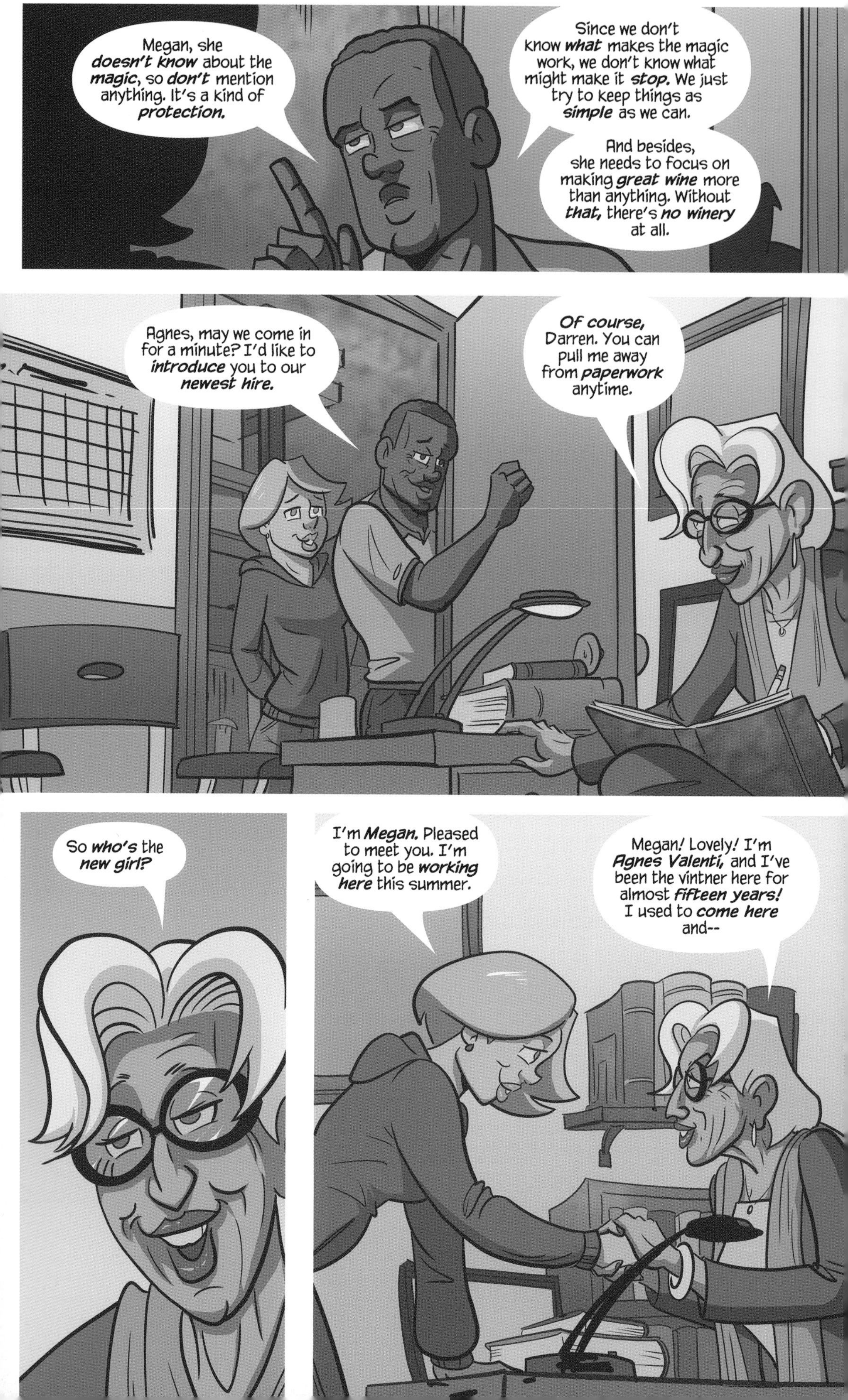
Megan, she *doesn't know* about the *magic*, so *don't* mention anything. It's a kind of *protection.*
Since we don't know *what* makes the magic work, we don't know what might make it *stop.* We just try to keep things as *simple* as we can.
And besides, she needs to focus on making *great wine* more than anything. Without *that,* there's *no winery* at all.
Agnes, may we come in for a minute? I'd like to *introduce* you to our *newest hire.*
*Of course,* Darren. You can pull me away from *paperwork* anytime.
So *who's* the *new girl?*
I'm *Megan.* Pleased to meet you. I'm going to be *working here* this summer.
Megan! Lovely! I'm *Agnes Valenti,* and I've been the vintner here for almost *fifteen years!* I used to *come here* and--

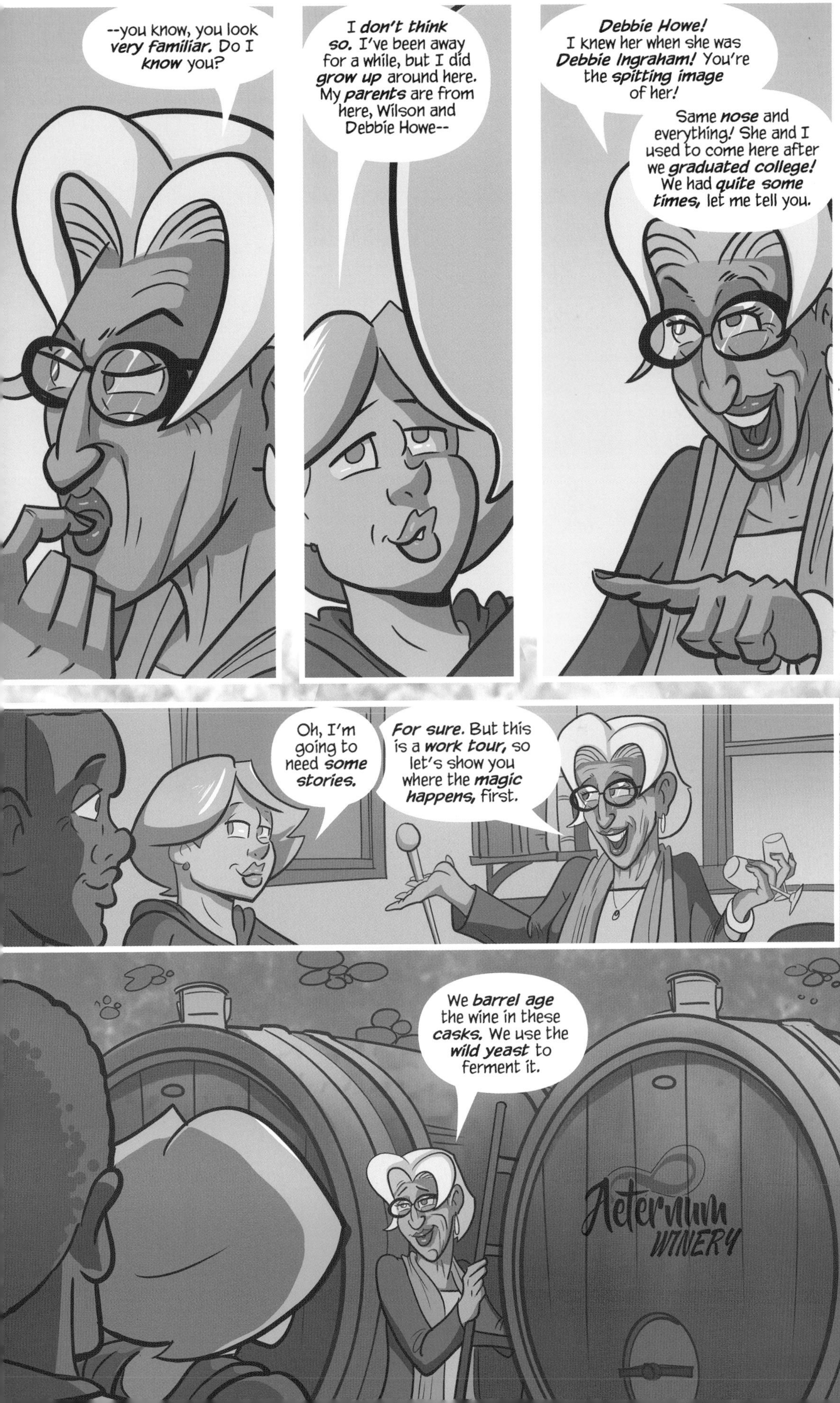
--you know, you look *very familiar.* Do I *know* you?
I *don't think so.* I've been away for a while, but I did *grow up* around here. My *parents* are from here, Wilson and Debbie Howe--
*Debbie Howe!* I knew her when she was *Debbie Ingraham!* You're the *spitting image* of her!
Same *nose* and everything! She and I used to come here after we *graduated college!* We had *quite some times,* let me tell you.
Oh, I'm going to need *some stories.*
*For sure.* But this is a *work tour,* so let's show you where the *magic happens,* first.
We *barrel age* the wine in these *casks.* We use the *wild yeast* to ferment it.
Aeternum
WINERY

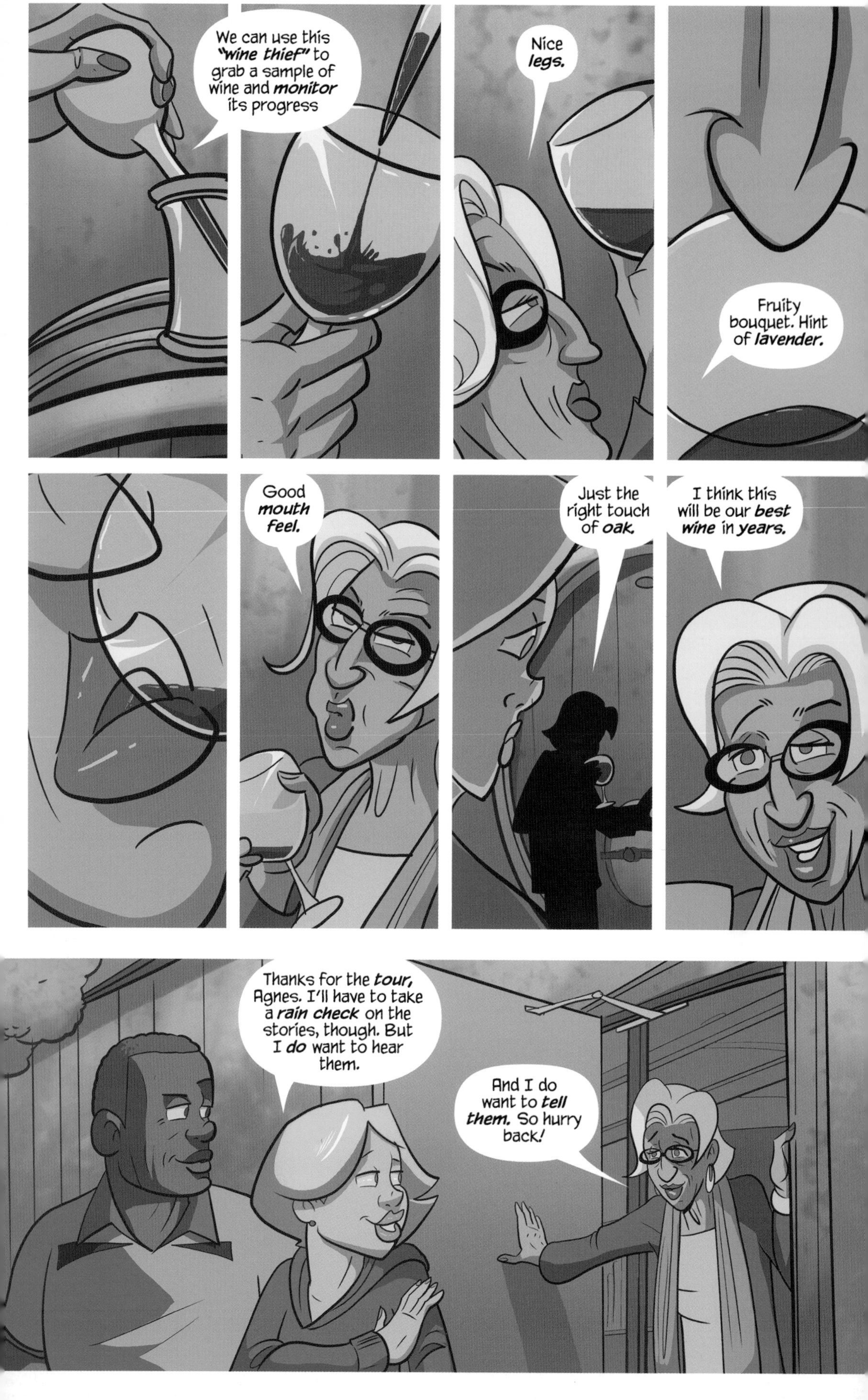
We can use this *"wine thief"* to grab a sample of wine and *monitor* its progress
Nice *legs.*
Fruity bouquet. Hint of *lavender.*
Good *mouth feel.*
Just the right touch of *oak.*
I think this will be our *best wine* in *years.*
Thanks for the *tour,* Agnes. I'll have to take a *rain check* on the stories, though. But I *do* want to hear them.
And I do want to *tell them.* So hurry back!

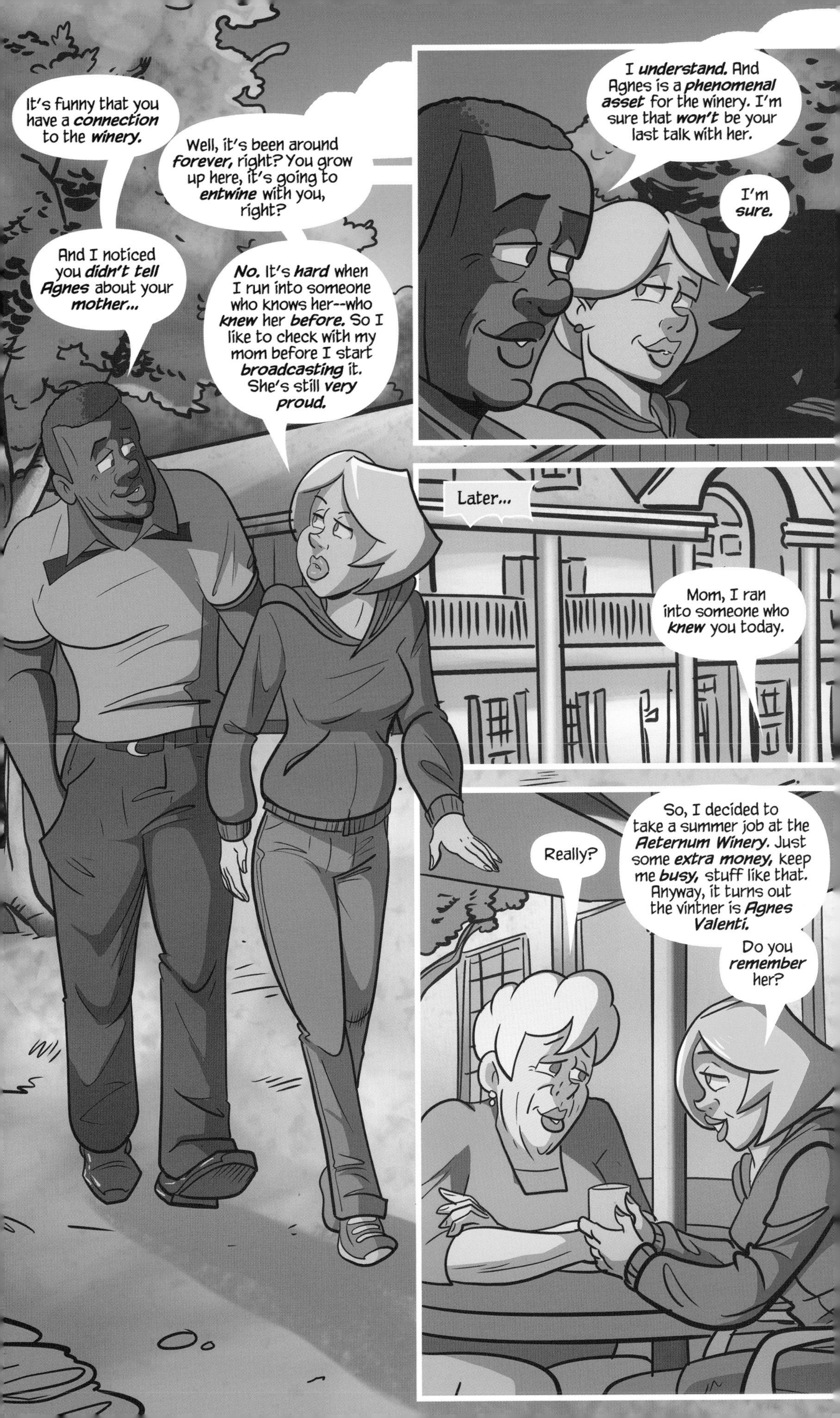
It's funny that you have a connection to the winery.
Well, it's been around forever, right? You grow up here, it's going to entwine with you, right?
And I noticed you didn't tell Agnes about your mother...
No. It's hard when I run into someone who knows her--who knew her before. So I like to check with my mom before I start broadcasting it. She's still very proud.
I understand. And Agnes is a phenomenal asset for the winery. I'm sure that won't be your last talk with her.
I'm sure.
Later...
Mom, I ran into someone who knew you today.
So, I decided to take a summer job at the Aeternum Winery. Just some extra money, keep me busy, stuff like that. Anyway, it turns out the vintner is Agnes Valenti.
Really?
Do you remember her?

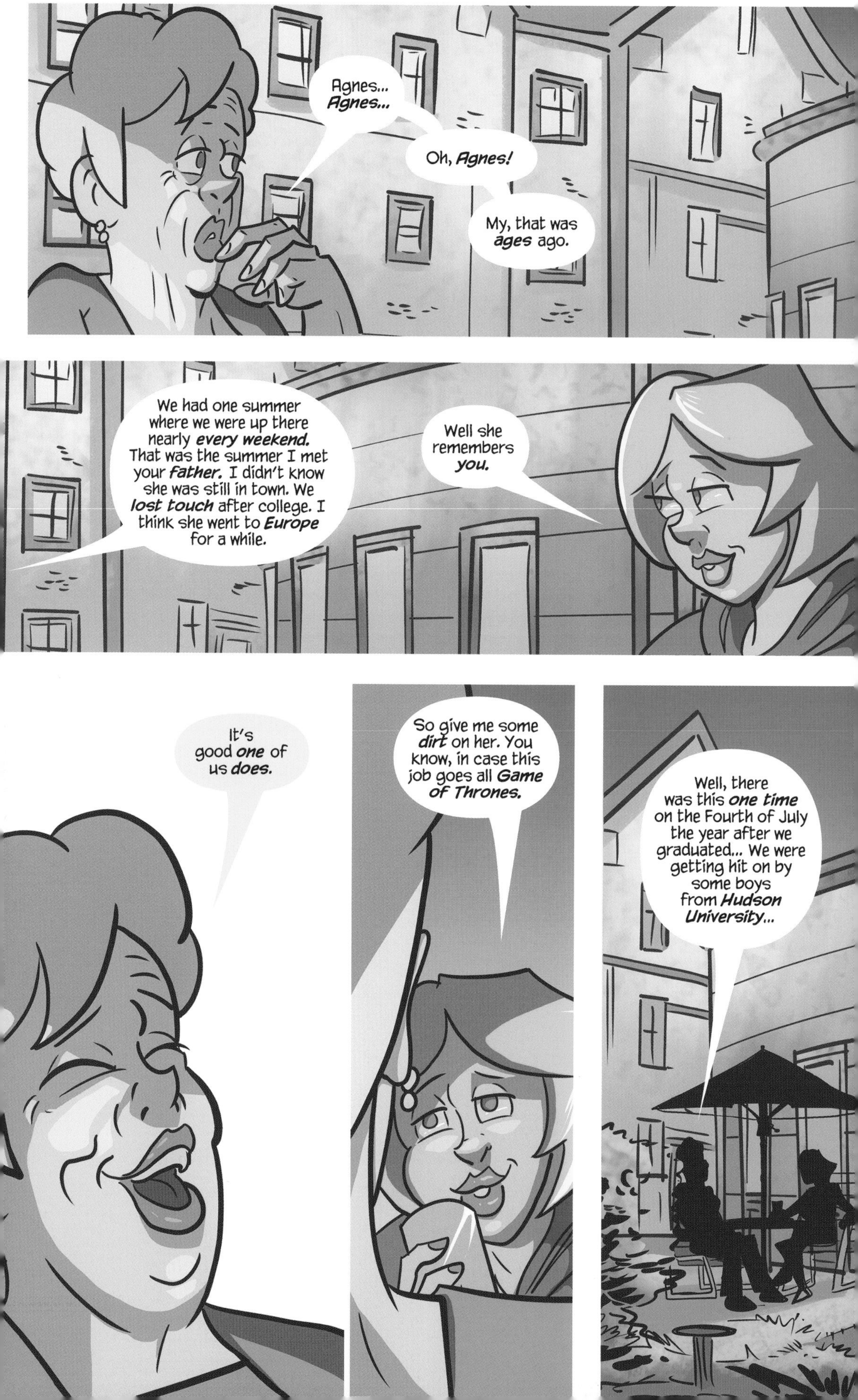
Agnes... Agnes...
Oh, Agnes!
My, that was ages ago.
We had one summer where we were up there nearly every weekend. That was the summer I met your father. I didn't know she was still in town. We lost touch after college. I think she went to Europe for a while.
Well she remembers you.
It's good one of us does.
So give me some dirt on her. You know, in case this job goes all Game of Thrones.
Well, there was this one time on the Fourth of July the year after we graduated... We were getting hit on by some boys from Hudson University...

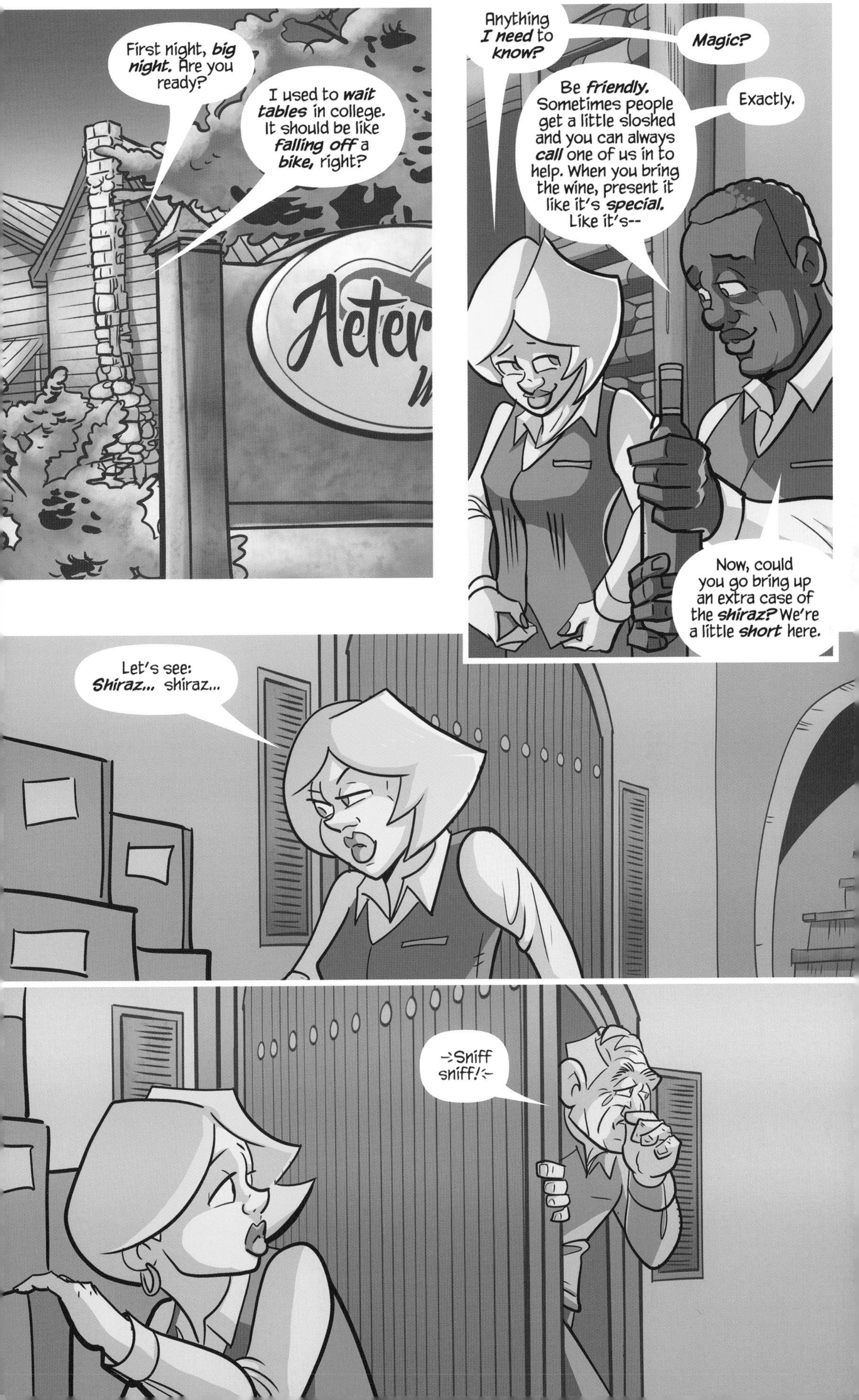

First night, big night. Are you ready?
I used to wait tables in college. It should be like falling off a bike, right?
Aeter
Anything I need to know?
Magic?
Be friendly. Sometimes people get a little sloshed and you can always call one of us in to help. When you bring the wine, present it like it's special. Like it's--
Exactly.
Now, could you go bring up an extra case of the shiraz? We're a little short here.
Let's see: Shiraz... shiraz...
Sniff sniff!

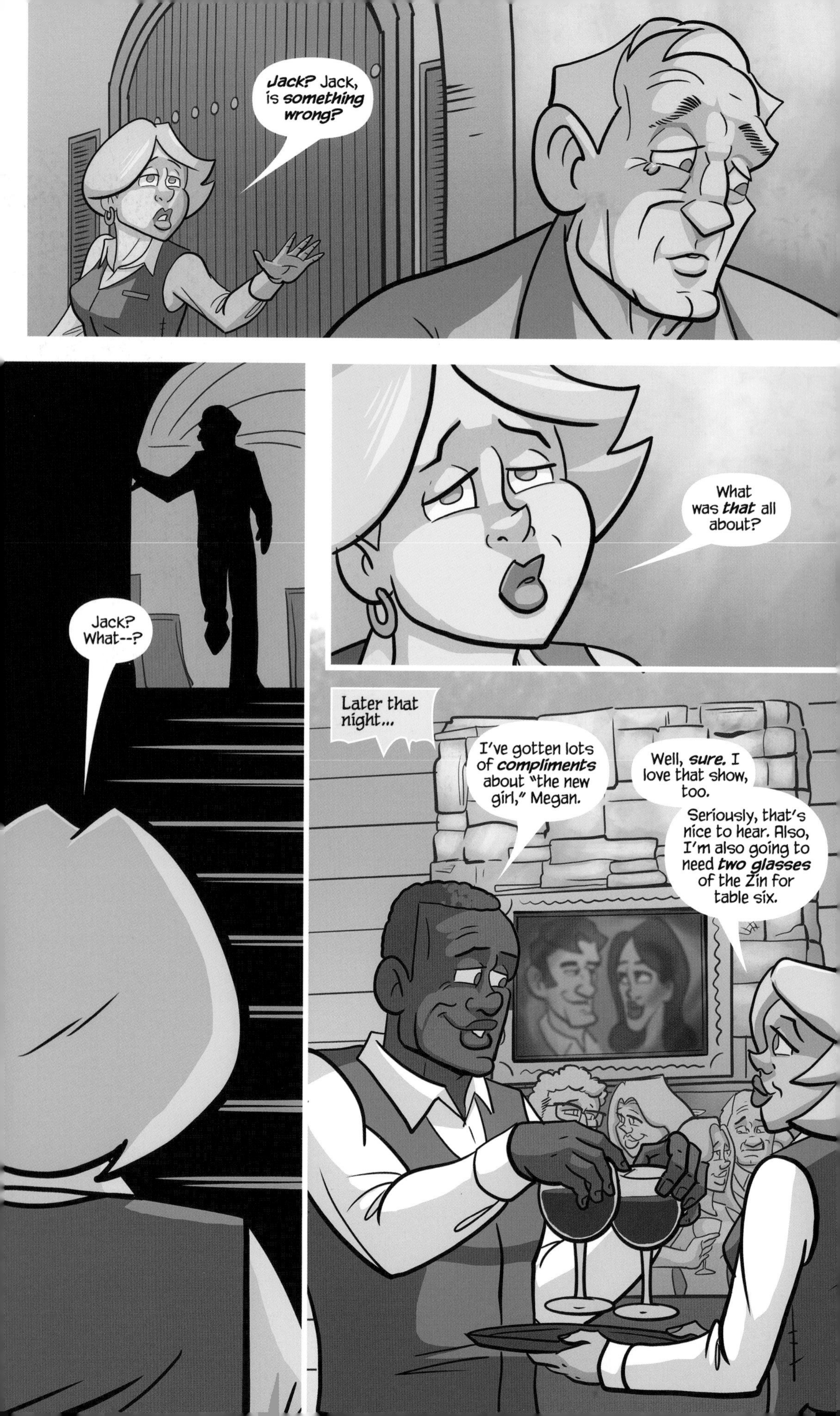

Jack? Jack, is something wrong?
Jack? What--?
What was that all about?
Later that night...
I've gotten lots of compliments about "the new girl," Megan.
Well, sure. I love that show, too.
Seriously, that's nice to hear. Also, I'm also going to need two glasses of the Zin for table six.

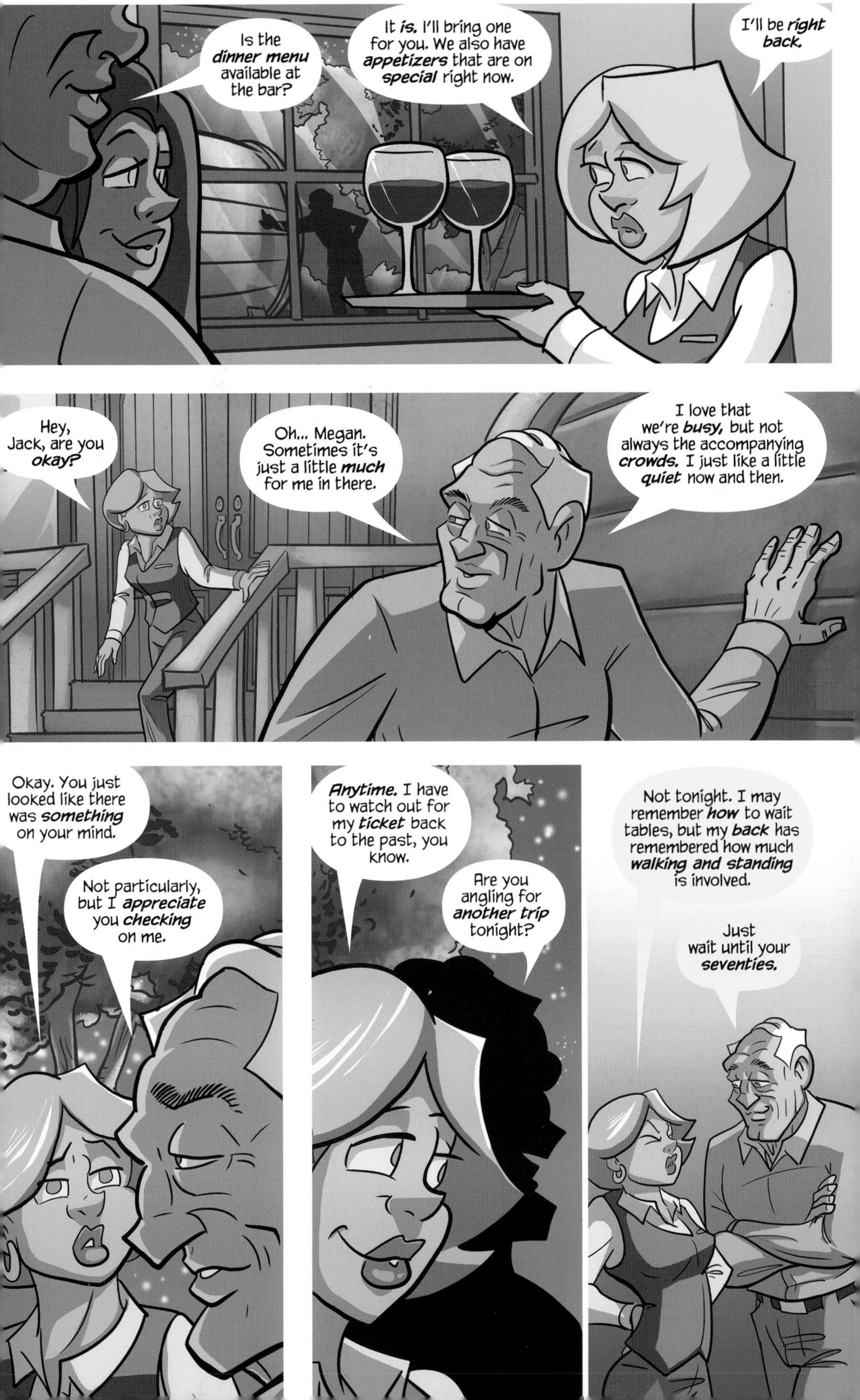
Is the dinner menu available at the bar?
It is. I'll bring one for you. We also have appetizers that are on special right now.
I'll be right back.
Hey, Jack, are you okay?
Oh... Megan. Sometimes it's just a little much for me in there.
I love that we're busy, but not always the accompanying crowds. I just like a little quiet now and then.
Okay. You just looked like there was something on your mind.
Not particularly, but I appreciate you checking on me.
Anytime. I have to watch out for my ticket back to the past, you know.
Are you angling for another trip tonight?
Not tonight. I may remember how to wait tables, but my back has remembered how much walking and standing is involved.
Just wait until your seventies.

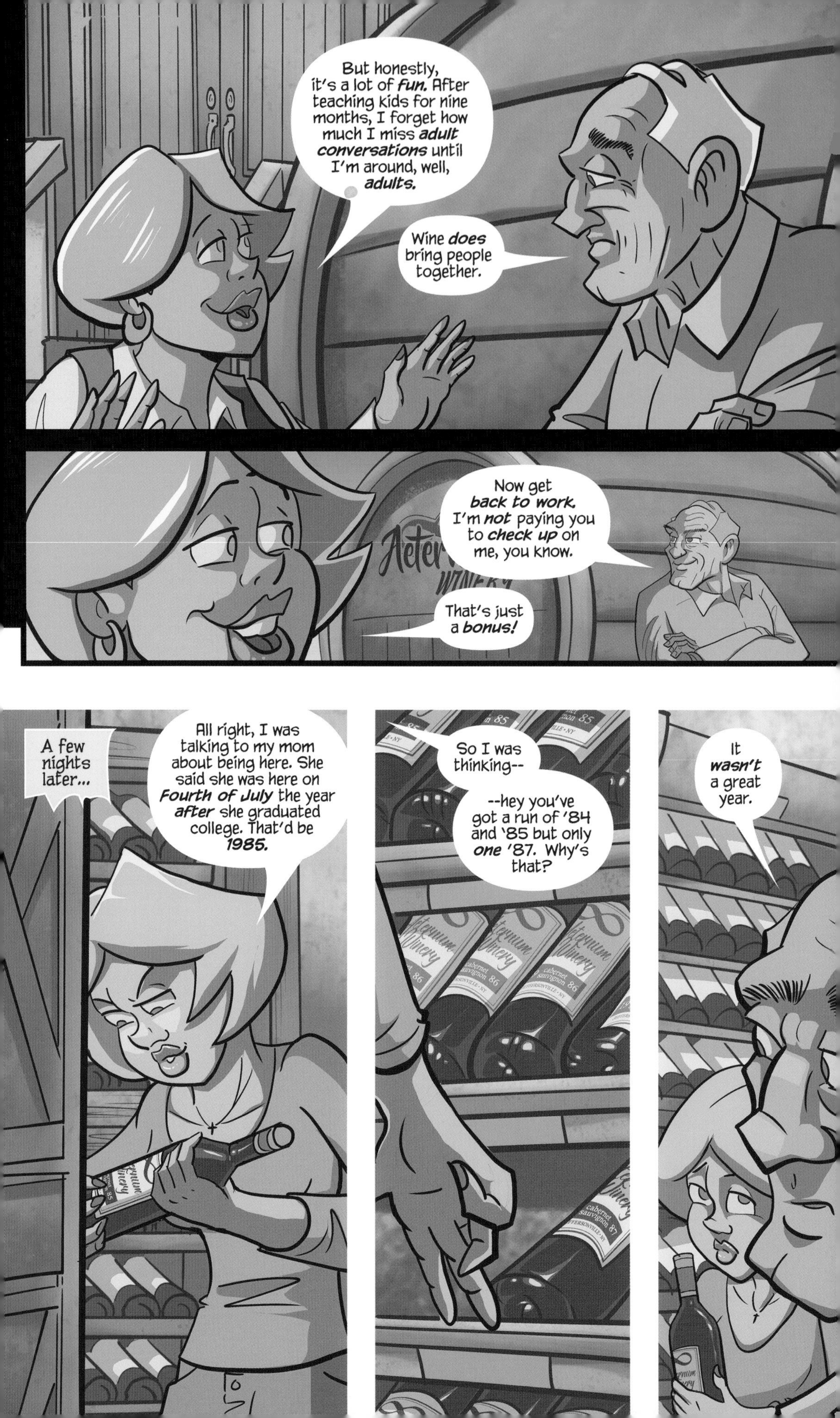
But honestly, it's a lot of *fun.* After teaching kids for nine months, I forget how much I miss *adult conversations* until I'm around, well, *adults.*
Wine *does* bring people together.
Now get *back to work.* I'm *not* paying you to *check up* on me, you know.
That's just a *bonus!*
A few nights later...
All right, I was talking to my mom about being here. She said she was here on *Fourth of July* the year *after* she graduated college. That'd be *1985.*
So I was thinking--
--hey you've got a run of '84 and '85 but only *one* '87. Why's that?
It *wasn't* a great year.

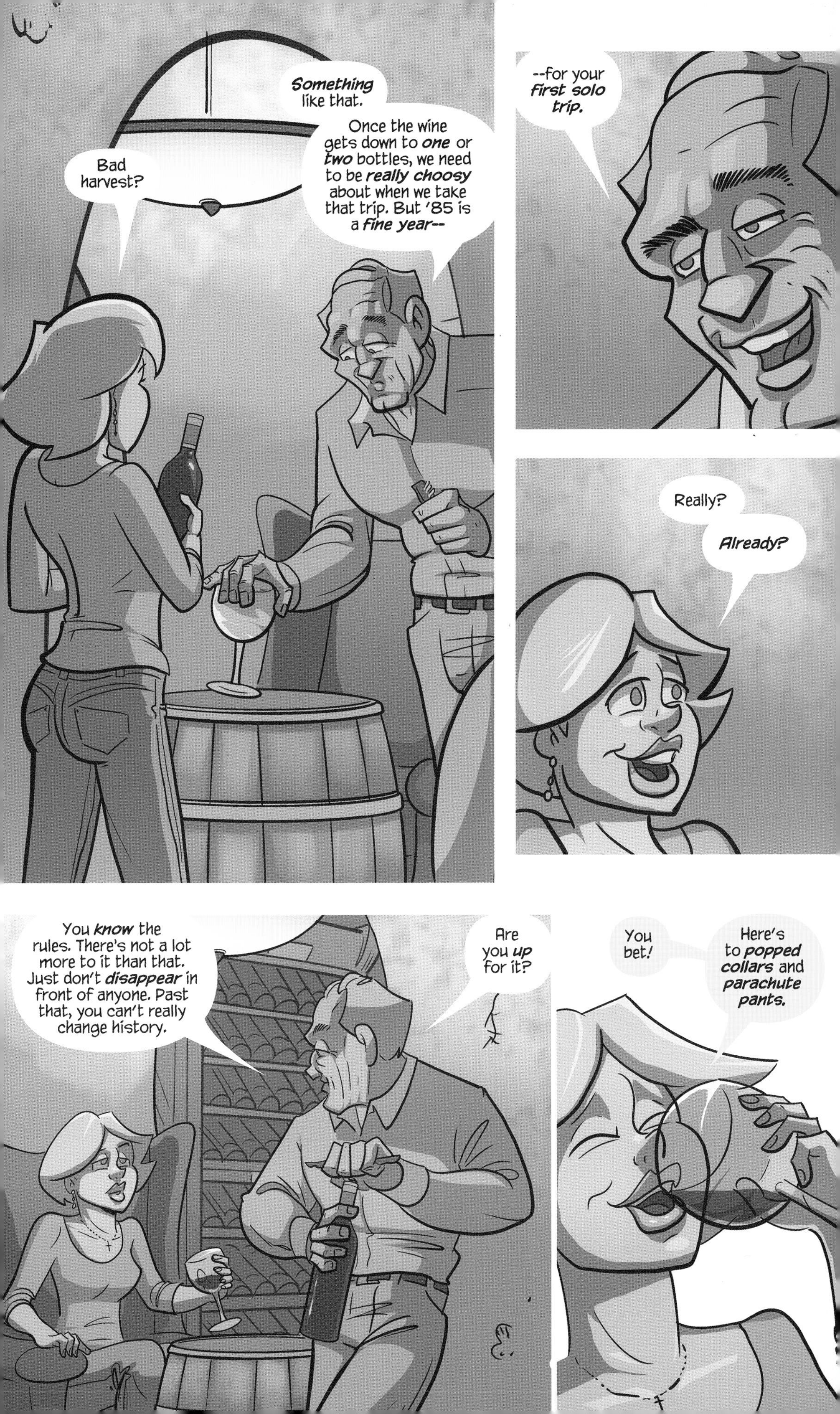
Something like that.
Bad harvest?
Once the wine gets down to one or two bottles, we need to be really choosy about when we take that trip. But '85 is a fine year--
--for your first solo trip.
Really?
Already?
You know the rules. There's not a lot more to it than that. Just don't disappear in front of anyone. Past that, you can't really change history.
Are you up for it?
You bet!
Here's to popped collars and parachute pants.

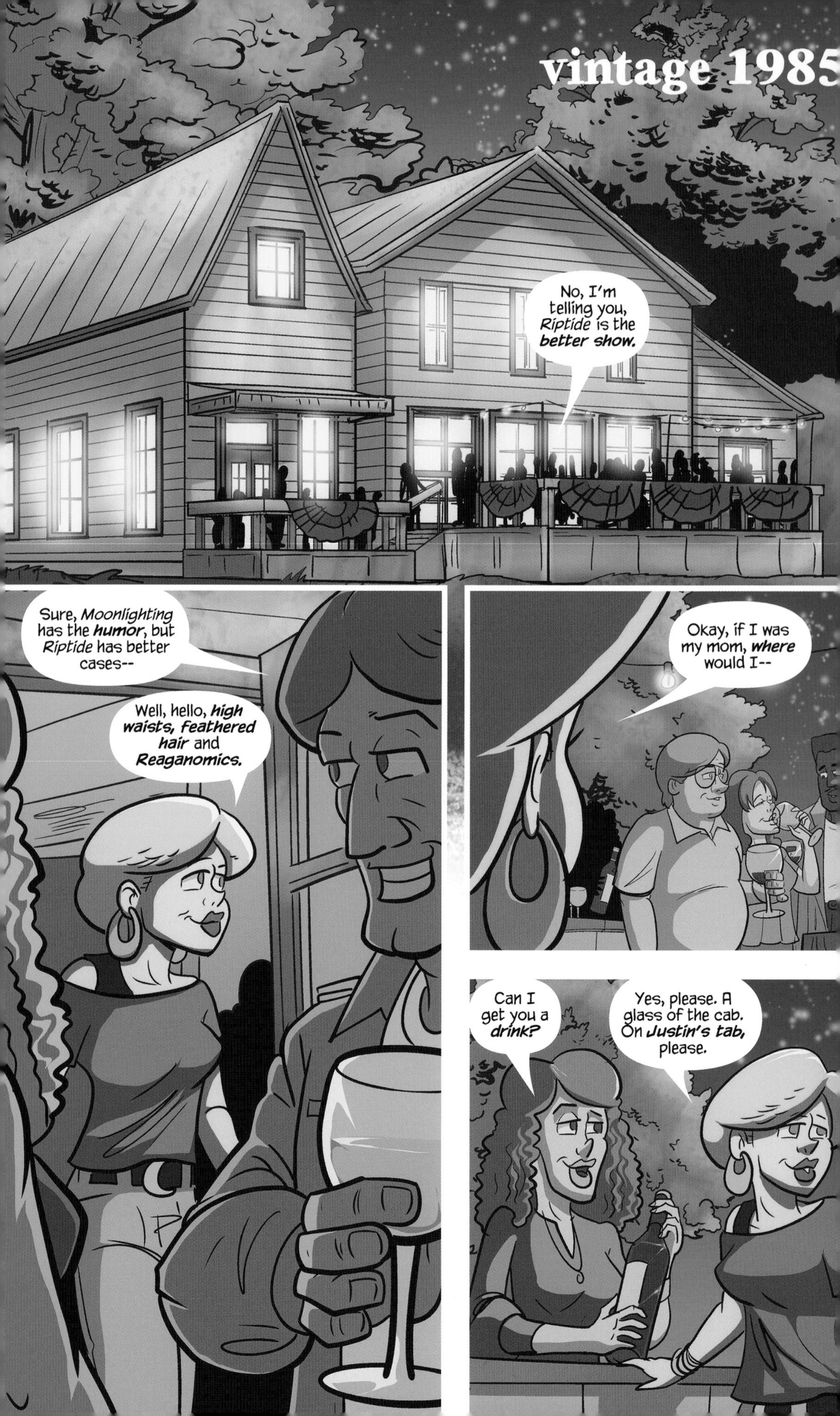
vintage 1985
No, I'm telling you, *Riptide* is the ***better show.***
Sure, *Moonlighting* has the ***humor***, but *Riptide* has better cases--
Well, hello, ***high waists, feathered hair*** and ***Reaganomics.***
Okay, if I was my mom, ***where*** would I--
Can I get you a ***drink?***
Yes, please. A glass of the cab. On ***Justin's tab***, please.

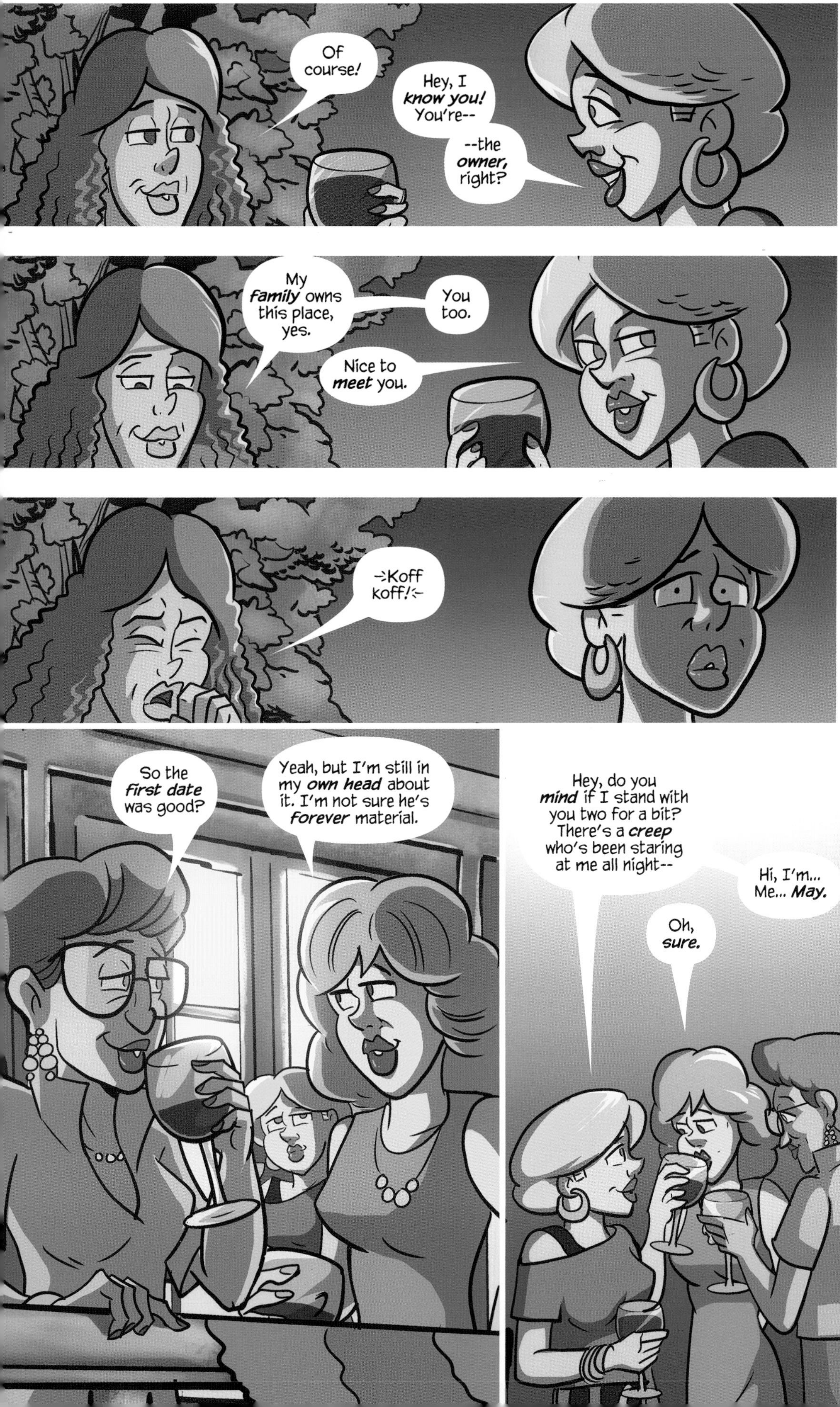
Of course!
Hey, I **know you!** You're--
--the **owner,** right?
My **family** owns this place, yes.
You too.
Nice to **meet** you.
-Koff koff!-
So the **first date** was good?
Yeah, but I'm still in my **own head** about it. I'm not sure he's **forever** material.
Hey, do you **mind** if I stand with you two for a bit? There's a **creep** who's been staring at me all night--
Hi, I'm... Me... **May.**
Oh, **sure.**

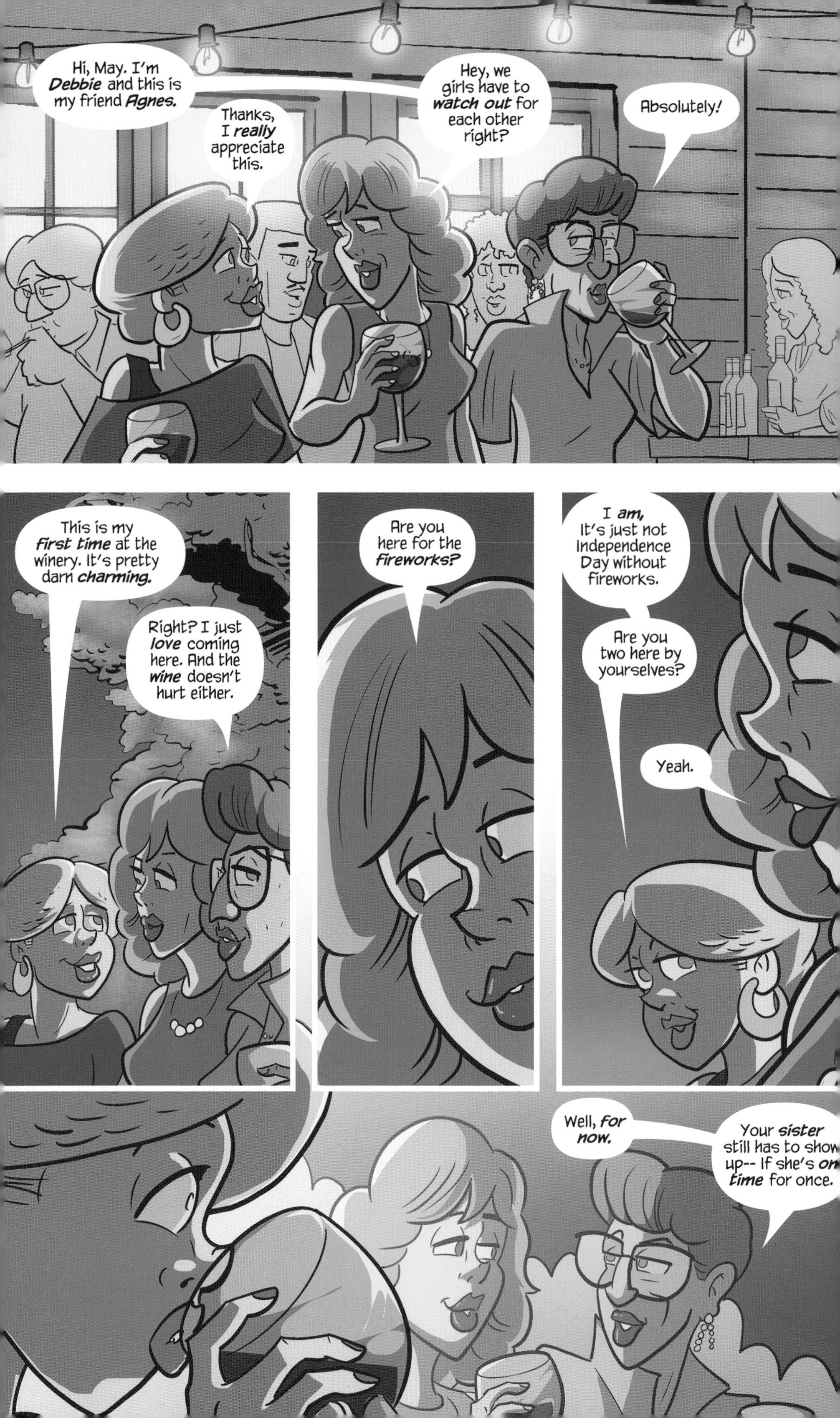
Hi, May. I'm *Debbie* and this is my friend *Agnes.*
Thanks, I *really* appreciate this.
Hey, we girls have to *watch out* for each other right?
Absolutely!
This is my *first time* at the winery. It's pretty darn *charming.*
Right? I just *love* coming here. And the *wine* doesn't hurt either.
Are you here for the *fireworks?*
I *am,* It's just not Independence Day without fireworks.
Are you two here by yourselves?
Yeah.
Well, *for now.*
Your *sister* still has to show up-- If she's *on time* for once.

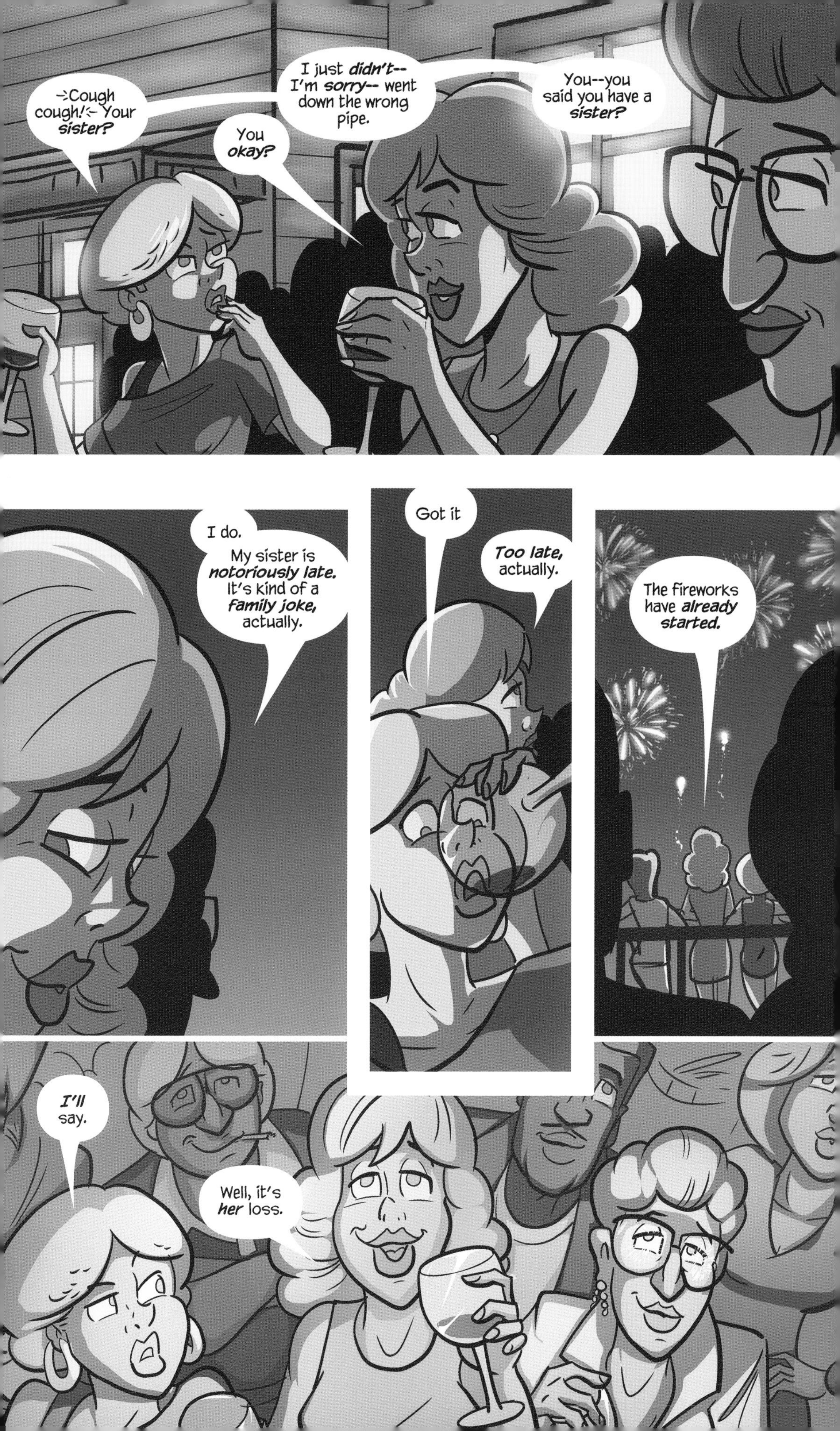

-Cough cough!- Your *sister?*
You *okay?*
I just *didn't--* I'm *sorry--* went down the wrong pipe.
You--you said you have a *sister?*
I do.
My sister is *notoriously late.* It's kind of a *family joke,* actually.
Got it
*Too late,* actually.
The fireworks have *already started.*
*I'll* say.
Well, it's *her* loss.

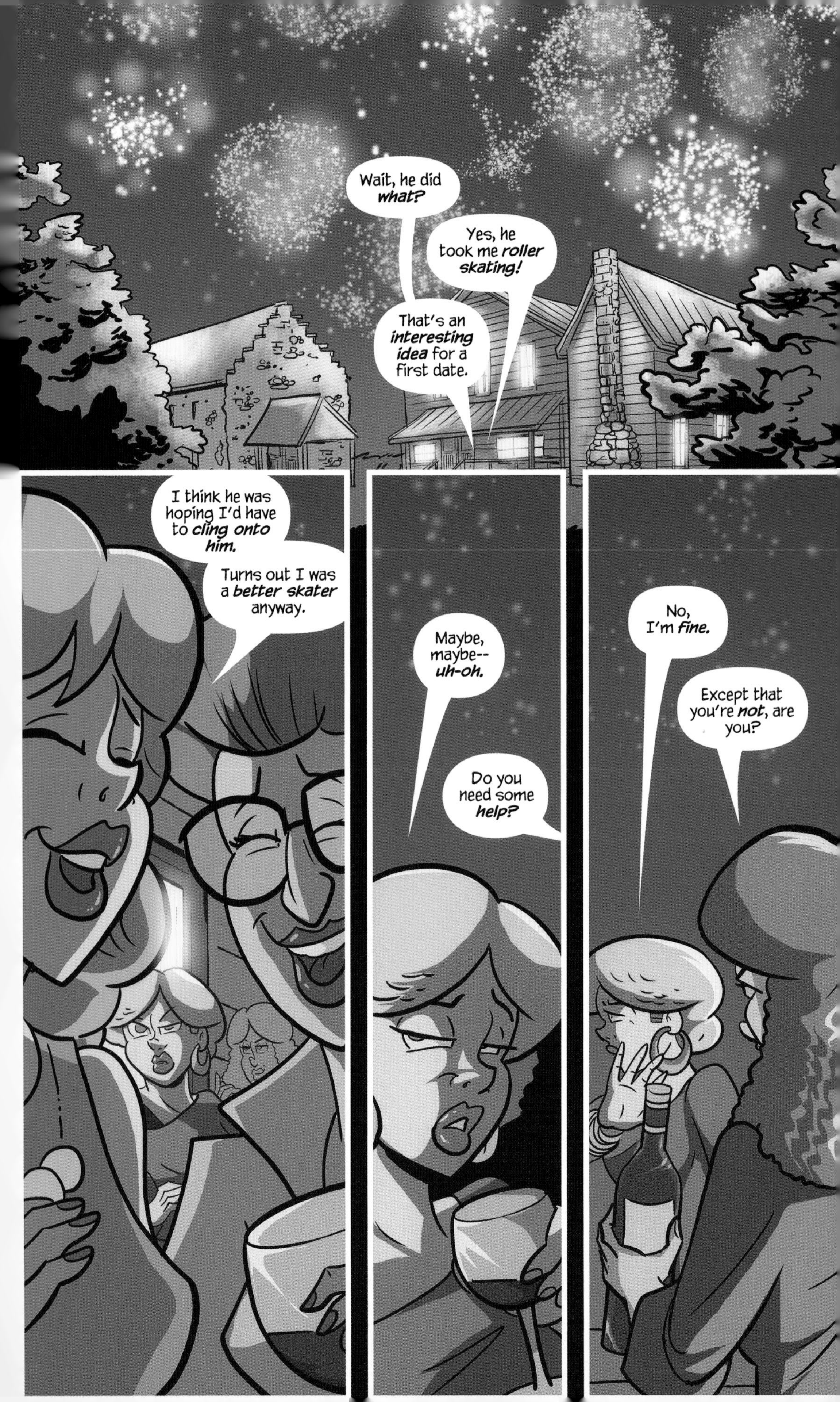

Wait, he did *what?*
Yes, he took me *roller skating!*
That's an *interesting idea* for a first date.
I think he was hoping I'd have to *cling onto him.*
Turns out I was a *better skater* anyway.
Maybe, maybe-- *uh-oh.*
Do you need some *help?*
No, I'm *fine.*
Except that you're *not*, are you?

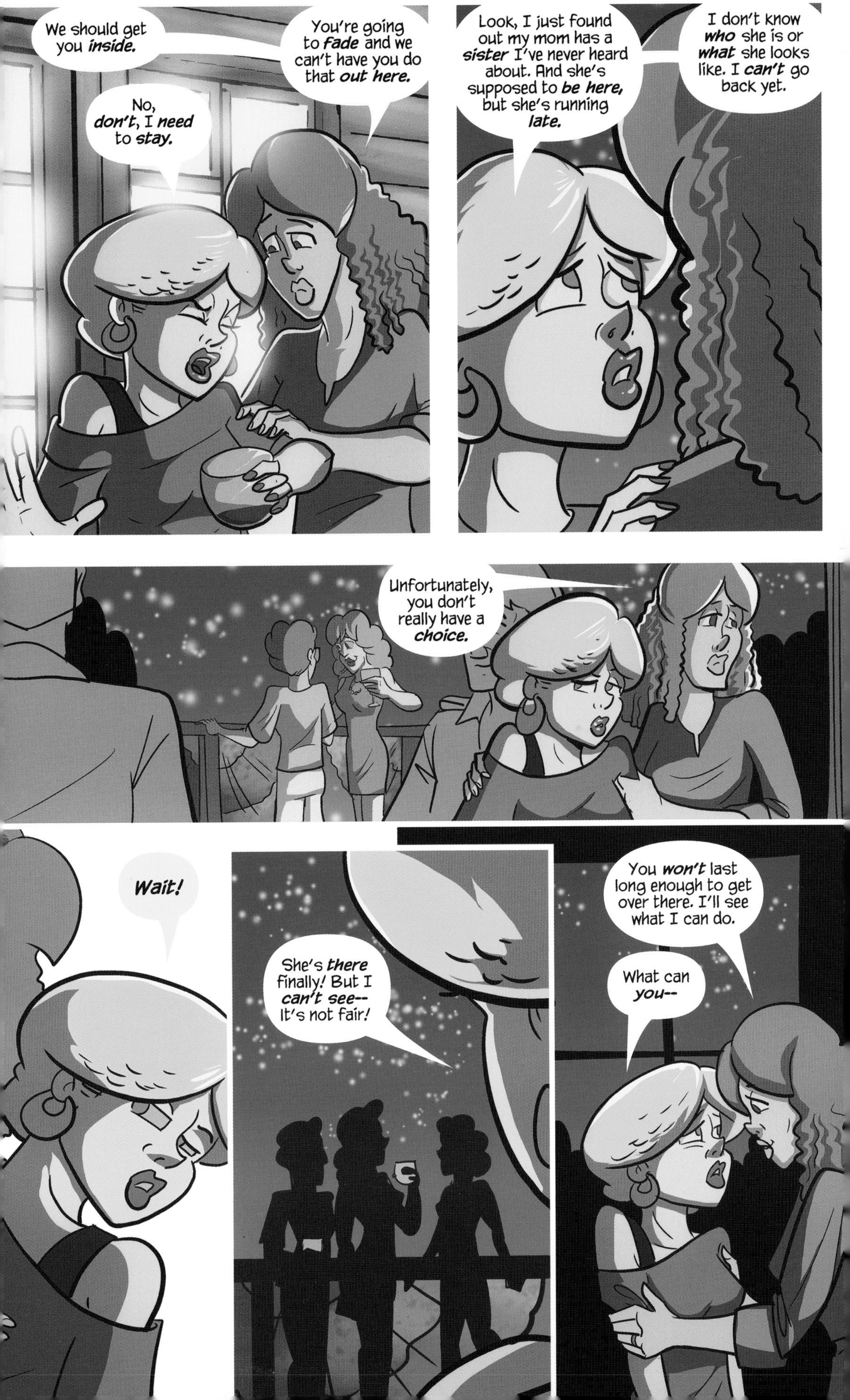
We should get you inside.
You're going to fade and we can't have you do that out here.
No, don't, I need to stay.
Look, I just found out my mom has a sister I've never heard about. And she's supposed to be here, but she's running late.
I don't know who she is or what she looks like. I can't go back yet.
Unfortunately, you don't really have a choice.
Wait!
She's there finally! But I can't see-- It's not fair!
You won't last long enough to get over there. I'll see what I can do.
What can you--

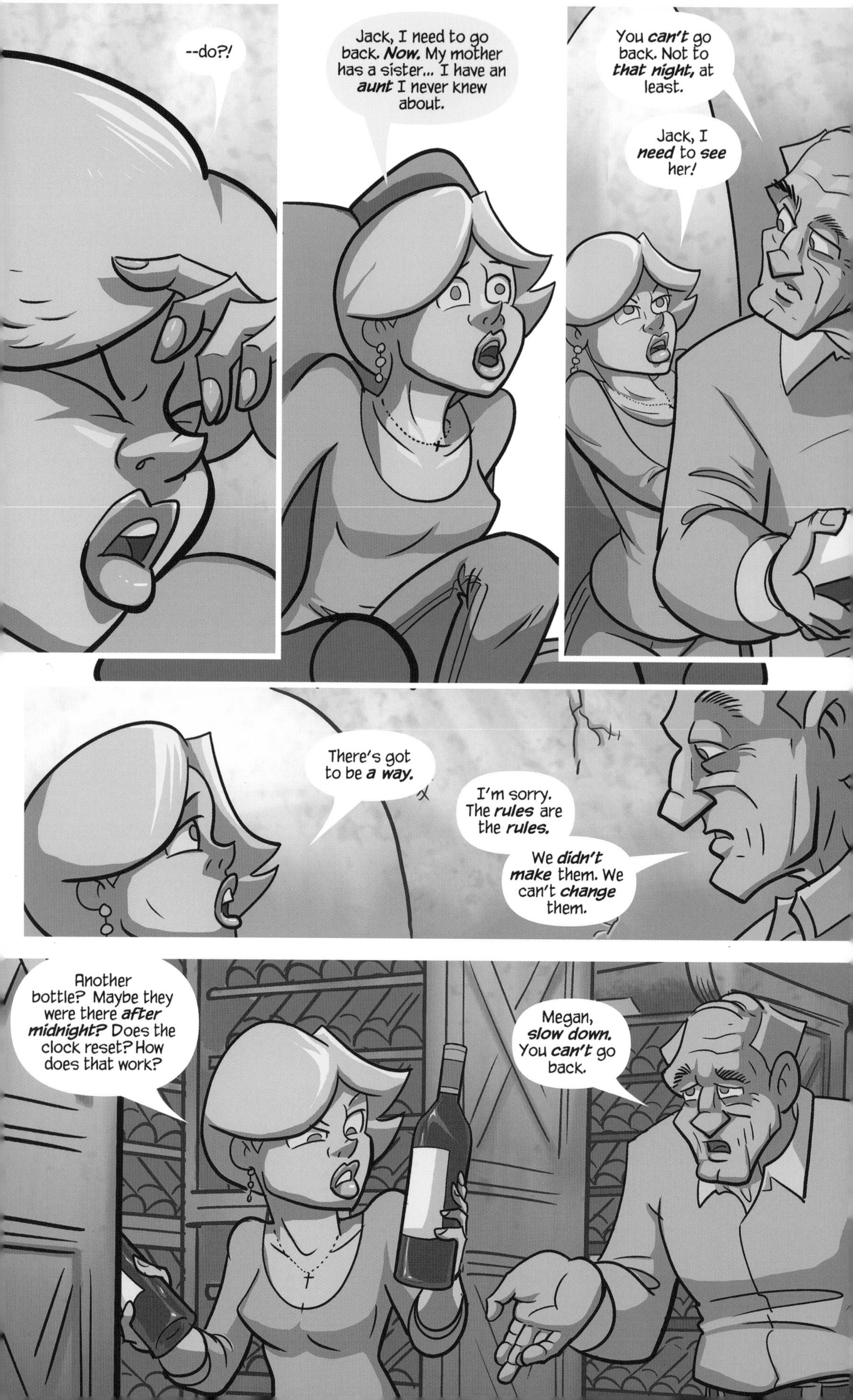
--do?!
Jack, I need to go back. *Now.* My mother has a sister... I have an *aunt* I never knew about.
You *can't* go back. Not to *that night,* at least.
Jack, I *need* to *see* her!
There's got to be *a way.*
I'm sorry. The *rules* are the *rules.*
We *didn't make* them. We can't *change* them.
Another bottle? Maybe they were there *after midnight?* Does the clock reset? How does that work?
Megan, *slow down.* You *can't* go back.

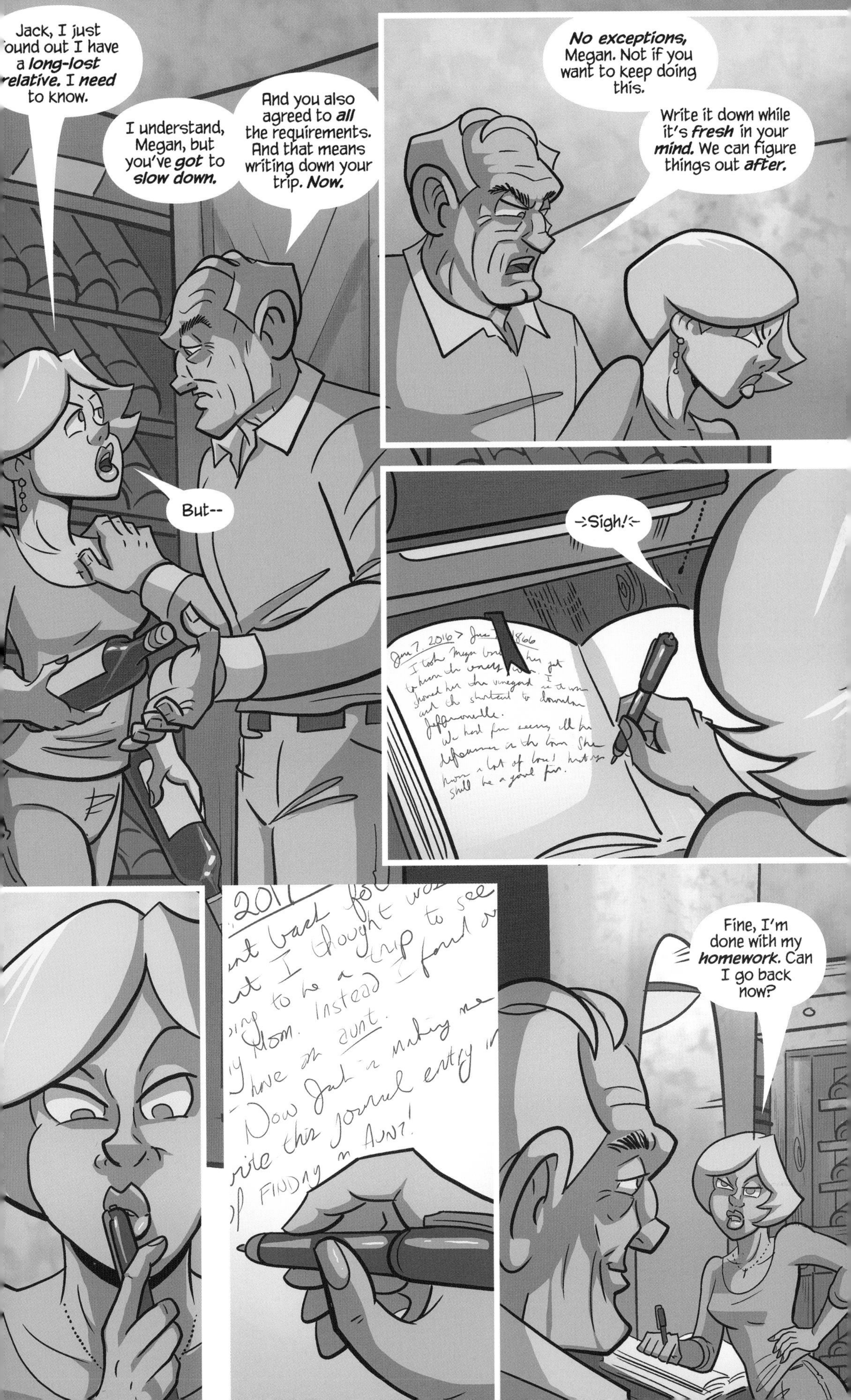
Jack, I just found out I have a long-lost relative. I need to know.
I understand, Megan, but you've got to slow down.
And you also agreed to all the requirements. And that means writing down your trip. Now.
But--
No exceptions, Megan. Not if you want to keep doing this.
Write it down while it's fresh in your mind. We can figure things out after.
Sigh!
Fine, I'm done with my homework. Can I go back now?

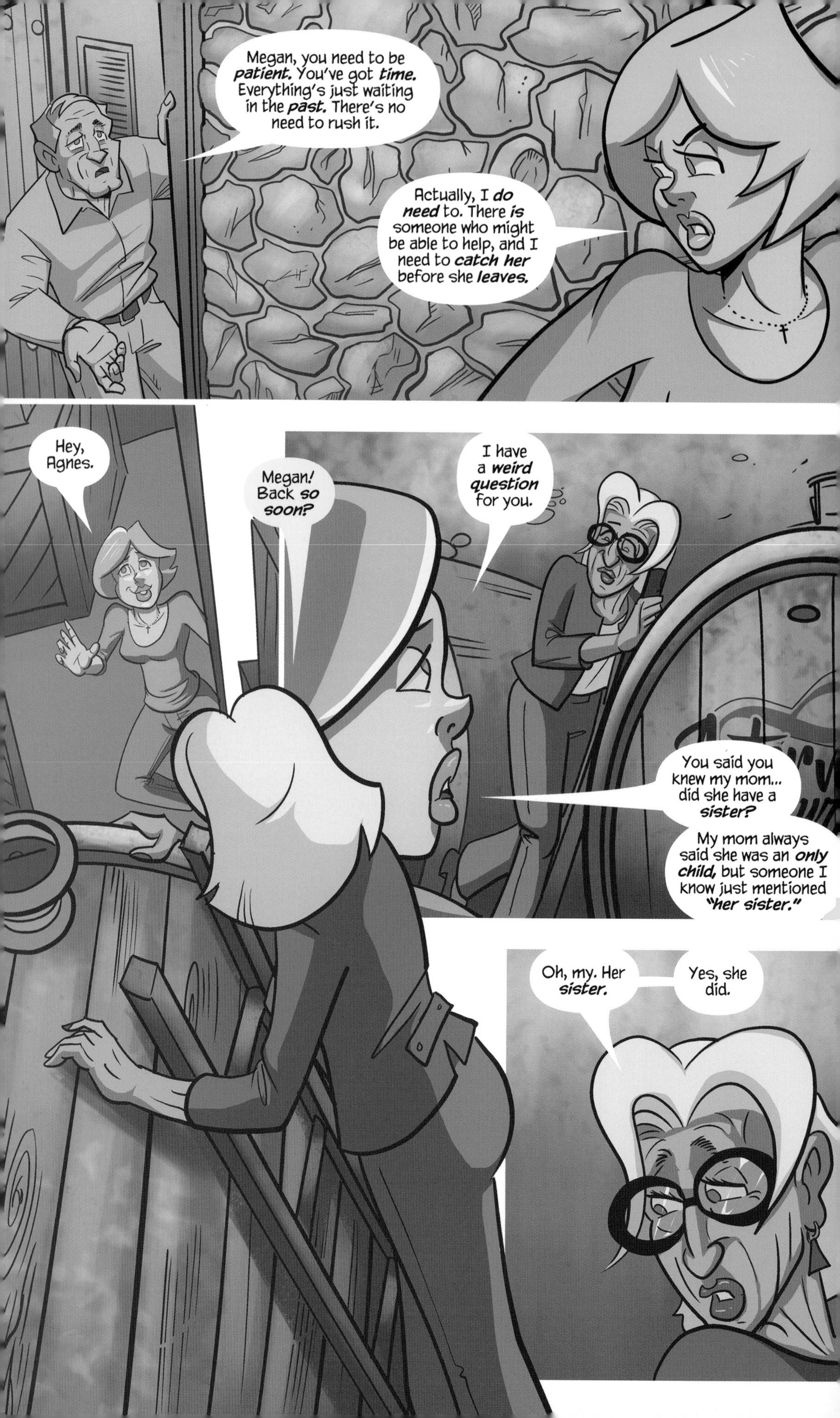
Megan, you need to be *patient.* You've got *time.* Everything's just waiting in the *past.* There's no need to rush it.
Actually, I *do need* to. There *is* someone who might be able to help, and I need to *catch her* before she *leaves.*
Hey, Agnes.
Megan! Back *so soon?*
I have a *weird question* for you.
You said you knew my mom... did she have a *sister?*
My mom always said she was an *only child,* but someone I know just mentioned *"her sister."*
Oh, my. Her *sister.*
Yes, she did.

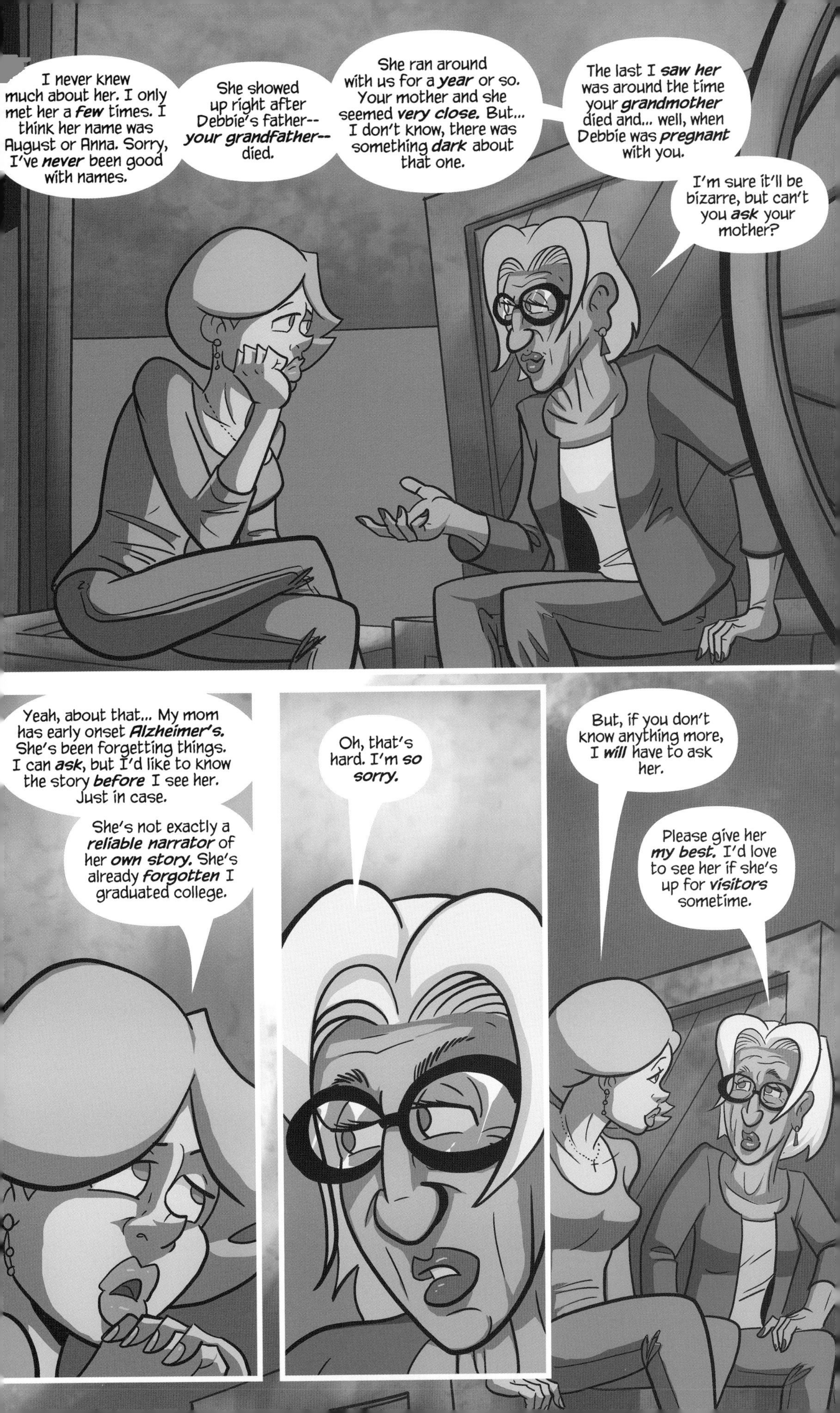
I never knew much about her. I only met her a few times. I think her name was August or Anna. Sorry, I've never been good with names.
She showed up right after Debbie's father-- your grandfather-- died.
She ran around with us for a year or so. Your mother and she seemed very close. But... I don't know, there was something dark about that one.
The last I saw her was around the time your grandmother died and... well, when Debbie was pregnant with you.
I'm sure it'll be bizarre, but can't you ask your mother?
Yeah, about that... My mom has early onset Alzheimer's. She's been forgetting things. I can ask, but I'd like to know the story before I see her. Just in case.
She's not exactly a reliable narrator of her own story. She's already forgotten I graduated college.
Oh, that's hard. I'm so sorry.
But, if you don't know anything more, I will have to ask her.
Please give her my best. I'd love to see her if she's up for visitors sometime.

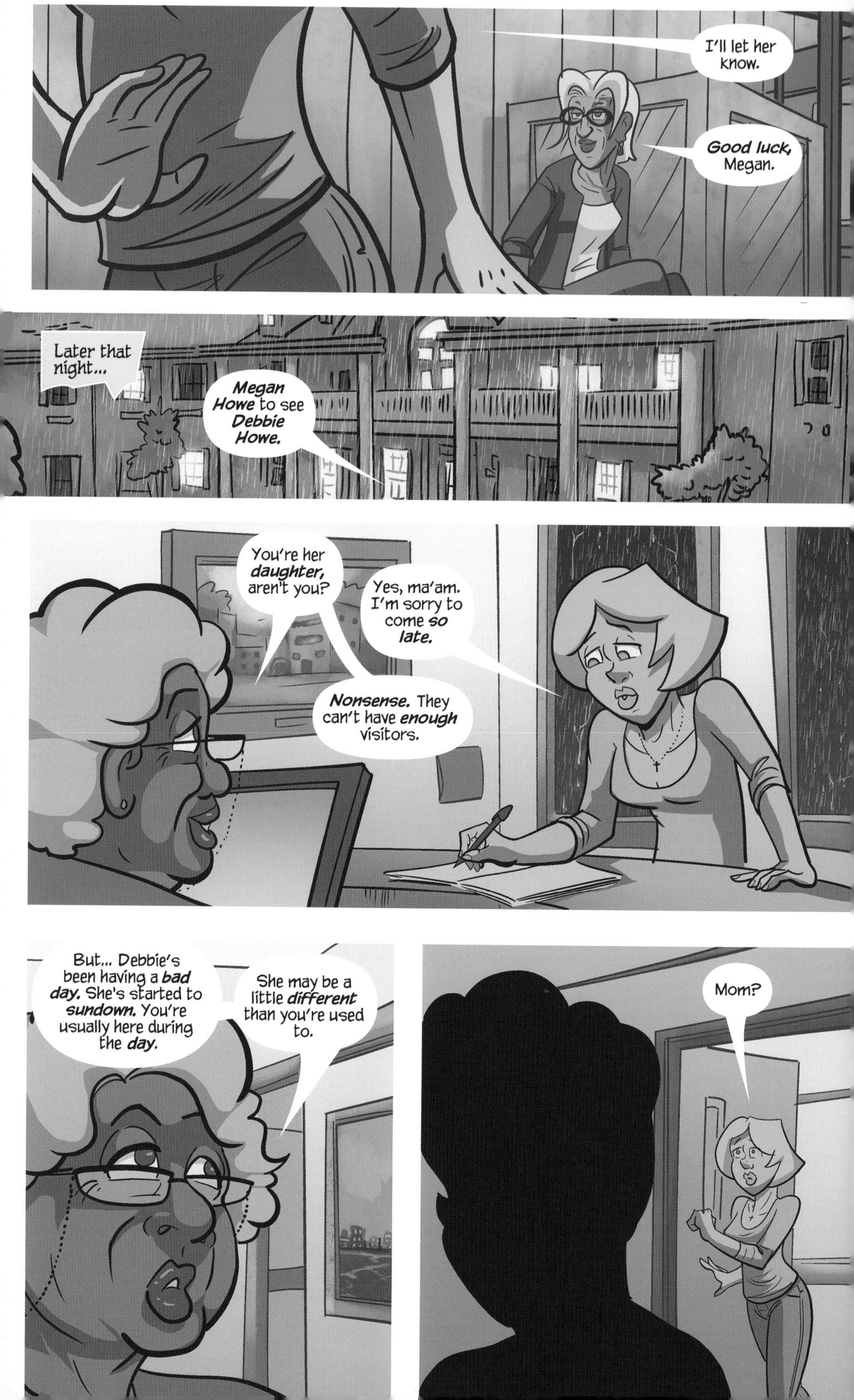
I'll let her know.
Good luck, Megan.
Later that night...
Megan Howe to see Debbie Howe.
You're her daughter, aren't you?
Yes, ma'am. I'm sorry to come so late.
Nonsense. They can't have enough visitors.
But... Debbie's been having a bad day. She's started to sundown. You're usually here during the day.
She may be a little different than you're used to.
Mom?

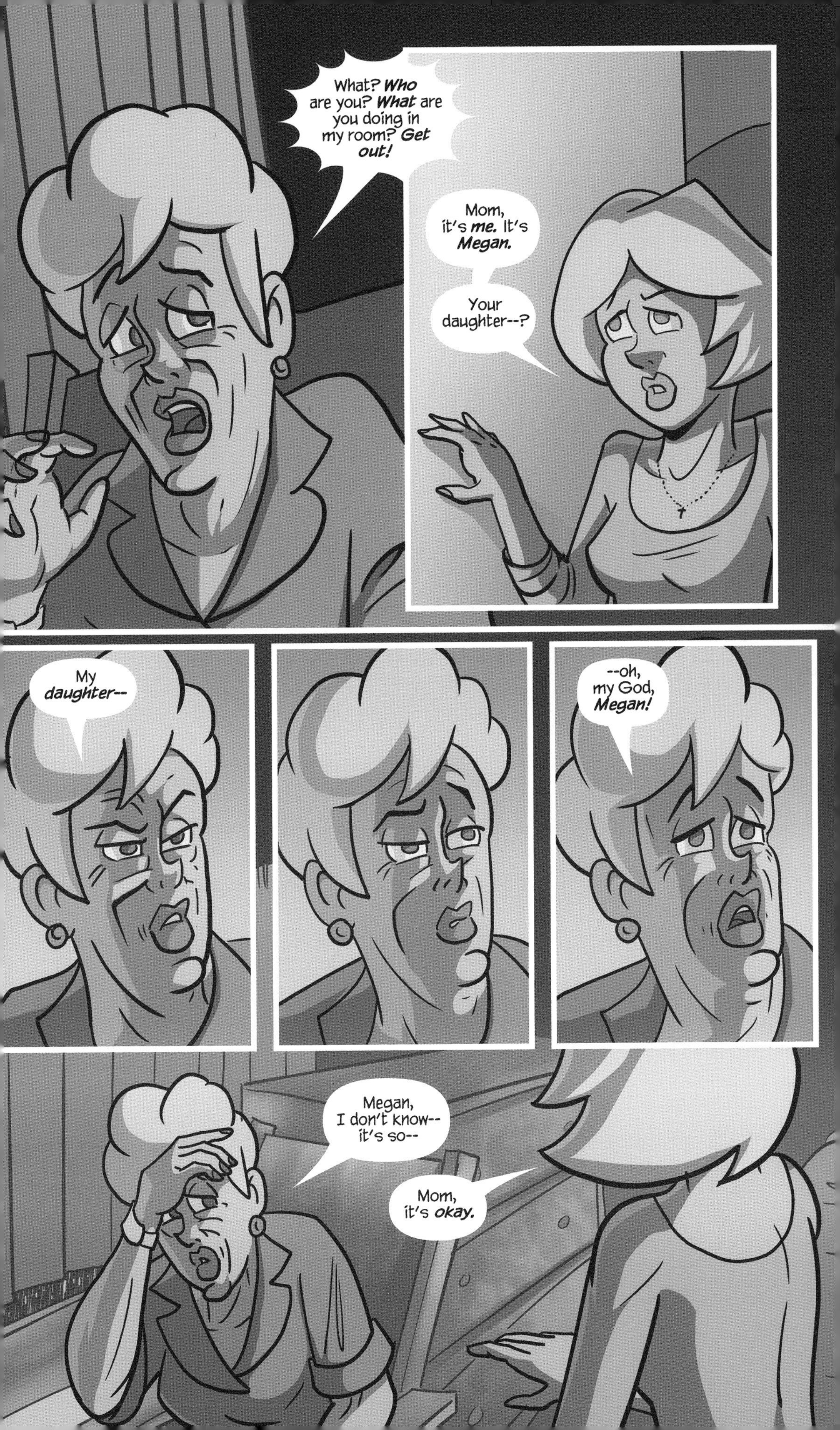

What? *Who* are you? *What* are you doing in my room? *Get out!*
Mom, it's *me.* It's *Megan.*
Your daughter--?
My *daughter*--
--oh, my God, *Megan!*
Megan, I don't know-- it's so--
Mom, it's *okay.*

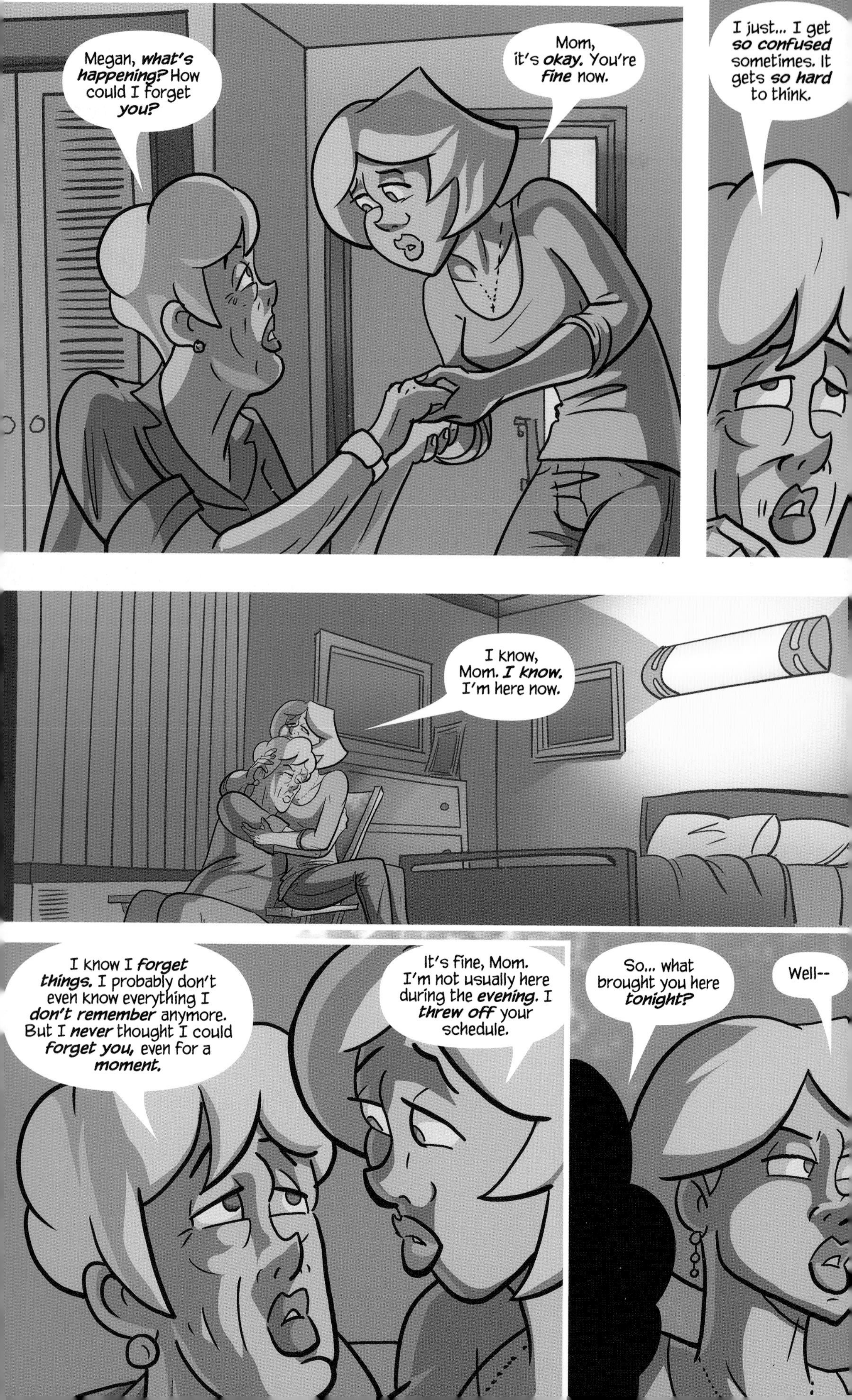
Megan, what's happening? How could I forget you?
Mom, it's okay. You're fine now.
I just... I get so confused sometimes. It gets so hard to think.
I know, Mom. I know. I'm here now.
I know I forget things. I probably don't even know everything I don't remember anymore. But I never thought I could forget you, even for a moment.
It's fine, Mom. I'm not usually here during the evening. I threw off your schedule.
So... what brought you here tonight?
Well--

--I had a **question.**

I was talking with **Agnes,** your old friend who works at the winery, and--

--well, this **weird thing** came up. She mentioned something that made it sound like you had a **sister.** But you never told me about one.

No--

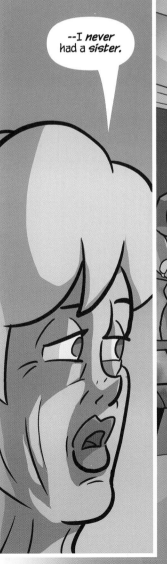

--I **never** had a **sister.**

Will you help me **up?**

Of course.

I think maybe I'll see about getting some **tea** to calm my nerves.

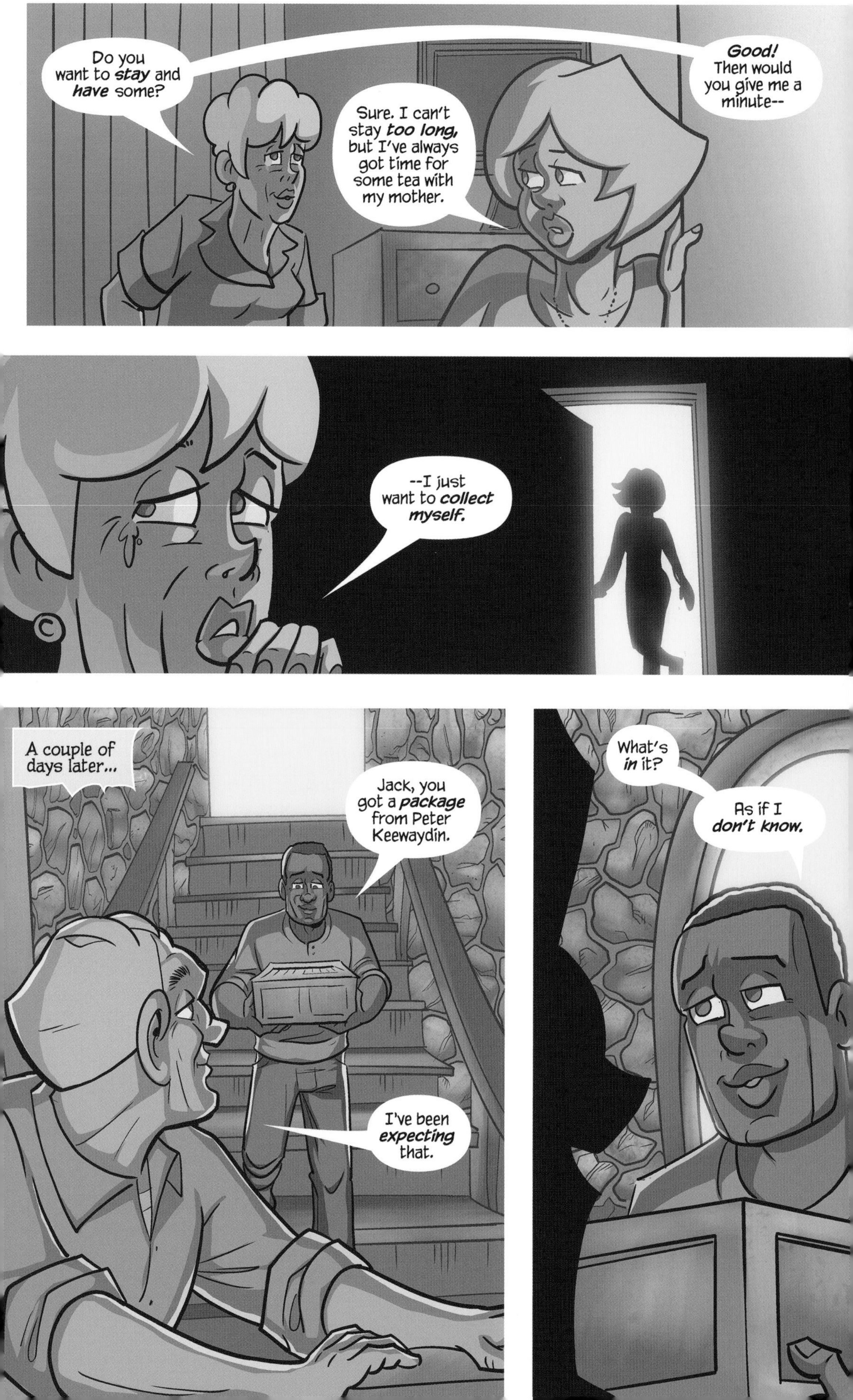
Do you want to *stay* and *have* some?
Sure. I can't stay *too long,* but I've always got time for some tea with my mother.
*Good!* Then would you give me a minute--
--I just want to *collect myself.*
A couple of days later...
Jack, you got a *package* from Peter Keewaydin.
I've been *expecting* that.
What's *in* it?
As if I *don't know.*

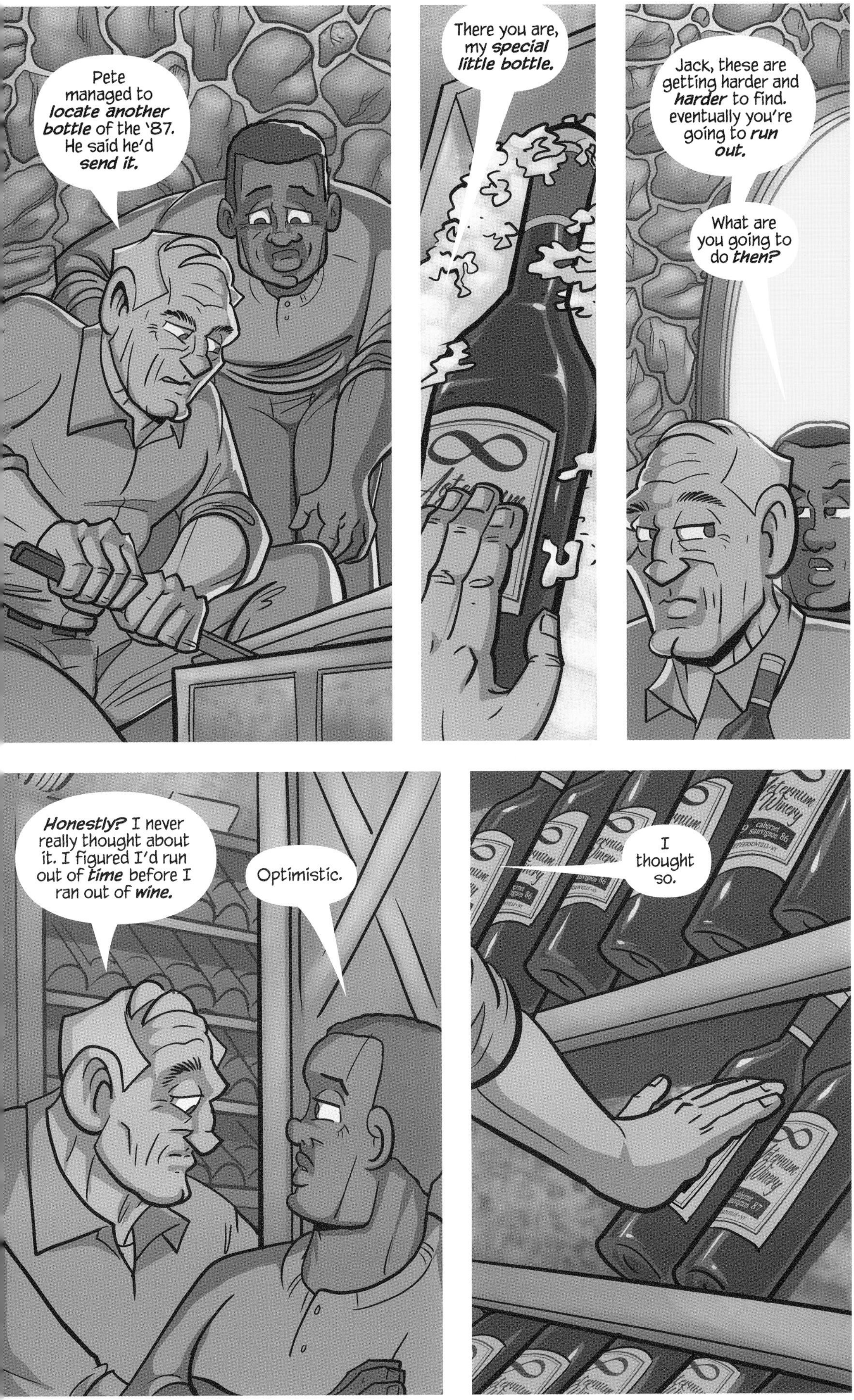

Pete managed to *locate another bottle* of the '87. He said he'd *send it.*
There you are, my *special little bottle.*
Jack, these are getting harder and *harder* to find. eventually you're going to *run out.*
What are you going to do *then?*
*Honestly?* I never really thought about it. I figured I'd run out of *time* before I ran out of *wine.*
Optimistic.
I thought so.

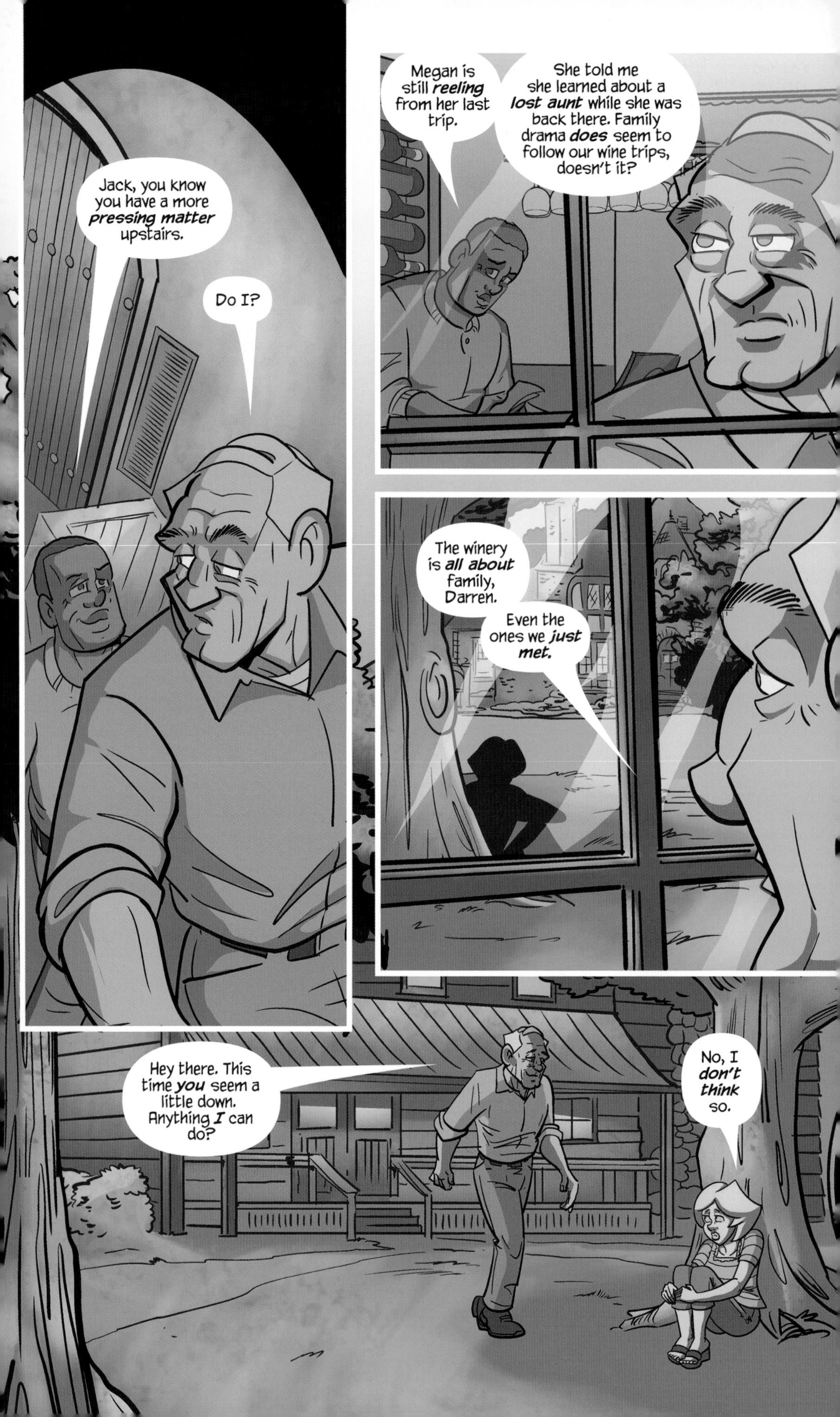
Jack, you know you have a more *pressing matter* upstairs.
Do I?
Megan is still *reeling* from her last trip.
She told me she learned about a *lost aunt* while she was back there. Family drama *does* seem to follow our wine trips, doesn't it?
The winery is *all about* family, Darren.
Even the ones we *just met.*
Hey there. This time *you* seem a little down. Anything *I* can do?
No, I *don't think* so.

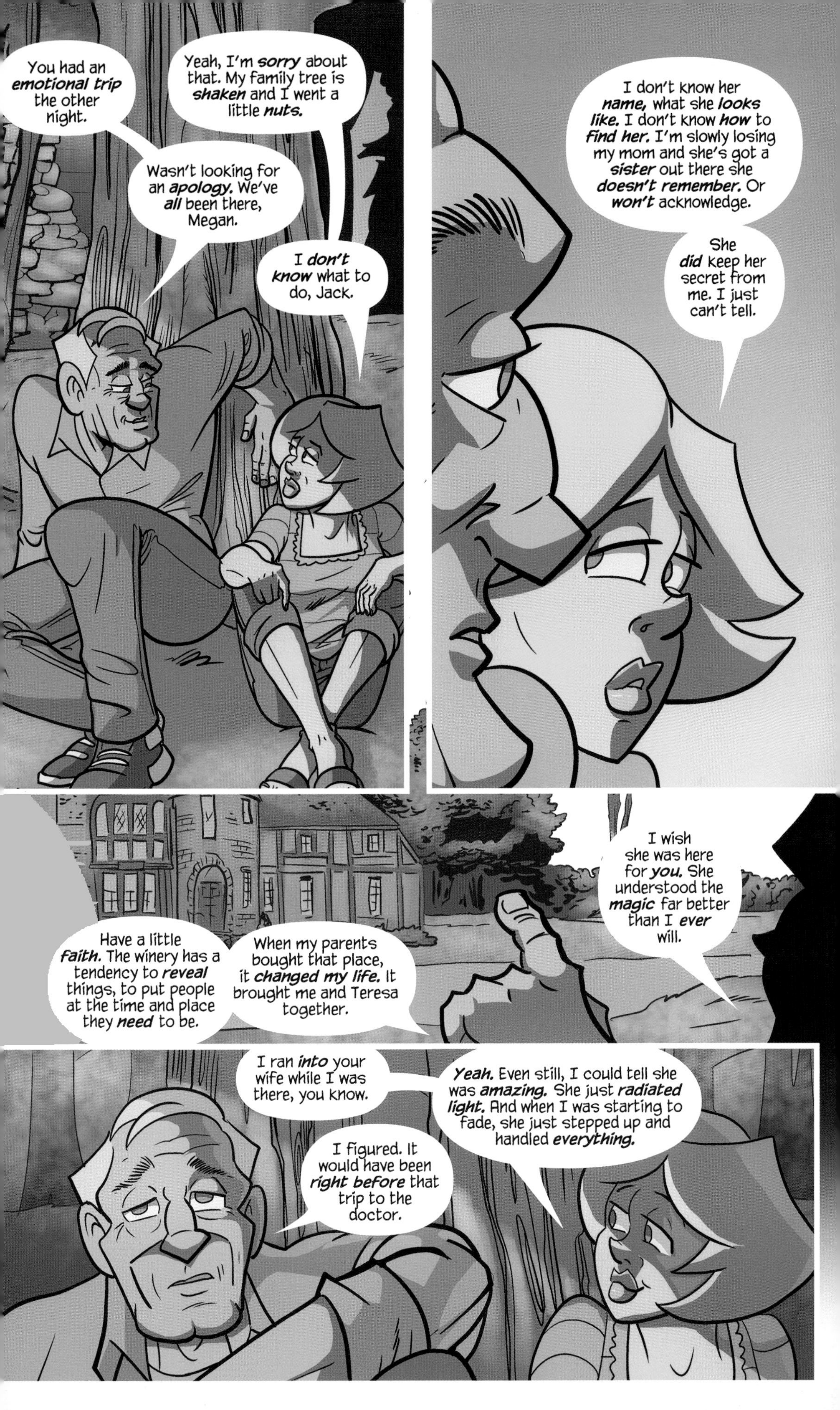

You had an *emotional trip* the other night.
Yeah, I'm *sorry* about that. My family tree is *shaken* and I went a little *nuts.*
Wasn't looking for an *apology.* We've *all* been there, Megan.
I *don't know* what to do, Jack.
I don't know her *name,* what she *looks like.* I don't know *how* to *find her.* I'm slowly losing my mom and she's got a *sister* out there she *doesn't remember.* Or *won't* acknowledge.
She *did* keep her secret from me. I just can't tell.
Have a little *faith.* The winery has a tendency to *reveal* things, to put people at the time and place they *need* to be.
When my parents bought that place, it *changed my life.* It brought me and Teresa together.
I wish she was here for *you.* She understood the *magic* far better than I *ever* will.
I ran *into* your wife while I was there, you know.
I figured. It would have been *right before* that trip to the doctor.
*Yeah.* Even still, I could tell she was *amazing.* She just *radiated light.* And when I was starting to fade, she just stepped up and handled *everything.*

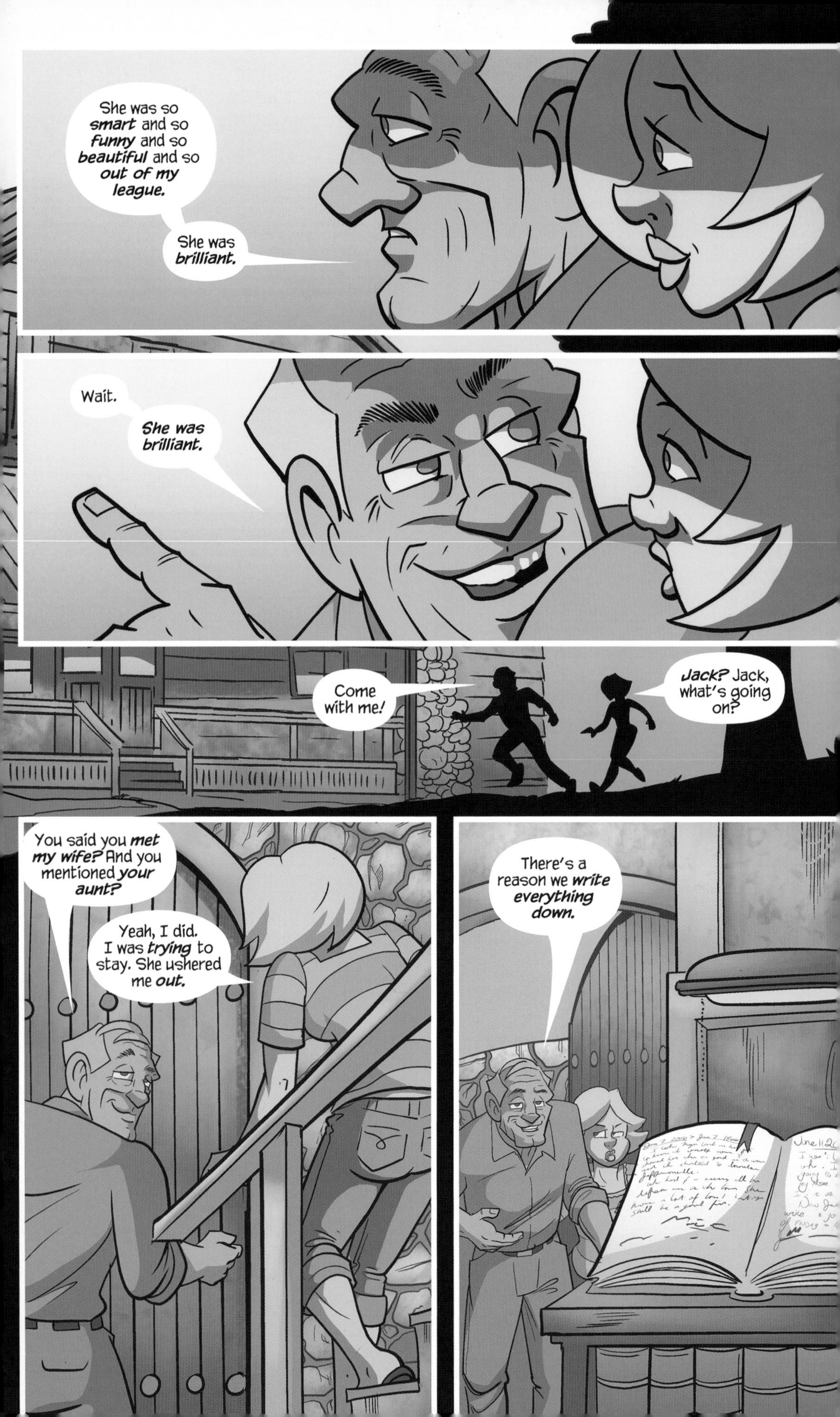
She was so smart and so funny and so beautiful and so out of my league.
She was brilliant.
Wait.
She was brilliant.
Come with me!
Jack? Jack, what's going on?
You said you met my wife? And you mentioned your aunt?
Yeah, I did. I was trying to stay. She ushered me out.
There's a reason we write everything down.

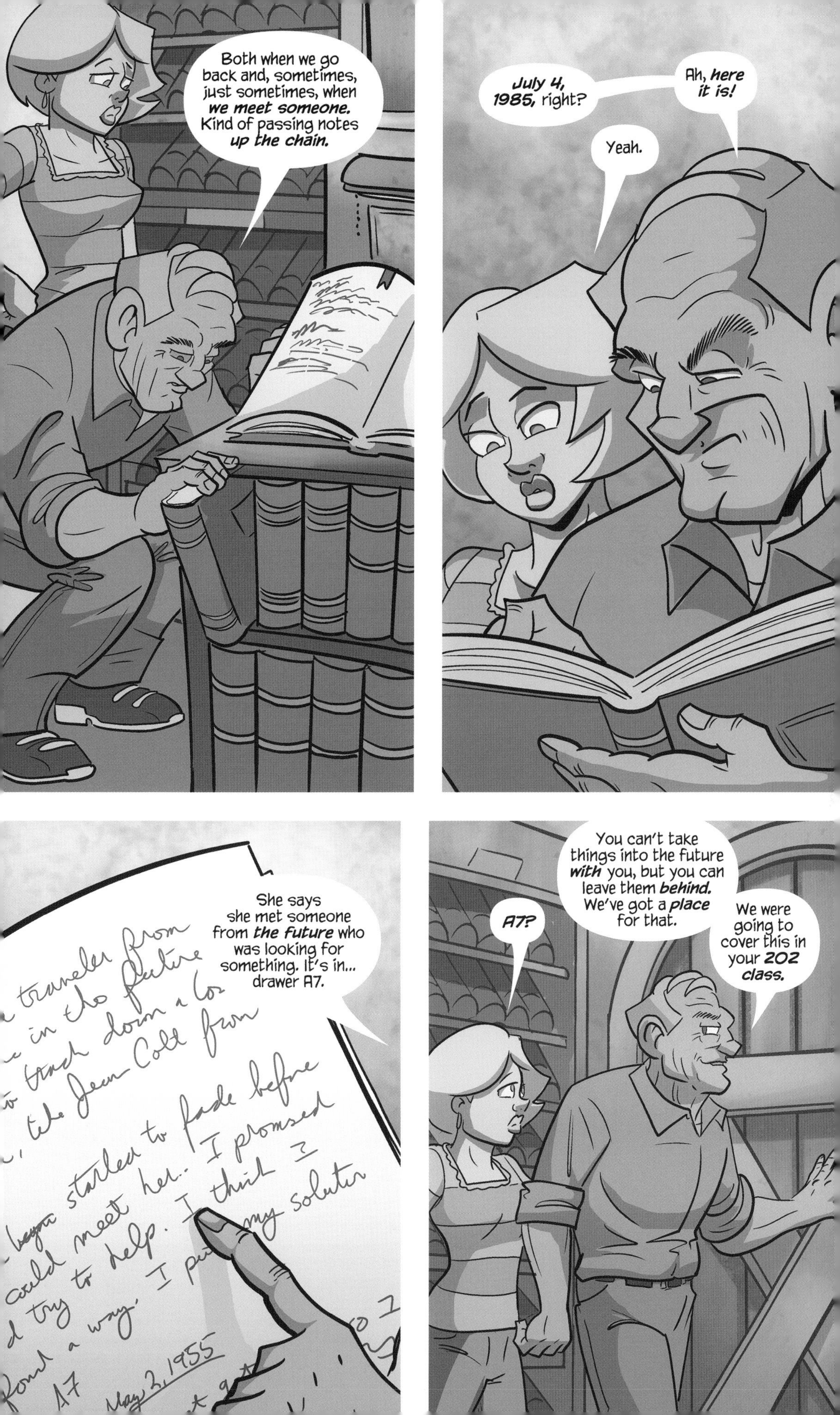
Both when we go back and, sometimes, just sometimes, when *we meet someone.* Kind of passing notes *up the chain.*
*July 4, 1985,* right?
Ah, *here it is!*
Yeah.
She says she met someone from *the future* who was looking for something. It's in... drawer A7.
A7
May 2, 1955
*A7?*
You can't take things into the future *with* you, but you can leave them *behind.* We've got a *place* for that.
We were going to cover this in your *202 class.*

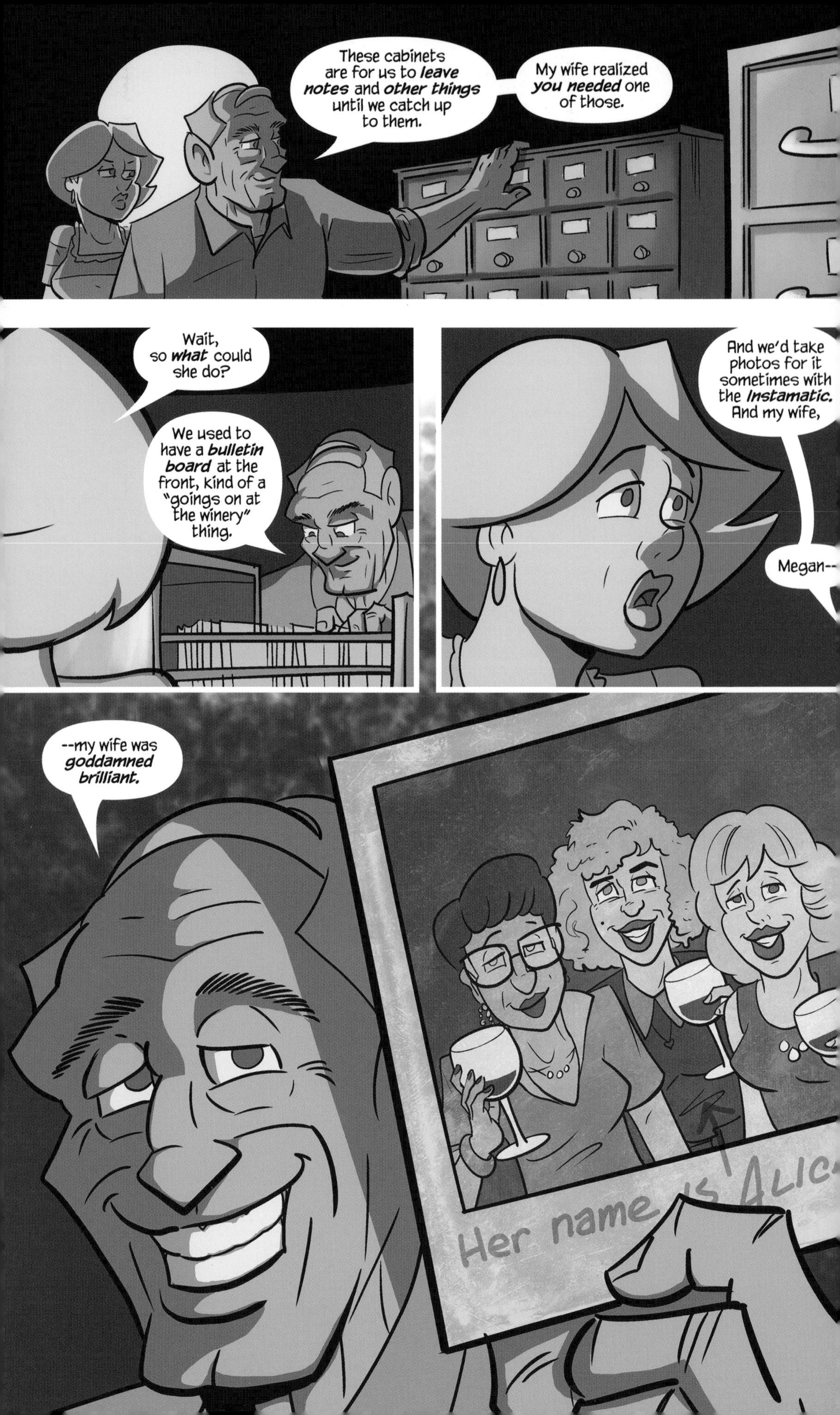
These cabinets are for us to *leave notes* and *other things* until we catch up to them.
My wife realized *you needed* one of those.
Wait, so *what* could she do?
We used to have a *bulletin board* at the front, kind of a "goings on at the winery" thing.
And we'd take photos for it sometimes with the *Instamatic.* And my wife,
Megan--
--my wife was *goddamned brilliant.*
Her name is ALIC

# Chapter Three

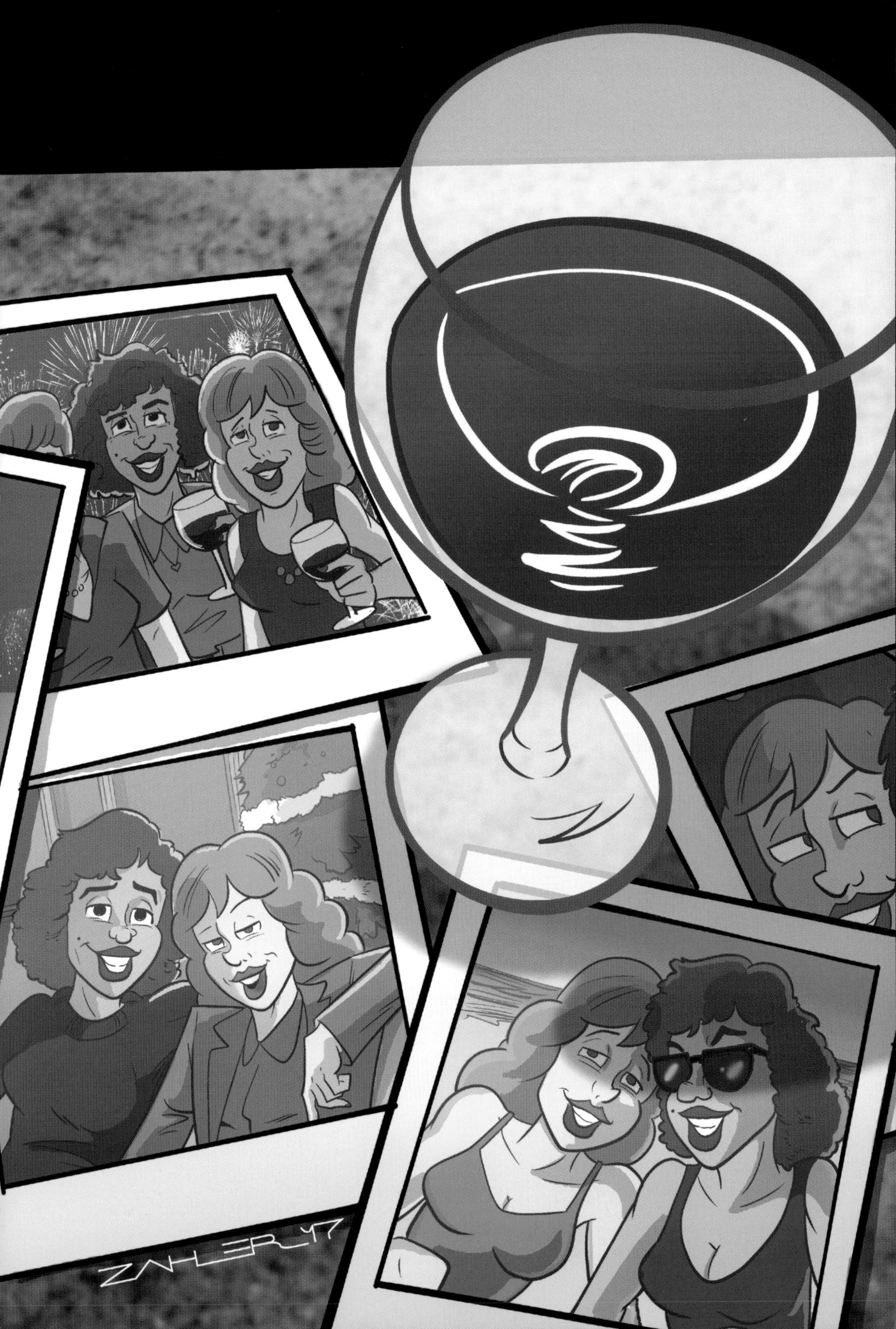
ZAHLER 17

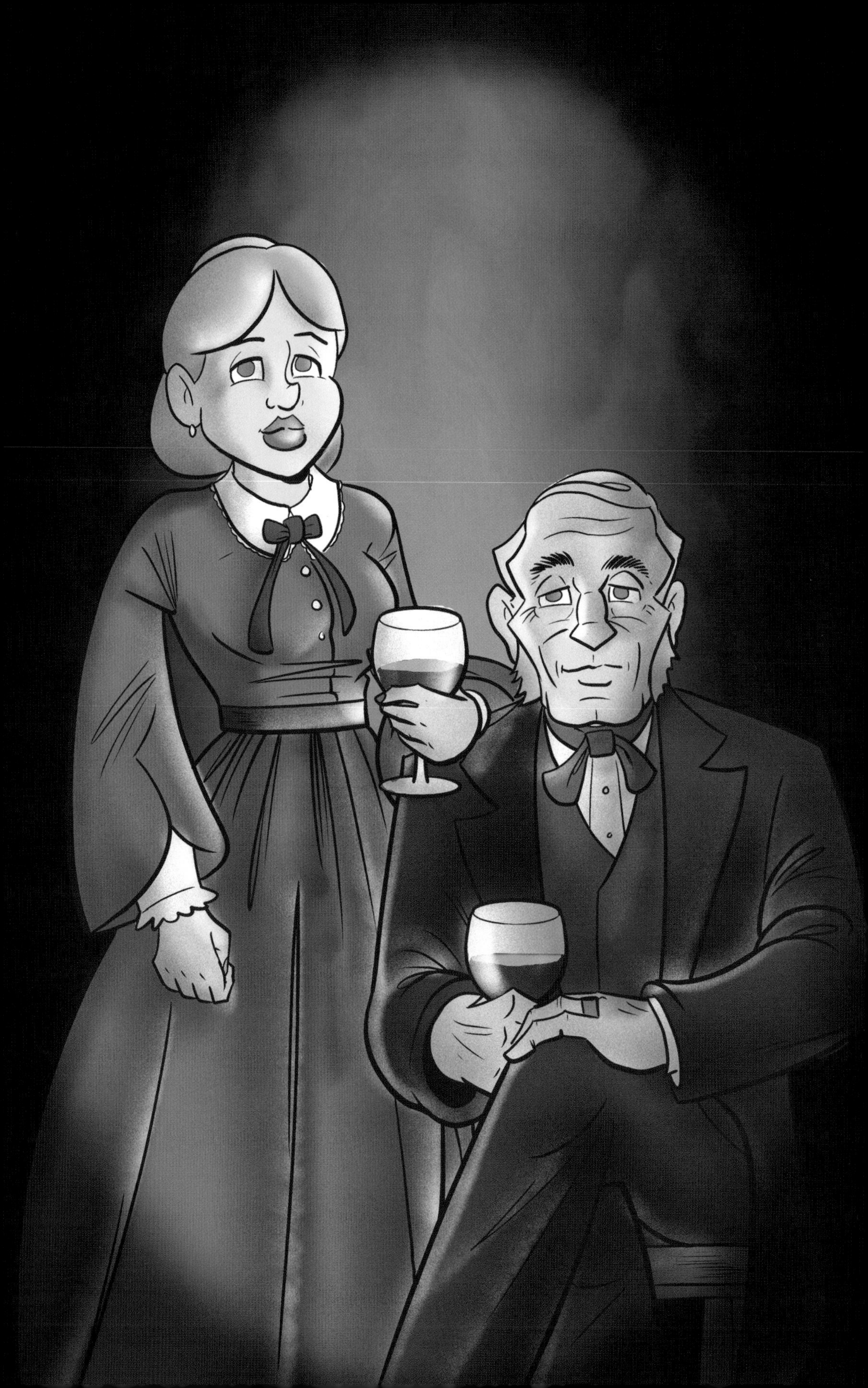

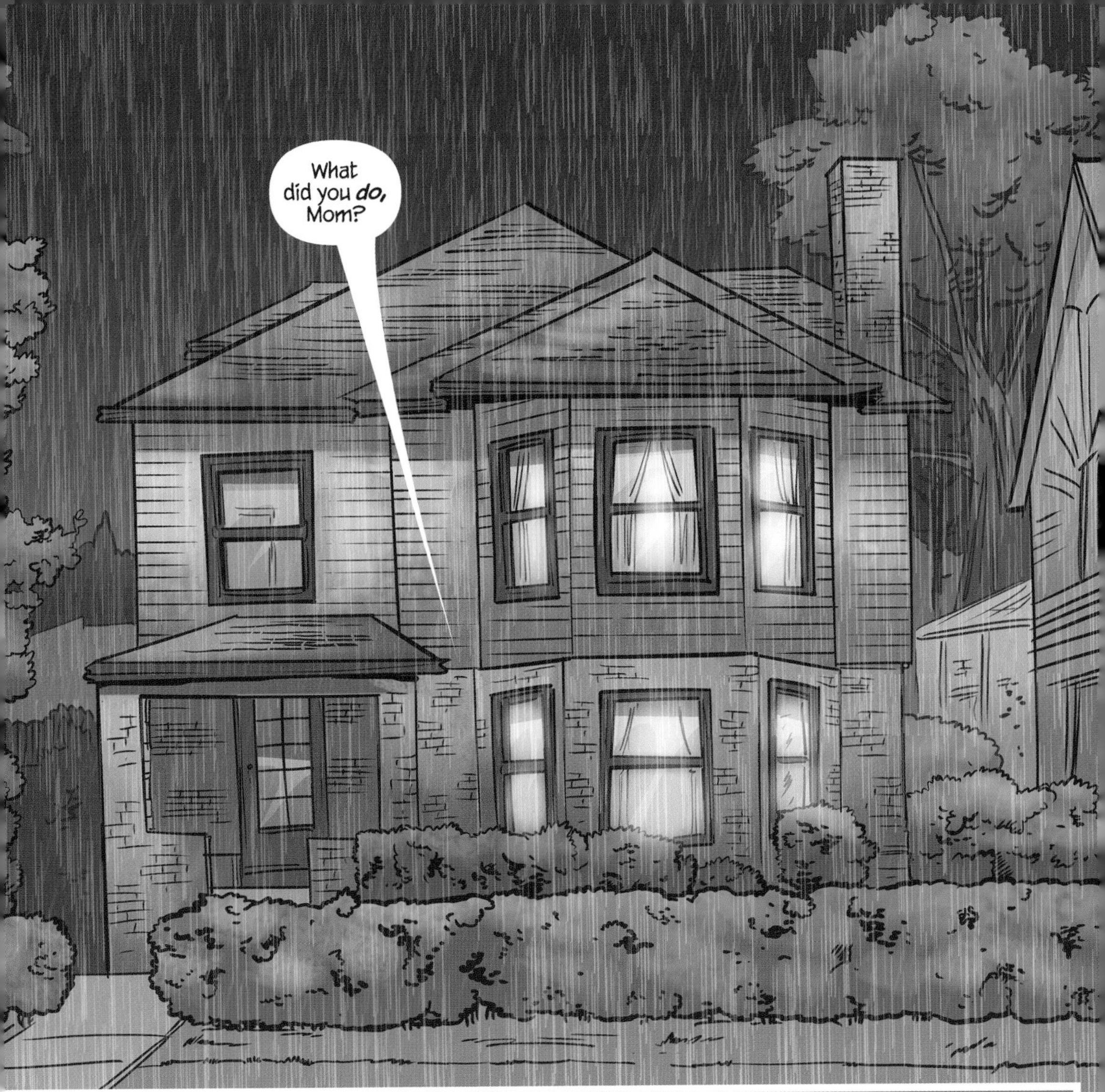
What did you ***do,*** Mom?

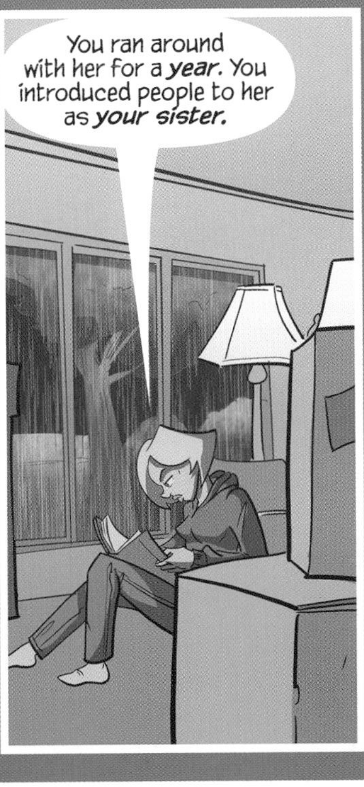
You ran around with her for a ***year.*** You introduced people to her as ***your sister.***

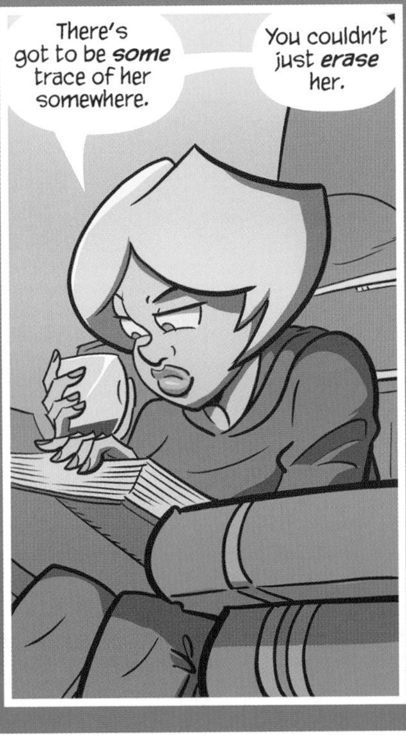
There's got to be ***some*** trace of her somewhere.
You couldn't just ***erase*** her.

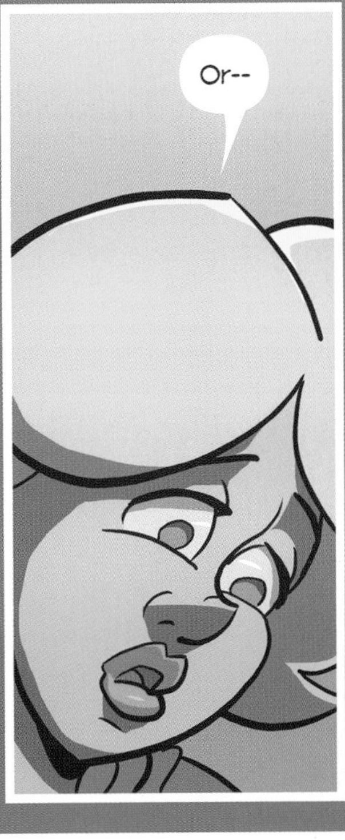
Or--

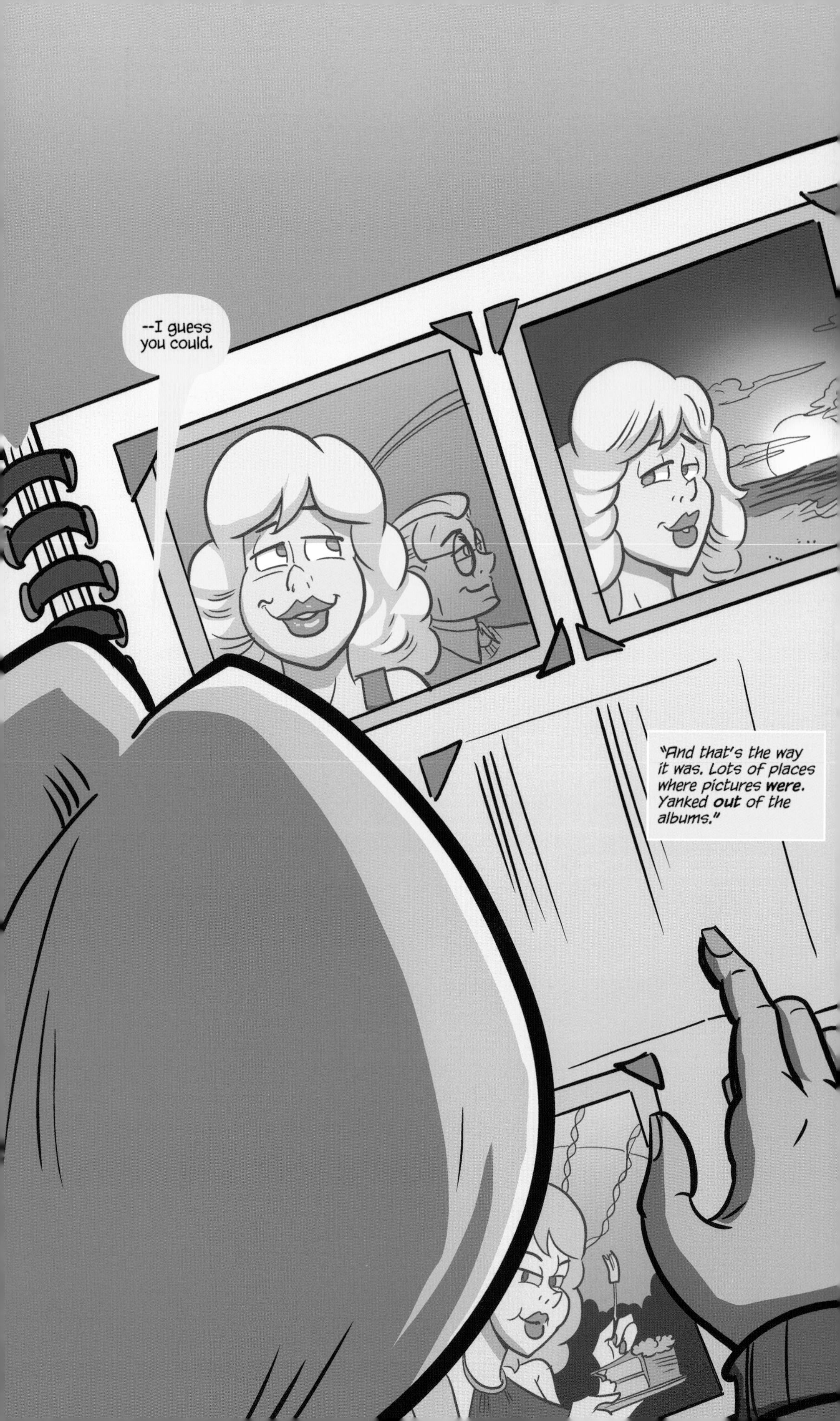
--I guess you could.
"And that's the way it was. Lots of places where pictures **were.** Yanked **out** of the albums."

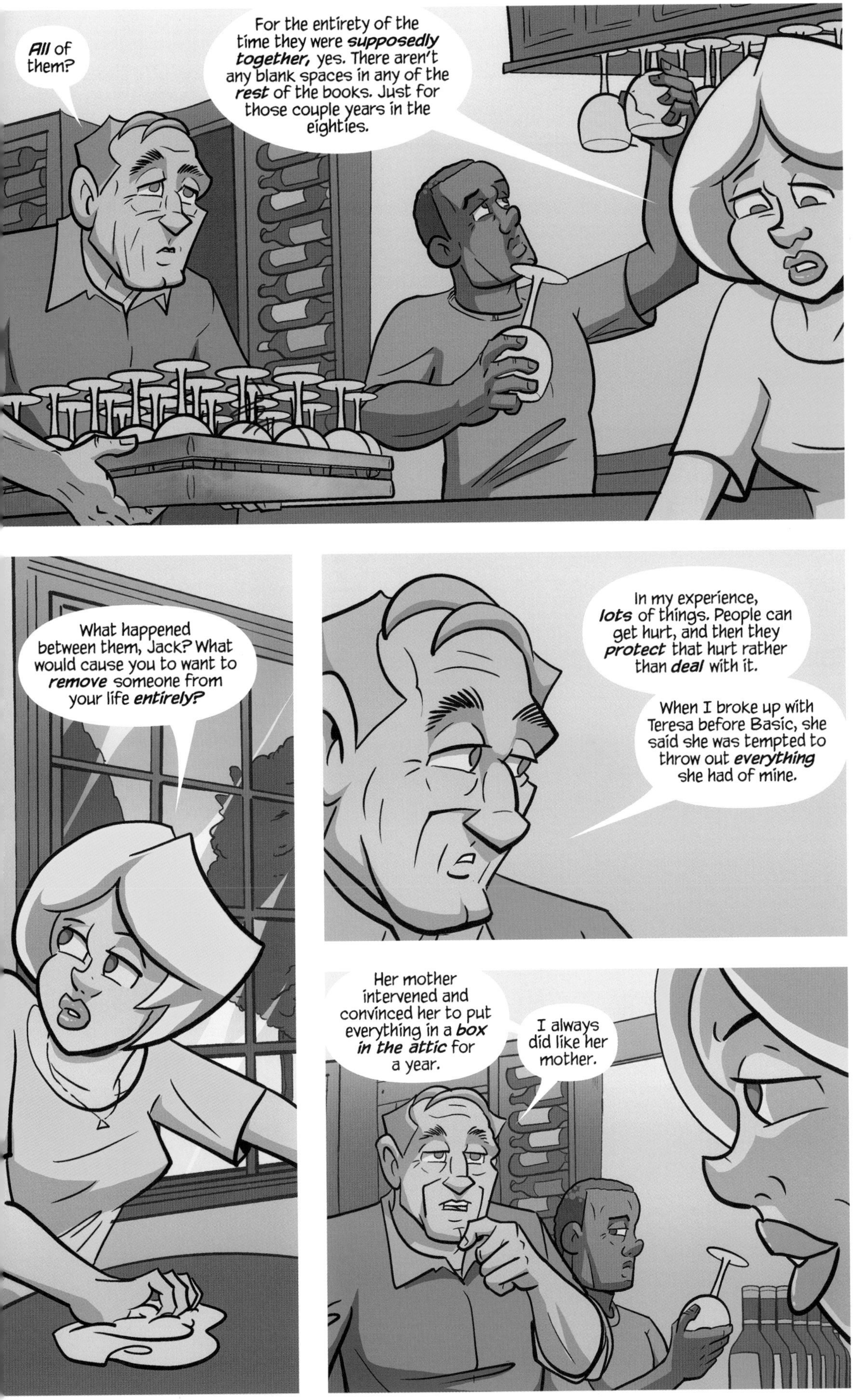
All of them?
For the entirety of the time they were supposedly together, yes. There aren't any blank spaces in any of the rest of the books. Just for those couple years in the eighties.
What happened between them, Jack? What would cause you to want to remove someone from your life entirely?
In my experience, lots of things. People can get hurt, and then they protect that hurt rather than deal with it.
When I broke up with Teresa before Basic, she said she was tempted to throw out everything she had of mine.
Her mother intervened and convinced her to put everything in a box in the attic for a year.
I always did like her mother.

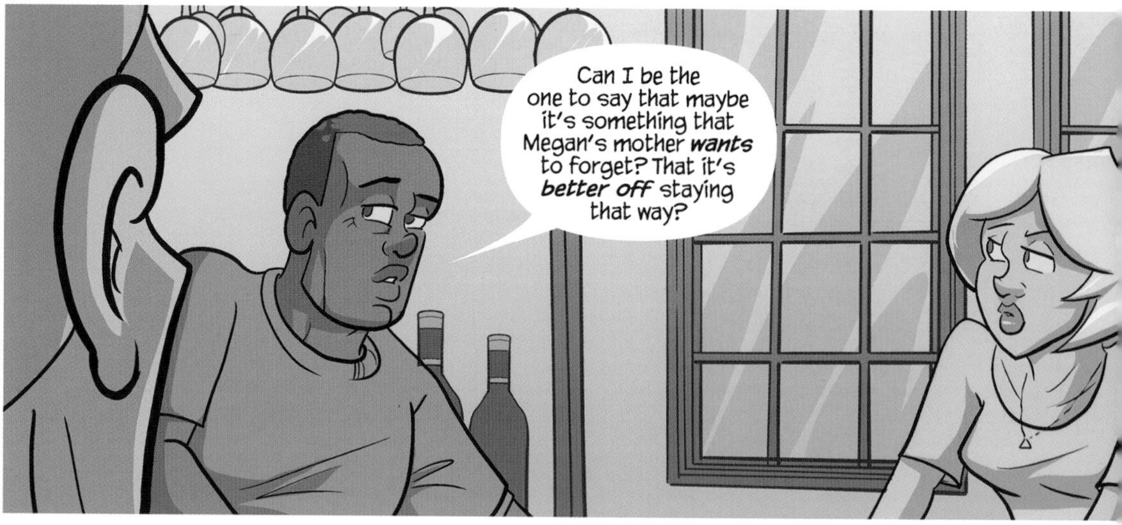
Can I be the one to say that maybe it's something that Megan's mother wants to forget? That it's better off staying that way?

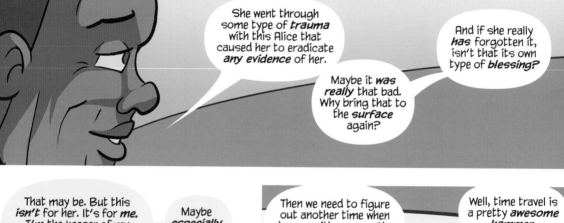

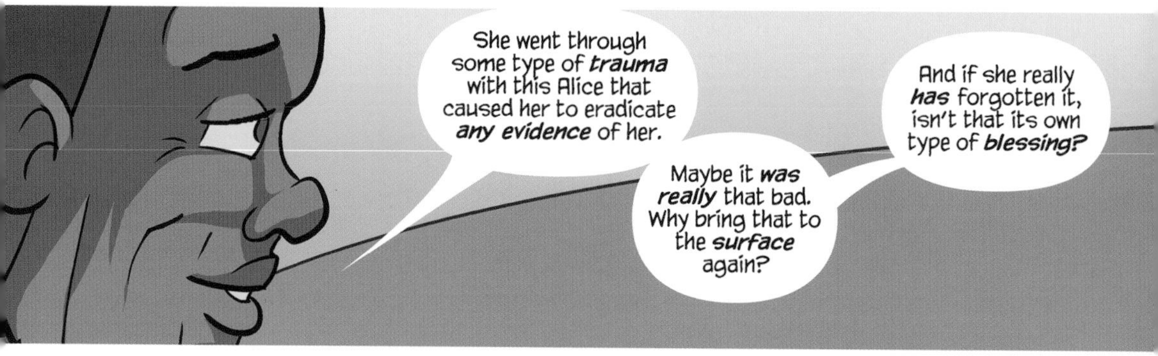
She went through some type of trauma with this Alice that caused her to eradicate any evidence of her.
Maybe it was really that bad. Why bring that to the surface again?
And if she really has forgotten it, isn't that its own type of blessing?

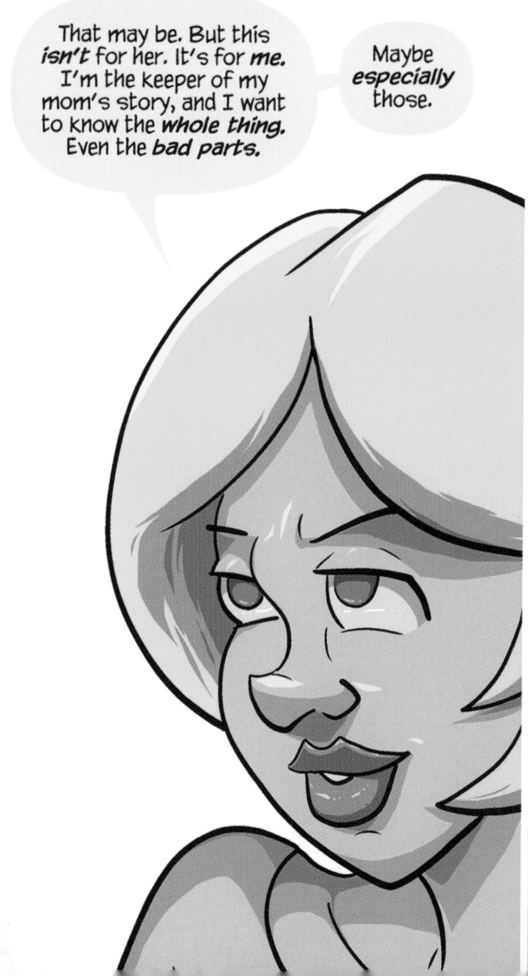
That may be. But this isn't for her. It's for me. I'm the keeper of my mom's story, and I want to know the whole thing. Even the bad parts.
Maybe especially those.

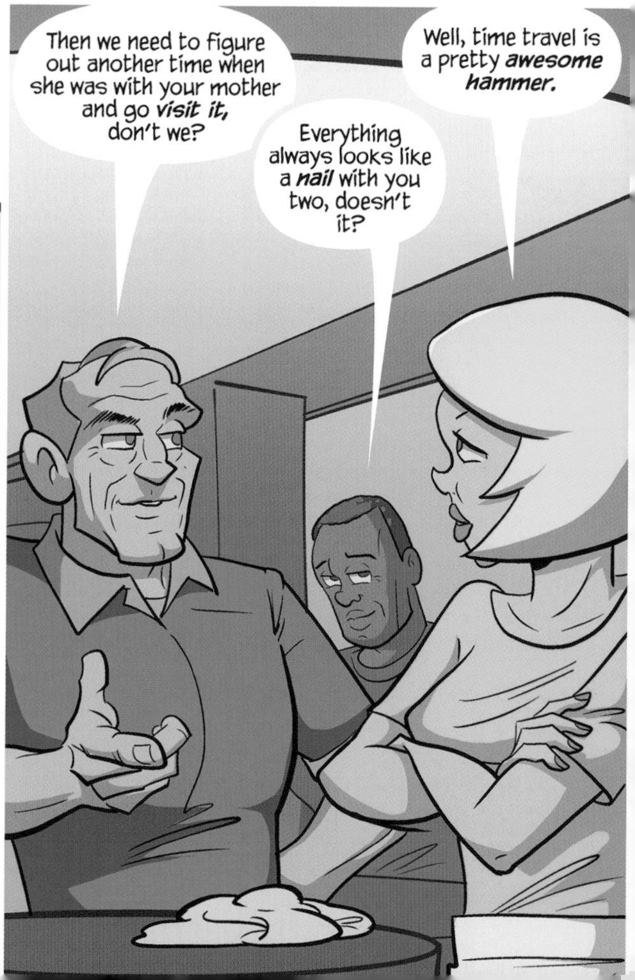
Then we need to figure out another time when she was with your mother and go visit it, don't we?
Everything always looks like a nail with you two, doesn't it?
Well, time travel is a pretty awesome hammer.

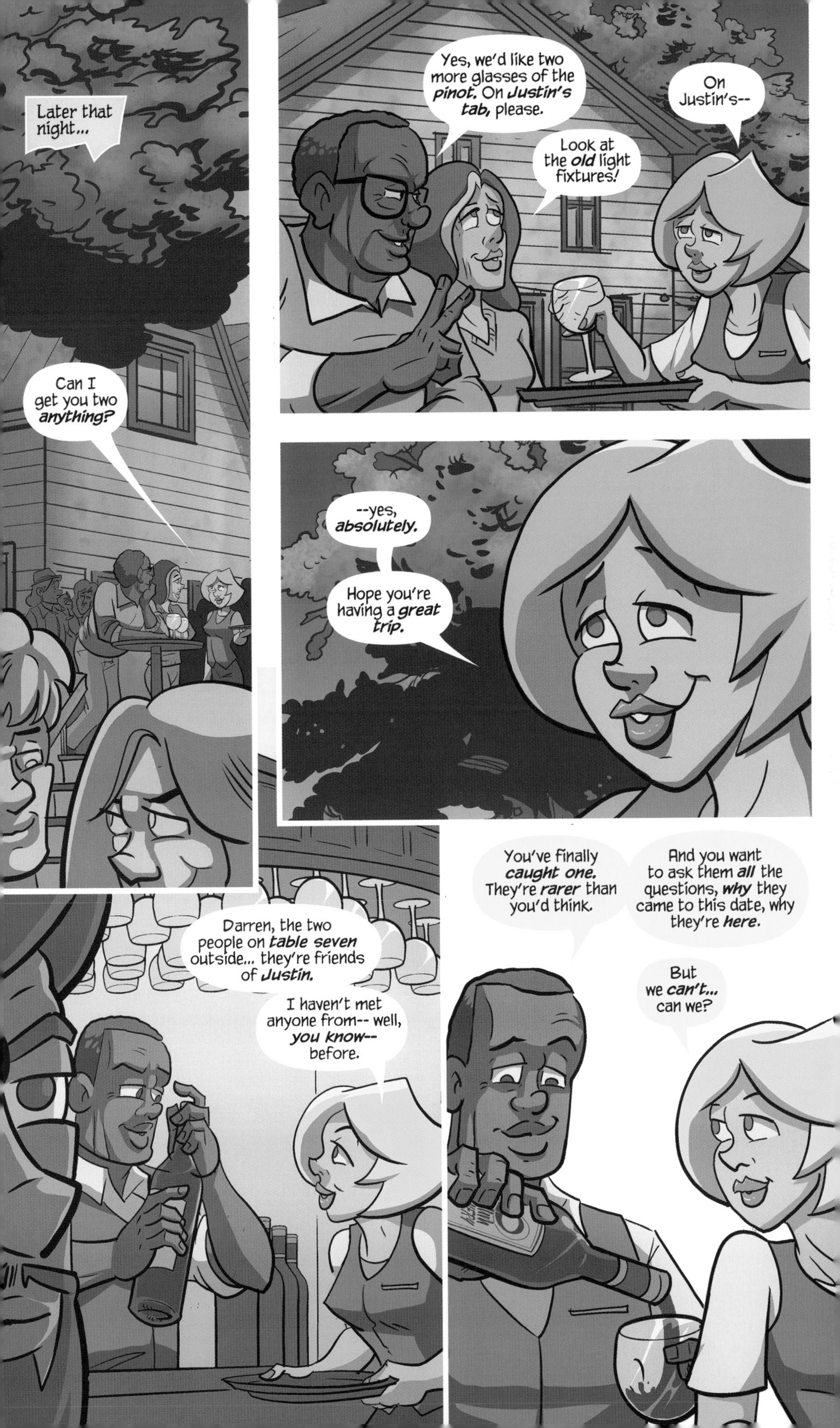

Later that night...
Can I get you two anything?
Yes, we'd like two more glasses of the pinot. On Justin's tab, please.
Look at the old light fixtures!
On Justin's--
--yes, absolutely.
Hope you're having a great trip.
Darren, the two people on table seven outside... they're friends of Justin.
I haven't met anyone from-- well, you know-- before.
You've finally caught one. They're rarer than you'd think.
And you want to ask them all the questions, why they came to this date, why they're here.
But we can't... can we?

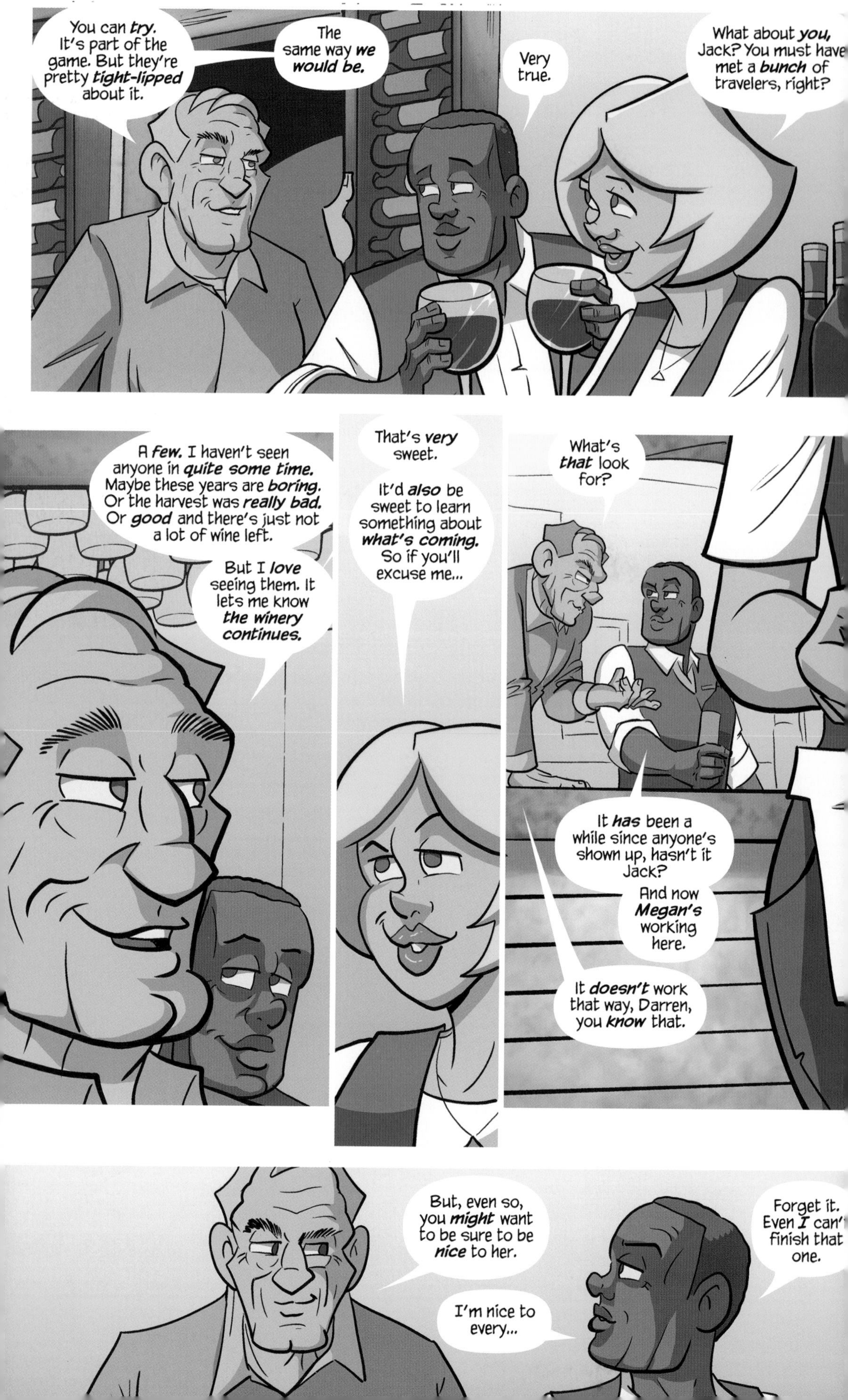
You can *try*. It's part of the game. But they're pretty *tight-lipped* about it.
The same way *we would be.*
Very true.
What about *you*, Jack? You must have met a *bunch* of travelers, right?
A *few*. I haven't seen anyone in *quite some time*. Maybe these years are *boring*. Or the harvest was *really bad*. Or *good* and there's just not a lot of wine left.
But I *love* seeing them. It lets me know *the winery continues.*
That's *very* sweet.
It'd *also* be sweet to learn something about *what's coming.* So if you'll excuse me...
What's *that* look for?
It *has* been a while since anyone's shown up, hasn't it Jack?
And now *Megan's* working here.
It *doesn't* work that way, Darren, you *know* that.
But, even so, you *might* want to be sure to be *nice* to her.
I'm nice to every...
Forget it. Even *I* can't finish that one.

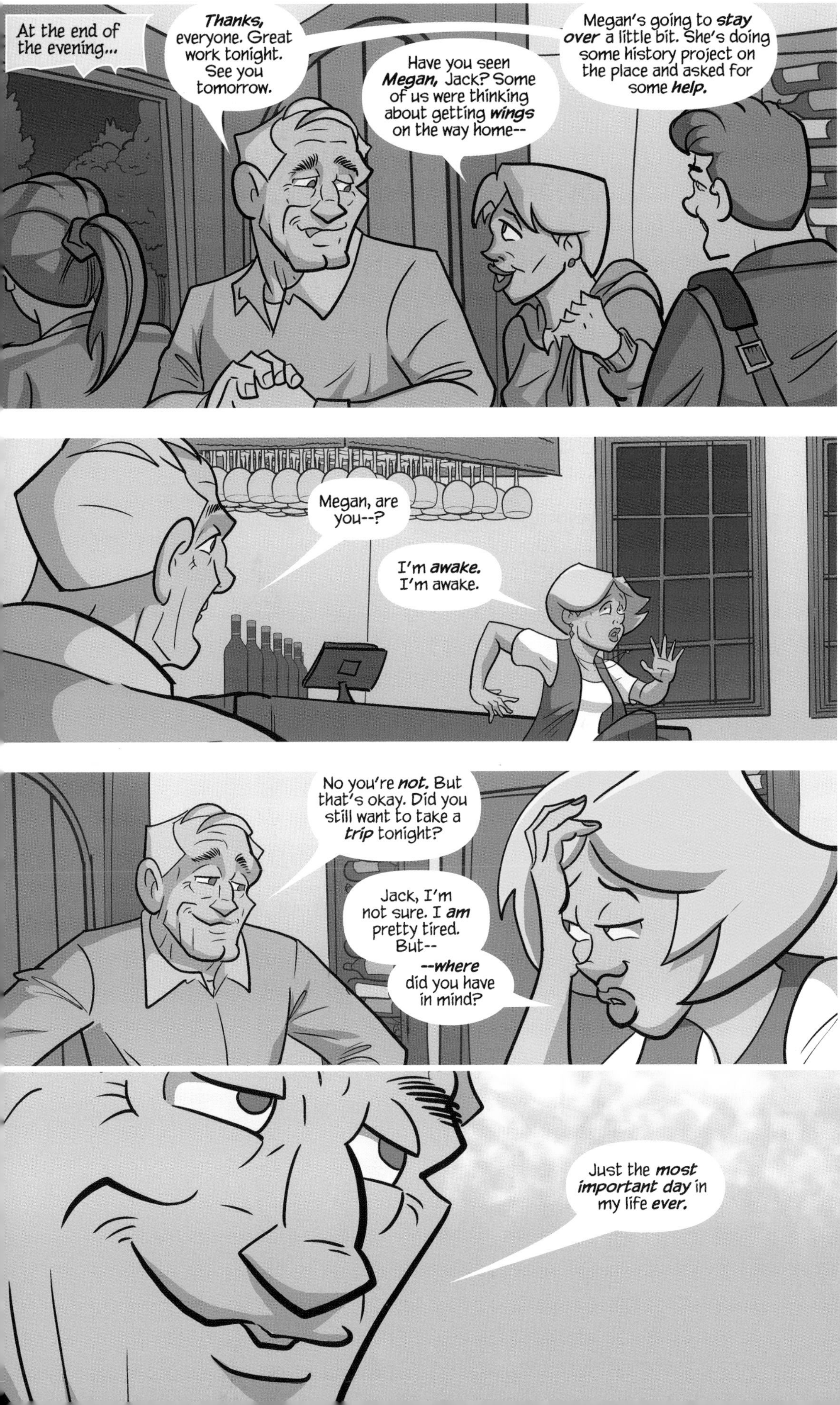
At the end of the evening...
*Thanks,* everyone. Great work tonight. See you tomorrow.
Have you seen *Megan,* Jack? Some of us were thinking about getting *wings* on the way home--
Megan's going to *stay over* a little bit. She's doing some history project on the place and asked for some *help.*
Megan, are you--?
I'm *awake.* I'm awake.
No you're *not.* But that's okay. Did you still want to take a *trip* tonight?
Jack, I'm not sure. I *am* pretty tired. But--
--*where* did you have in mind?
Just the *most important day* in my life *ever.*

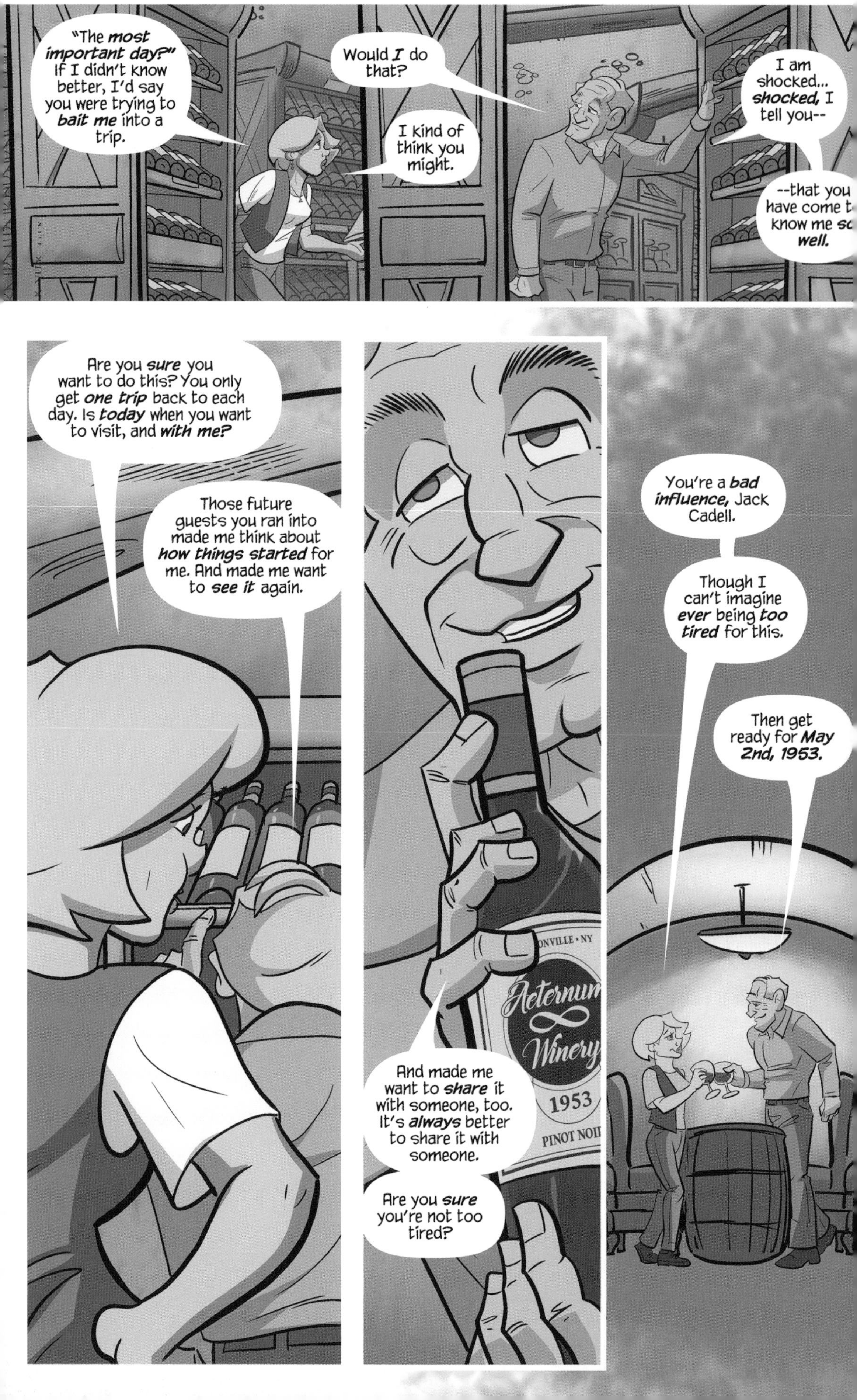
"The most important day?" If I didn't know better, I'd say you were trying to bait me into a trip.
Would I do that?
I kind of think you might.
I am shocked... shocked, I tell you--
--that you have come t know me s well.
Are you sure you want to do this? You only get one trip back to each day. Is today when you want to visit, and with me?
Those future guests you ran into made me think about how things started for me. And made me want to see it again.
ONVILLE • NY
Aeternum Winery
1953
PINOT NOI
And made me want to share it with someone, too. It's always better to share it with someone.
Are you sure you're not too tired?
You're a bad influence, Jack Cadell.
Though I can't imagine ever being too tired for this.
Then get ready for May 2nd, 1953.

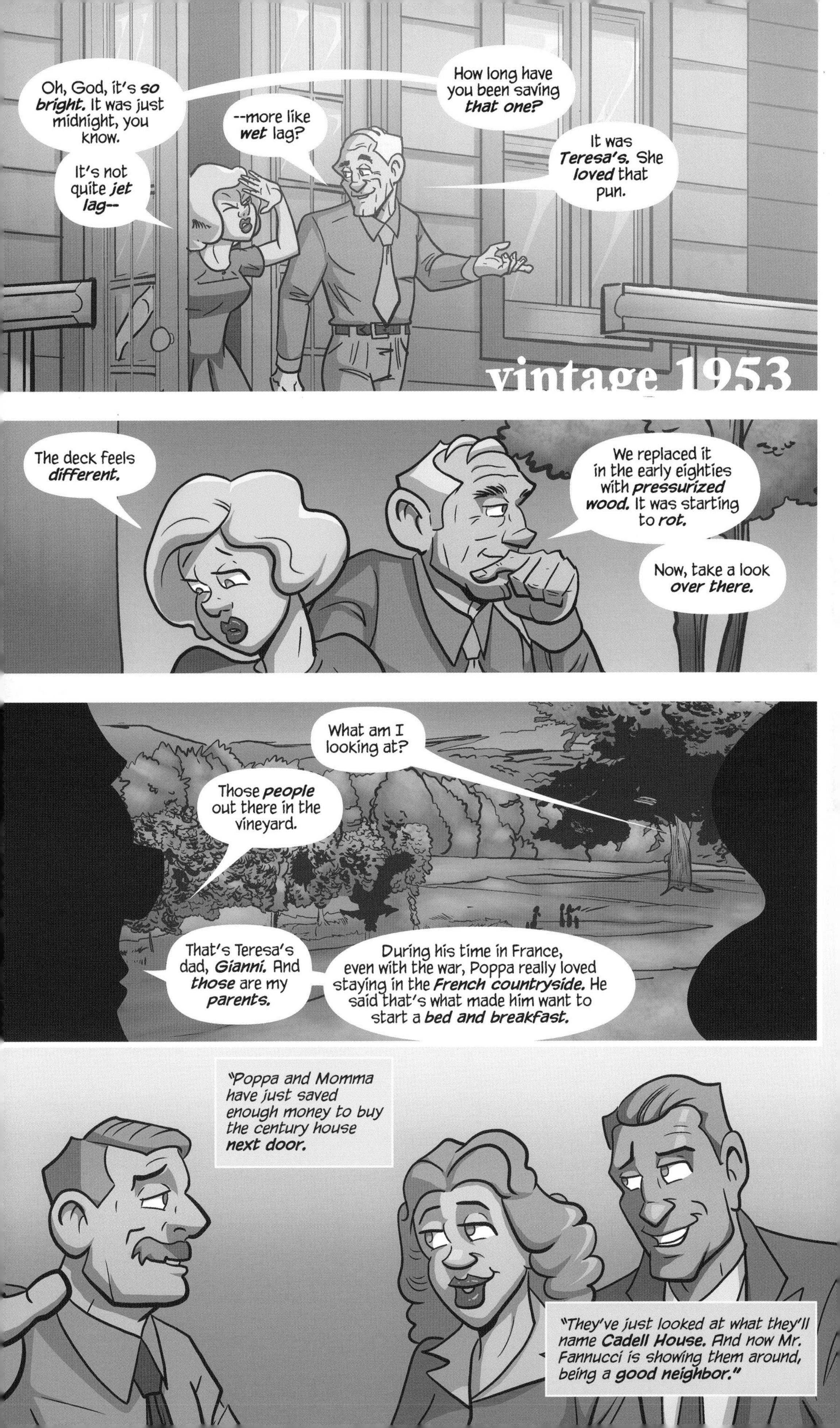
Oh, God, it's **so bright.** It was just midnight, you know.
It's not quite ***jet* lag--**
--more like ***wet*** lag?
How long have you been saving ***that one?***
It was ***Teresa's.*** She ***loved*** that pun.
vintage 1953
The deck feels ***different.***
We replaced it in the early eighties with ***pressurized wood.*** It was starting to ***rot.***
Now, take a look ***over there.***
What am I looking at?
Those ***people*** out there in the vineyard.
That's Teresa's dad, ***Gianni.*** And ***those*** are my ***parents.***
During his time in France, even with the war, Poppa really loved staying in the ***French countryside.*** He said that's what made him want to start a ***bed and breakfast.***
*"Poppa and Momma have just saved enough money to buy the century house* ***next door.***
*"They've just looked at what they'll name* ***Cadell House.*** *And now Mr. Fannucci is showing them around, being a* ***good neighbor."***

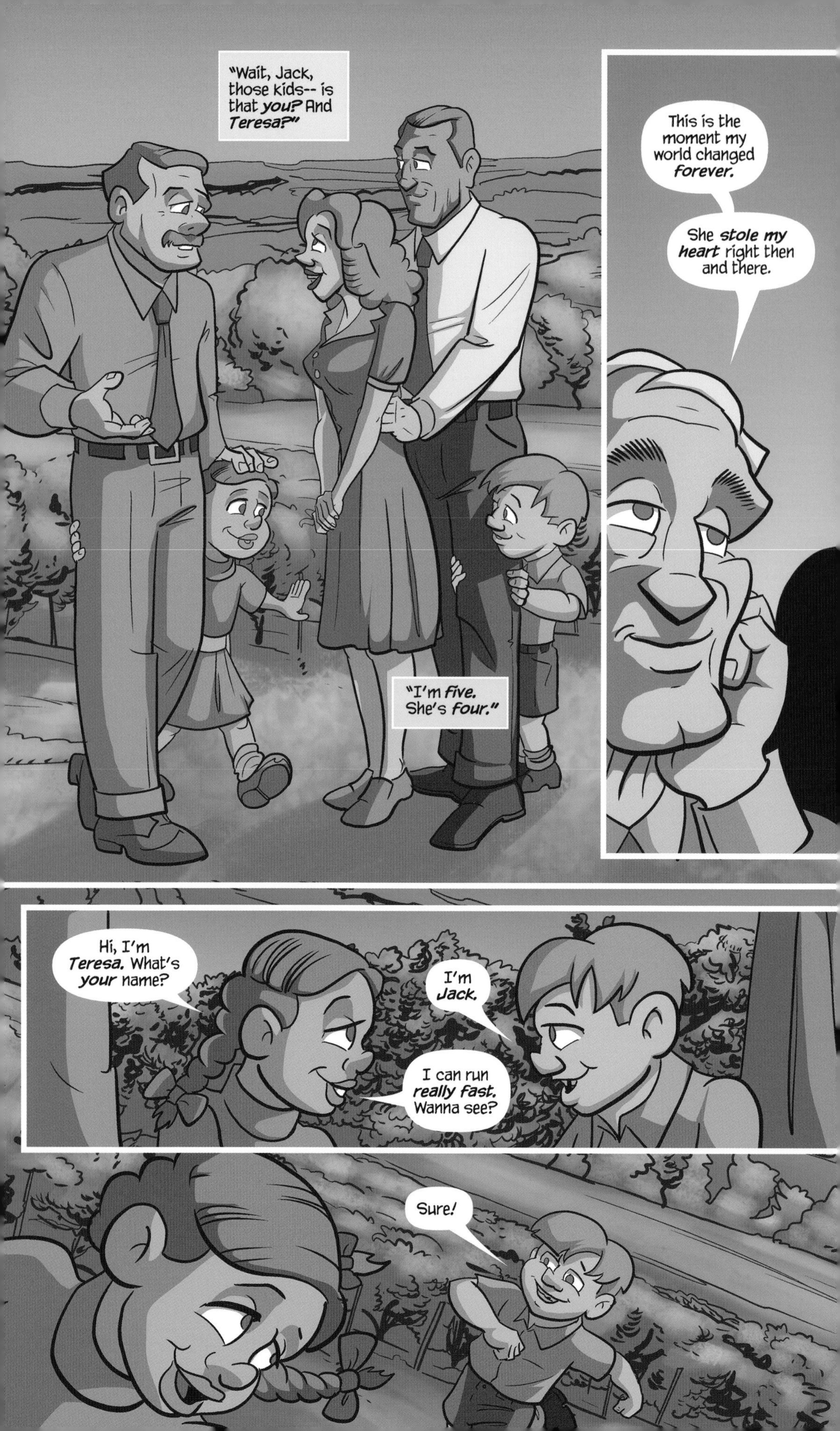
"Wait, Jack, those kids-- is that *you?* And *Teresa?"*
"I'm *five.* She's *four."*
This is the moment my world changed *forever.*
She ***stole my heart*** right then and there.
Hi, I'm ***Teresa.*** What's ***your*** name?
I'm ***Jack.***
I can run ***really fast.*** Wanna see?
Sure!

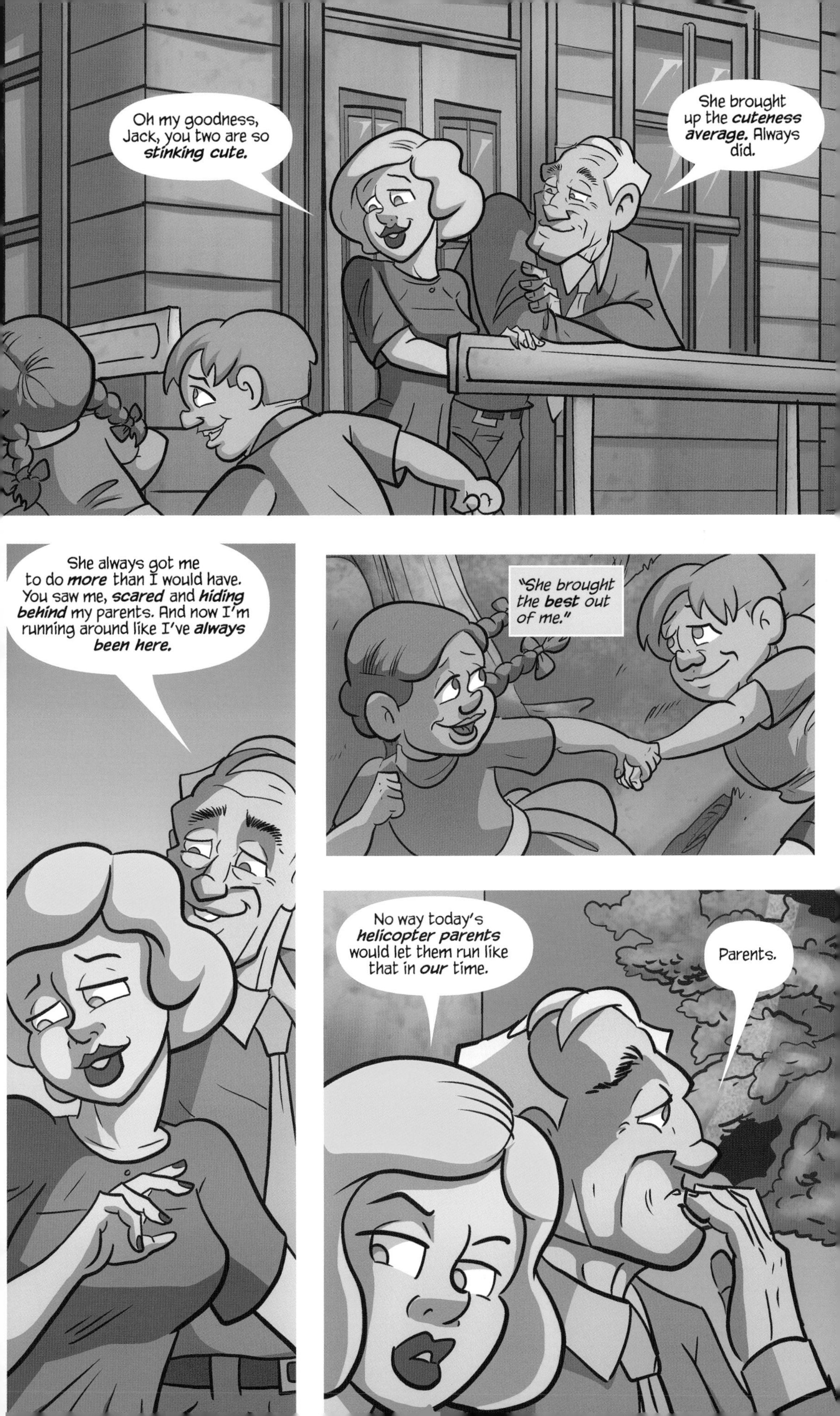
Oh my goodness, Jack, you two are so ***stinking cute.***
She brought up the ***cuteness average.*** Always did.
She always got me to do ***more*** than I would have. You saw me, ***scared*** and ***hiding behind*** my parents. And now I'm running around like I've ***always been here.***
*"She brought the **best** out of me."*
No way today's ***helicopter parents*** would let them run like that in ***our*** time.
Parents.

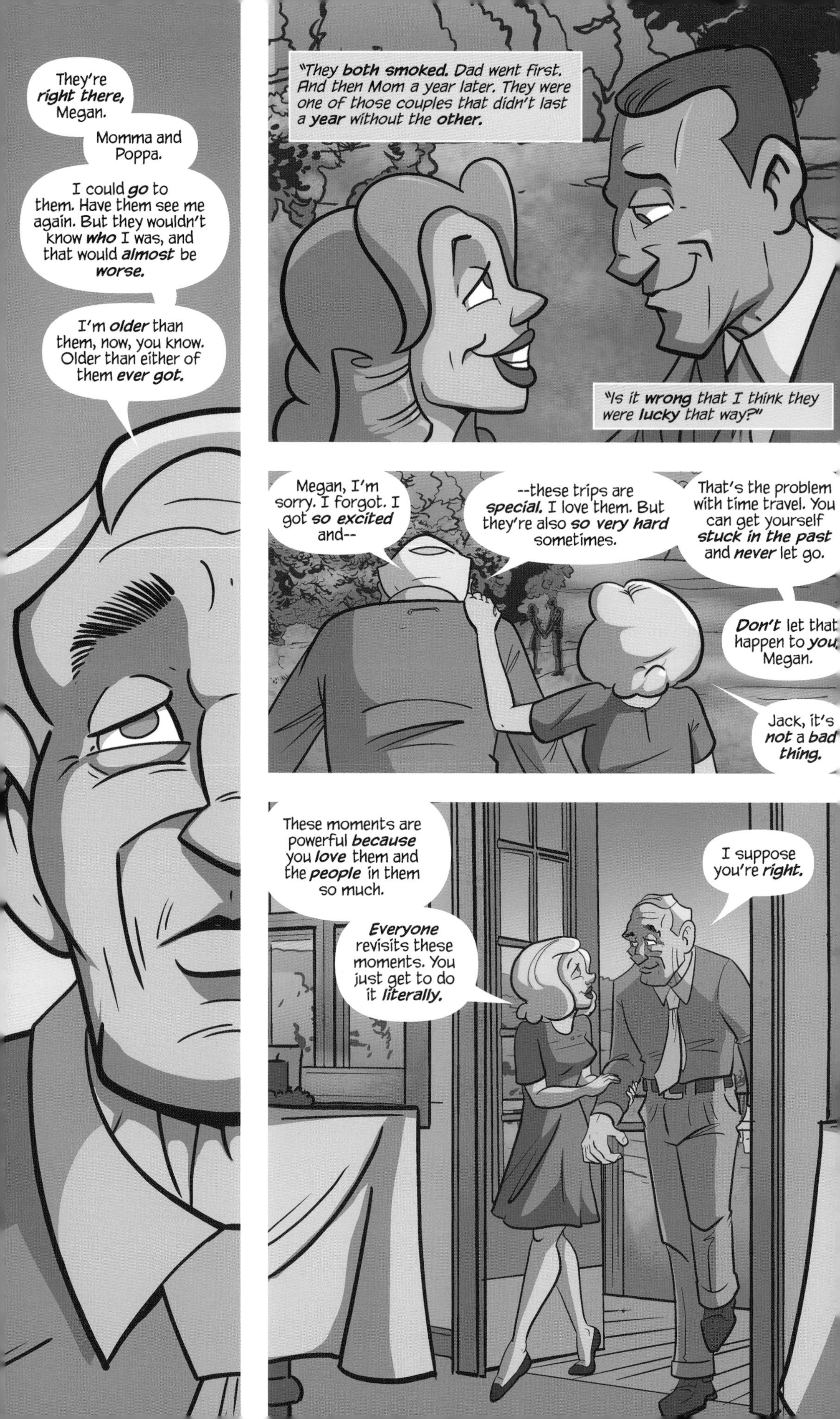
They're *right there,* Megan.
Momma and Poppa.
I could *go* to them. Have them see me again. But they wouldn't know *who* I was, and that would *almost* be *worse.*
I'm *older* than them, now, you know. Older than either of them *ever got.*
"They **both smoked.** Dad went first. And then Mom a year later. They were one of those couples that didn't last a **year** without the **other.**
"Is it **wrong** that I think they were **lucky** that way?"
Megan, I'm sorry. I forgot. I got *so excited* and--
--these trips are *special.* I love them. But they're also *so very hard* sometimes.
That's the problem with time travel. You can get yourself *stuck in the past* and *never* let go.
*Don't* let that happen to *you,* Megan.
Jack, it's *not* a *bad thing.*
These moments are powerful *because* you *love* them and the *people* in them so much.
*Everyone* revisits these moments. You just get to do it *literally.*
I suppose you're *right.*

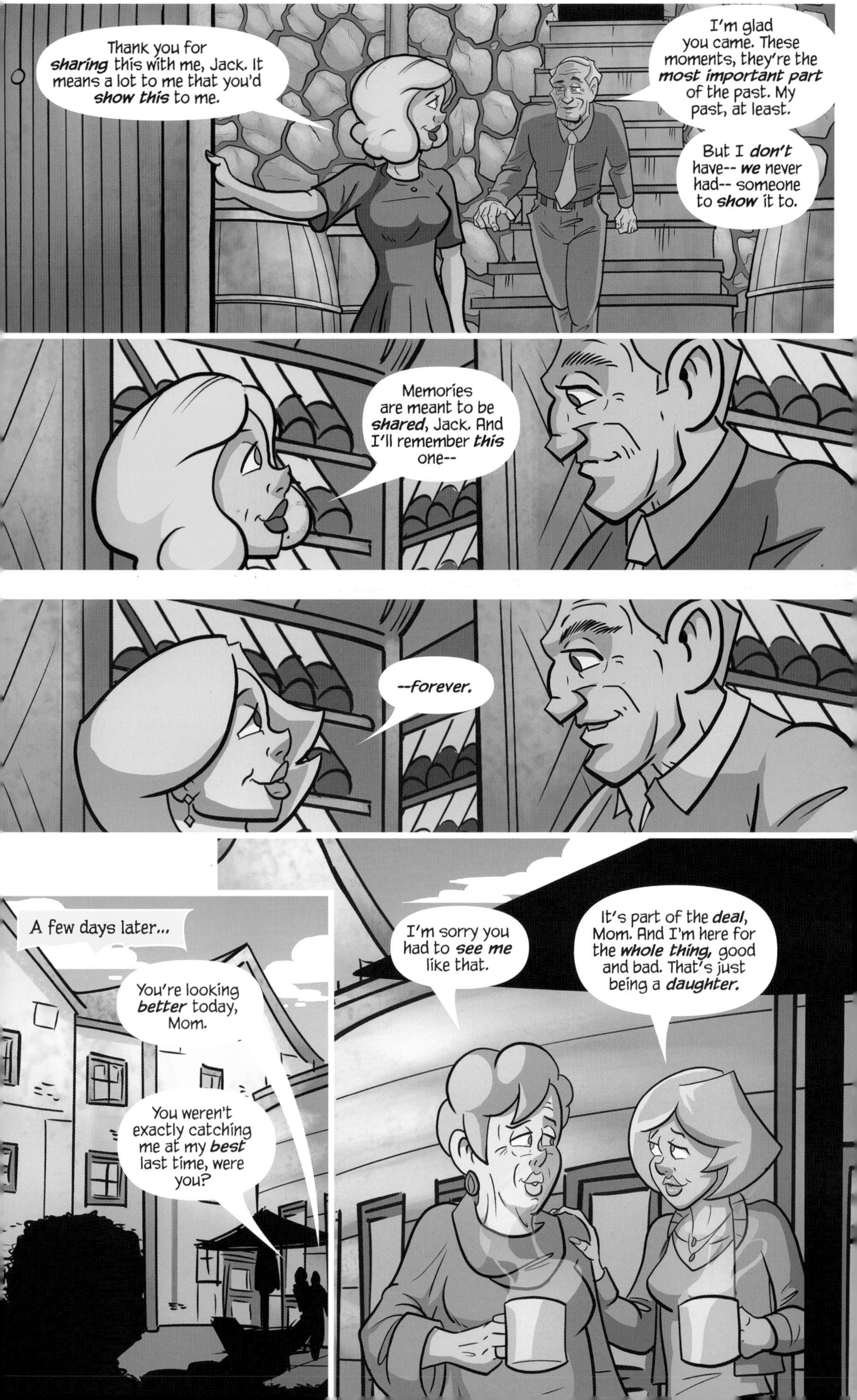
Thank you for *sharing* this with me, Jack. It means a lot to me that you'd *show this* to me.
I'm glad you came. These moments, they're the ***most important part*** of the past. My past, at least.
But I ***don't*** have-- ***we*** never had-- someone to ***show*** it to.
Memories are meant to be ***shared***, Jack. And I'll remember ***this*** one--
***--forever.***
A few days later...
You're looking ***better*** today, Mom.
You weren't exactly catching me at my ***best*** last time, were you?
I'm sorry you had to ***see me*** like that.
It's part of the ***deal***, Mom. And I'm here for the ***whole thing,*** good and bad. That's just being a ***daughter.***

No, it's being a *good* daughter.

*Thank you,* Mom. But--

--look, this is going to sound *weird* but I had a *moment* with a friend today and--

--I'm *sorry* you don't have grand-children.

I hope you *do* have them, Megan. Children are the *most* special thing. But have them when *you're ready,* and for God's sake, with the *right* person.

There's no rush *either.* You're still young.

Besides, I don't know that I'd *want* my grandchildren to have to *see me* like this.

That's the part I *hate* about getting older. There's *so much* I'm going to *miss.* And, in my case, so much I'm *not going to remember.*

I hope you have them, I hope I *see them,* and that they *never* have to have me look at them like I *don't know* who they are.

We *live on* in our children and our stories, Megan.

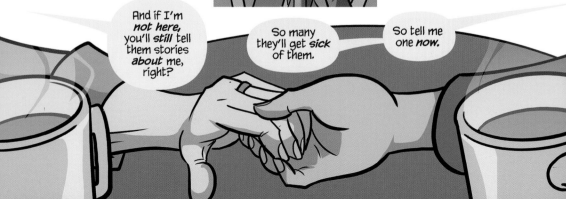

And if I'm *not here,* you'll *still* tell them stories *about* me, right?

So many they'll get *sick* of them.

So tell me one *now.*

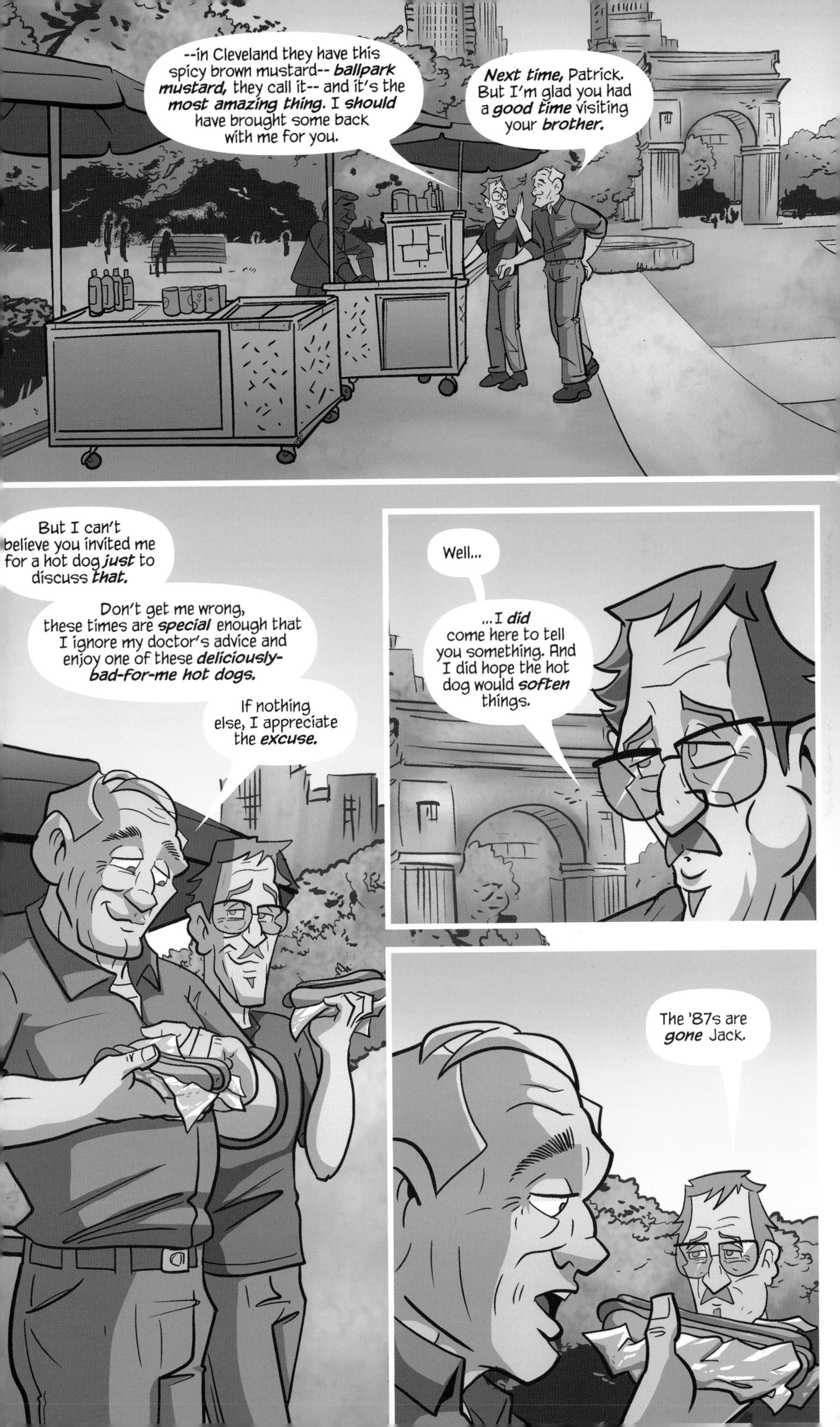
--in Cleveland they have this spicy brown mustard-- *ballpark mustard,* they call it-- and it's the *most amazing thing.* I *should* have brought some back with me for you.
*Next time,* Patrick. But I'm glad you had a *good time* visiting your *brother.*
But I can't believe you invited me for a hot dog *just* to discuss *that.*
Don't get me wrong, these times are *special* enough that I ignore my doctor's advice and enjoy one of these *deliciously-bad-for-me hot dogs.*
If nothing else, I appreciate the *excuse.*
Well...
...I *did* come here to tell you something. And I did hope the hot dog would *soften* things.
The '87s are *gone* Jack.

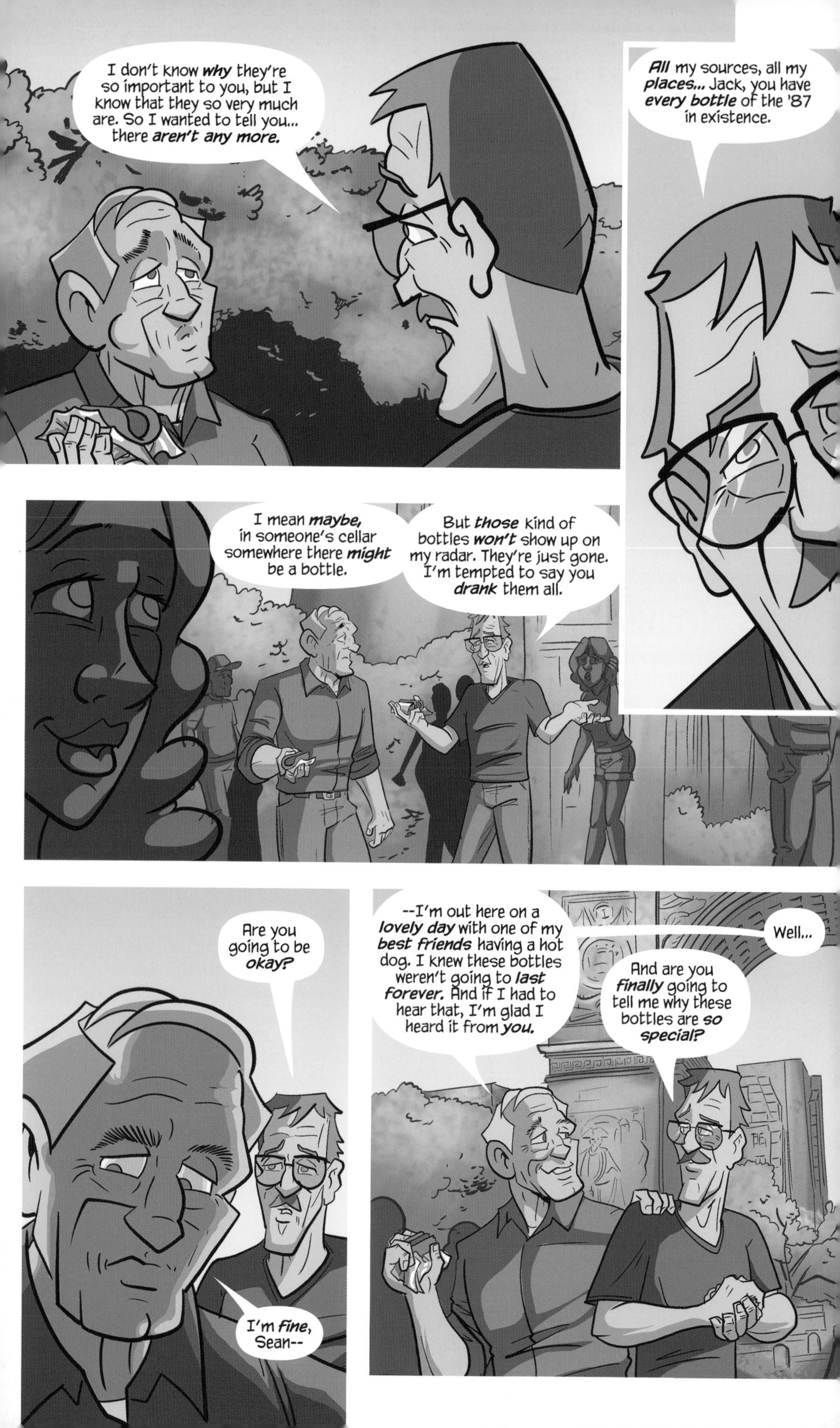

I don't know *why* they're so important to you, but I know that they so very much are. So I wanted to tell you... there *aren't any more.*
*All* my sources, all my *places...* Jack, you have *every bottle* of the '87 in existence.
I mean *maybe,* in someone's cellar somewhere there *might* be a bottle.
But *those* kind of bottles *won't* show up on my radar. They're just gone. I'm tempted to say you *drank* them all.
Are you going to be *okay?*
I'm *fine,* Sean--
--I'm out here on a *lovely day* with one of my *best friends* having a hot dog. I knew these bottles weren't going to *last forever.* And if I had to hear that, I'm glad I heard it from *you.*
Well...
And are you *finally* going to tell me why these bottles are *so special?*

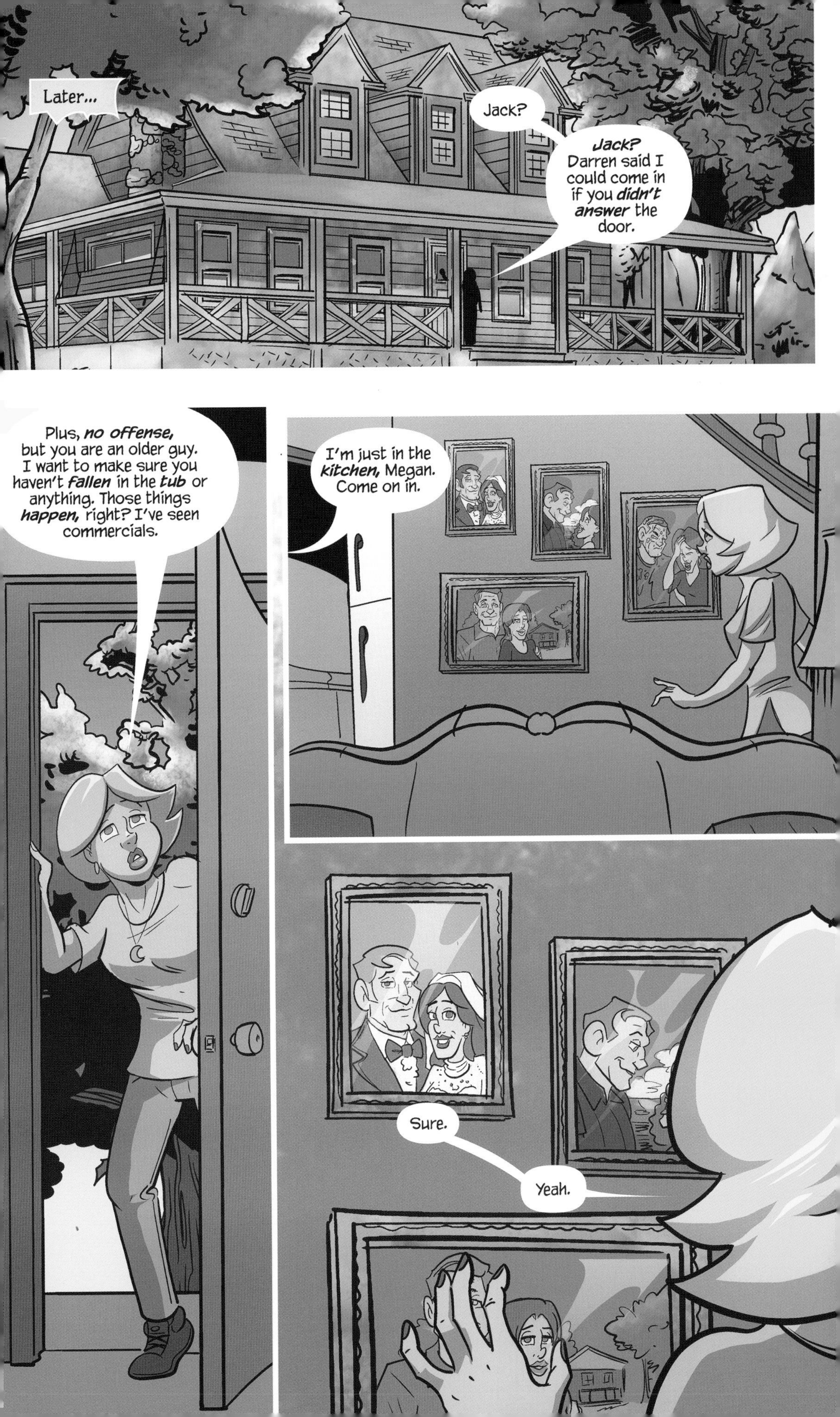

Later...
Jack?
Jack? Darren said I could come in if you didn't answer the door.
Plus, no offense, but you are an older guy. I want to make sure you haven't fallen in the tub or anything. Those things happen, right? I've seen commercials.
I'm just in the kitchen, Megan. Come on in.
Sure.
Yeah.

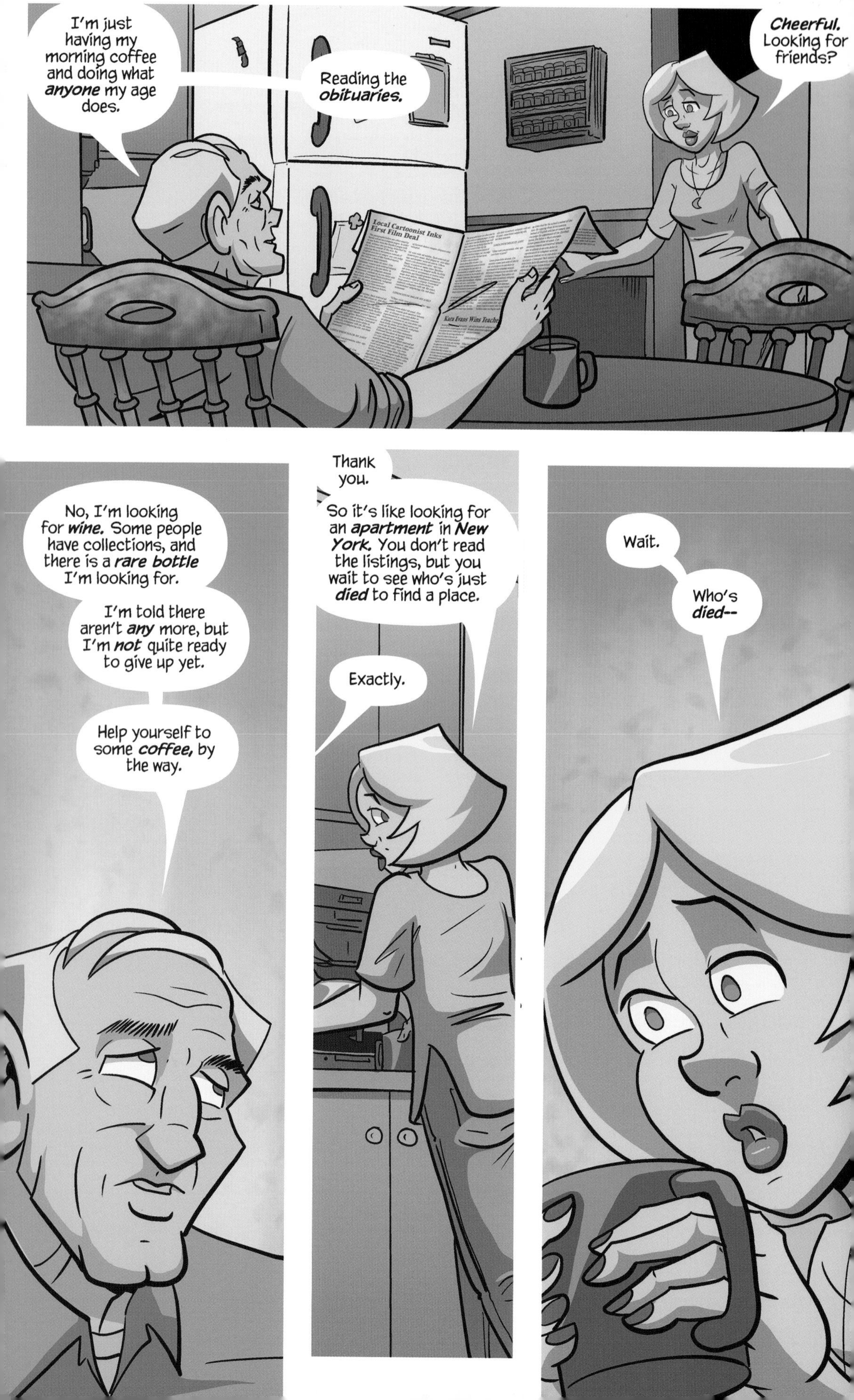
I'm just having my morning coffee and doing what *anyone* my age does.
Reading the *obituaries.*
Local Cartoonist Inks First Film Deal
Cheerful. Looking for friends?
No, I'm looking for *wine.* Some people have collections, and there is a *rare bottle* I'm looking for.
I'm told there aren't *any* more, but I'm *not* quite ready to give up yet.
Help yourself to some *coffee,* by the way.
Thank you.
So it's like looking for an *apartment* in *New York.* You don't read the listings, but you wait to see who's just *died* to find a place.
Exactly.
Wait.
Who's *died--*

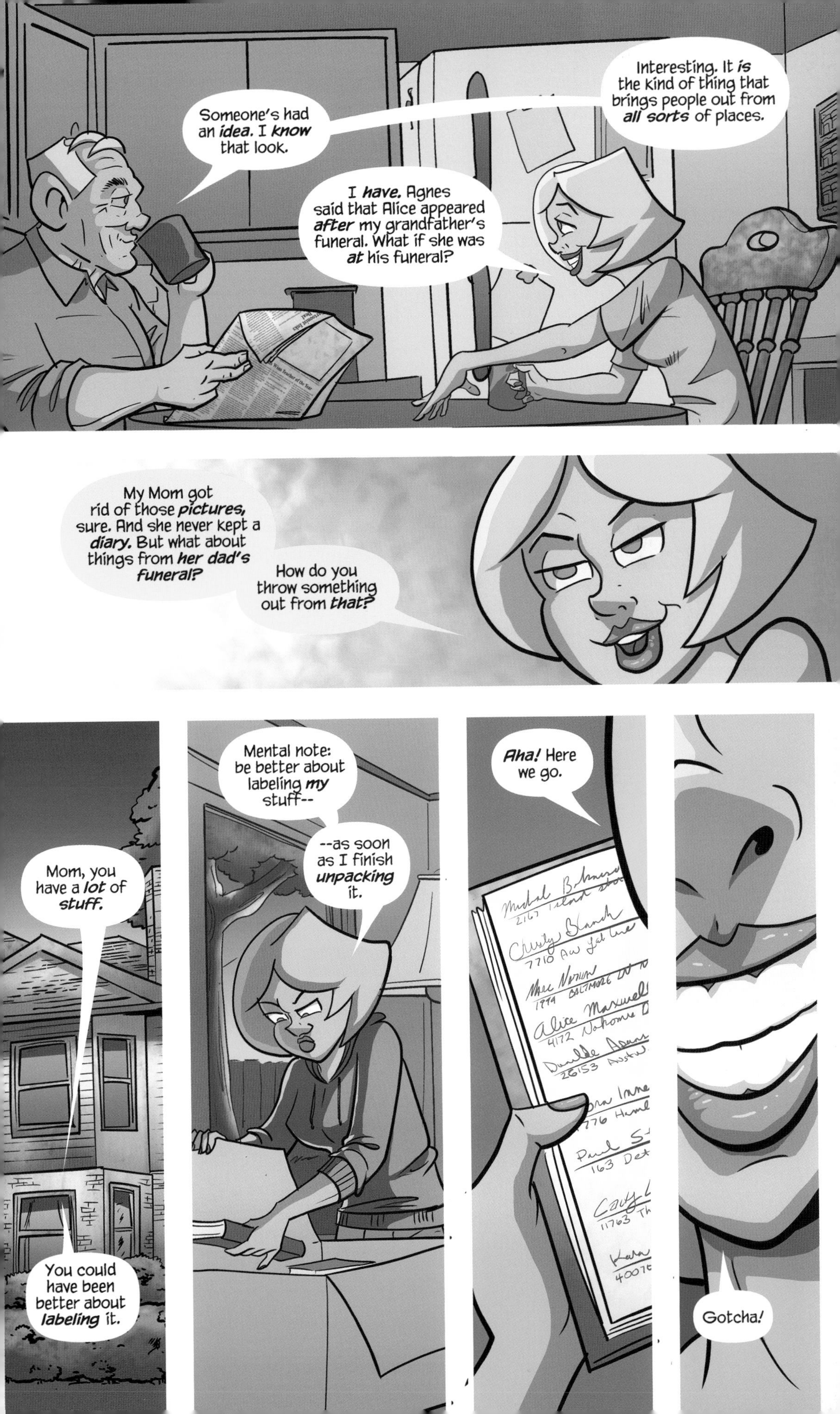
Someone's had an *idea.* I *know* that look.
Interesting. It *is* the kind of thing that brings people out from *all sorts* of places.
I *have.* Agnes said that Alice appeared *after* my grandfather's funeral. What if she was *at* his funeral?
My Mom got rid of those *pictures,* sure. And she never kept a *diary.* But what about things from *her dad's funeral?*
How do you throw something out from *that?*
Mom, you have a *lot* of *stuff.*
You could have been better about *labeling* it.
Mental note: be better about labeling *my* stuff--
--as soon as I finish *unpacking* it.
*Aha!* Here we go.
Gotcha!

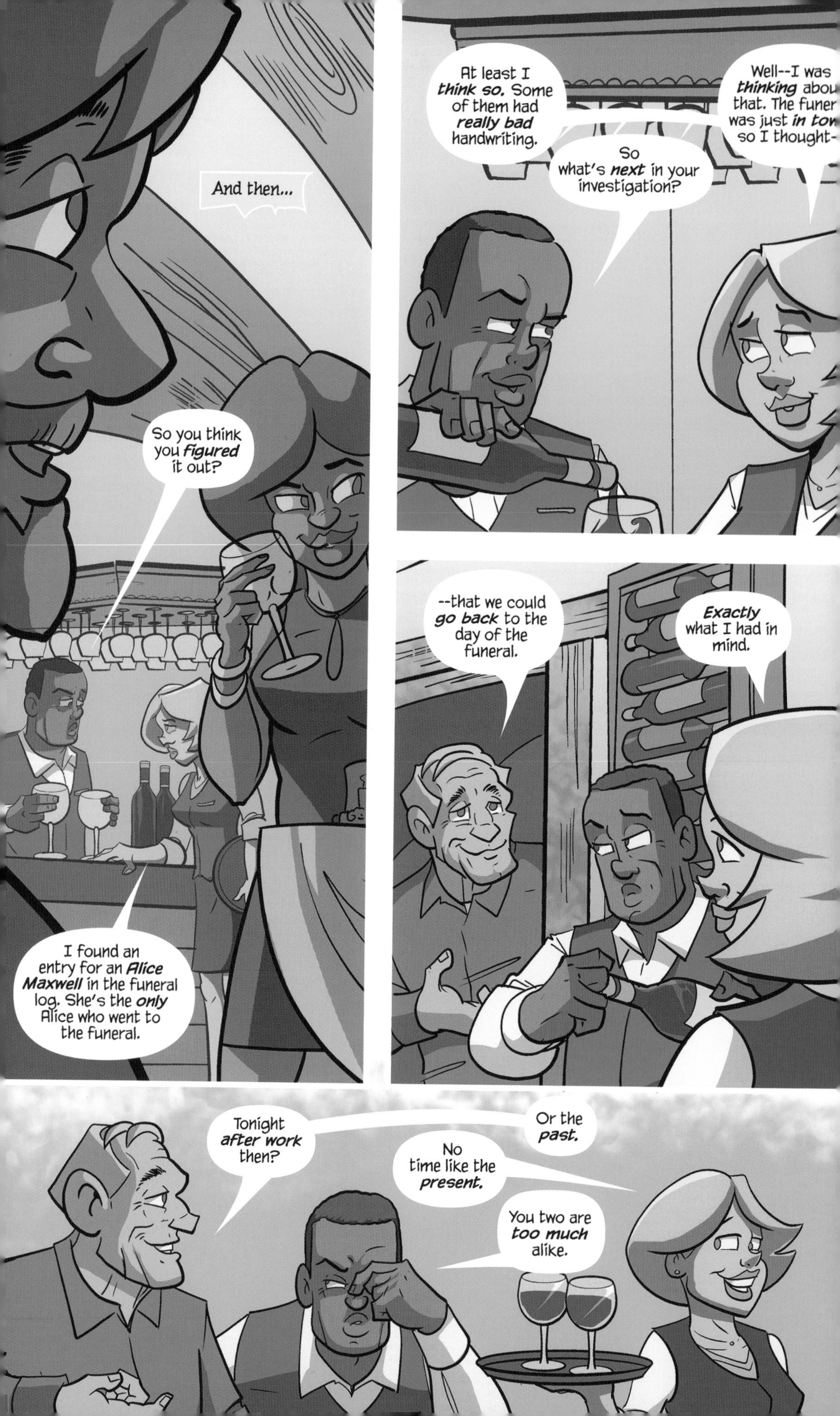
And then...
So you think you *figured* it out?
I found an entry for an *Alice Maxwell* in the funeral log. She's the *only* Alice who went to the funeral.
At least I *think so.* Some of them had *really bad* handwriting.
So what's *next* in your investigation?
Well--I was *thinking* abou that. The funer was just *in tow* so I thought-
--that we could *go back* to the day of the funeral.
*Exactly* what I had in mind.
Tonight *after work* then?
Or the *past.*
No time like the *present.*
You two are *too much* alike.

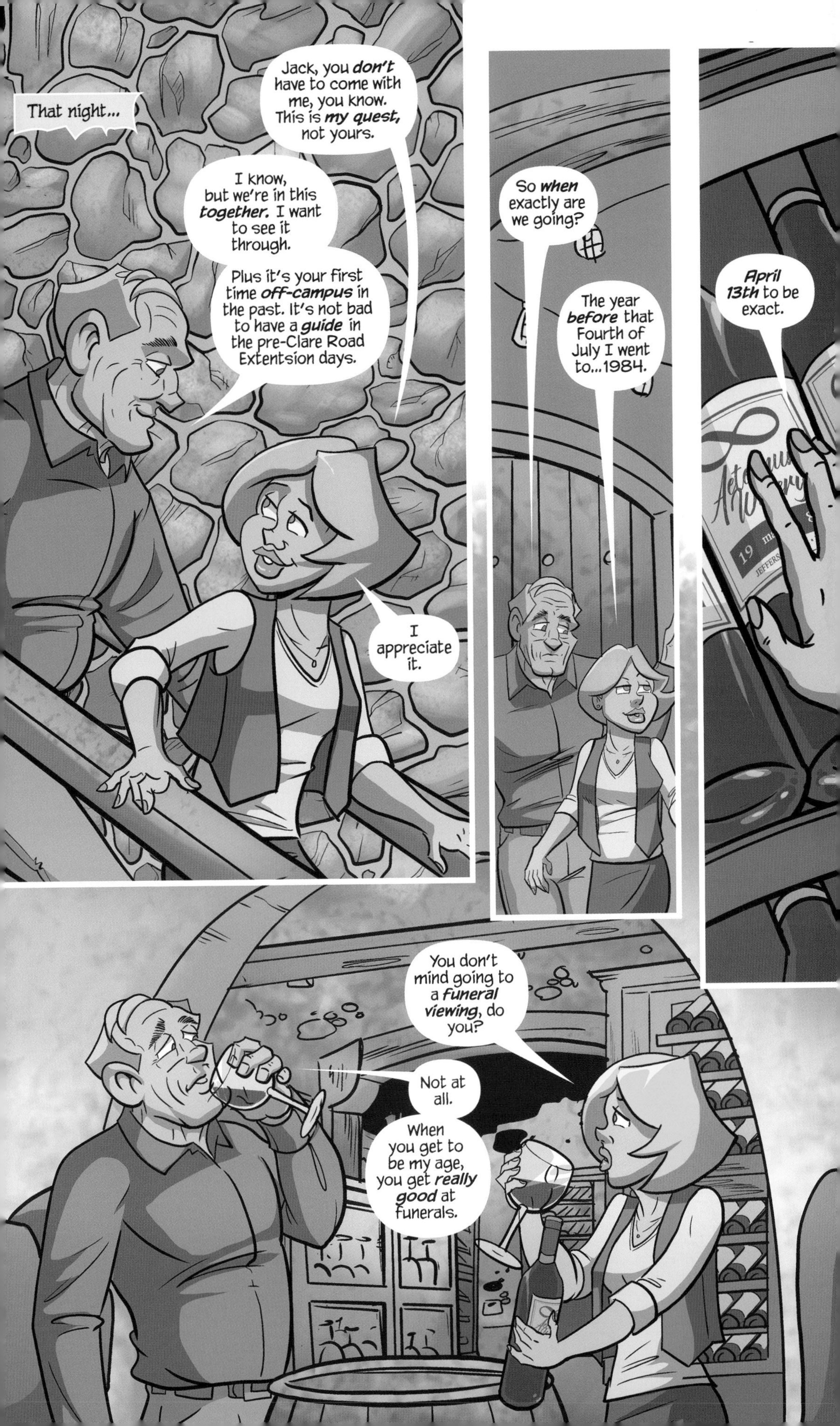
That night...
Jack, you don't have to come with me, you know. This is my quest, not yours.
I know, but we're in this together. I want to see it through.
Plus it's your first time off-campus in the past. It's not bad to have a guide in the pre-Clare Road Extentsion days.
I appreciate it.
So when exactly are we going?
The year before that Fourth of July I went to...1984.
April 13th to be exact.
You don't mind going to a funeral viewing, do you?
Not at all.
When you get to be my age, you get really good at funerals.

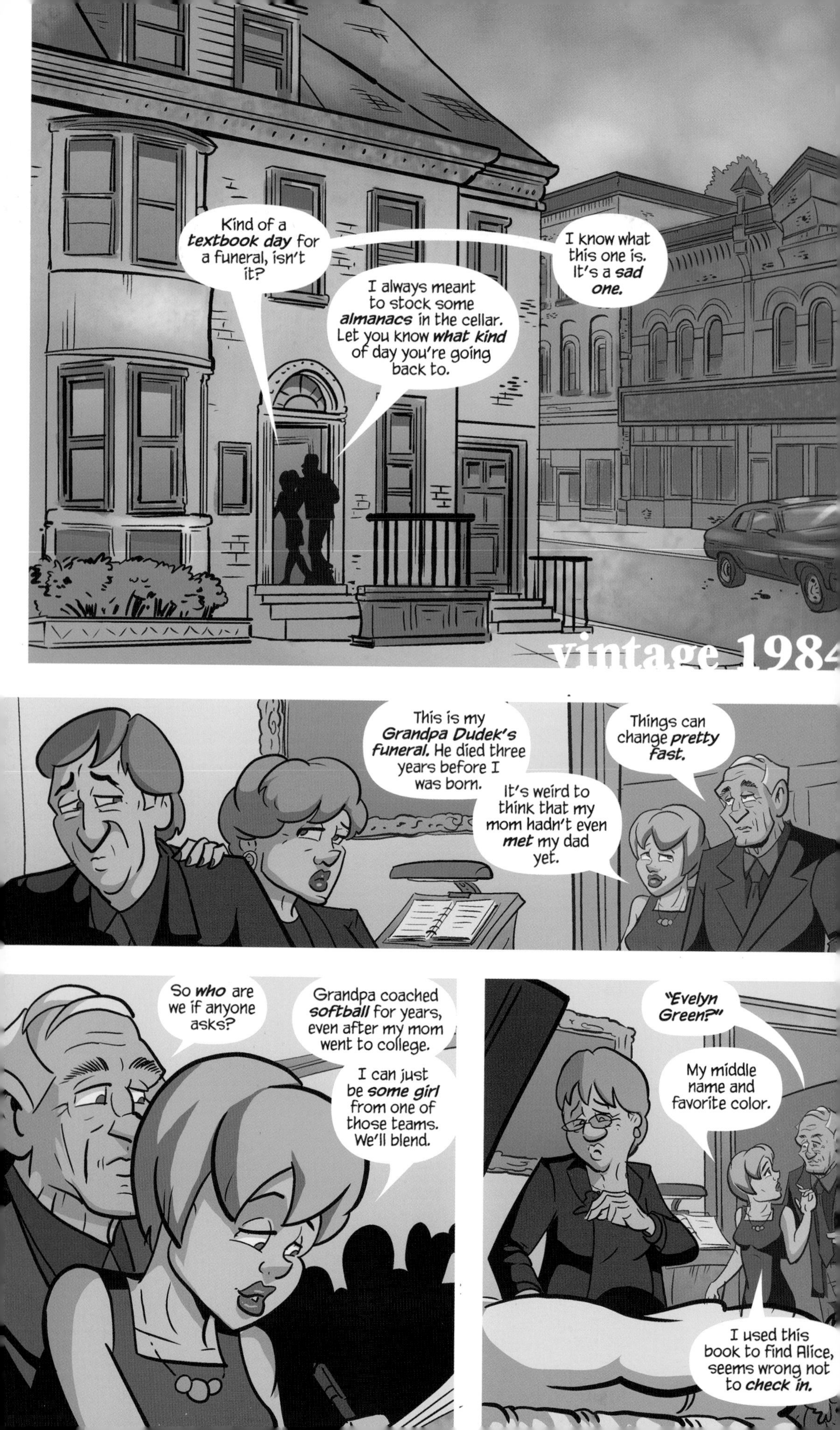
Kind of a textbook day for a funeral, isn't it?
I know what this one is. It's a sad one.
I always meant to stock some almanacs in the cellar. Let you know what kind of day you're going back to.
vintage 1984
This is my Grandpa Dudek's funeral. He died three years before I was born.
It's weird to think that my mom hadn't even met my dad yet.
Things can change pretty fast.
So who are we if anyone asks?
Grandpa coached softball for years, even after my mom went to college.
I can just be some girl from one of those teams. We'll blend.
"Evelyn Green?"
My middle name and favorite color.
I used this book to find Alice, seems wrong not to check in.

Come on, we should pay our respects.

Oh my.

*What* is it?

"I came here for *Alice*, but I didn't expect this. Jack, it's *my family*."

"That's *Uncle Charlie*. He had the best laugh. He's going to die of a heart attack fifteen years from now.

"That's *Great Aunt Grace*. I've only seen pictures of her. She moved to Florida not long after I was born.

"That's *Dave* and *Miko*. He worked for Toyota, and met her on one of his trips to Japan. They always used to *yell* at each other, but they're still married today. Just much, much grayer.

"Oh my God, *Parker* was so young. He's grandpa's youngest nephew.

"And that's *Karen*, Parker's cousin. She let me have my first sip of *wine* at one of Mom's birthday parties.

"I haven't seen them in so long."

And this is my *grandfather*. I never knew him, Jack, but I heard *so many* stories.

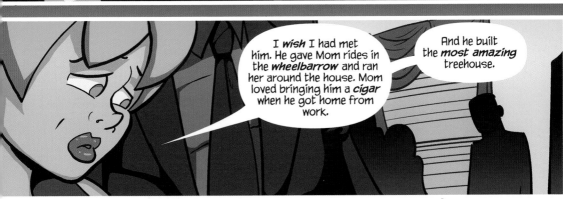

I *wish* I had met him. He gave Mom rides in the *wheelbarrow* and ran her around the house. Mom loved bringing him a *cigar* when he got home from work.

And he built the *most amazing* treehouse.

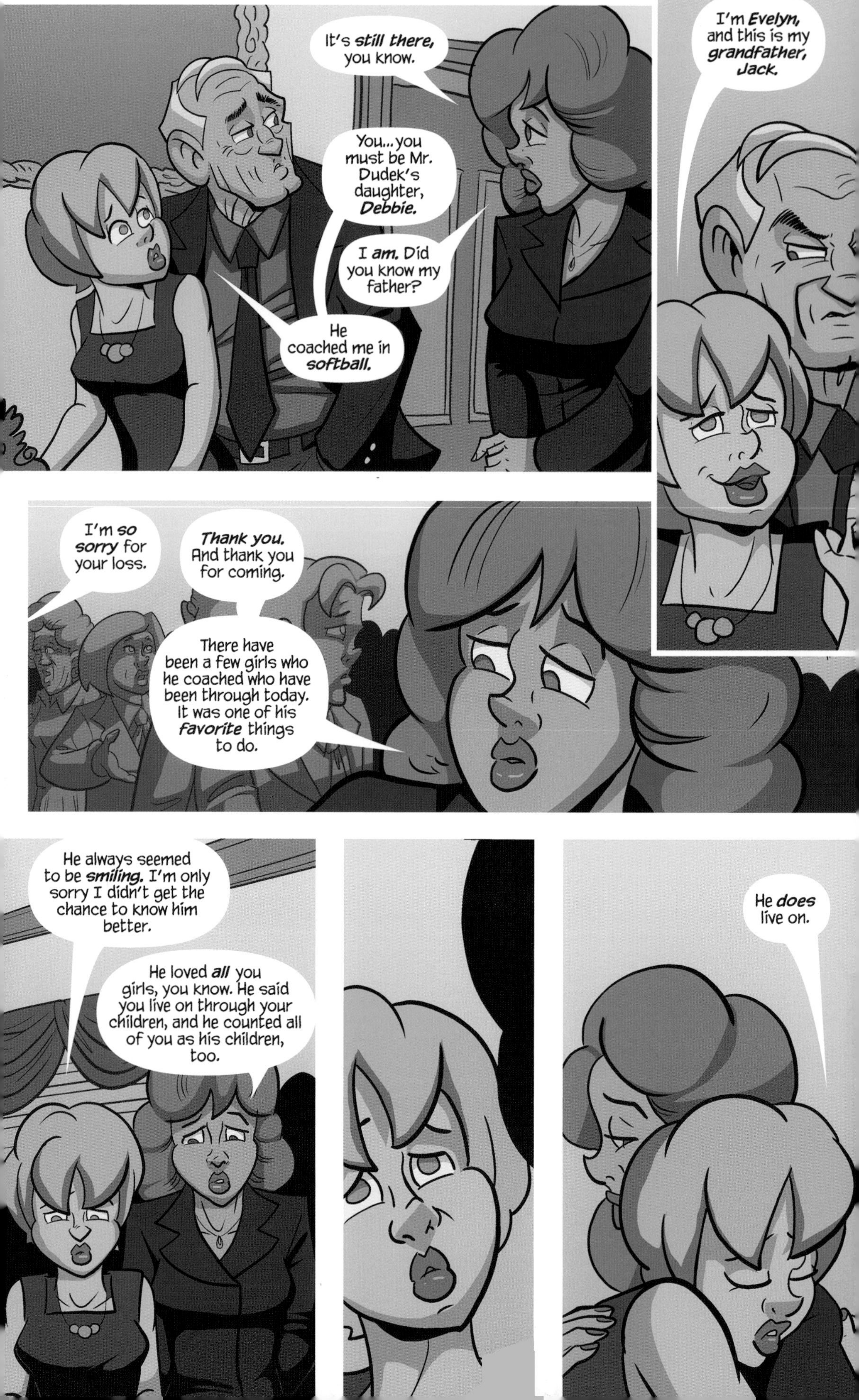
It's *still there,* you know.
You... you must be Mr. Dudek's daughter, *Debbie.*
I *am.* Did you know my father?
He coached me in *softball.*
I'm *Evelyn,* and this is my *grandfather, Jack.*
I'm *so sorry* for your loss.
*Thank you.* And thank you for coming.
There have been a few girls who he coached who have been through today. It was one of his *favorite* things to do.
He always seemed to be *smiling.* I'm only sorry I didn't get the chance to know him better.
He loved *all* you girls, you know. He said you live on through your children, and he counted all of you as his children, too.
He *does* live on.

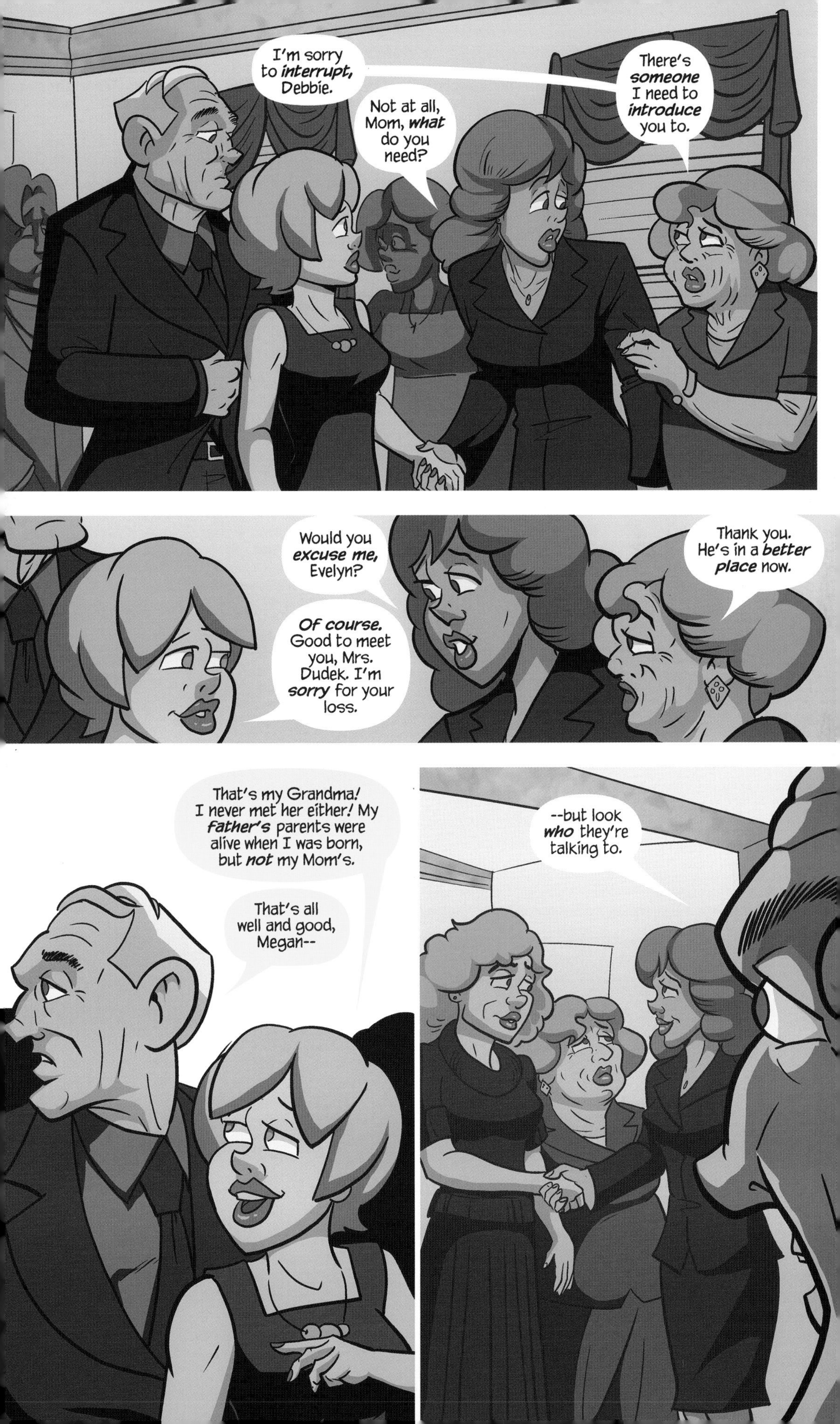
I'm sorry to *interrupt*, Debbie.
There's *someone* I need to *introduce* you to.
Not at all, Mom, *what* do you need?
Would you *excuse me*, Evelyn?
*Of course.* Good to meet you, Mrs. Dudek. I'm *sorry* for your loss.
Thank you. He's in a *better place* now.
That's my Grandma! I never met her either! My *father's* parents were alive when I was born, but *not* my Mom's.
That's all well and good, Megan--
--but look *who* they're talking to.

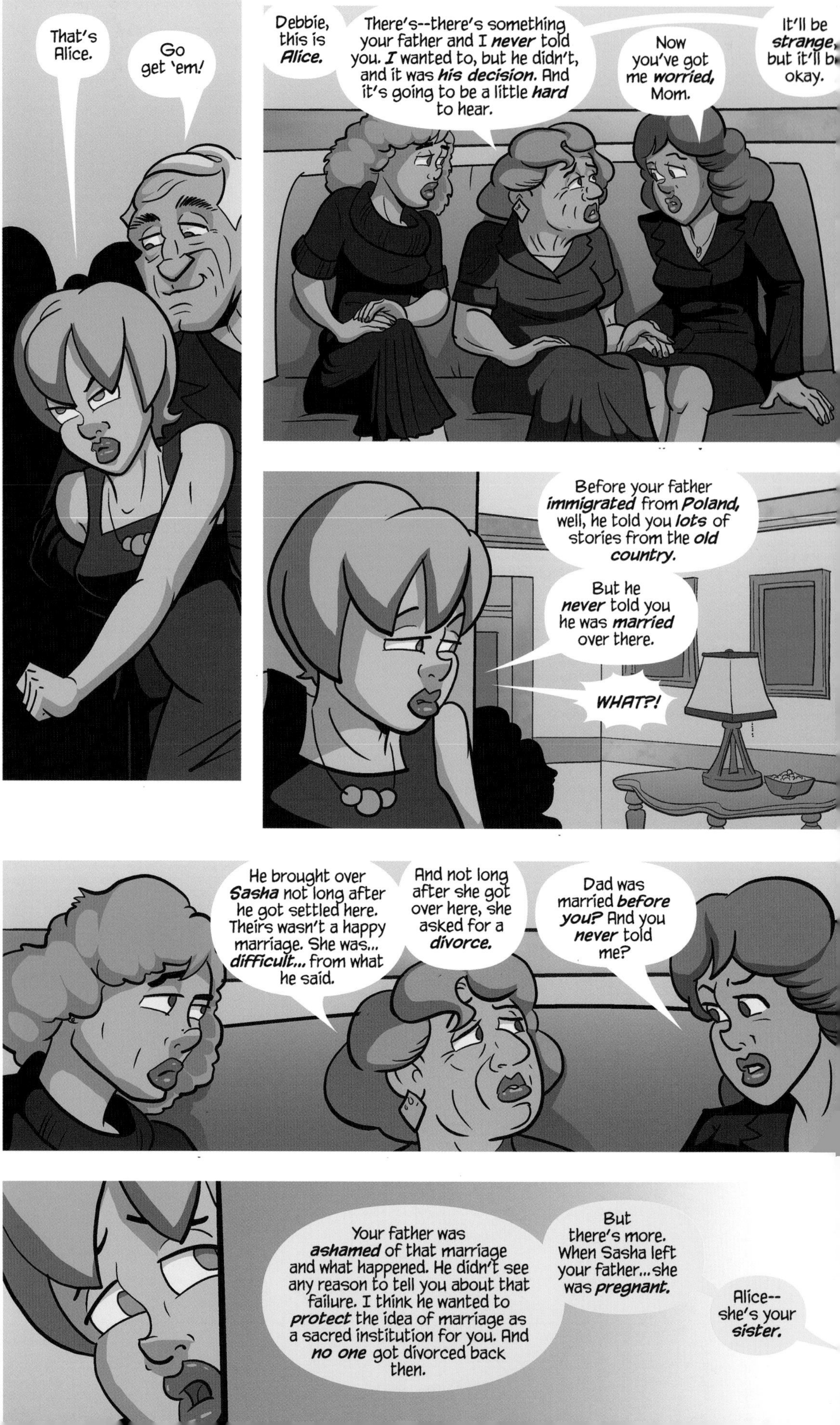

That's Alice.
Go get 'em!
Debbie, this is Alice.
There's--there's something your father and I never told you. I wanted to, but he didn't, and it was his decision. And it's going to be a little hard to hear.
Now you've got me worried, Mom.
It'll be strange, but it'll b okay.
Before your father immigrated from Poland, well, he told you lots of stories from the old country.
But he never told you he was married over there.
WHAT?!
He brought over Sasha not long after he got settled here. Theirs wasn't a happy marriage. She was... difficult... from what he said.
And not long after she got over here, she asked for a divorce.
Dad was married before you? And you never told me?
Your father was ashamed of that marriage and what happened. He didn't see any reason to tell you about that failure. I think he wanted to protect the idea of marriage as a sacred institution for you. And no one got divorced back then.
But there's more. When Sasha left your father...she was pregnant.
Alice--she's your sister.

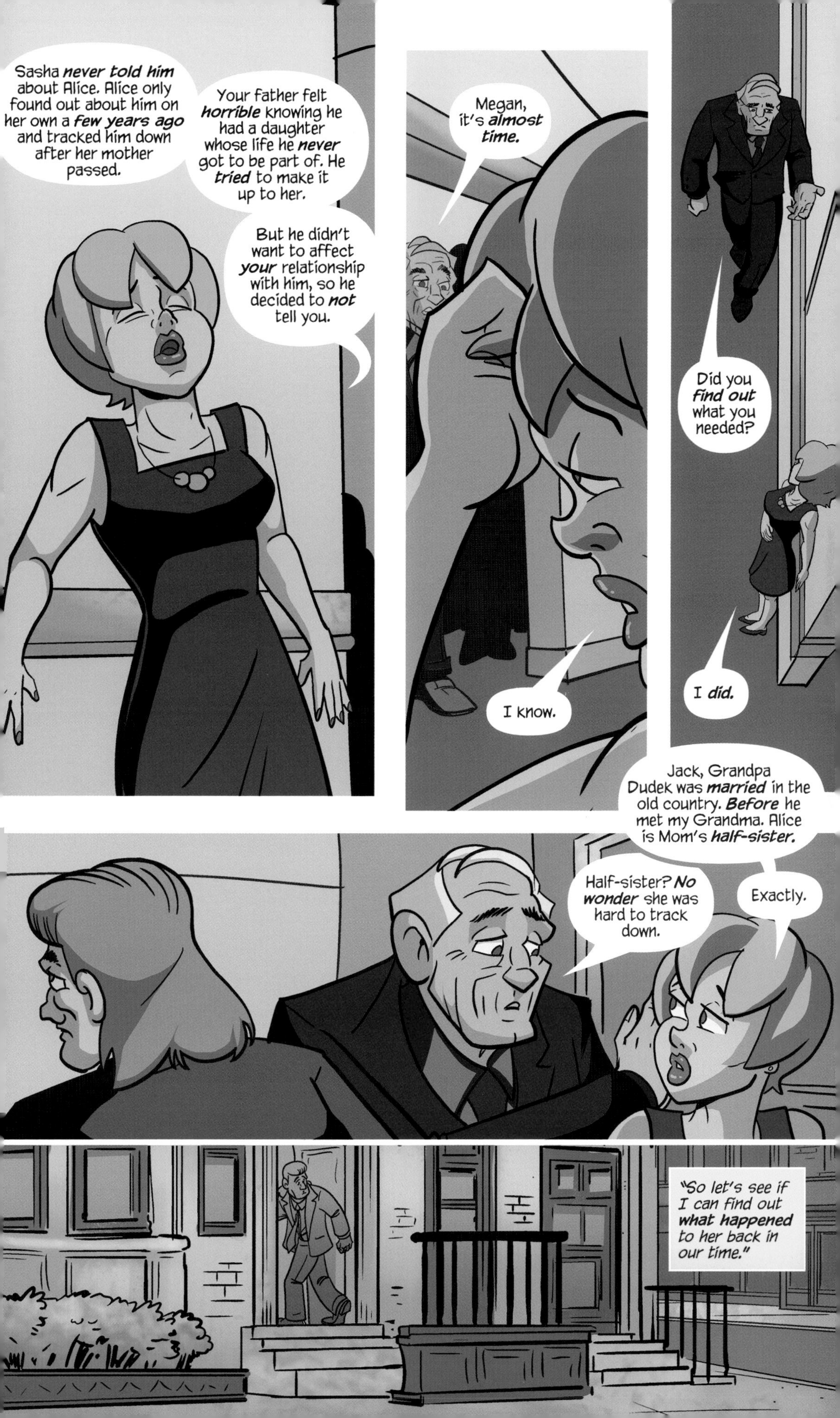

Sasha *never told him* about Alice. Alice only found out about him on her own a *few years ago* and tracked him down after her mother passed.
Your father felt *horrible* knowing he had a daughter whose life he *never* got to be part of. He *tried* to make it up to her.
But he didn't want to affect *your* relationship with him, so he decided to *not* tell you.
Megan, it's *almost time.*
I know.
Did you *find out* what you needed?
I *did.*
Jack, Grandpa Dudek was *married* in the old country. *Before* he met my Grandma. Alice is Mom's *half-sister.*
Half-sister? *No wonder* she was hard to track down.
Exactly.
*"So let's see if I can find out* ***what happened*** *to her back in our time."*

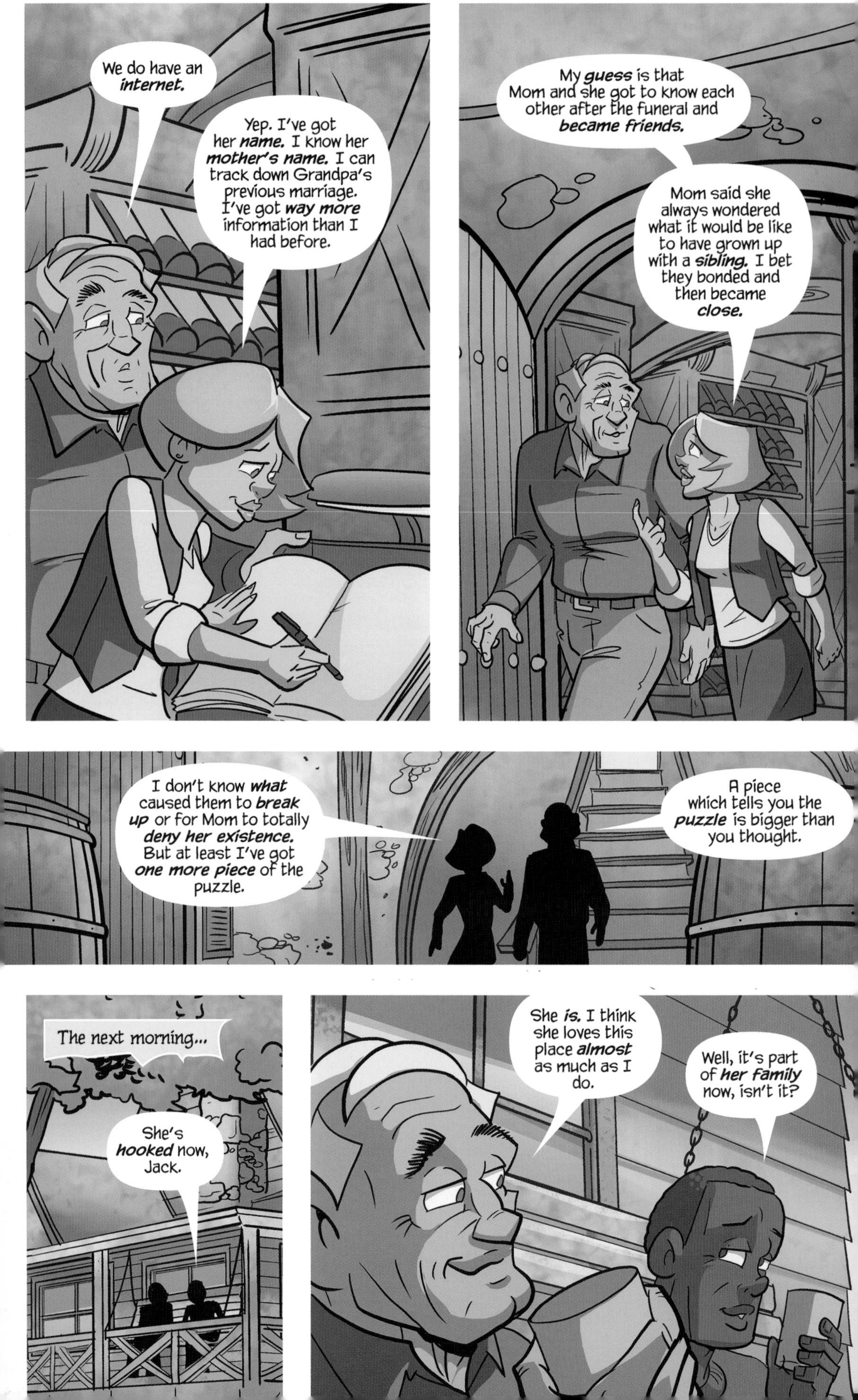

We do have an *internet.*
Yep. I've got her *name.* I know her *mother's name.* I can track down Grandpa's previous marriage. I've got *way more* information than I had before.
My *guess* is that Mom and she got to know each other after the funeral and *became friends.*
Mom said she always wondered what it would be like to have grown up with a *sibling.* I bet they bonded and then became *close.*
I don't know *what* caused them to *break up* or for Mom to totally *deny her existence.* But at least I've got *one more piece* of the puzzle.
A piece which tells you the *puzzle* is bigger than you thought.
The next morning...
She's *hooked* now, Jack.
She *is.* I think she loves this place *almost* as much as I do.
Well, it's part of *her family* now, isn't it?

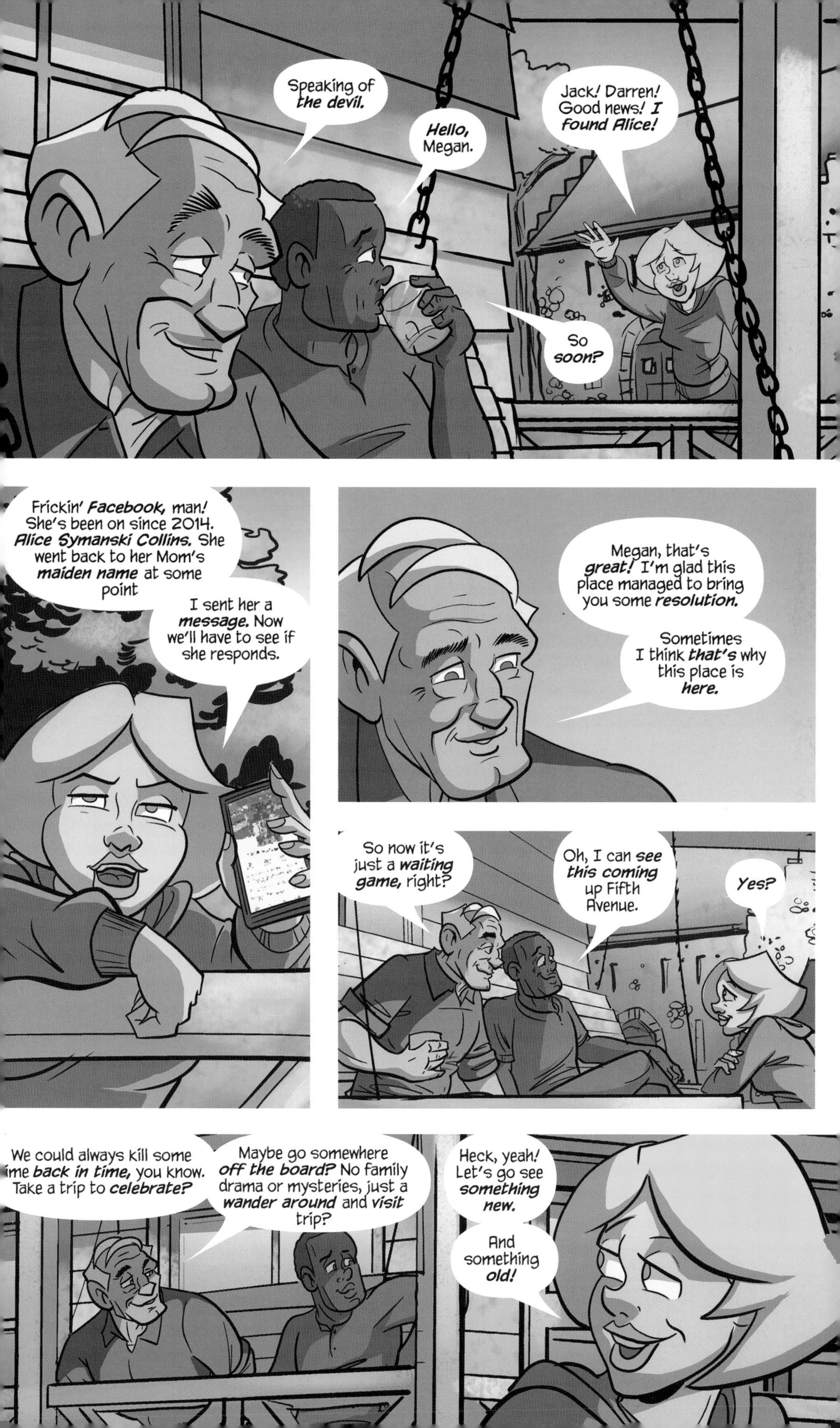
Speaking of *the devil.*
*Hello,* Megan.
Jack! Darren! Good news! *I found Alice!*
So *soon?*
Frickin' *Facebook,* man! She's been on since 2014. *Alice Symanski Collins.* She went back to her Mom's *maiden name* at some point
I sent her a *message.* Now we'll have to see if she responds.
Megan, that's *great!* I'm glad this place managed to bring you some *resolution.*
Sometimes I think *that's* why this place is *here.*
So now it's just a *waiting game,* right?
Oh, I can *see this coming* up Fifth Avenue.
*Yes?*
We could always kill some ime *back in time,* you know. Take a trip to *celebrate?*
Maybe go somewhere *off the board?* No family drama or mysteries, just a *wander around* and *visit* trip?
Heck, yeah! Let's go see *something new.*
And something *old!*

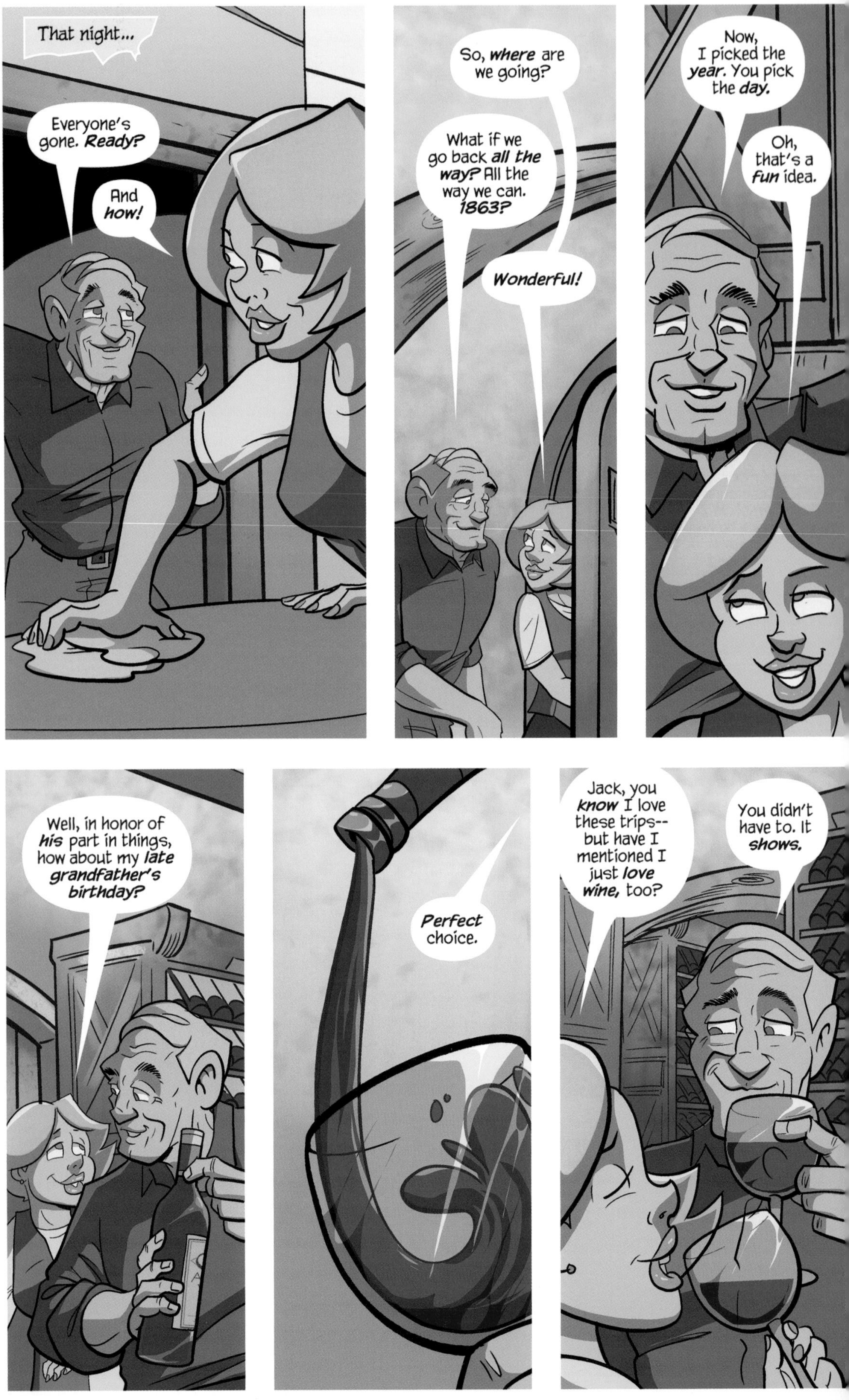
That night...
Everyone's gone. *Ready?*
And *how!*
So, *where* are we going?
What if we go back *all the way?* All the way we can. *1863?*
*Wonderful!*
Now, I picked the *year*. You pick the *day.*
Oh, that's a *fun* idea.
Well, in honor of *his* part in things, how about my *late grandfather's birthday?*
*Perfect* choice.
Jack, you *know* I love these trips-- but have I mentioned I just *love wine,* too?
You didn't have to. It *shows.*

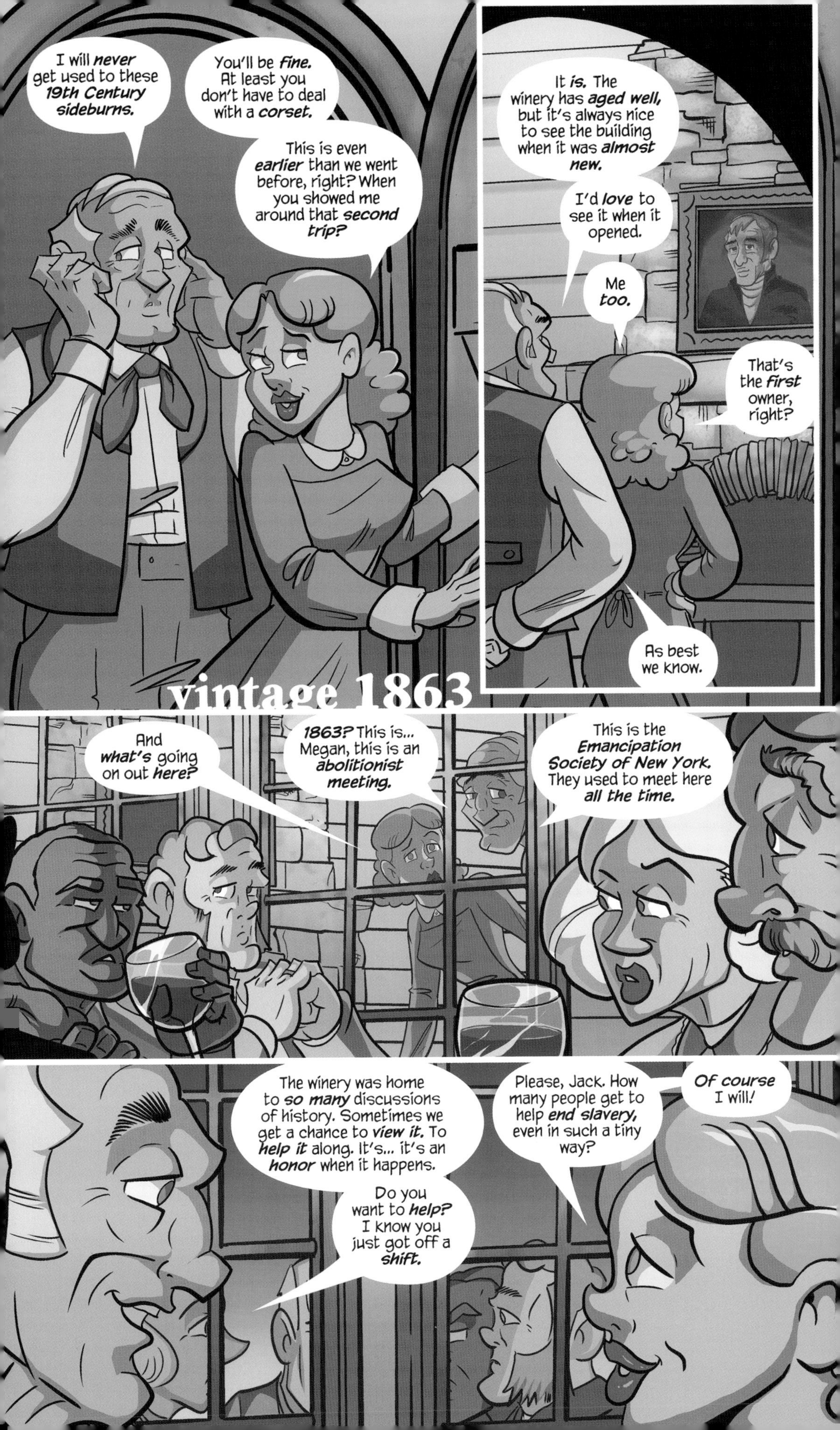
I will *never* get used to these *19th Century sideburns.*
You'll be *fine.* At least you don't have to deal with a *corset.*
This is even *earlier* than we went before, right? When you showed me around that *second trip?*
It *is.* The winery has *aged well,* but it's always nice to see the building when it was *almost new.*
I'd *love* to see it when it opened.
Me *too.*
That's the *first* owner, right?
As best we know.
vintage 1863
And *what's* going on out *here?*
*1863?* This is... Megan, this is an *abolitionist meeting.*
This is the *Emancipation Society of New York.* They used to meet here *all the time.*
The winery was home to *so many* discussions of history. Sometimes we get a chance to *view it.* To *help it* along. It's... it's an *honor* when it happens.
Do you want to *help?* I know you just got off a *shift.*
Please, Jack. How many people get to help *end slavery,* even in such a tiny way?
*Of course* I will!

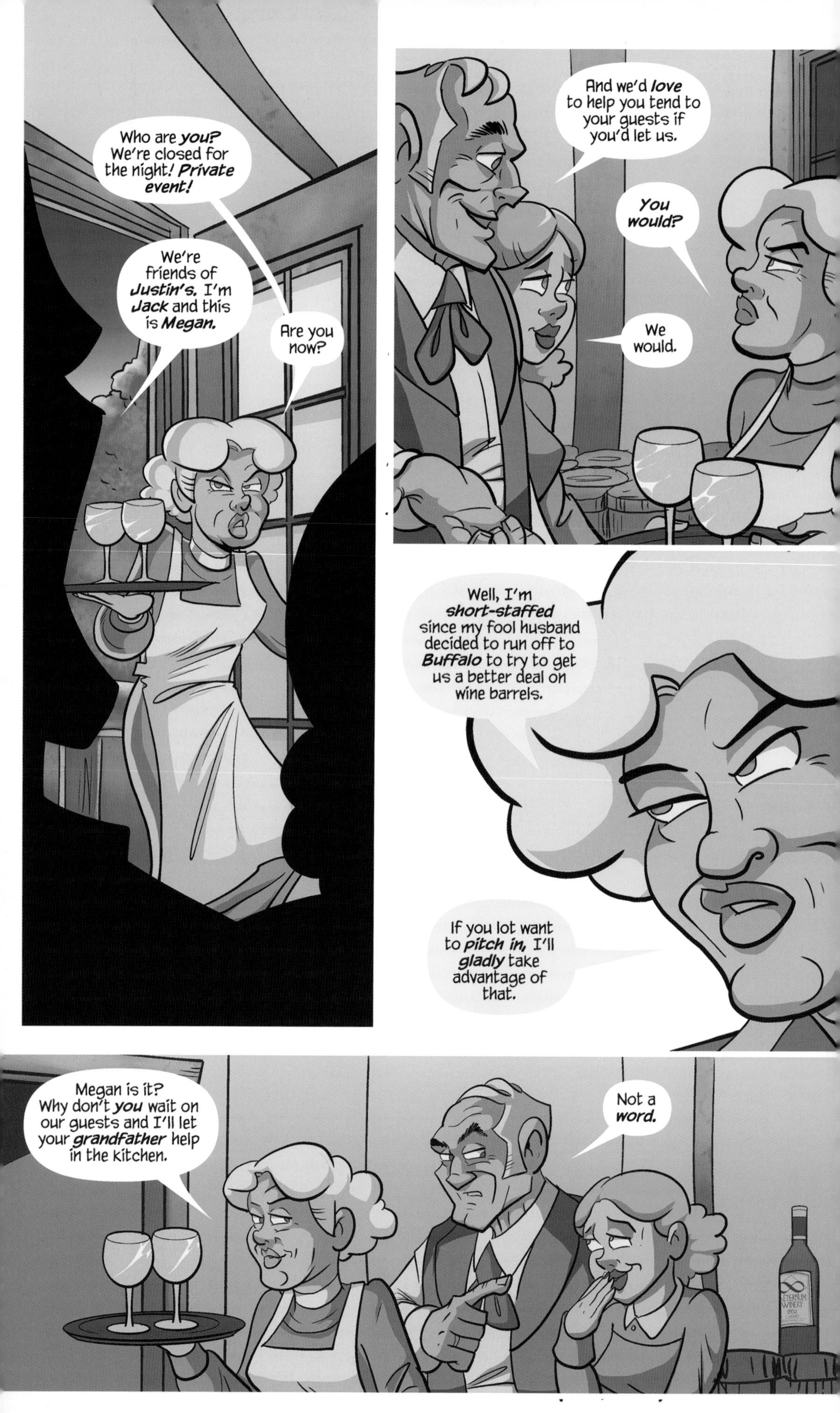
Who are *you?* We're closed for the night! *Private event!*
We're friends of *Justin's.* I'm *Jack* and this is *Megan.*
Are you now?
And we'd *love* to help you tend to your guests if you'd let us.
*You would?*
We would.
Well, I'm *short-staffed* since my fool husband decided to run off to *Buffalo* to try to get us a better deal on wine barrels.
If you lot want to *pitch in,* I'll *gladly* take advantage of that.
Megan is it? Why don't *you* wait on our guests and I'll let your *grandfather* help in the kitchen.
Not a *word.*

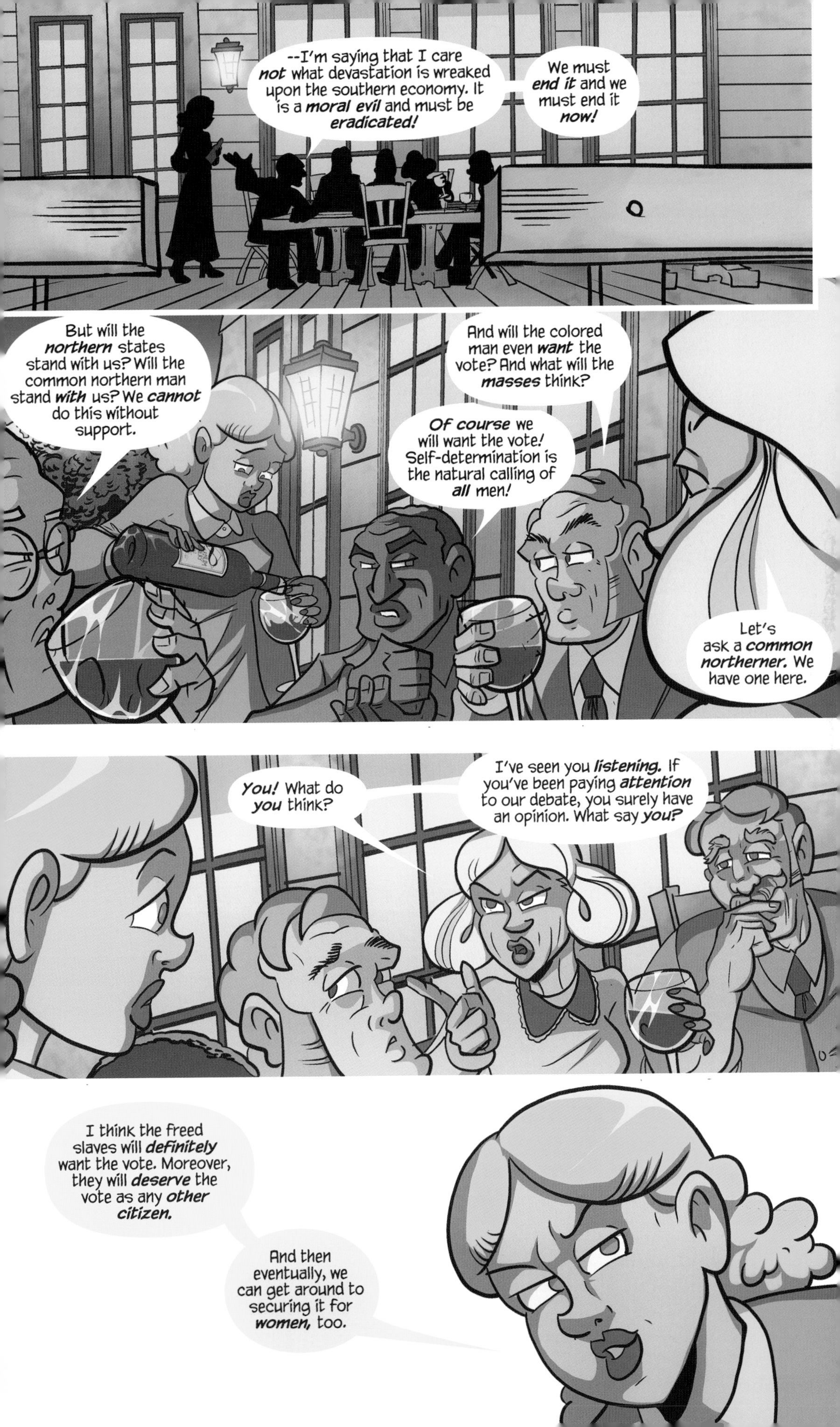
--I'm saying that I care *not* what devastation is wreaked upon the southern economy. It is a *moral evil* and must be *eradicated!*
We must *end it* and we must end it *now!*
But will the *northern* states stand with us? Will the common northern man stand *with* us? We *cannot* do this without support.
And will the colored man even *want* the vote? And what will the *masses* think?
*Of course* we will want the vote! Self-determination is the natural calling of *all* men!
Let's ask a *common northerner.* We have one here.
*You!* What do *you* think?
I've seen you *listening.* If you've been paying *attention* to our debate, you surely have an opinion. What say *you?*
I think the freed slaves will *definitely* want the vote. Moreover, they will *deserve* the vote as any *other citizen.*
And then eventually, we can get around to securing it for *women,* too.

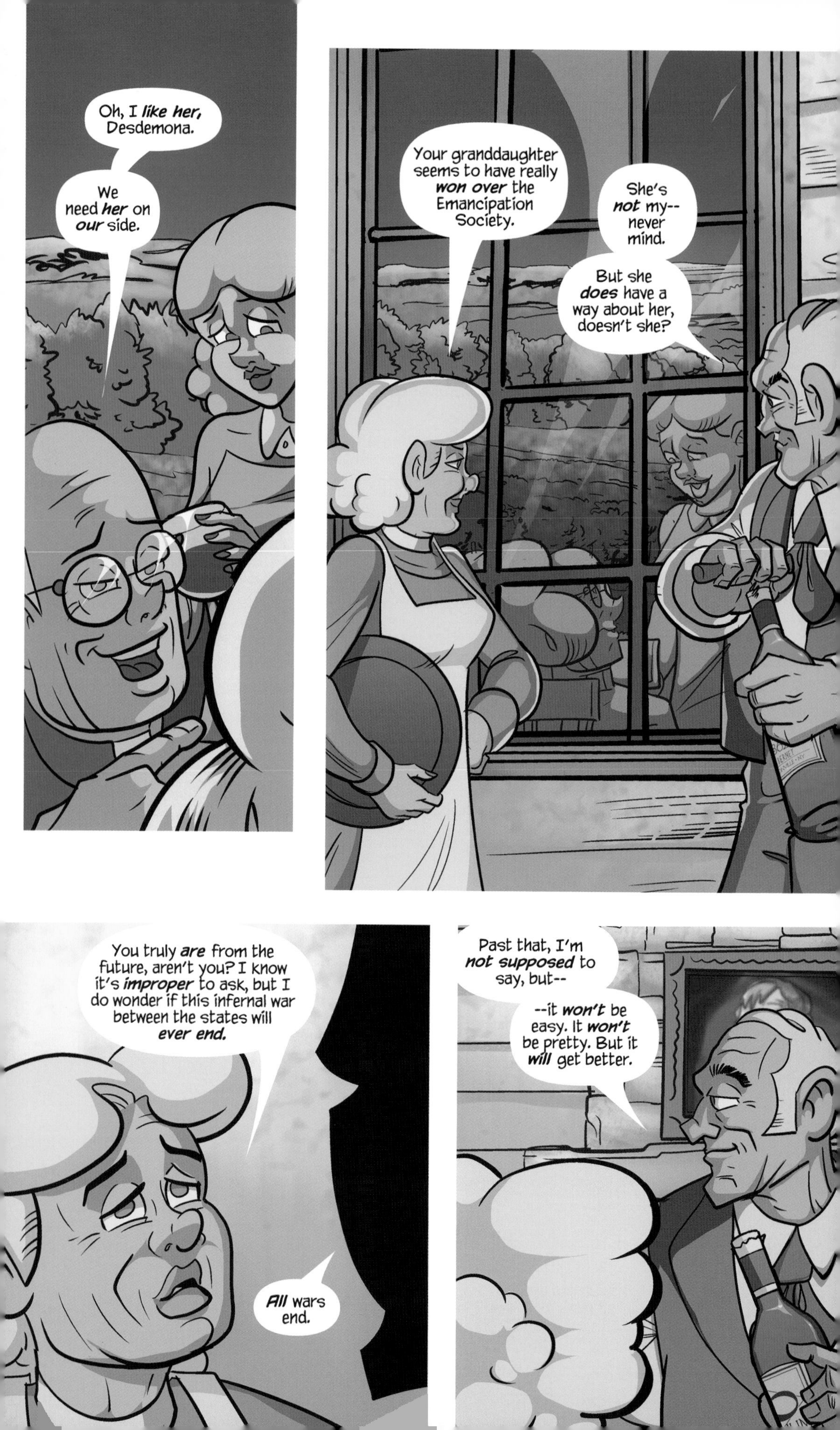

Oh, I *like her,* Desdemona.
We need *her* on *our* side.
Your granddaughter seems to have really *won over* the Emancipation Society.
She's *not* my-- never mind.
But she *does* have a way about her, doesn't she?
You truly *are* from the future, aren't you? I know it's *improper* to ask, but I do wonder if this infernal war between the states will *ever end.*
*All* wars end.
Past that, I'm *not supposed* to say, but--
--it *won't* be easy. It *won't* be pretty. But it *will* get better.

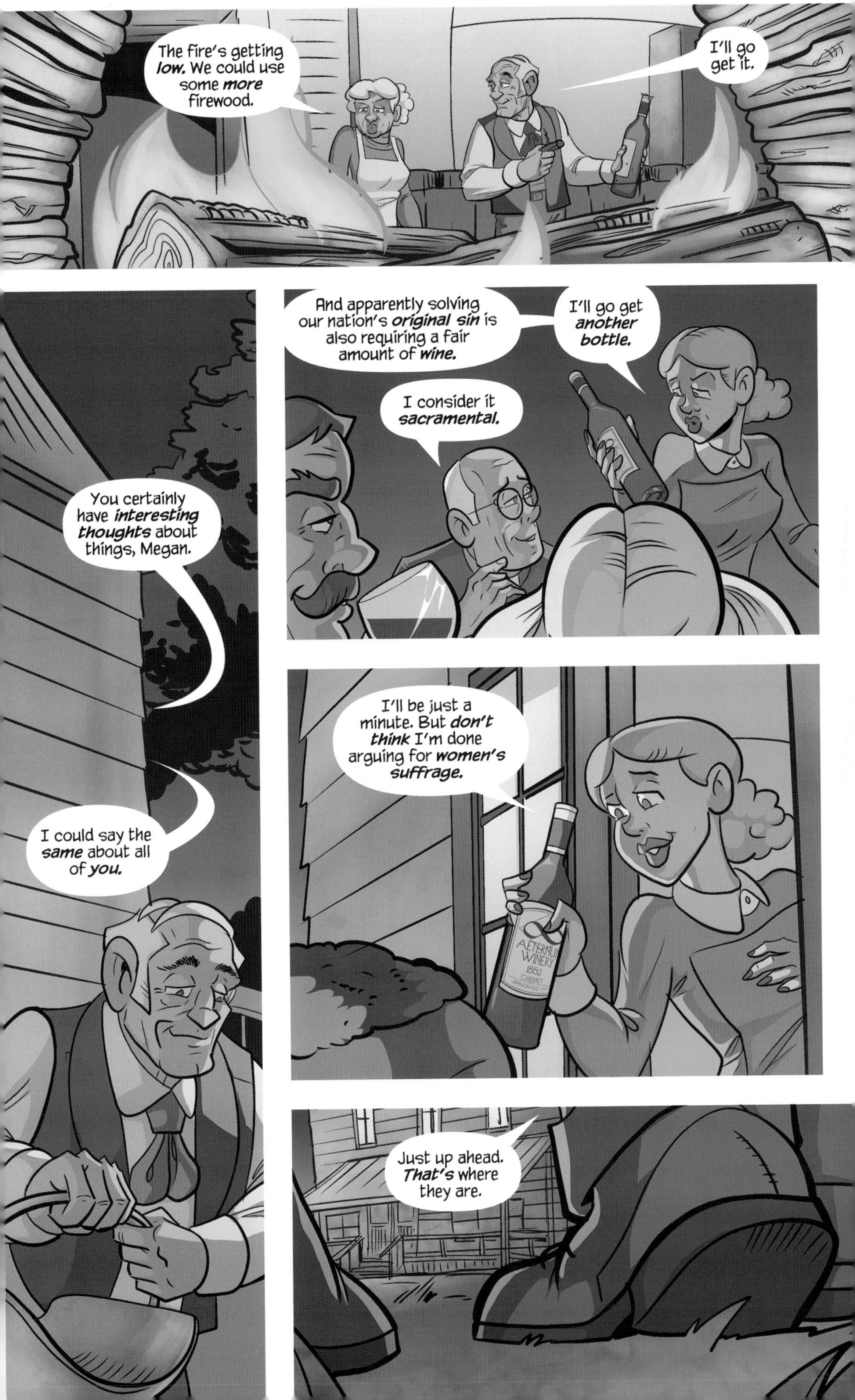

The fire's getting *low.* We could use some *more* firewood.
I'll go get it.
And apparently solving our nation's *original sin* is also requiring a fair amount of *wine.*
I'll go get *another bottle.*
I consider it *sacramental.*
You certainly have *interesting thoughts* about things, Megan.
I could say the *same* about all of *you.*
I'll be just a minute. But *don't think* I'm done arguing for *women's suffrage.*
AETERNUM WINERY
1862
CABERNET
Just up ahead. *That's* where they are.

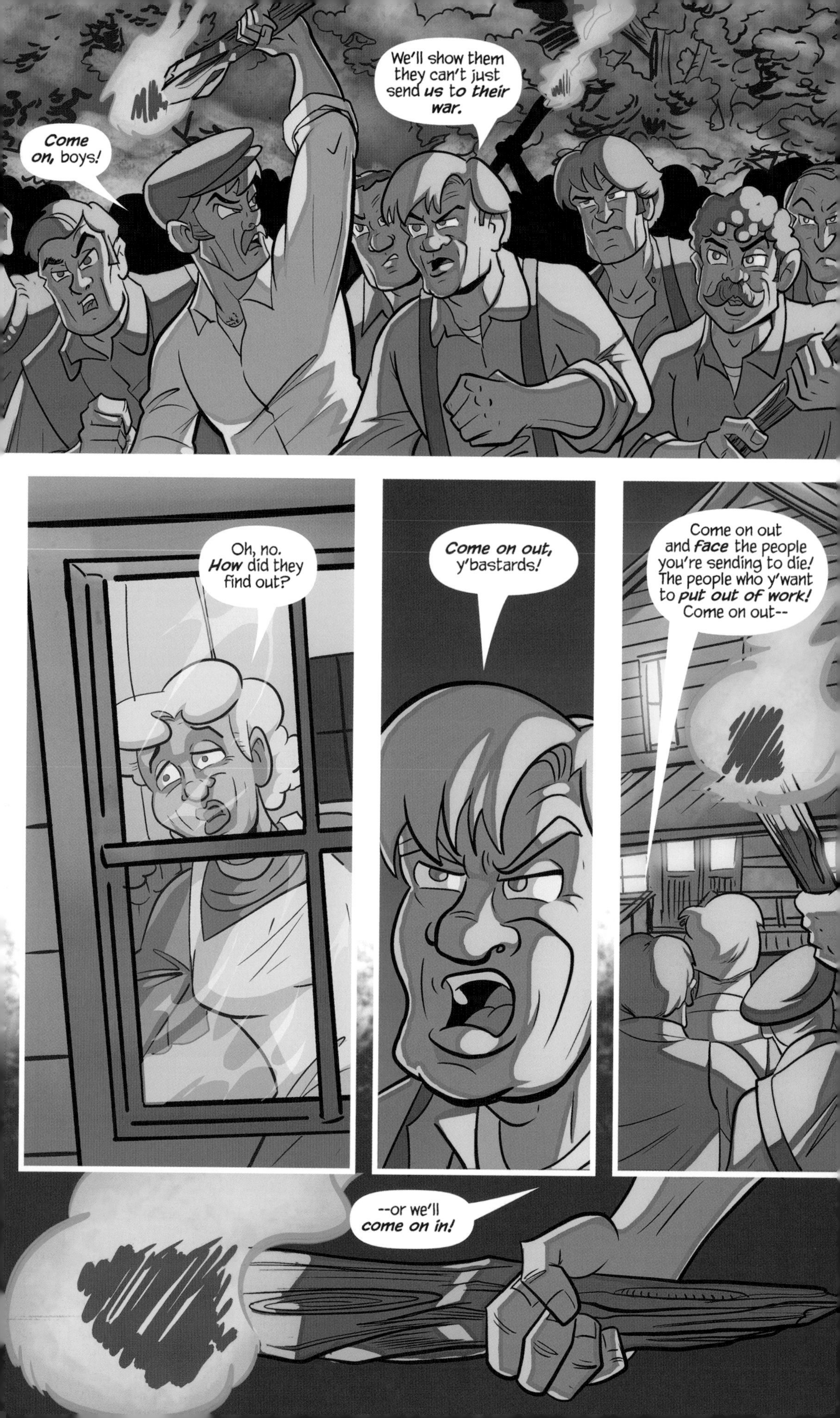

Come on, boys!
We'll show them they can't just send us to their war.
Oh, no. How did they find out?
Come on out, y'bastards!
Come on out and face the people you're sending to die! The people who y'want to put out of work! Come on out--
--or we'll come on in!

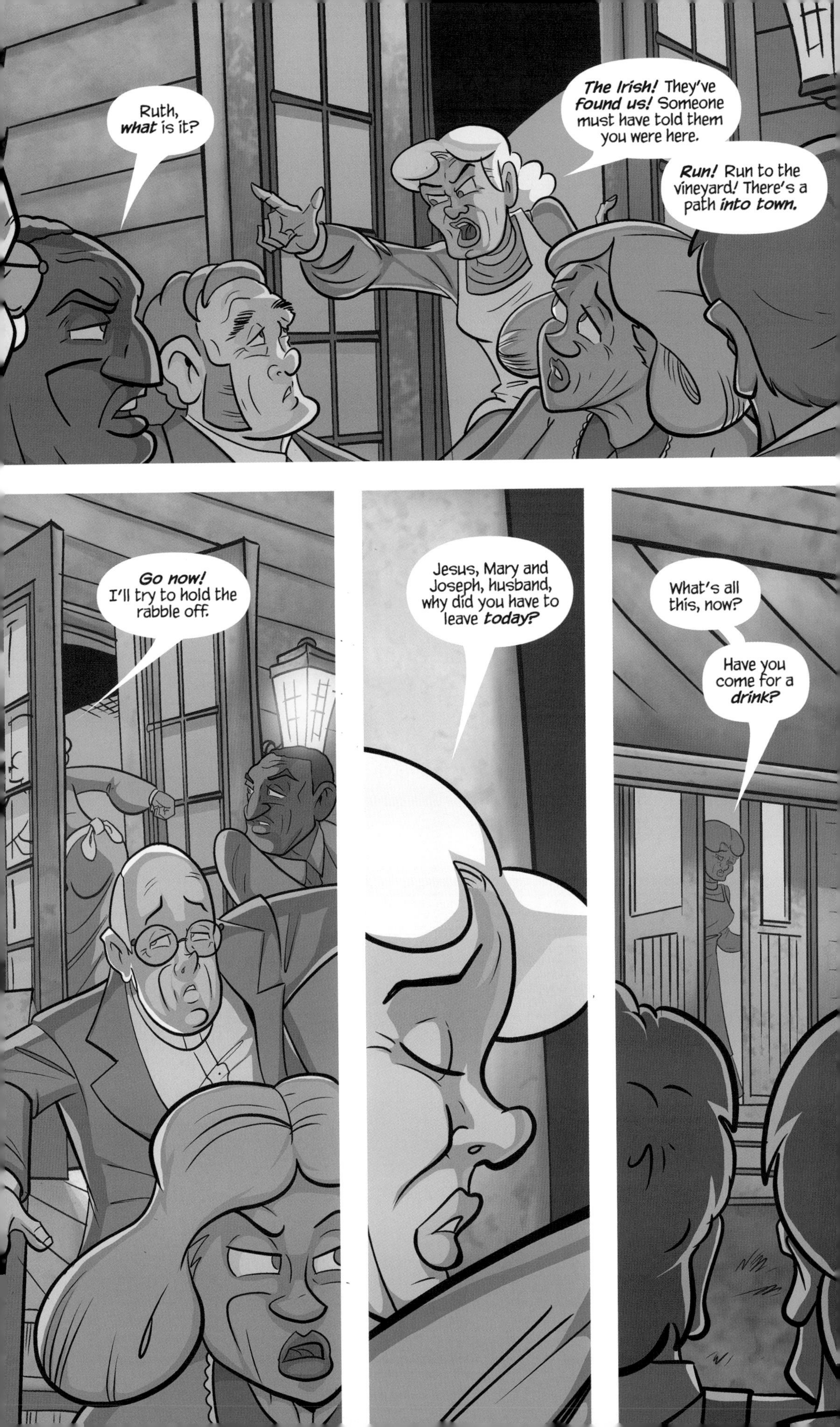

Ruth, *what* is it?
*The Irish!* They've *found us!* Someone must have told them you were here.
*Run!* Run to the vineyard! There's a path *into town.*
*Go now!* I'll try to hold the rabble off.
Jesus, Mary and Joseph, husband, why did you have to leave *today?*
What's all this, now?
Have you come for a *drink?*

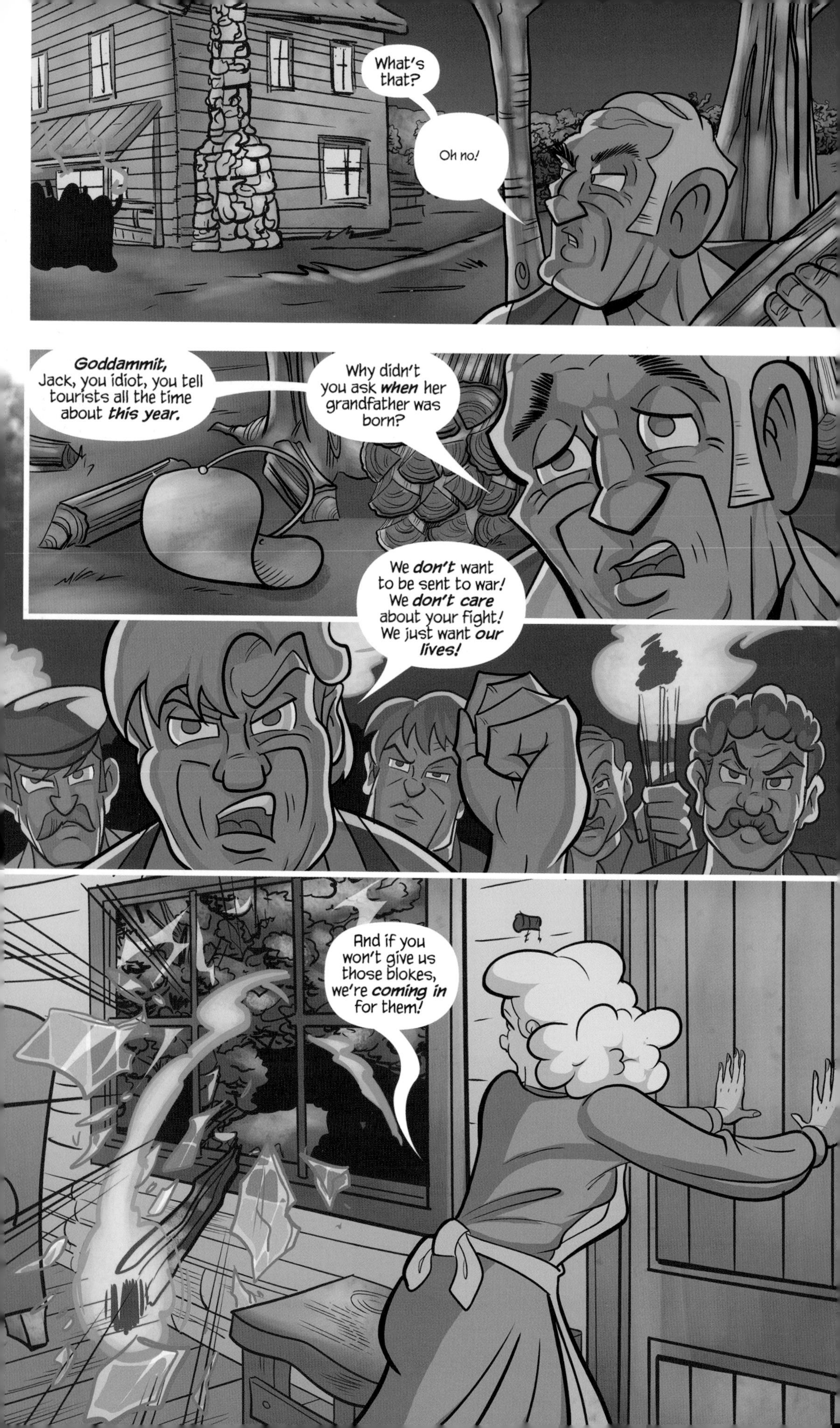
What's that?
Oh no!
Goddammit, Jack, you idiot, you tell tourists all the time about this year.
Why didn't you ask when her grandfather was born?
We don't want to be sent to war! We don't care about your fight! We just want our lives!
And if you won't give us those blokes, we're coming in for them!

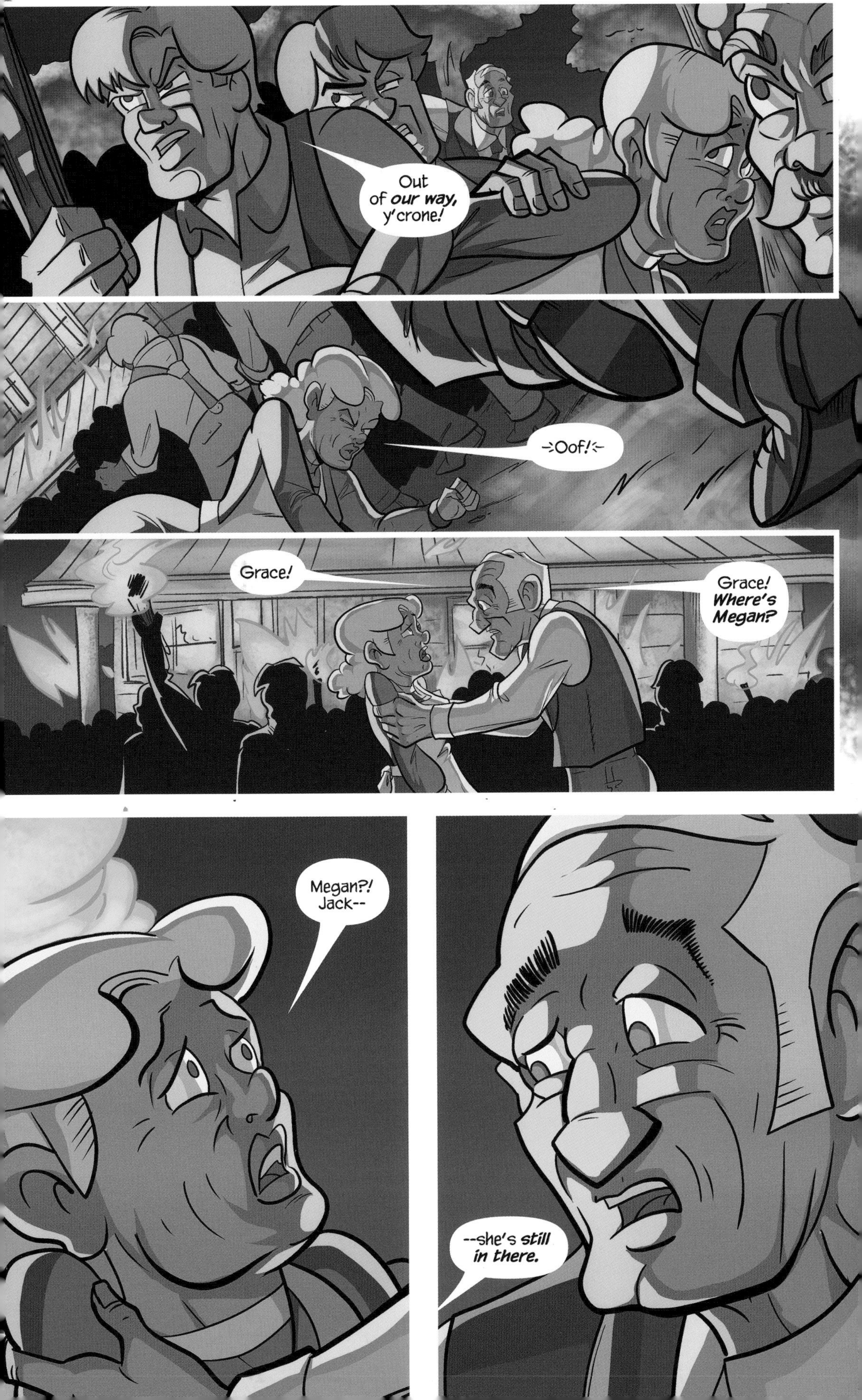
Out of our way, y'crone!
Oof!
Grace!
Grace! Where's Megan?
Megan?! Jack--
--she's still in there.

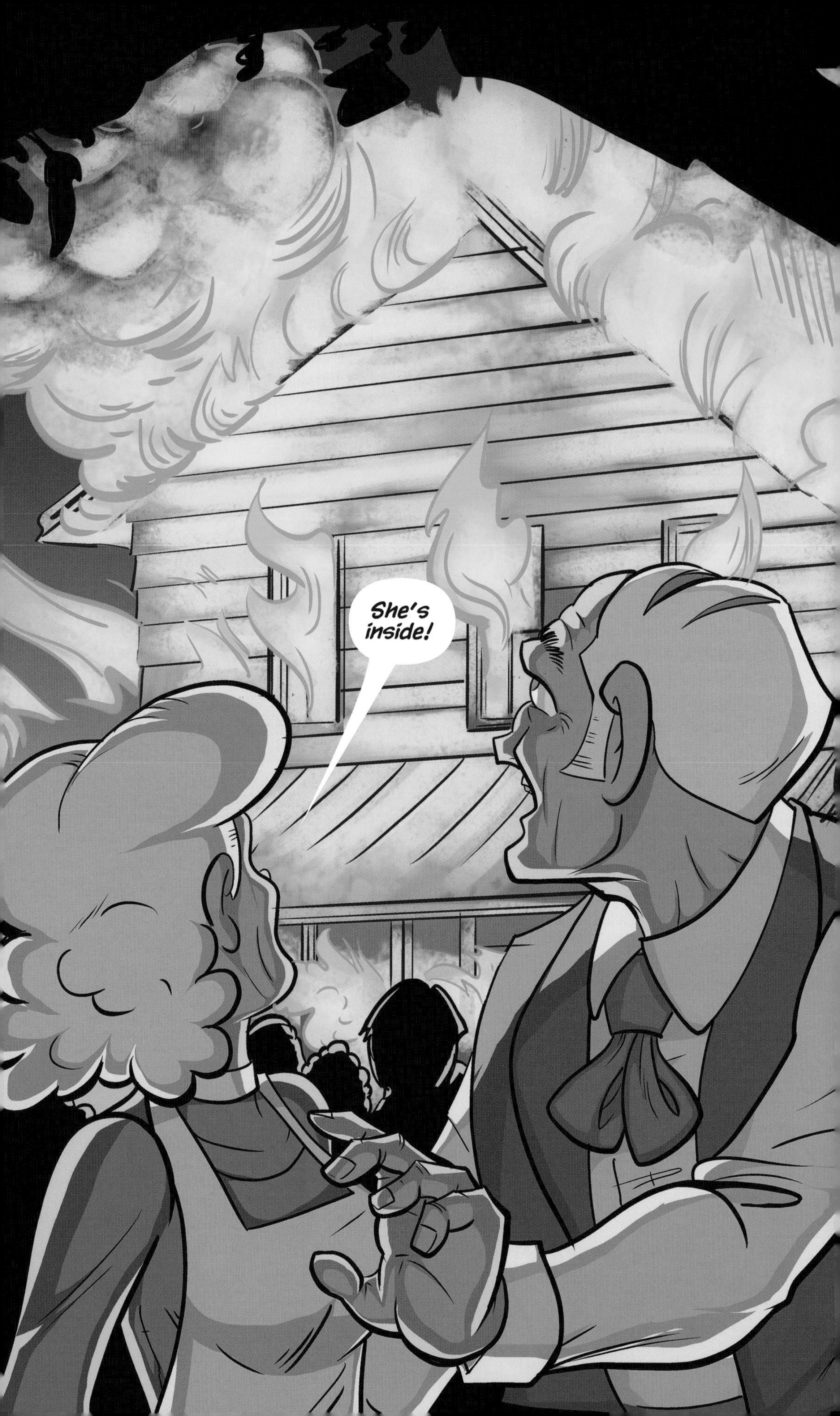
She's inside!

# Chapter Four

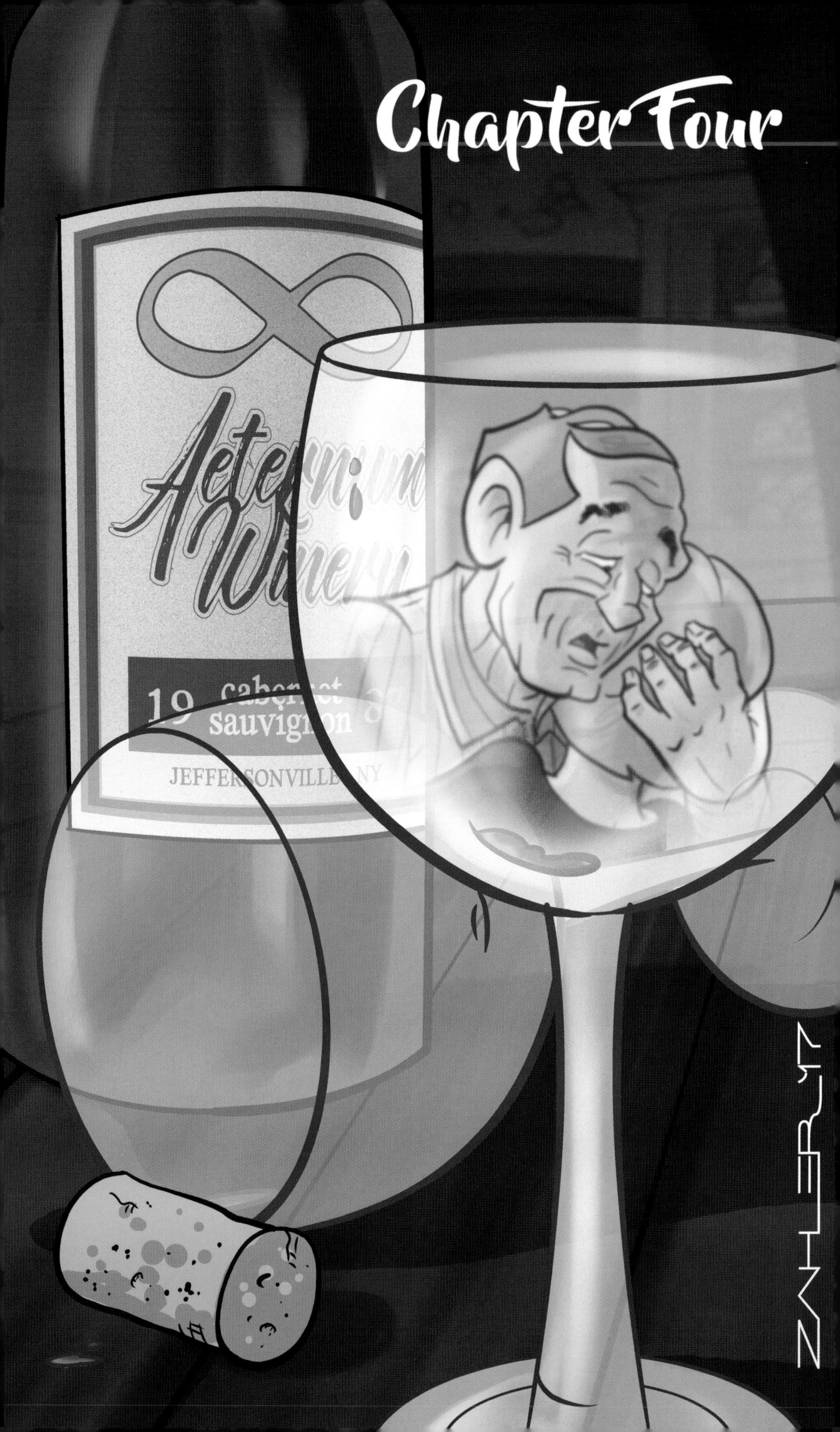

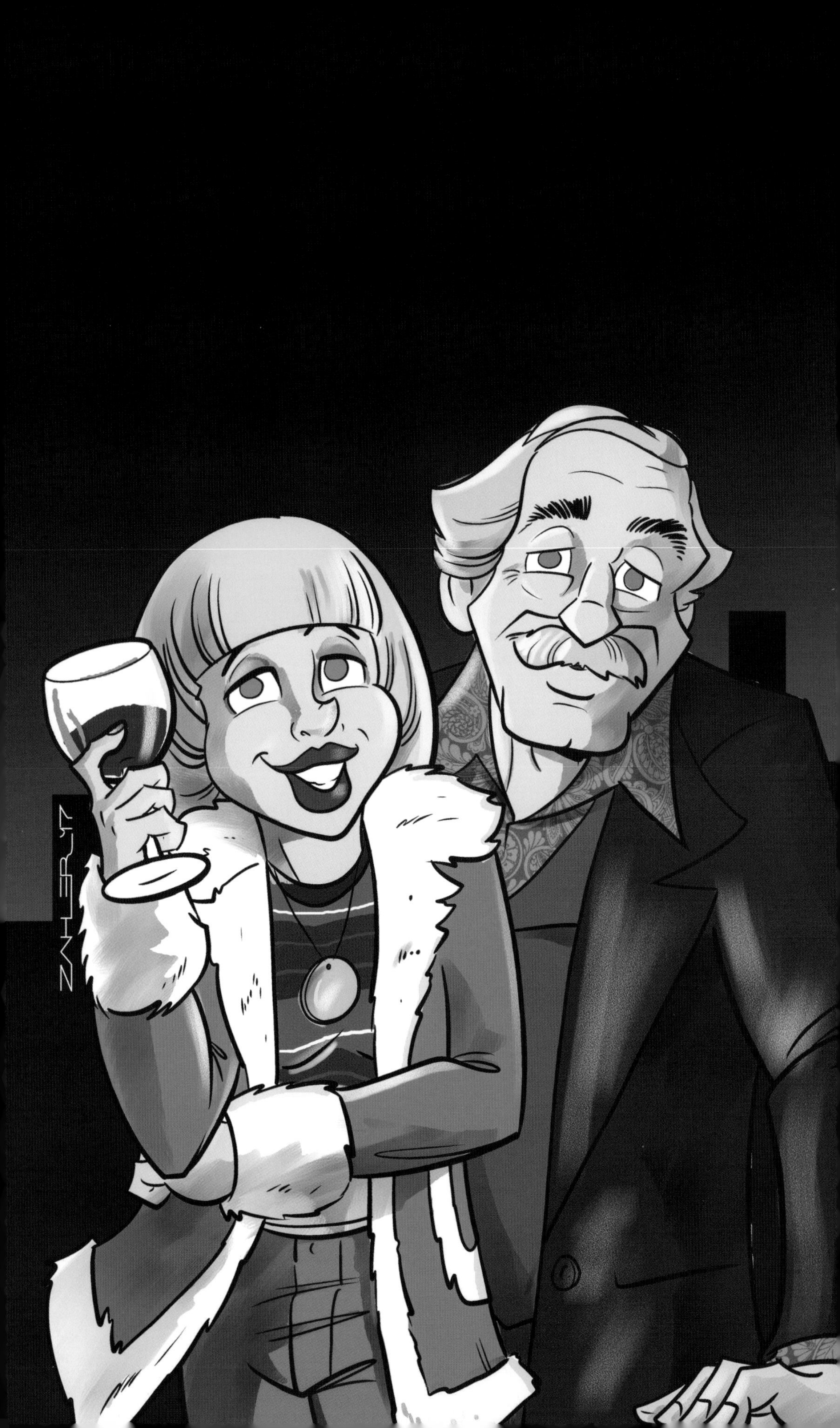
ZAHLER '17

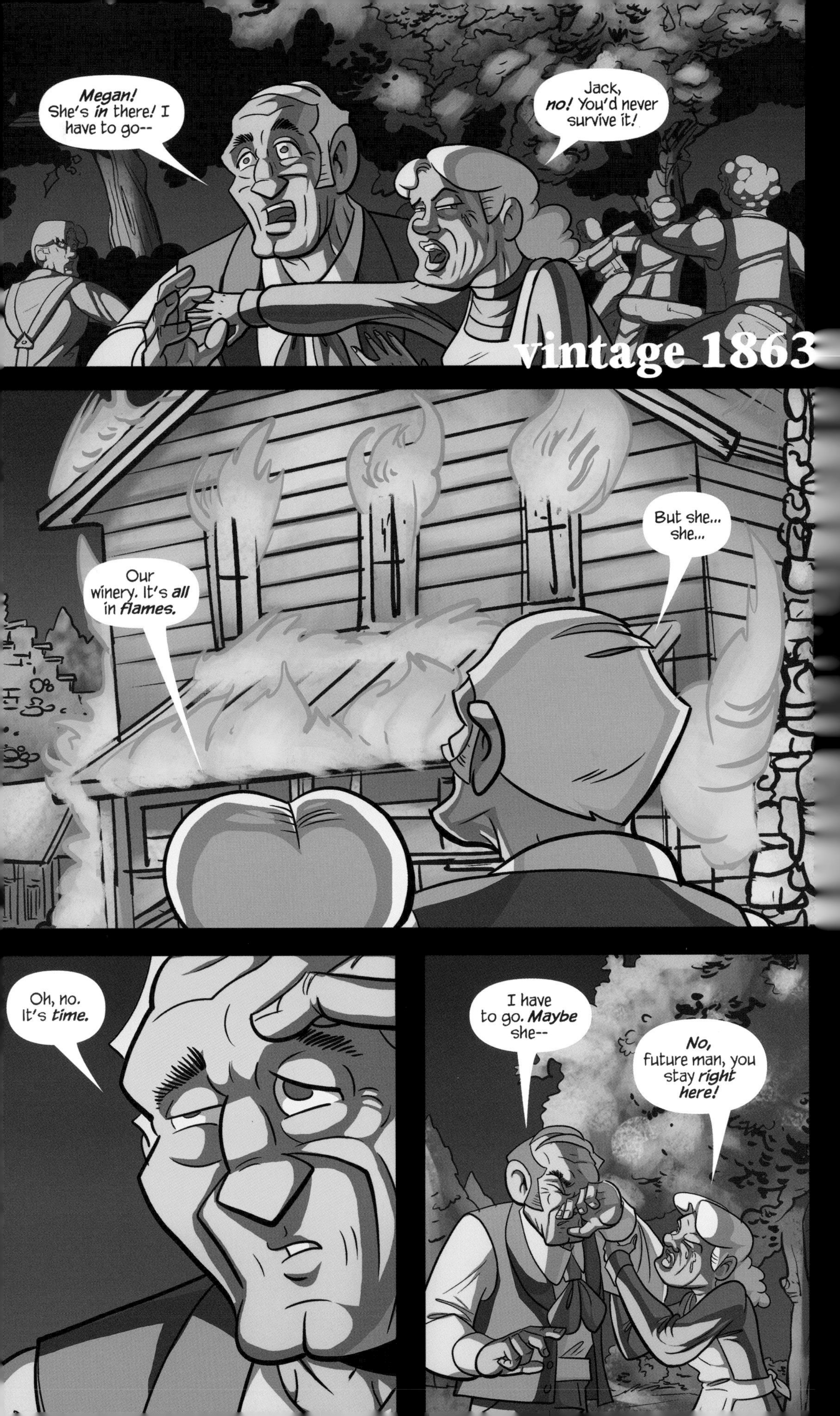
Megan! She's in there! I have to go--
Jack, no! You'd never survive it!
vintage 1863
Our winery. It's all in flames.
But she... she...
Oh, no. It's time.
I have to go. Maybe she--
No, future man, you stay right here!

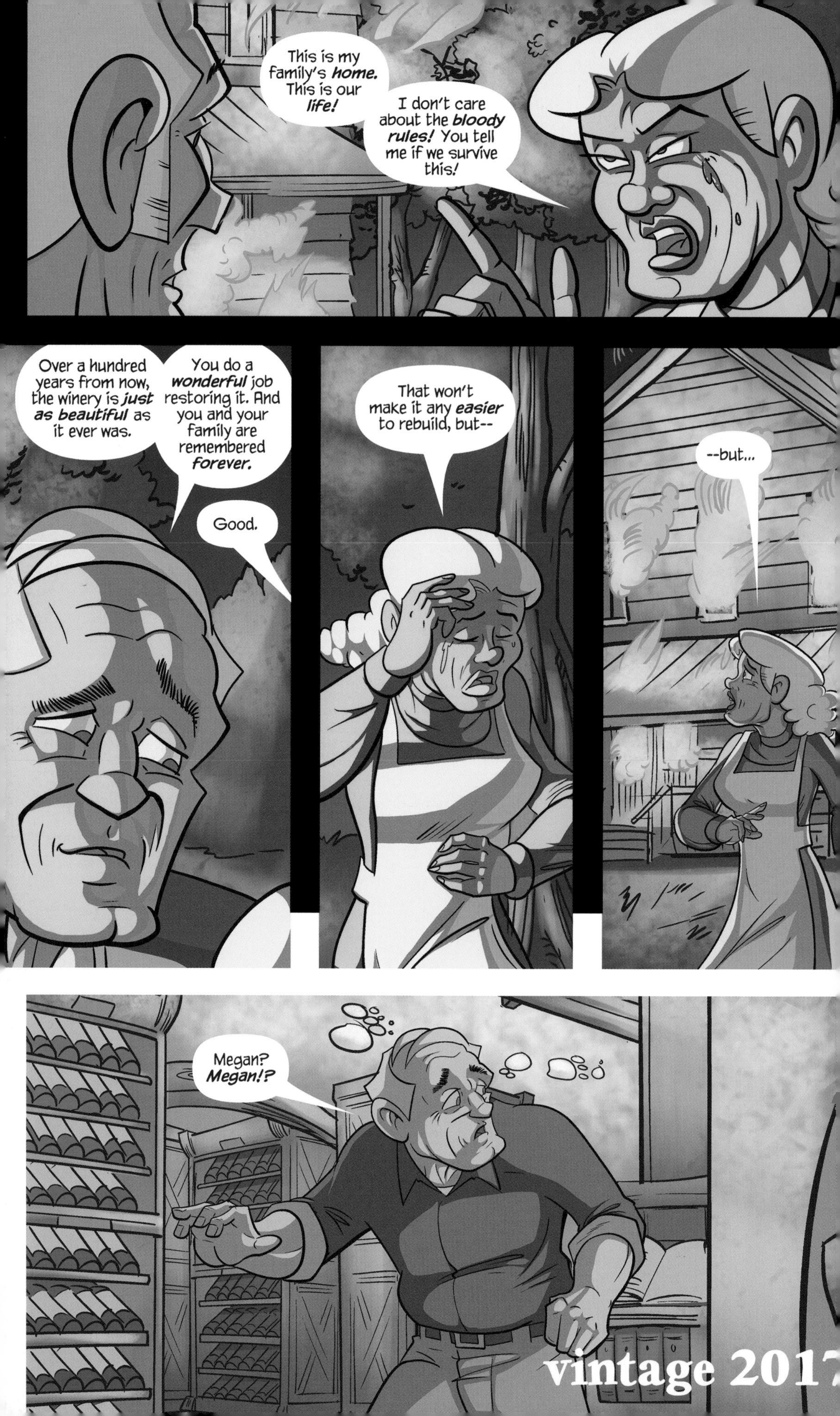
This is my family's *home.* This is our *life!*
I don't care about the *bloody rules!* You tell me if we survive this!
Over a hundred years from now, the winery is *just as beautiful* as it ever was.
You do a *wonderful* job restoring it. And you and your family are remembered *forever.*
Good.
That won't make it any *easier* to rebuild, but--
--but...
Megan? *Megan!?*
vintage 2017

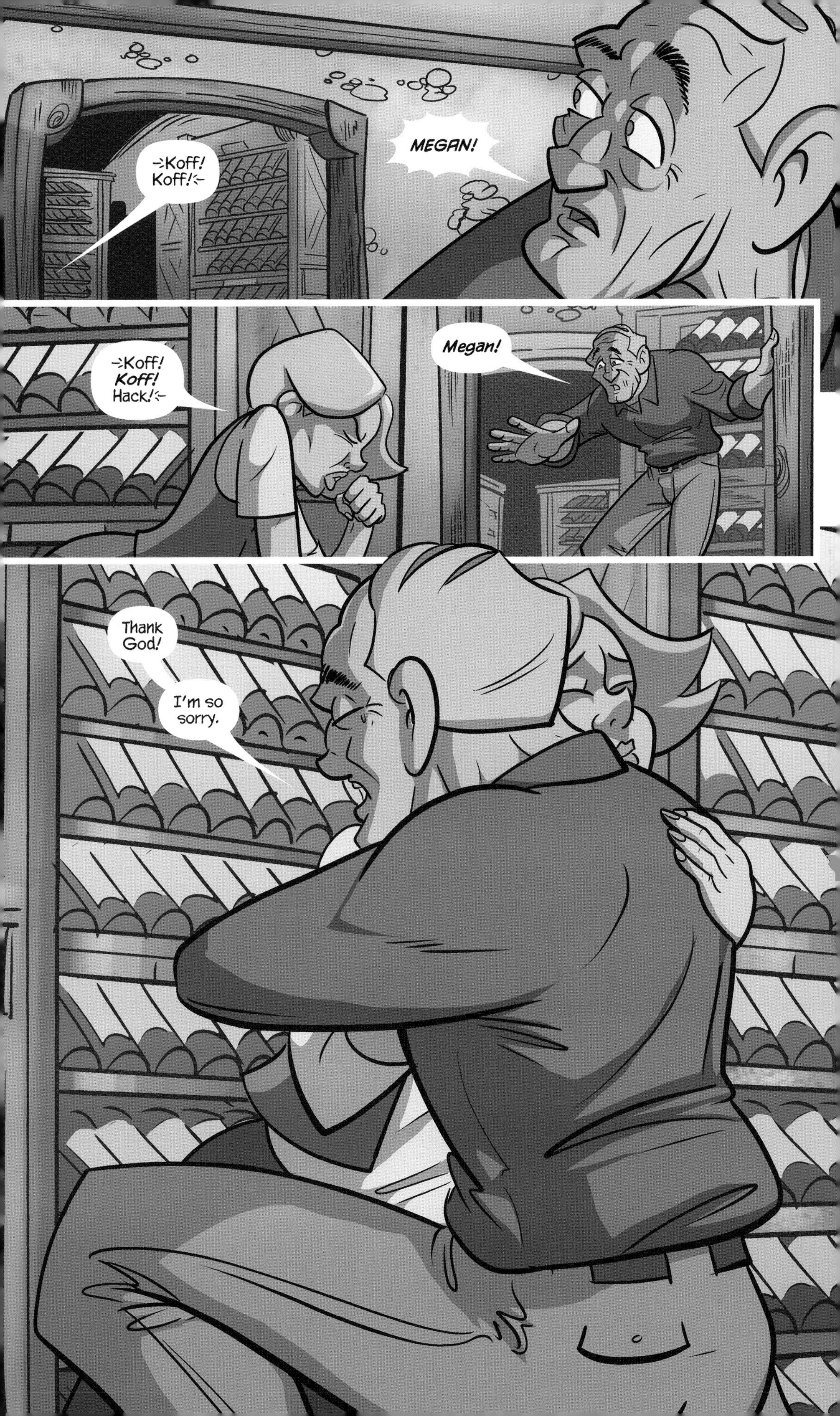
MEGAN!
Koff! Koff!
Koff! Koff! Hack!
Megan!
Thank God!
I'm so sorry.

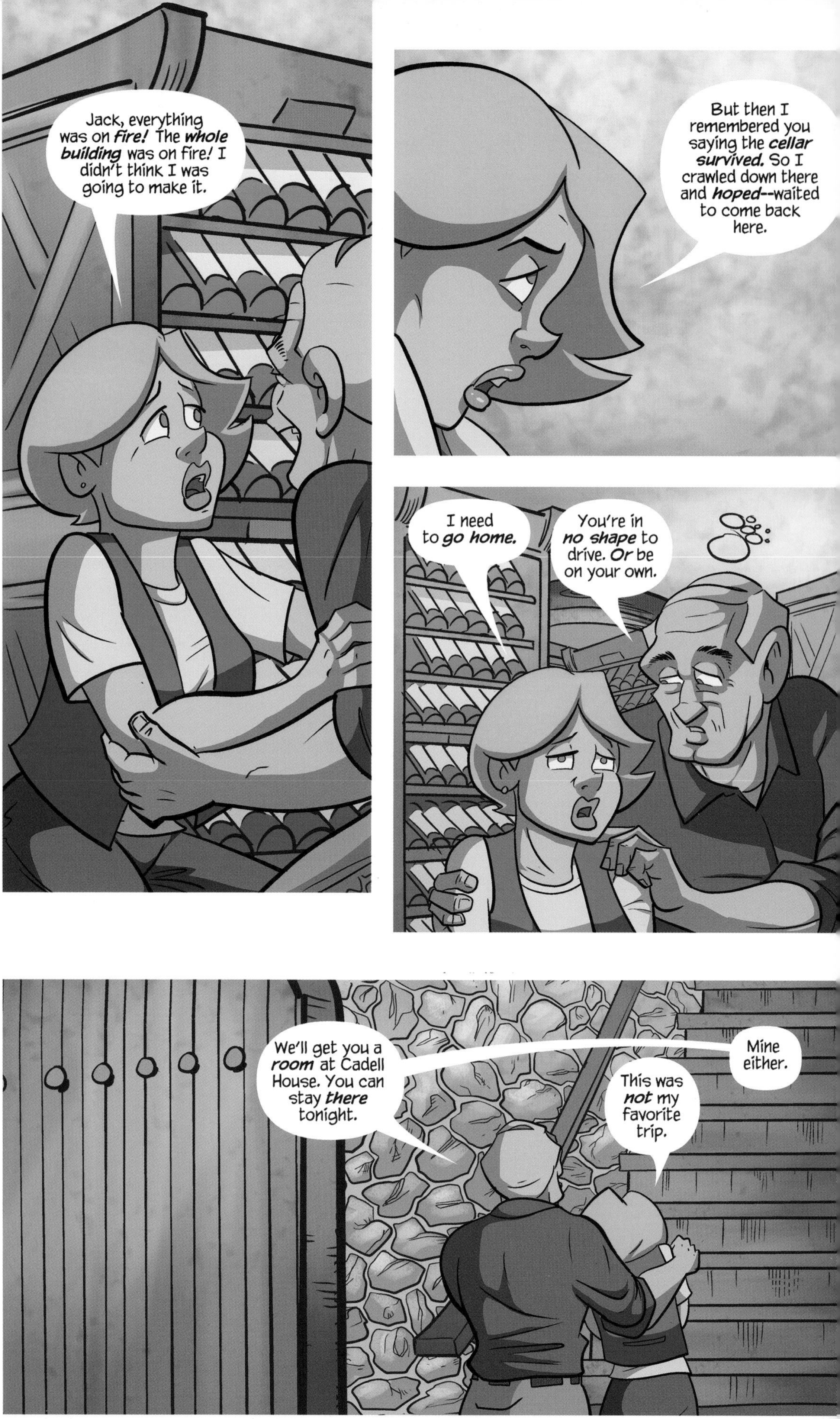
Jack, everything was on *fire!* The *whole building* was on fire! I didn't think I was going to make it.
But then I remembered you saying the *cellar survived.* So I crawled down there and *hoped*--waited to come back here.
I need to *go home.*
You're in *no shape* to drive. *Or* be on your own.
We'll get you a *room* at Cadell House. You can stay *there* tonight.
This was *not* my favorite trip.
Mine either.

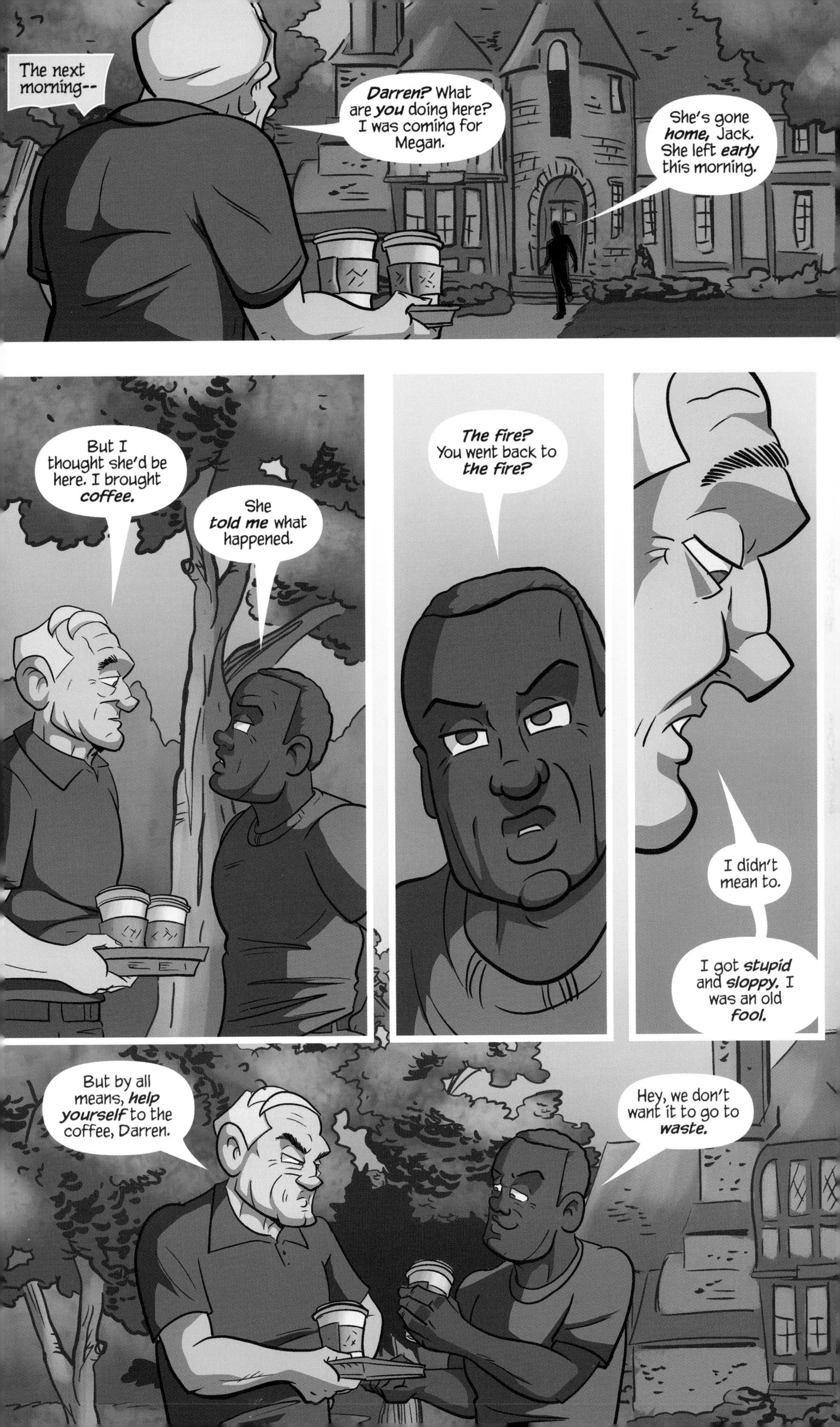
The next morning--
Darren? What are you doing here? I was coming for Megan.
She's gone home, Jack. She left early this morning.
But I thought she'd be here. I brought coffee.
She told me what happened.
The fire? You went back to the fire?
I didn't mean to.
I got stupid and sloppy. I was an old fool.
But by all means, help yourself to the coffee, Darren.
Hey, we don't want it to go to waste.

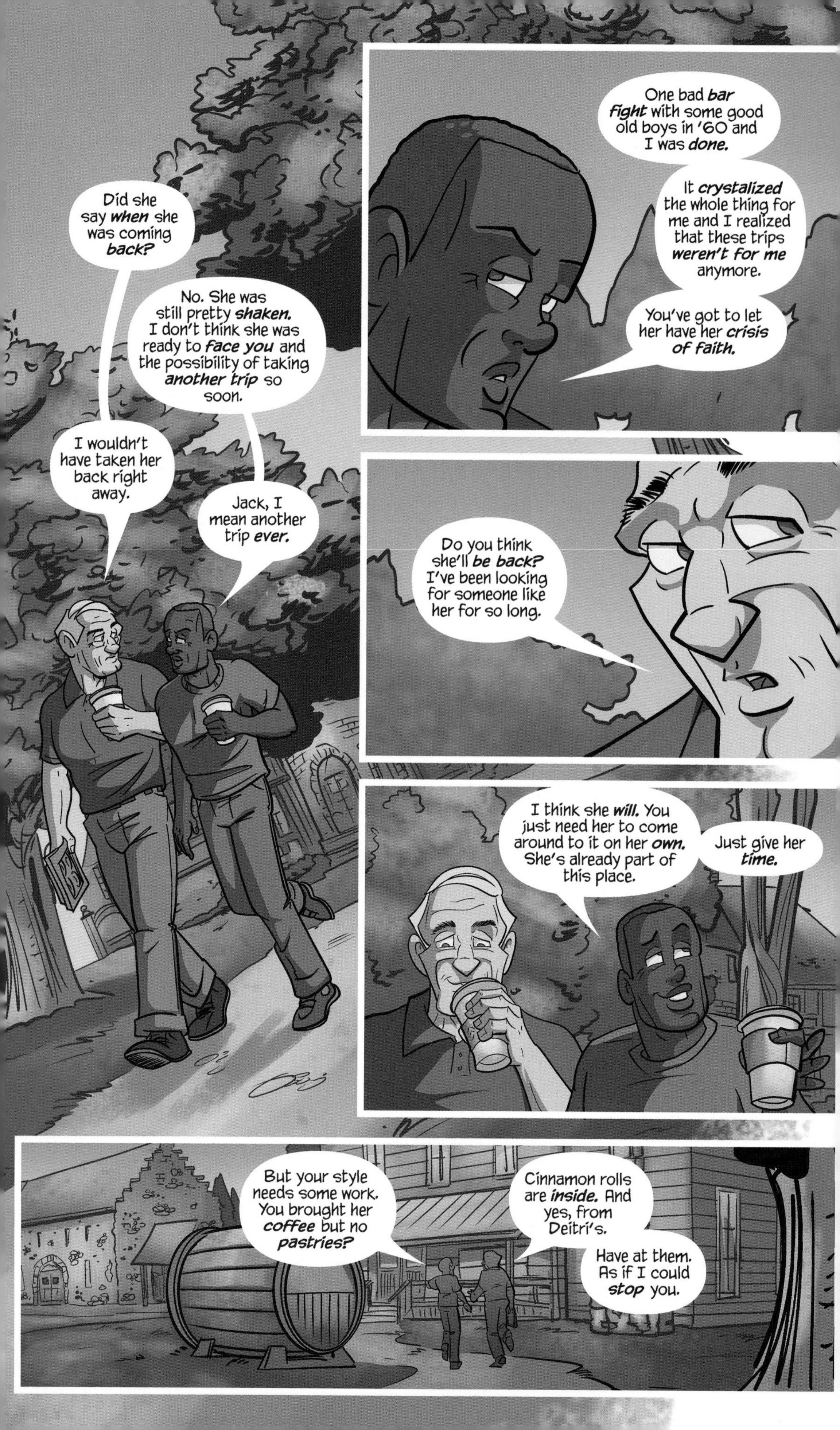
Did she say when she was coming back?
No. She was still pretty shaken. I don't think she was ready to face you and the possibility of taking another trip so soon.
I wouldn't have taken her back right away.
Jack, I mean another trip ever.
One bad bar fight with some good old boys in '60 and I was done.
It crystalized the whole thing for me and I realized that these trips weren't for me anymore.
You've got to let her have her crisis of faith.
Do you think she'll be back? I've been looking for someone like her for so long.
I think she will. You just need her to come around to it on her own. She's already part of this place.
Just give her time.
But your style needs some work. You brought her coffee but no pastries?
Cinnamon rolls are inside. And yes, from Deitri's.
Have at them. As if I could stop you.

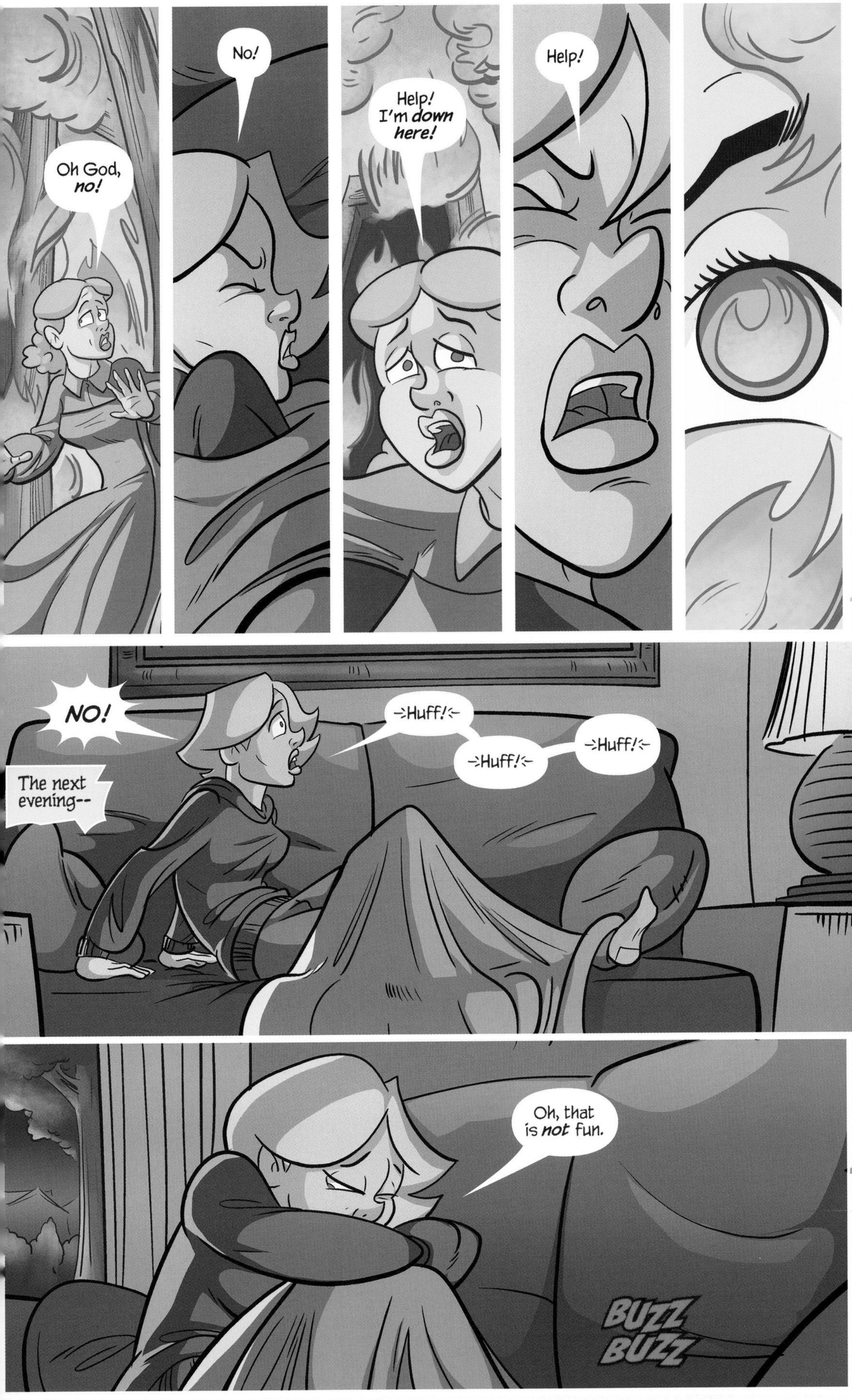
Oh God, no!
No!
Help! I'm down here!
Help!
NO!
The next evening--
Huff!
Huff!
Huff!
Oh, that is not fun.
BUZZ BUZZ

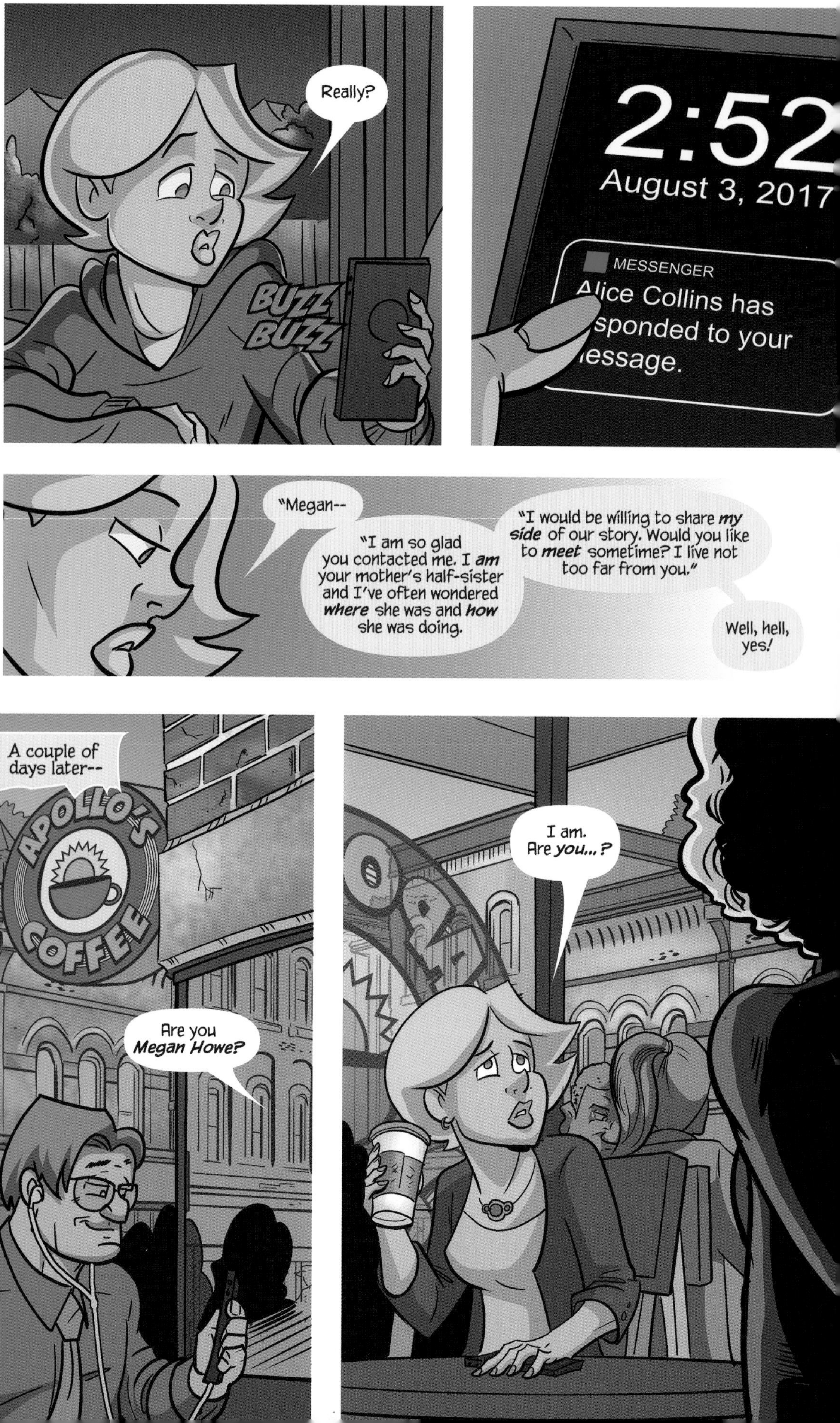
Really?
BUZZ BUZZ
2:52
August 3, 2017
MESSENGER
Alice Collins has
sponded to your
essage.
"Megan--
"I am so glad you contacted me. I *am* your mother's half-sister and I've often wondered *where* she was and *how* she was doing.
"I would be willing to share *my side* of our story. Would you like to *meet* sometime? I live not too far from you."
Well, hell, yes!
A couple of days later--
APOLLO'S COFFEE
Are you *Megan Howe?*
I am. Are *you...?*

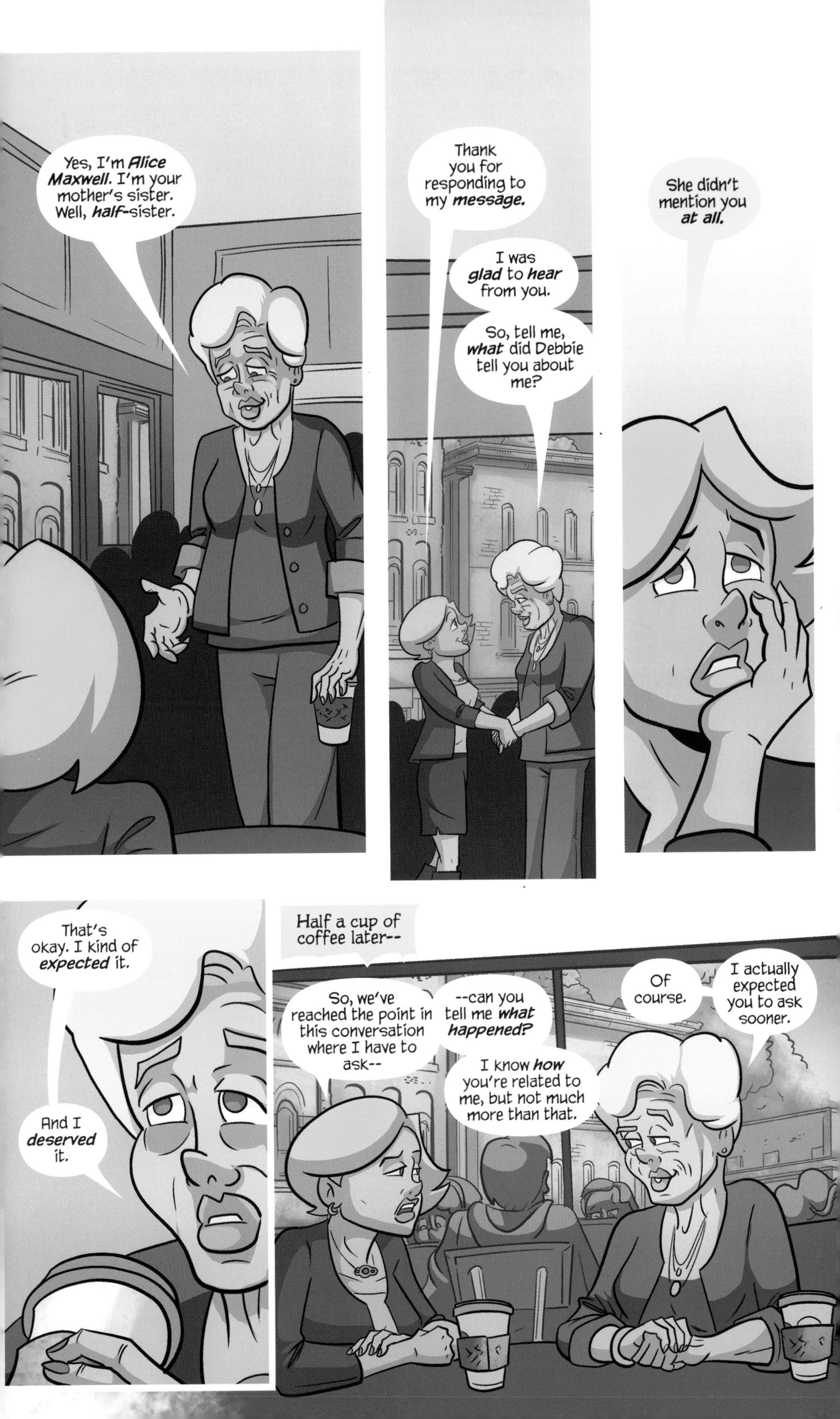
Yes, I'm *Alice Maxwell*. I'm your mother's sister. Well, *half*-sister.
Thank you for responding to my *message.*
I was *glad* to *hear* from you.
So, tell me, *what* did Debbie tell you about me?
She didn't mention you *at all.*
That's okay. I kind of *expected* it.
And I *deserved* it.
Half a cup of coffee later--
So, we've reached the point in this conversation where I have to ask--
--can you tell me *what happened?*
I know *how* you're related to me, but not much more than that.
Of course.
I actually expected you to ask sooner.

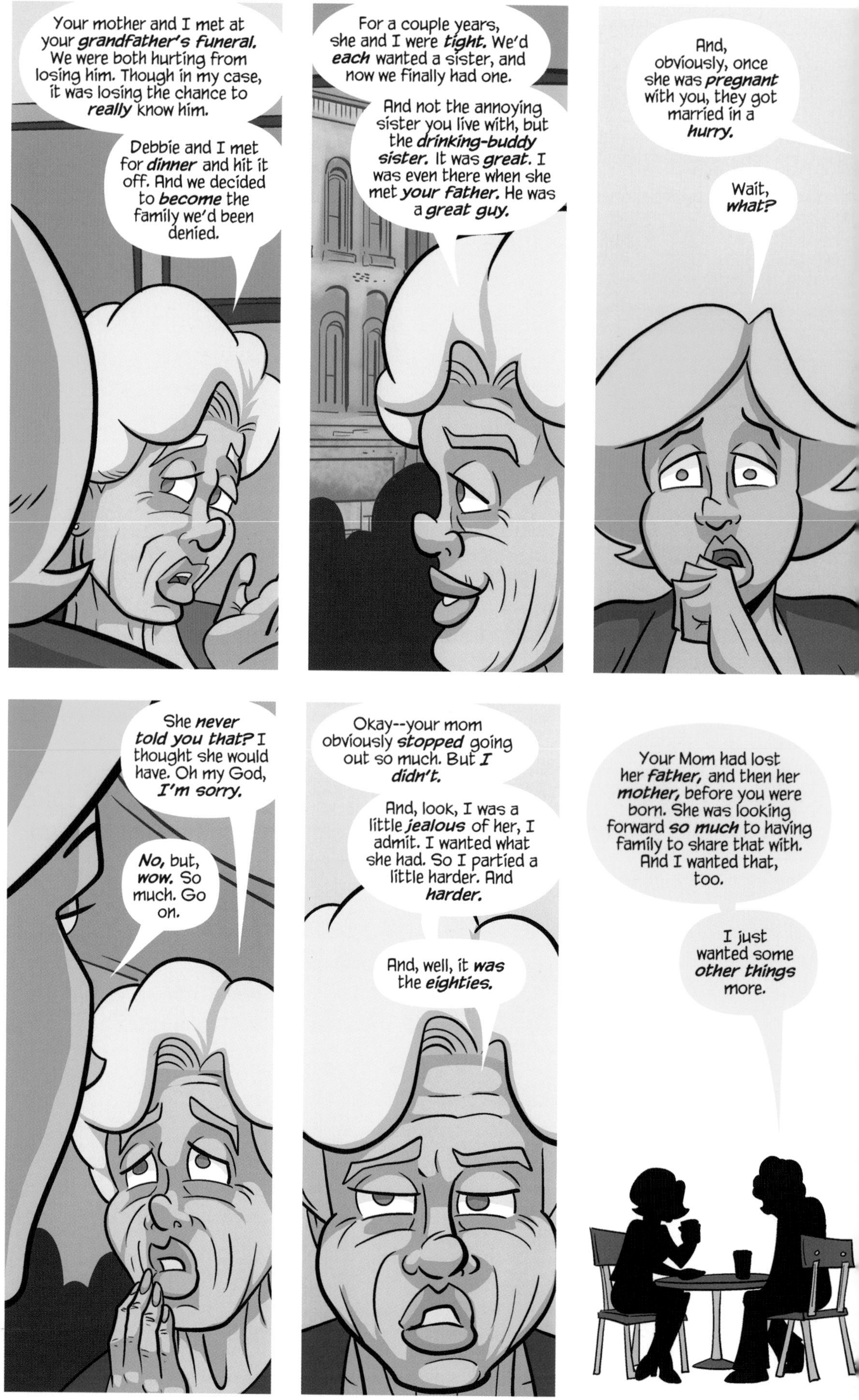
Your mother and I met at your grandfather's funeral. We were both hurting from losing him. Though in my case, it was losing the chance to really know him.
Debbie and I met for dinner and hit it off. And we decided to become the family we'd been denied.
For a couple years, she and I were tight. We'd each wanted a sister, and now we finally had one.
And not the annoying sister you live with, but the drinking-buddy sister. It was great. I was even there when she met your father. He was a great guy.
And, obviously, once she was pregnant with you, they got married in a hurry.
Wait, what?
She never told you that? I thought she would have. Oh my God, I'm sorry.
No, but, wow. So much. Go on.
Okay--your mom obviously stopped going out so much. But I didn't.
And, look, I was a little jealous of her, I admit. I wanted what she had. So I partied a little harder. And harder.
And, well, it was the eighties.
Your Mom had lost her father, and then her mother, before you were born. She was looking forward so much to having family to share that with. And I wanted that, too.
I just wanted some other things more.

I borrowed some *money* from her and *promised* to pay it back.

And then I ran to *California* with some guy whose name I can't even remember now.

I'm sure it *destroyed* your mom.

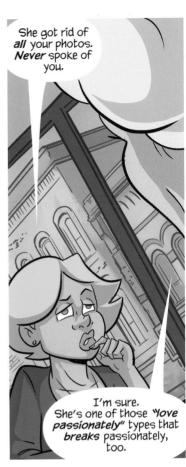

She got rid of *all* your photos. *Never* spoke of you.

I'm sure. She's one of those *"love passionately"* types that *breaks* passionately, too.

I tried a *couple of times* to get in touch with her, and she *never responded.* And then I lost track of her altogether. I moved back to the city, got married, had a *daughter* myself.

Wait, so *I* have a *new cousin,* too?

I *guess* so. I'll make the *introductions* if you'd like. *When* you're ready.

Thank you.

So how *is* your mother? I understand why she wouldn't want to *talk* about this, but--

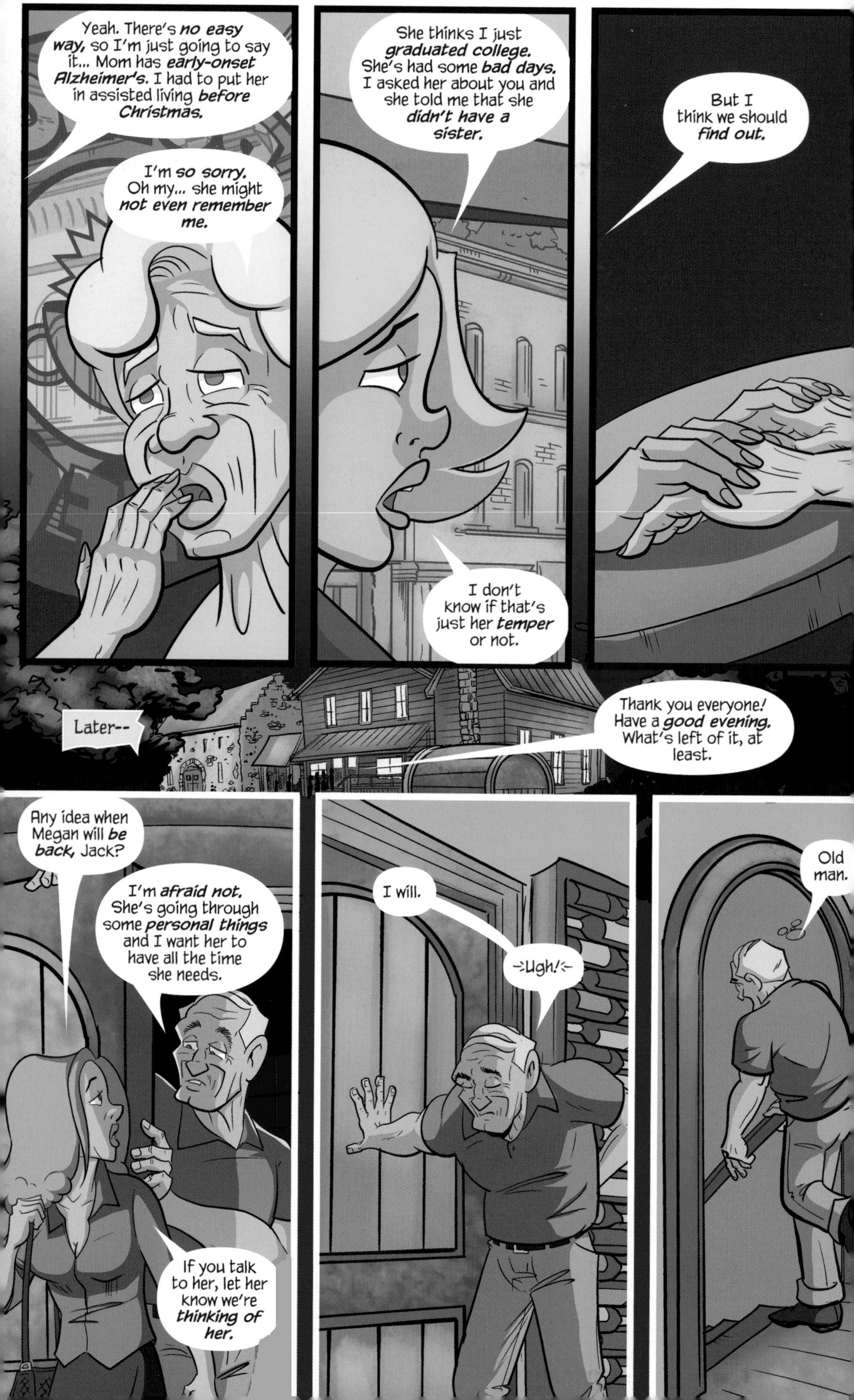
Yeah. There's no easy way, so I'm just going to say it... Mom has early-onset Alzheimer's. I had to put her in assisted living before Christmas.
I'm so sorry. Oh my... she might not even remember me.
She thinks I just graduated college. She's had some bad days. I asked her about you and she told me that she didn't have a sister.
I don't know if that's just her temper or not.
But I think we should find out.
Later--
Thank you everyone! Have a good evening. What's left of it, at least.
Any idea when Megan will be back, Jack?
I'm afraid not. She's going through some personal things and I want her to have all the time she needs.
If you talk to her, let her know we're thinking of her.
I will.
Ugh!
Old man.

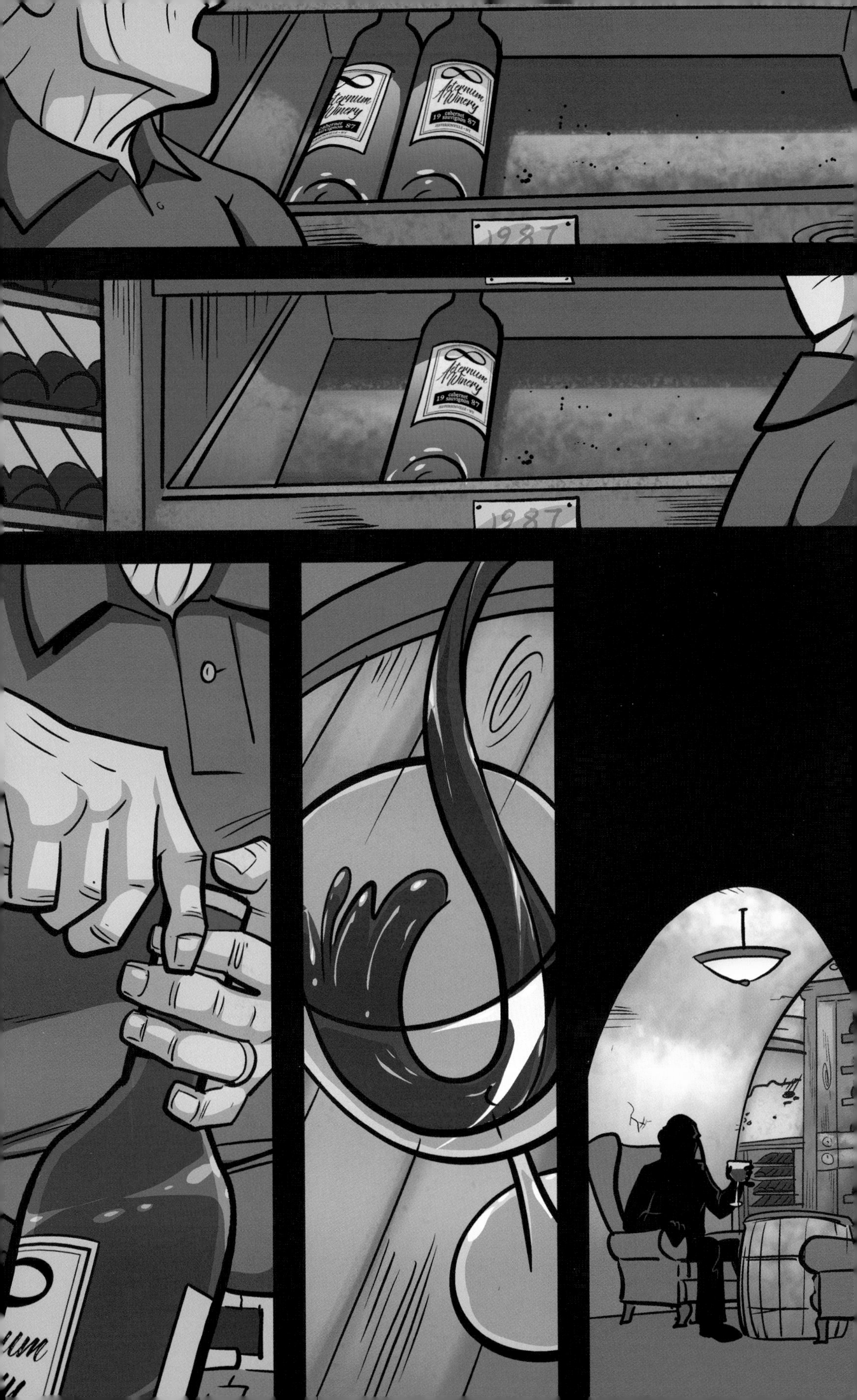
Æternum Winery
cabernet sauvignon 19 87
1987
Æternum Winery
cabernet sauvignon 19 87
1987

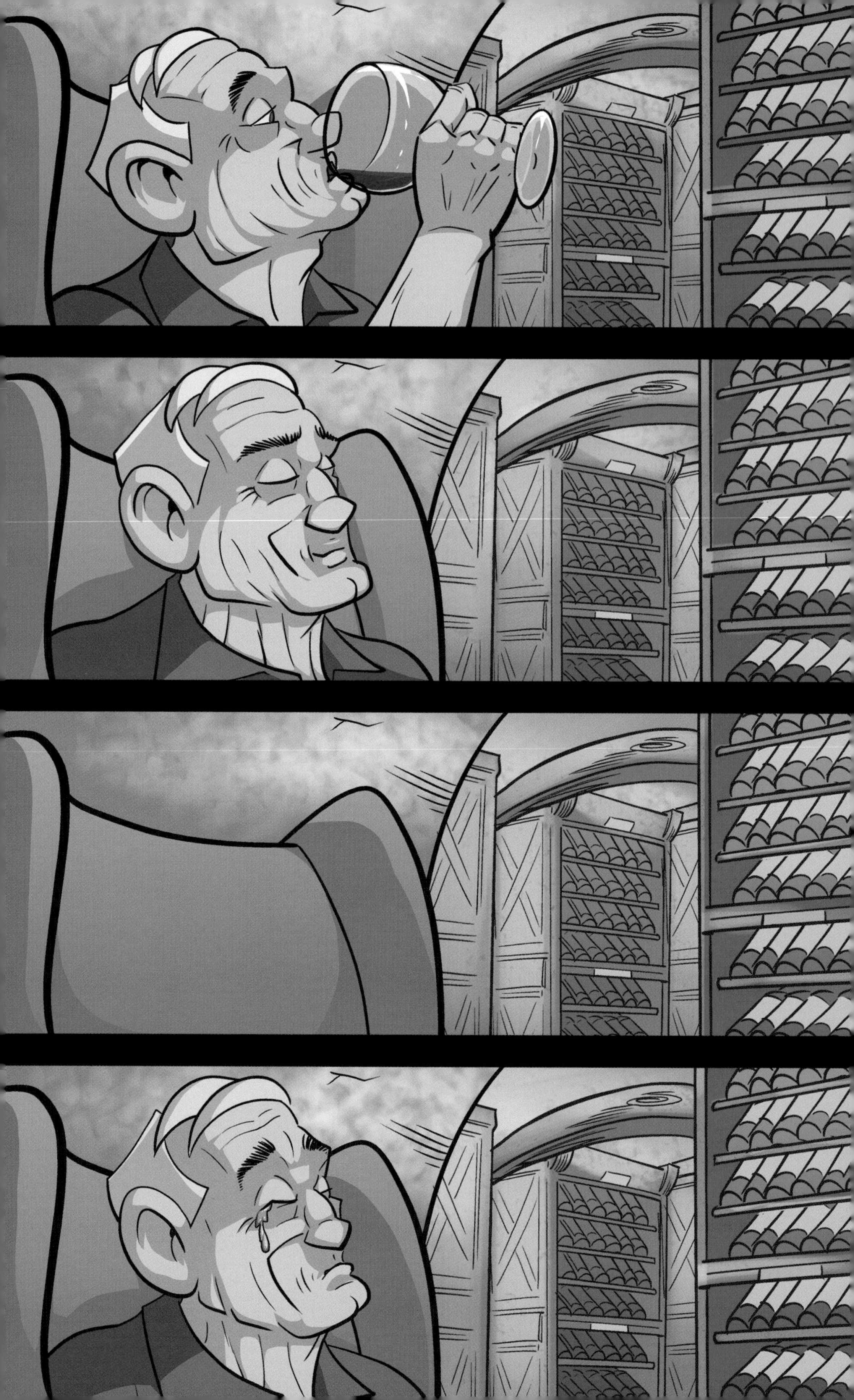

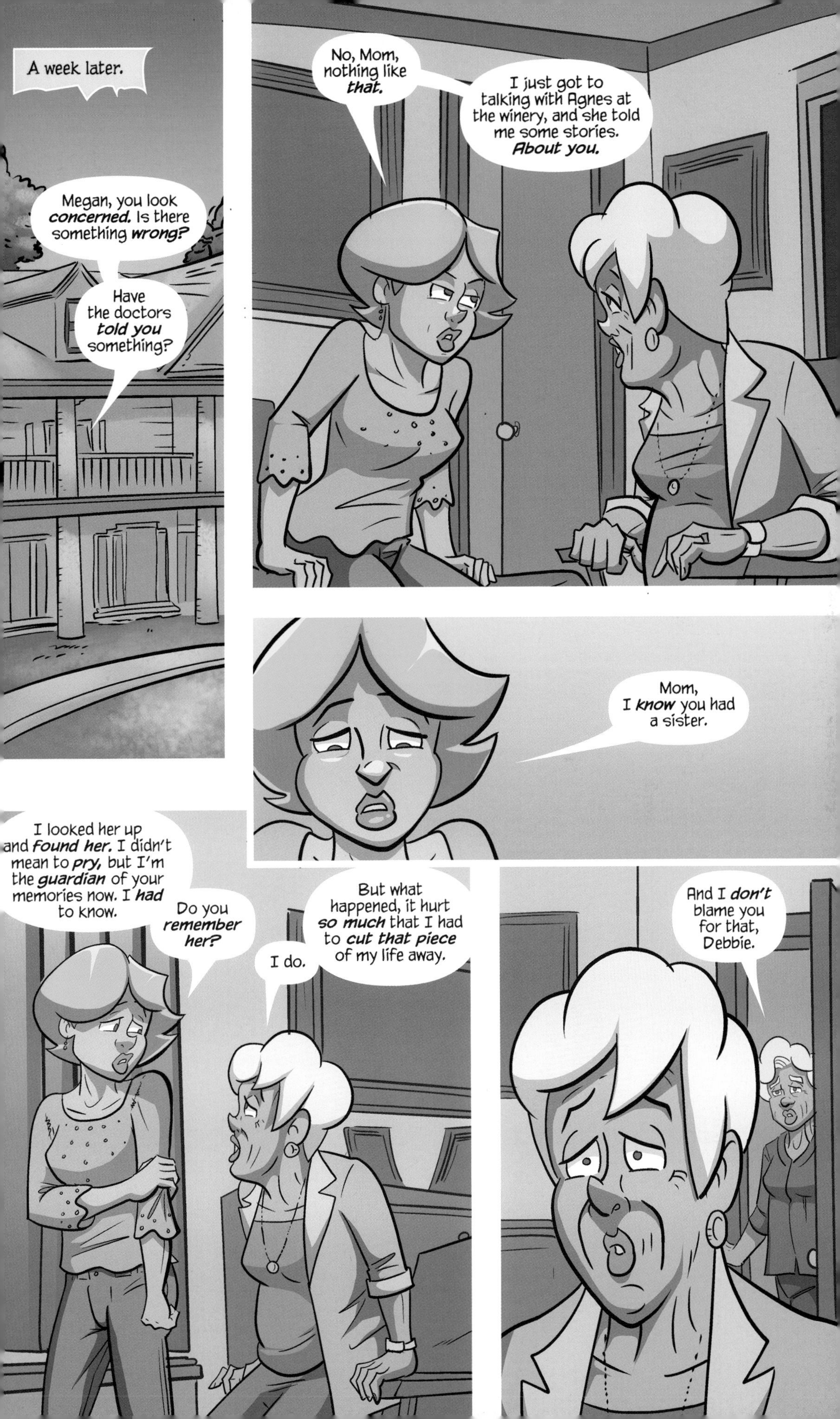
A week later.
Megan, you look concerned. Is there something wrong?
Have the doctors told you something?
No, Mom, nothing like that.
I just got to talking with Agnes at the winery, and she told me some stories. About you.
Mom, I know you had a sister.
I looked her up and found her. I didn't mean to pry, but I'm the guardian of your memories now. I had to know.
Do you remember her?
I do.
But what happened, it hurt so much that I had to cut that piece of my life away.
And I don't blame you for that, Debbie.

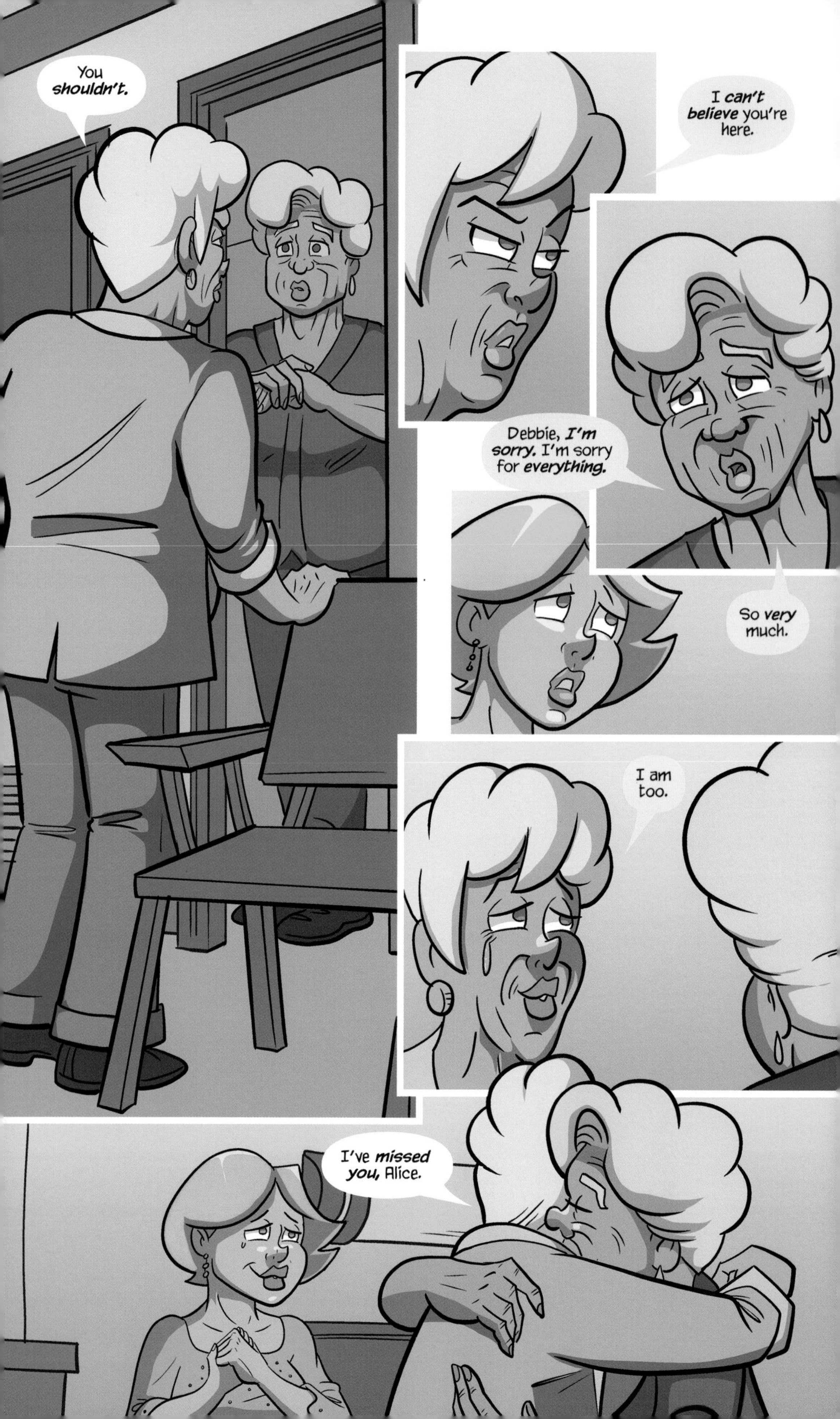
You *shouldn't.*
I *can't believe* you're here.
Debbie, *I'm sorry.* I'm sorry for *everything.*
So *very* much.
I am too.
I've *missed you,* Alice.

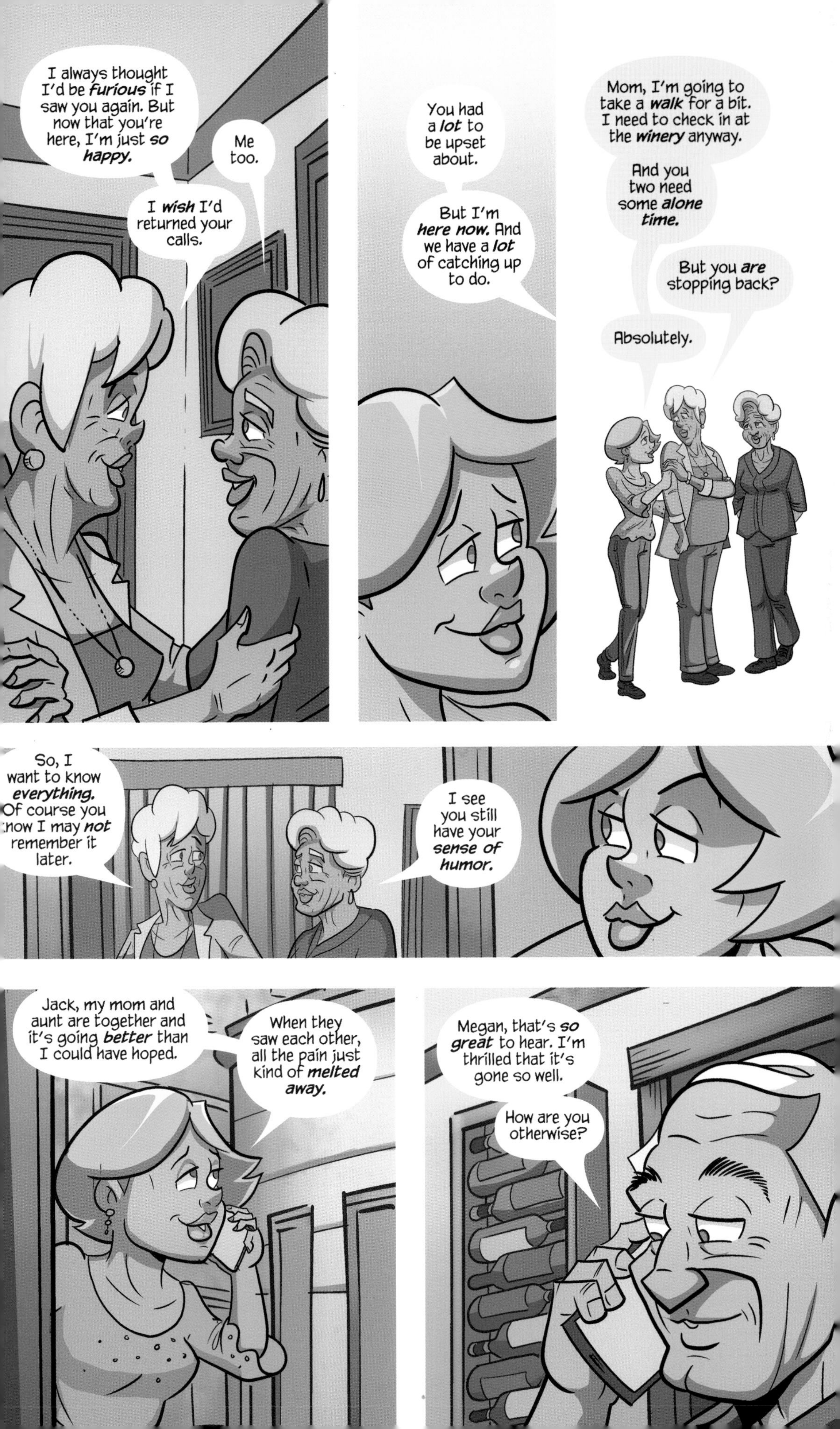
I always thought I'd be *furious* if I saw you again. But now that you're here, I'm just *so happy.*
Me too.
I *wish* I'd returned your calls.
You had a *lot* to be upset about.
But I'm *here now.* And we have a *lot* of catching up to do.
Mom, I'm going to take a *walk* for a bit. I need to check in at the *winery* anyway.
And you two need some *alone time.*
But you *are* stopping back?
Absolutely.
So, I want to know *everything.* Of course you know I may *not* remember it later.
I see you still have your *sense of humor.*
Jack, my mom and aunt are together and it's going *better* than I could have hoped.
When they saw each other, all the pain just kind of *melted away.*
Megan, that's *so great* to hear. I'm thrilled that it's gone so well.
How are you otherwise?

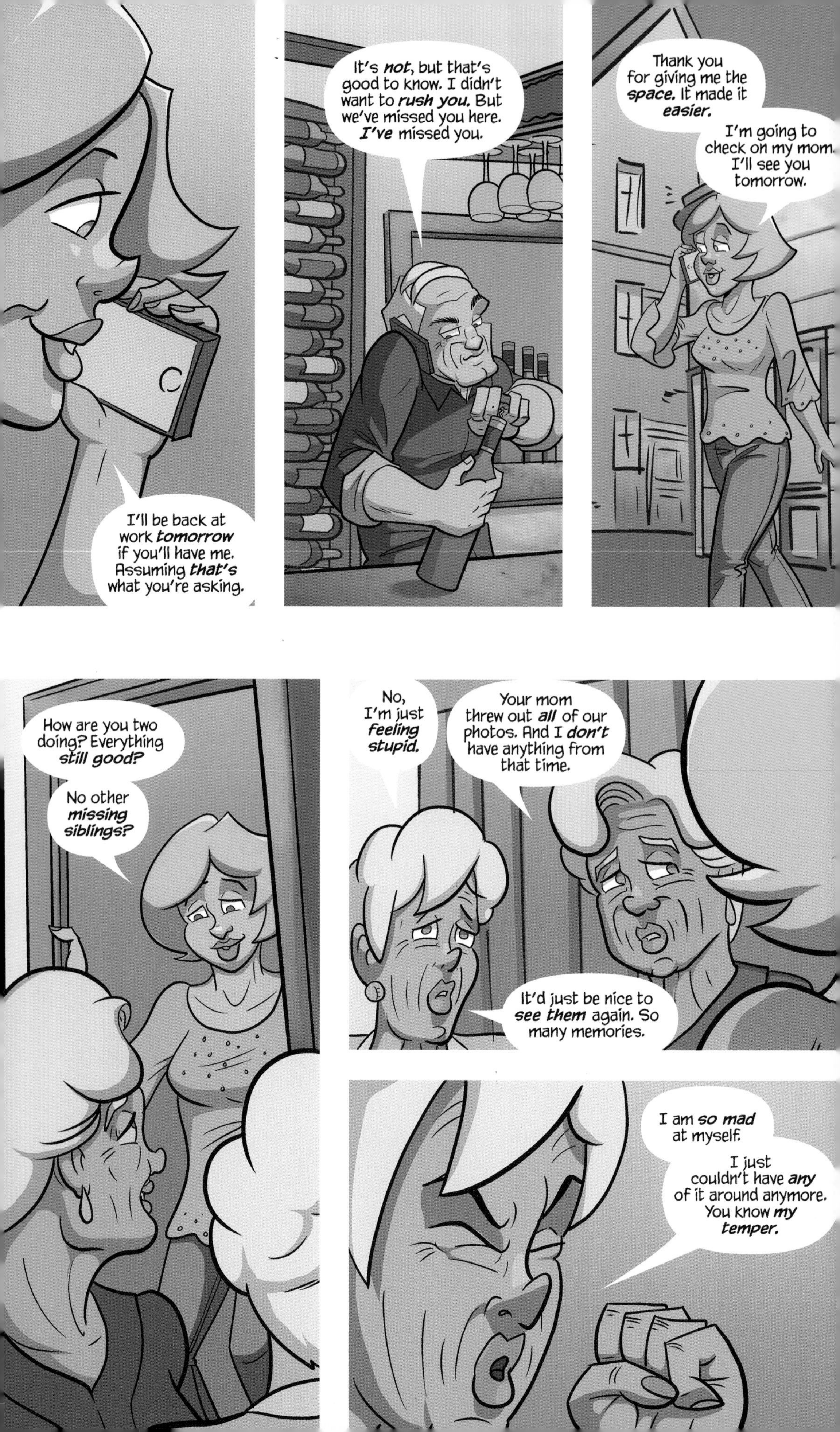

I'll be back at work *tomorrow* if you'll have me. Assuming *that's* what you're asking.
It's *not*, but that's good to know. I didn't want to *rush you.* But we've missed you here. *I've* missed you.
Thank you for giving me the *space.* It made it *easier.*
I'm going to check on my mom. I'll see you tomorrow.
How are you two doing? Everything *still good?*
No other *missing siblings?*
No, I'm just *feeling stupid.*
Your mom threw out *all* of our photos. And I *don't* have anything from that time.
It'd just be nice to *see them* again. So many memories.
I am *so mad* at myself.
I just couldn't have *any* of it around anymore. You know *my temper.*

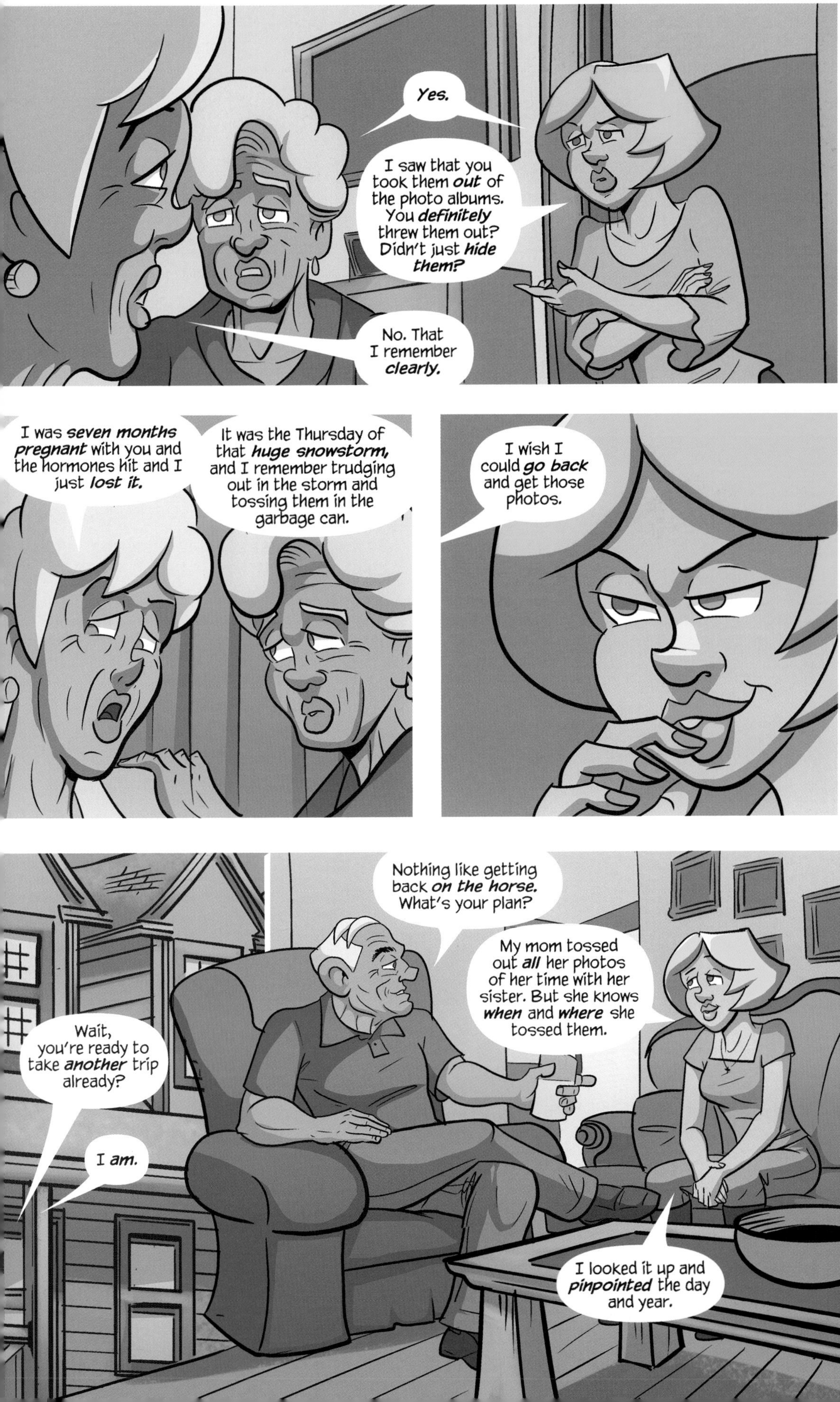
Yes.
I saw that you took them out of the photo albums. You definitely threw them out? Didn't just hide them?
No. That I remember clearly.
I was seven months pregnant with you and the hormones hit and I just lost it.
It was the Thursday of that huge snowstorm, and I remember trudging out in the storm and tossing them in the garbage can.
I wish I could go back and get those photos.
Wait, you're ready to take another trip already?
I am.
Nothing like getting back on the horse. What's your plan?
My mom tossed out all her photos of her time with her sister. But she knows when and where she tossed them.
I looked it up and pinpointed the day and year.

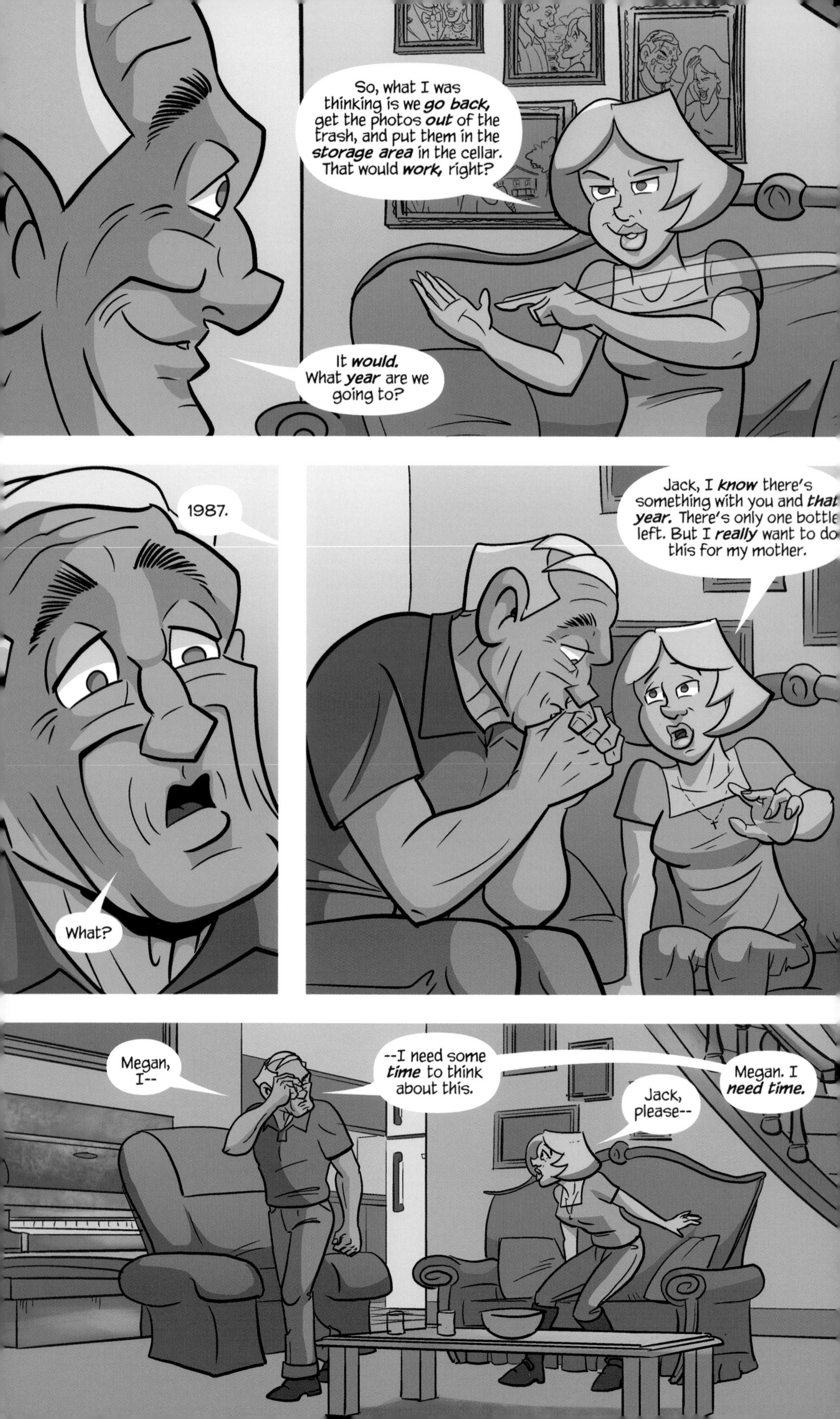

So, what I was thinking is we *go back,* get the photos *out* of the trash, and put them in the *storage area* in the cellar. That would *work,* right?
It *would.* What *year* are we going to?
1987.
What?
Jack, I *know* there's something with you and *that year.* There's only one bottle left. But I *really* want to do this for my mother.
Megan, I--
--I need some *time* to think about this.
Jack, please--
Megan. I *need time.*

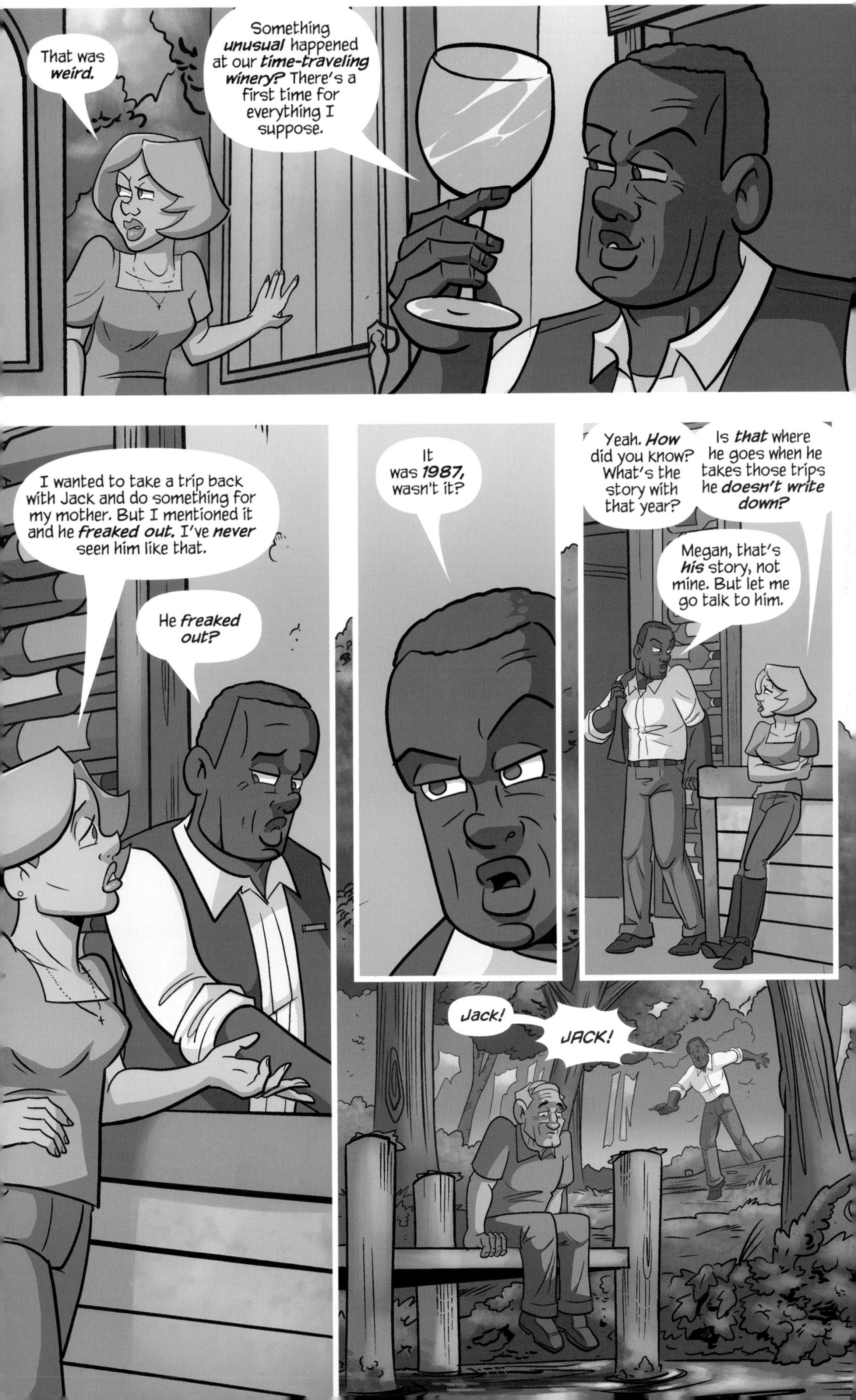
That was *weird.*
Something *unusual* happened at our *time-traveling winery?* There's a first time for everything I suppose.
I wanted to take a trip back with Jack and do something for my mother. But I mentioned it and he *freaked out.* I've *never* seen him like that.
He *freaked out?*
It was *1987,* wasn't it?
Yeah. *How* did you know? What's the story with that year?
Is *that* where he goes when he takes those trips he *doesn't write down?*
Megan, that's *his* story, not mine. But let me go talk to him.
*Jack!*
*JACK!*

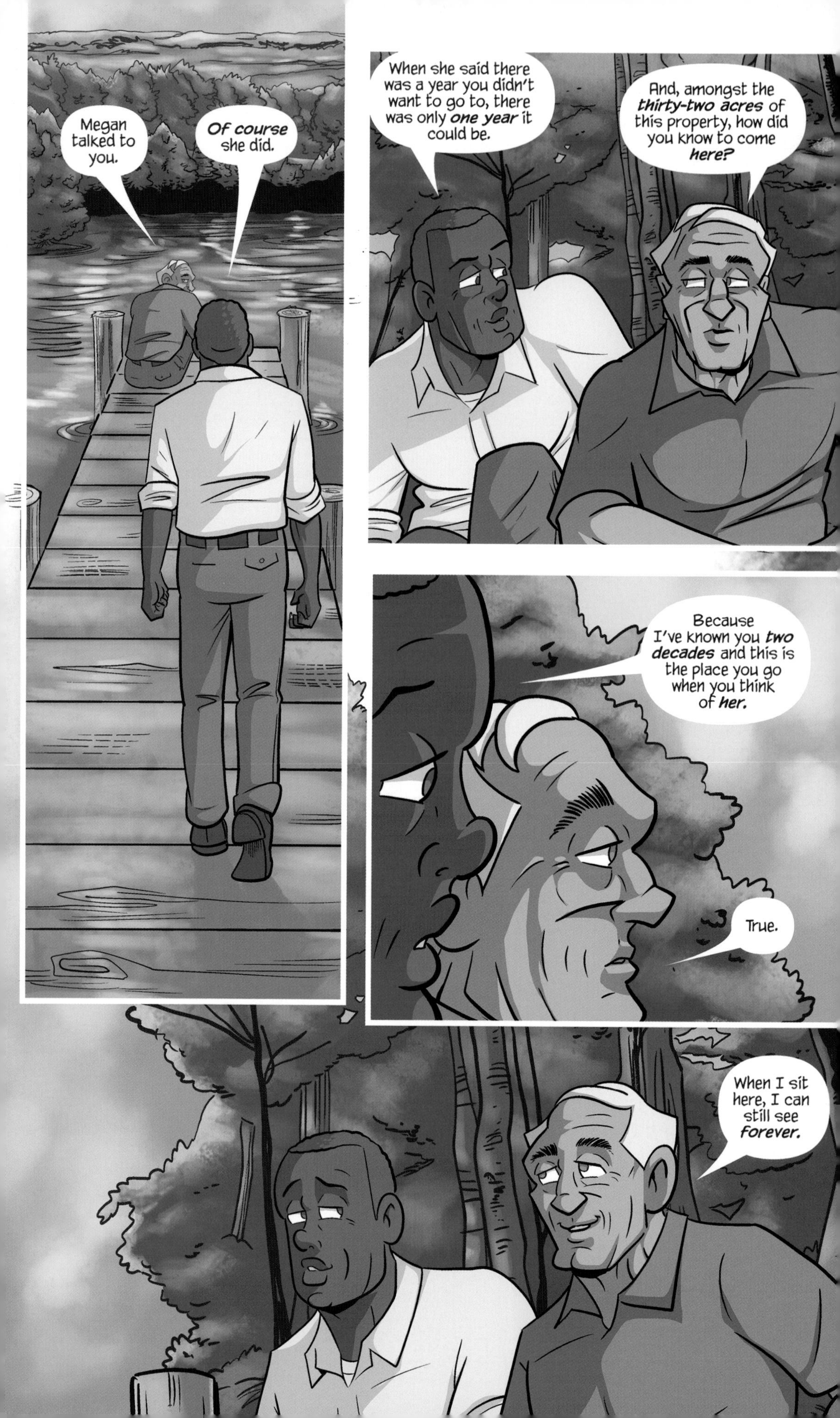
Megan talked to you.
Of course she did.
When she said there was a year you didn't want to go to, there was only one year it could be.
And, amongst the thirty-two acres of this property, how did you know to come here?
Because I've known you two decades and this is the place you go when you think of her.
True.
When I sit here, I can still see forever.

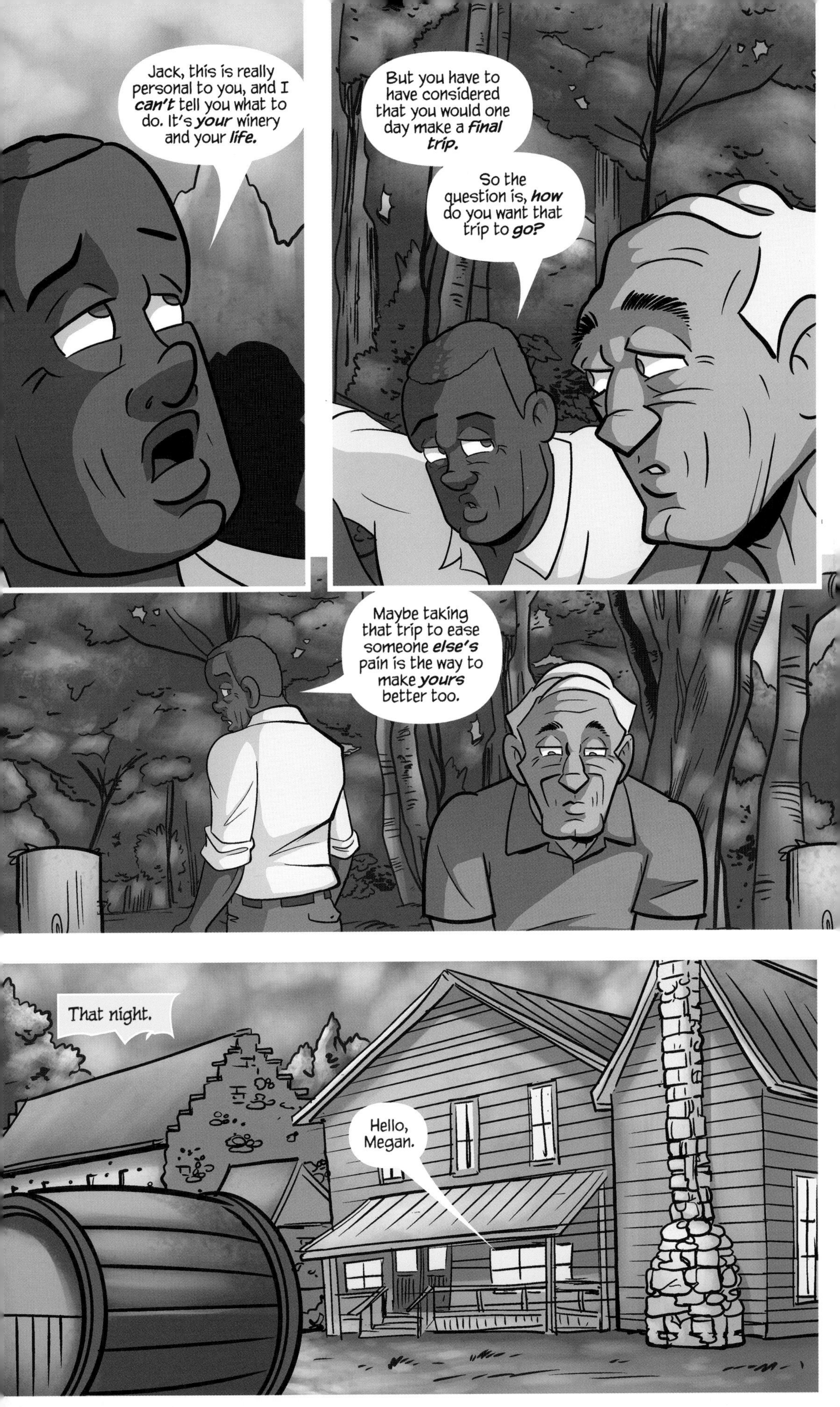
Jack, this is really personal to you, and I *can't* tell you what to do. It's *your* winery and your *life.*
But you have to have considered that you would one day make a *final trip.*
So the question is, *how* do you want that trip to *go?*
Maybe taking that trip to ease someone *else's* pain is the way to make *yours* better too.
That night.
Hello, Megan.

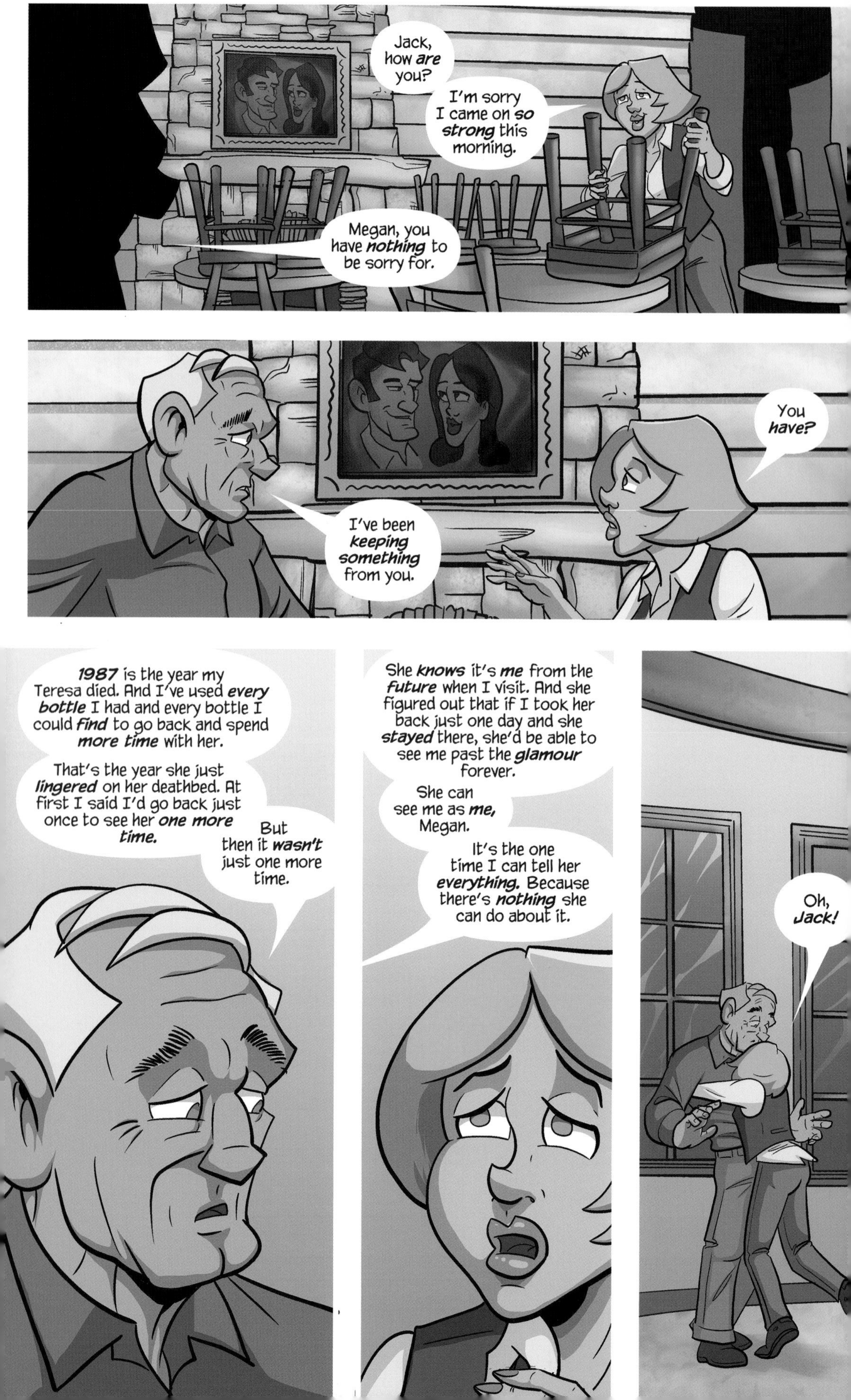

Jack, how are you?
I'm sorry I came on so strong this morning.
Megan, you have nothing to be sorry for.
You have?
I've been keeping something from you.
1987 is the year my Teresa died. And I've used every bottle I had and every bottle I could find to go back and spend more time with her.
That's the year she just lingered on her deathbed. At first I said I'd go back just once to see her one more time.
But then it wasn't just one more time.
She knows it's me from the future when I visit. And she figured out that if I took her back just one day and she stayed there, she'd be able to see me past the glamour forever.
She can see me as me, Megan.
It's the one time I can tell her everything. Because there's nothing she can do about it.
Oh, Jack!

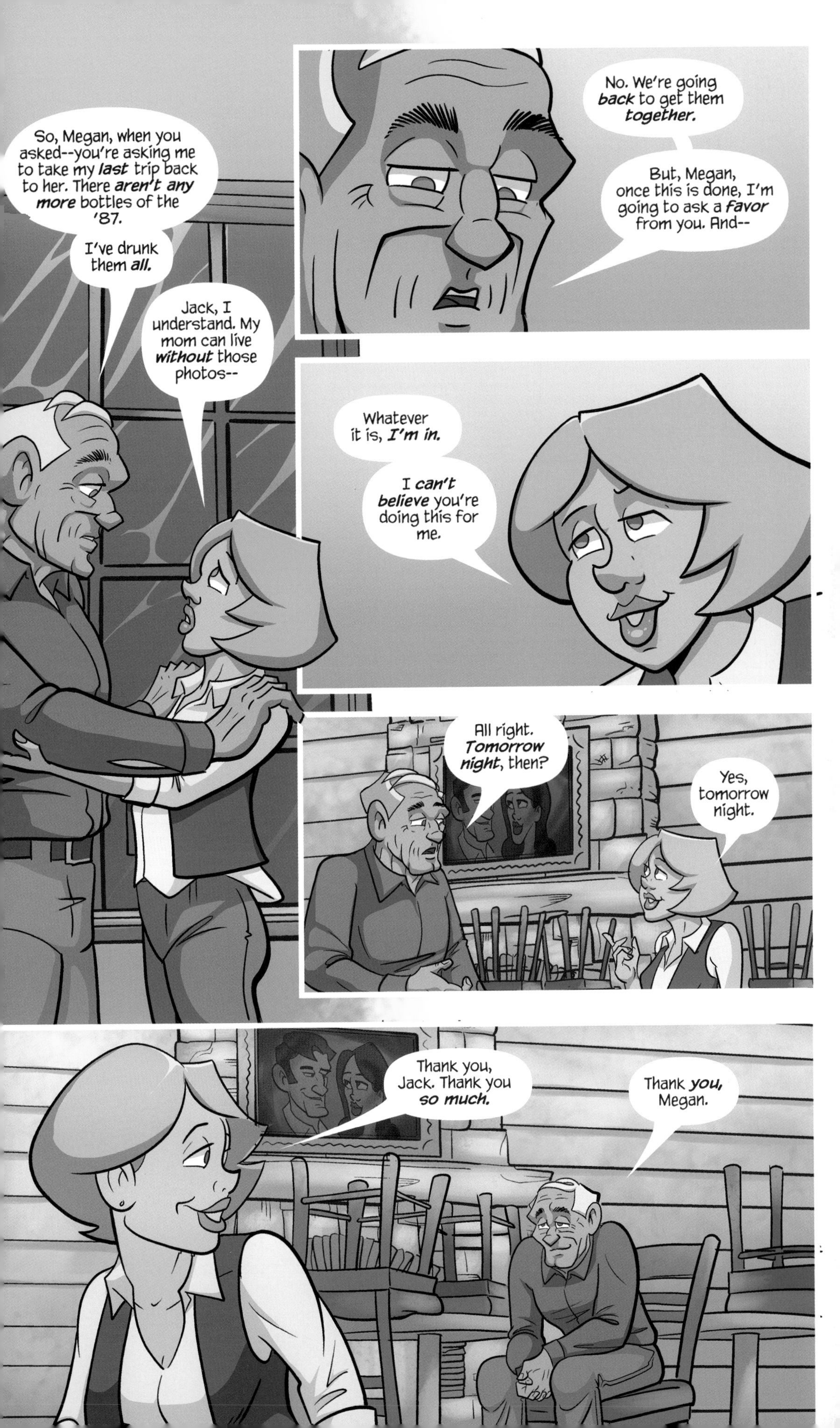
So, Megan, when you asked--you're asking me to take my *last* trip back to her. There *aren't any more* bottles of the '87.
I've drunk them *all.*
Jack, I understand. My mom can live *without* those photos--
No. We're going *back* to get them *together.*
But, Megan, once this is done, I'm going to ask a *favor* from you. And--
Whatever it is, *I'm in.*
I *can't believe* you're doing this for me.
All right. *Tomorrow night*, then?
Yes, tomorrow night.
Thank you, Jack. Thank you *so much.*
Thank *you,* Megan.

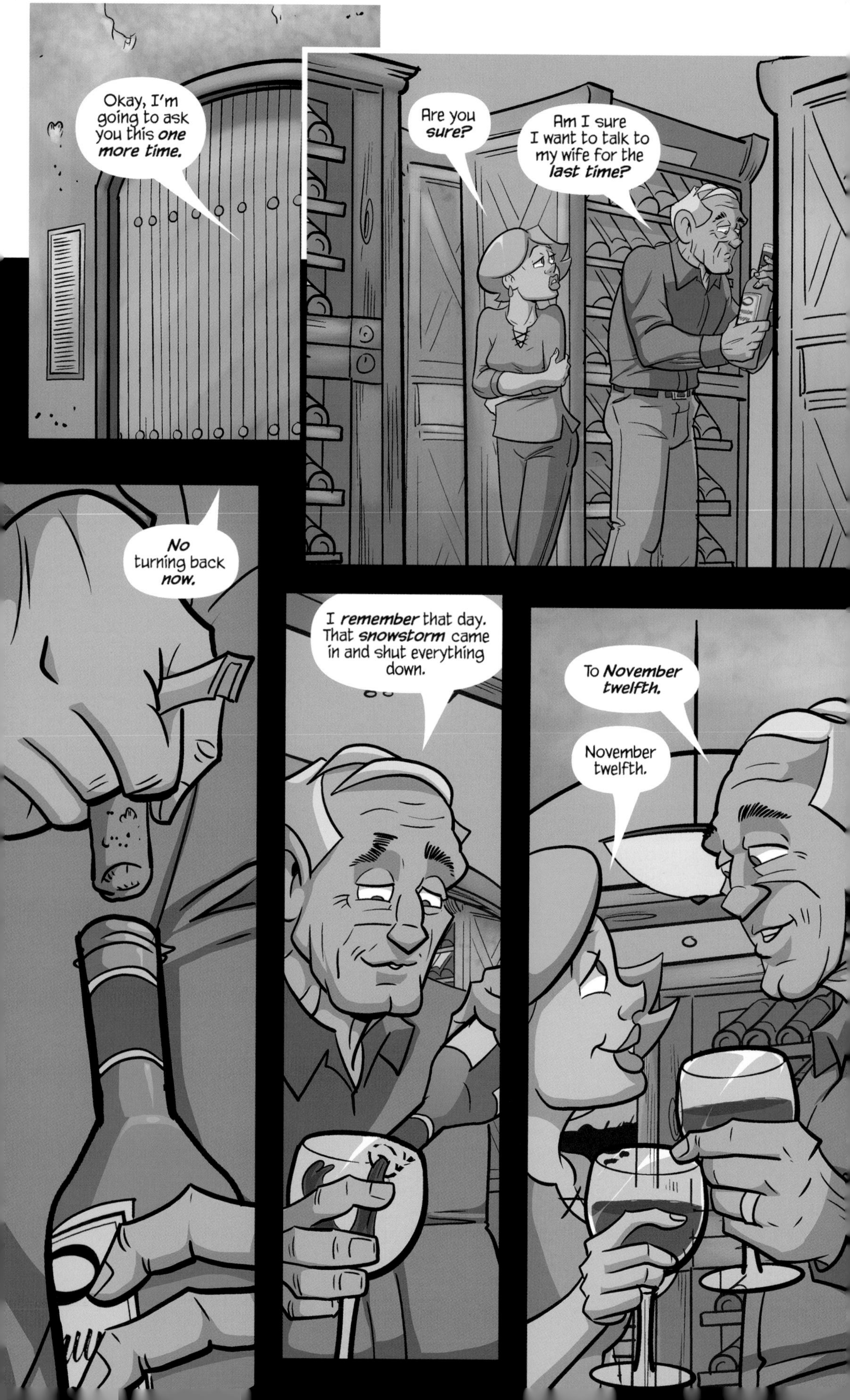
Okay, I'm going to ask you this *one more time.*
Are you *sure?*
Am I sure I want to talk to my wife for the *last time?*
*No* turning back *now.*
I *remember* that day. That *snowstorm* came in and shut everything down.
To *November twelfth.*
November twelfth.

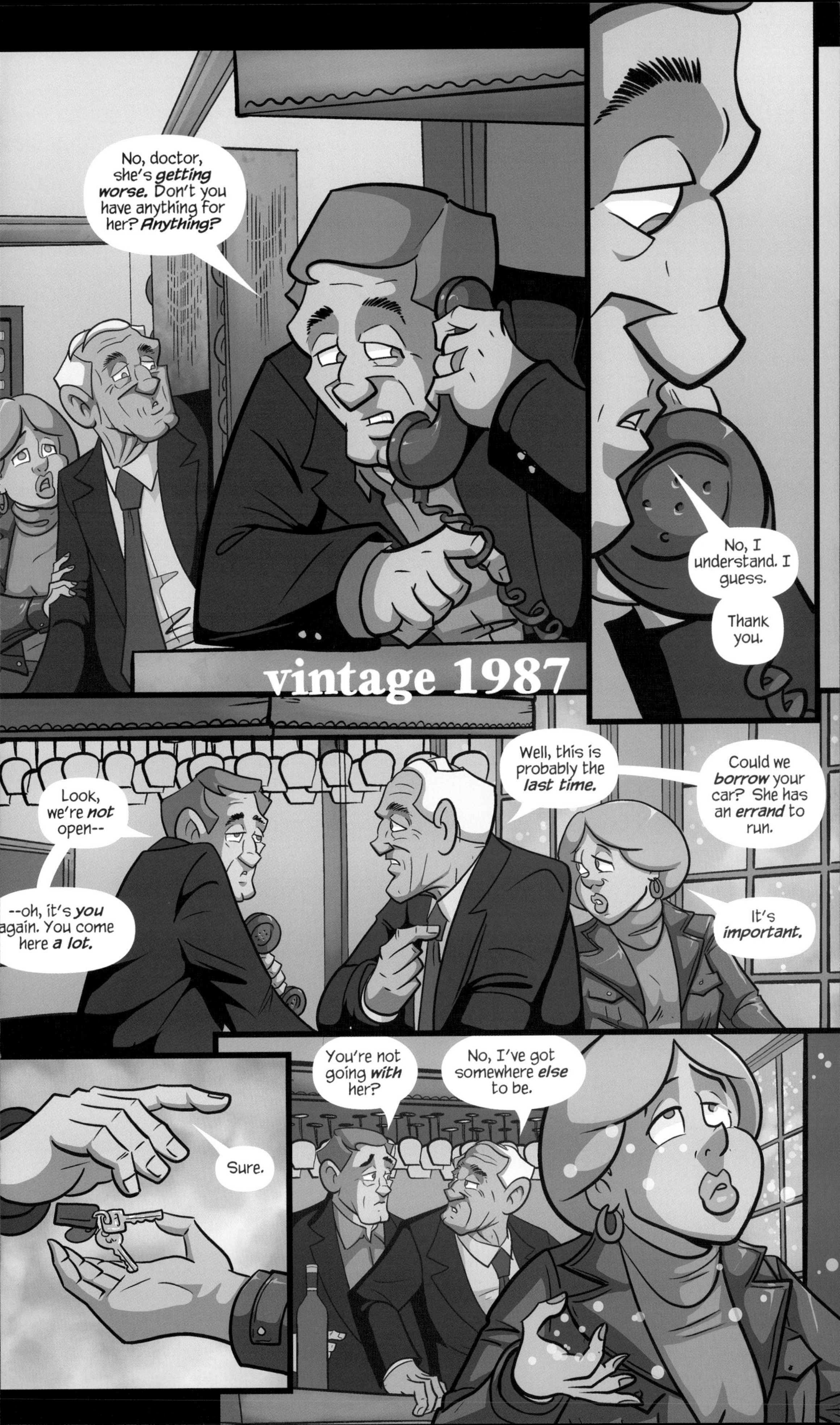
No, doctor, she's *getting worse.* Don't you have anything for her? *Anything?*
No, I understand. I guess.
Thank you.
vintage 1987
Look, we're *not* open--
--oh, it's *you* again. You come here *a lot.*
Well, this is probably the *last time.*
Could we *borrow* your car? She has an *errand* to run.
It's *important.*
Sure.
You're not going *with* her?
No, I've got somewhere *else* to be.

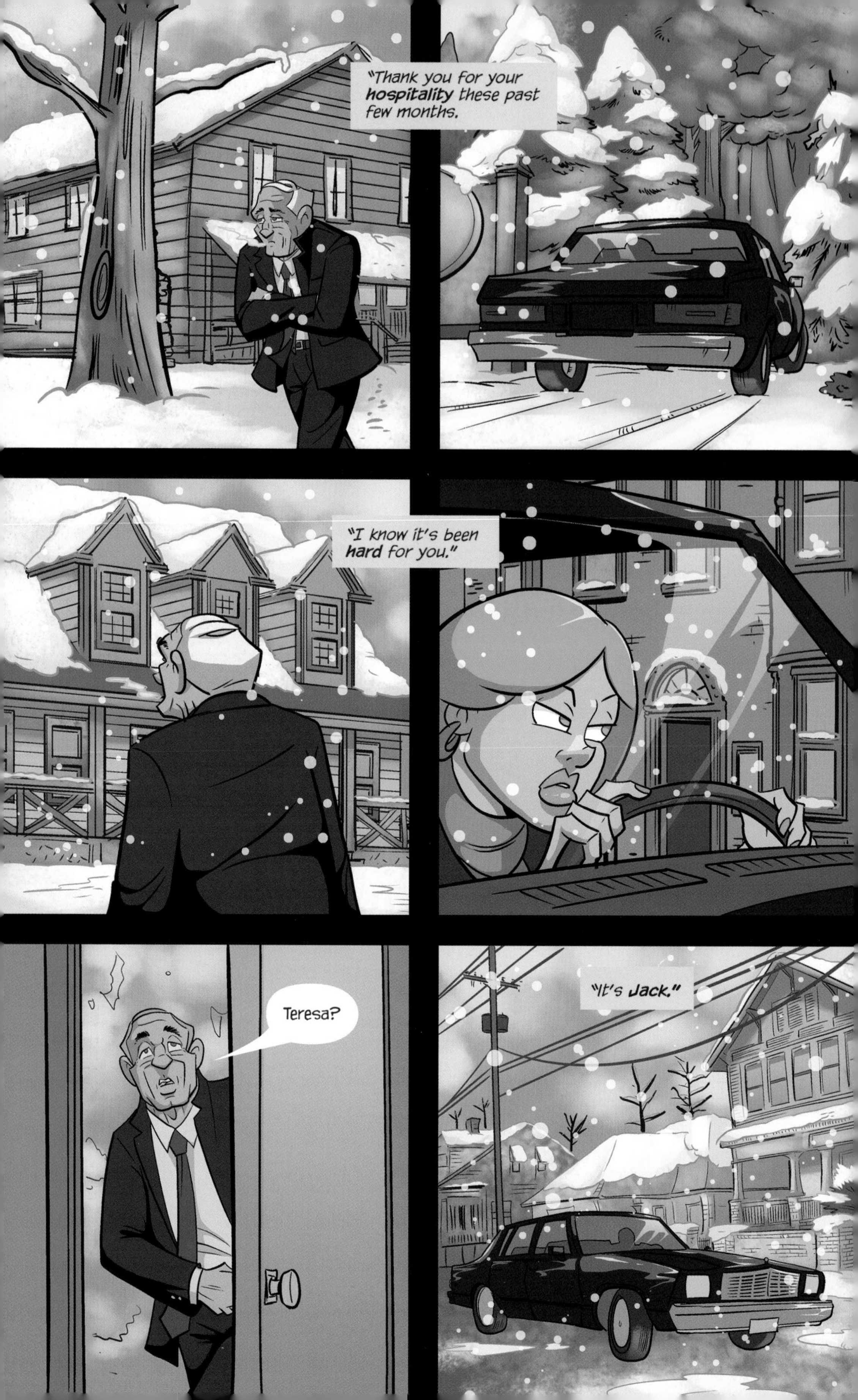
"Thank you for your **hospitality** these past few months.
"I know it's been **hard** for you."
Teresa?
"It's **Jack.**"

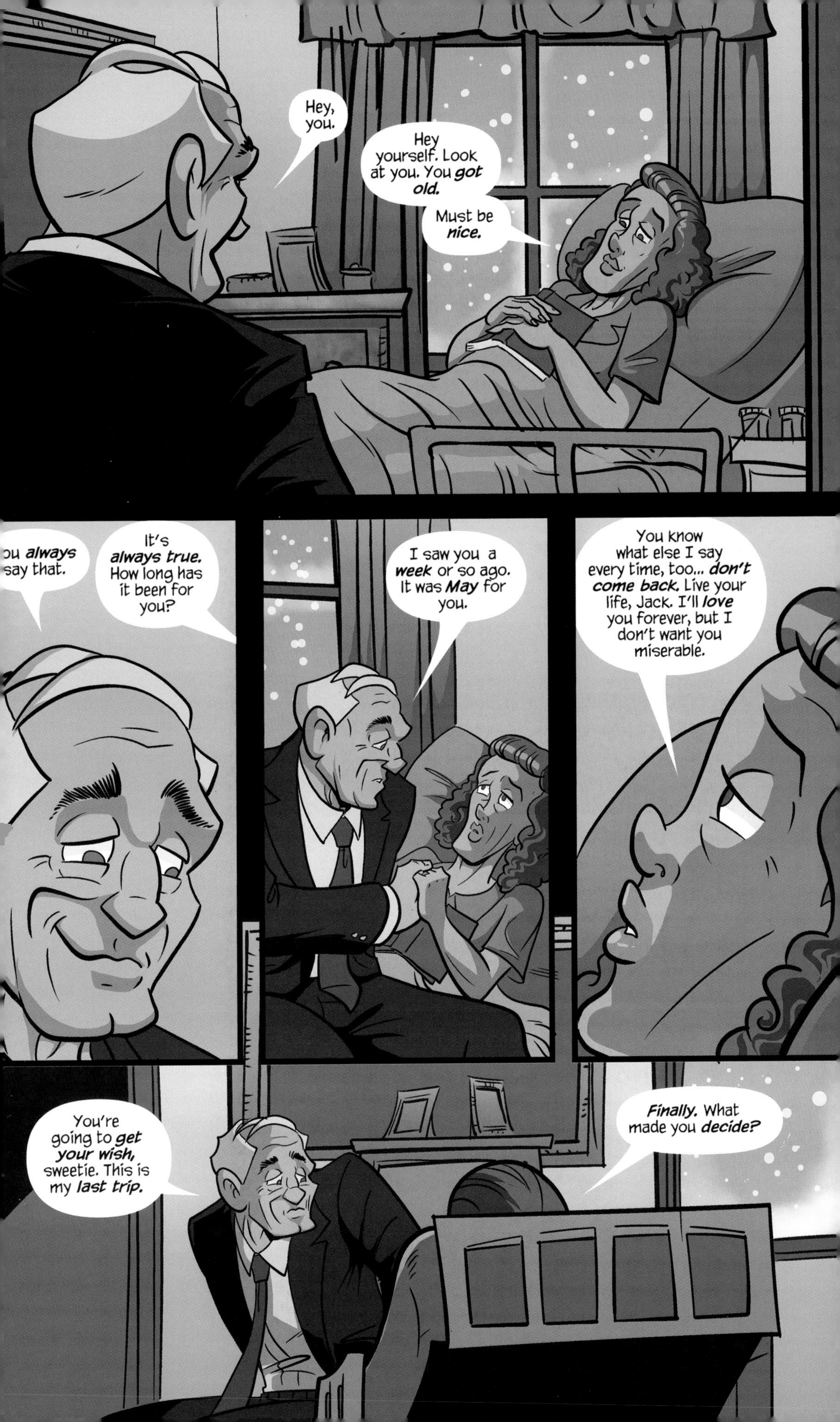
Hey, you.
Hey yourself. Look at you. You *got old.*
Must be *nice.*
...ou *always* say that.
It's *always true.* How long has it been for you?
I saw you a *week* or so ago. It was *May* for you.
You know what else I say every time, too... *don't come back.* Live your life, Jack. I'll *love* you forever, but I don't want you miserable.
You're going to *get your wish,* sweetie. This is my *last trip.*
*Finally.* What made you *decide?*

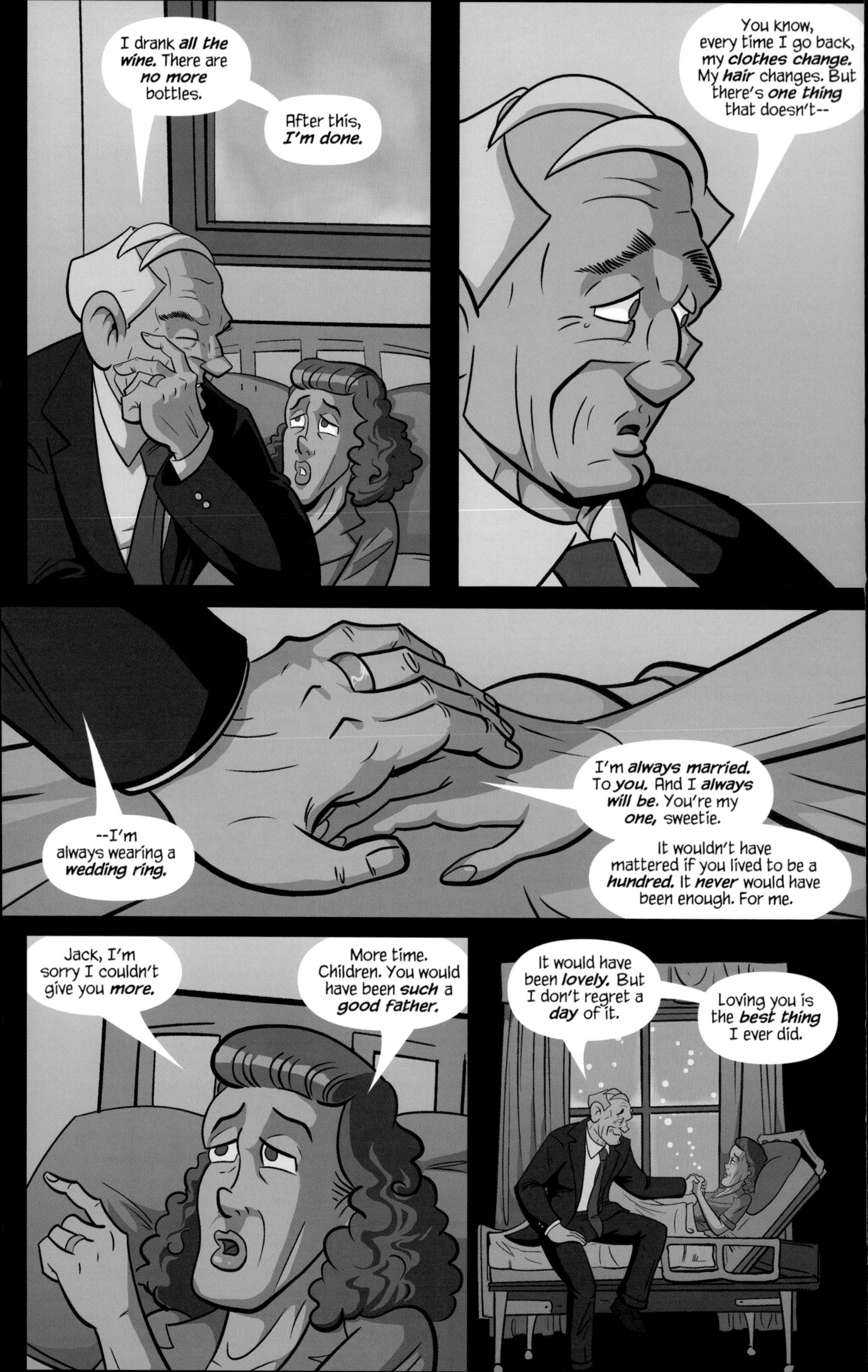
I drank all the wine. There are no more bottles.
After this, I'm done.
You know, every time I go back, my clothes change. My hair changes. But there's one thing that doesn't--
--I'm always wearing a wedding ring.
I'm always married. To you. And I always will be. You're my one, sweetie.
It wouldn't have mattered if you lived to be a hundred. It never would have been enough. For me.
Jack, I'm sorry I couldn't give you more.
More time. Children. You would have been such a good father.
It would have been lovely. But I don't regret a day of it.
Loving you is the best thing I ever did.

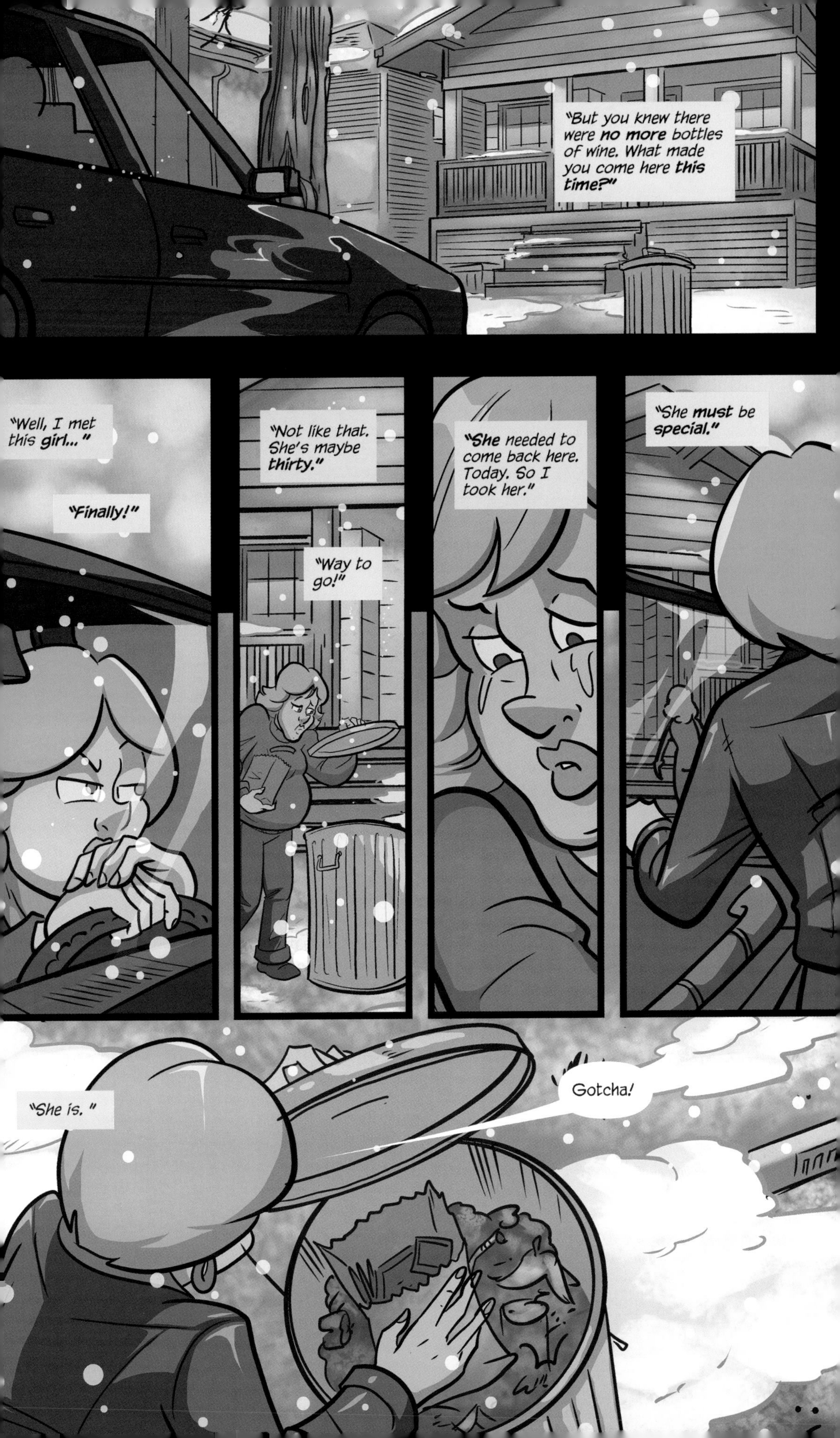

"But you knew there were **no more** bottles of wine. What made you come here **this time?**"
"Well, I met this **girl...**"
"Finally!"
"Not like that. She's maybe **thirty.**"
"Way to go!"
"**She** needed to come back here. Today. So I took her."
"She **must** be **special.**"
"She is."
Gotcha!

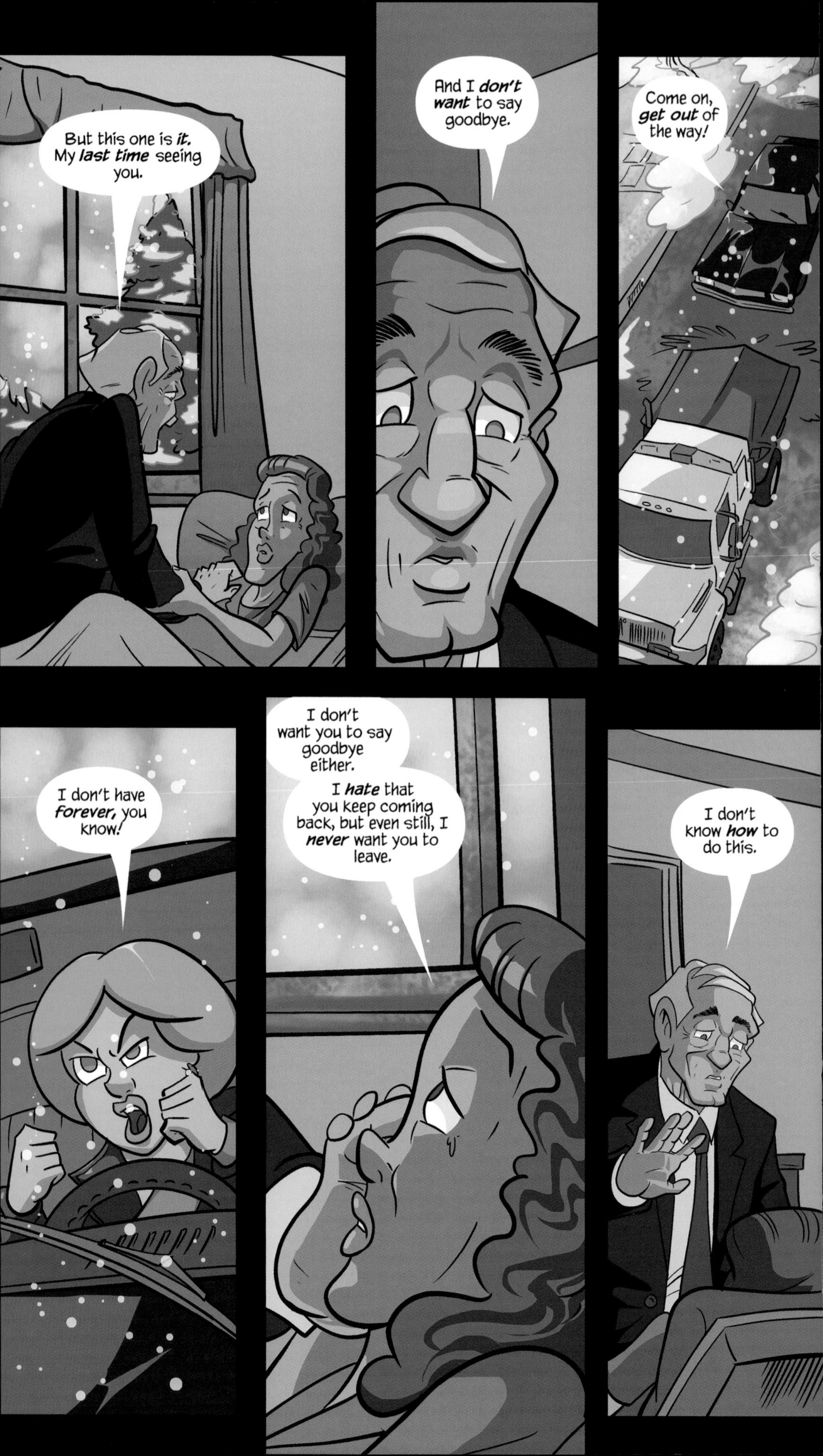

But this one is *it.* My *last time* seeing you.
And I *don't want* to say goodbye.
Come on, *get out* of the way!
I don't have *forever,* you know!
I don't want you to say goodbye either.
I *hate* that you keep coming back, but even still, I *never* want you to leave.
I don't know *how* to do this.

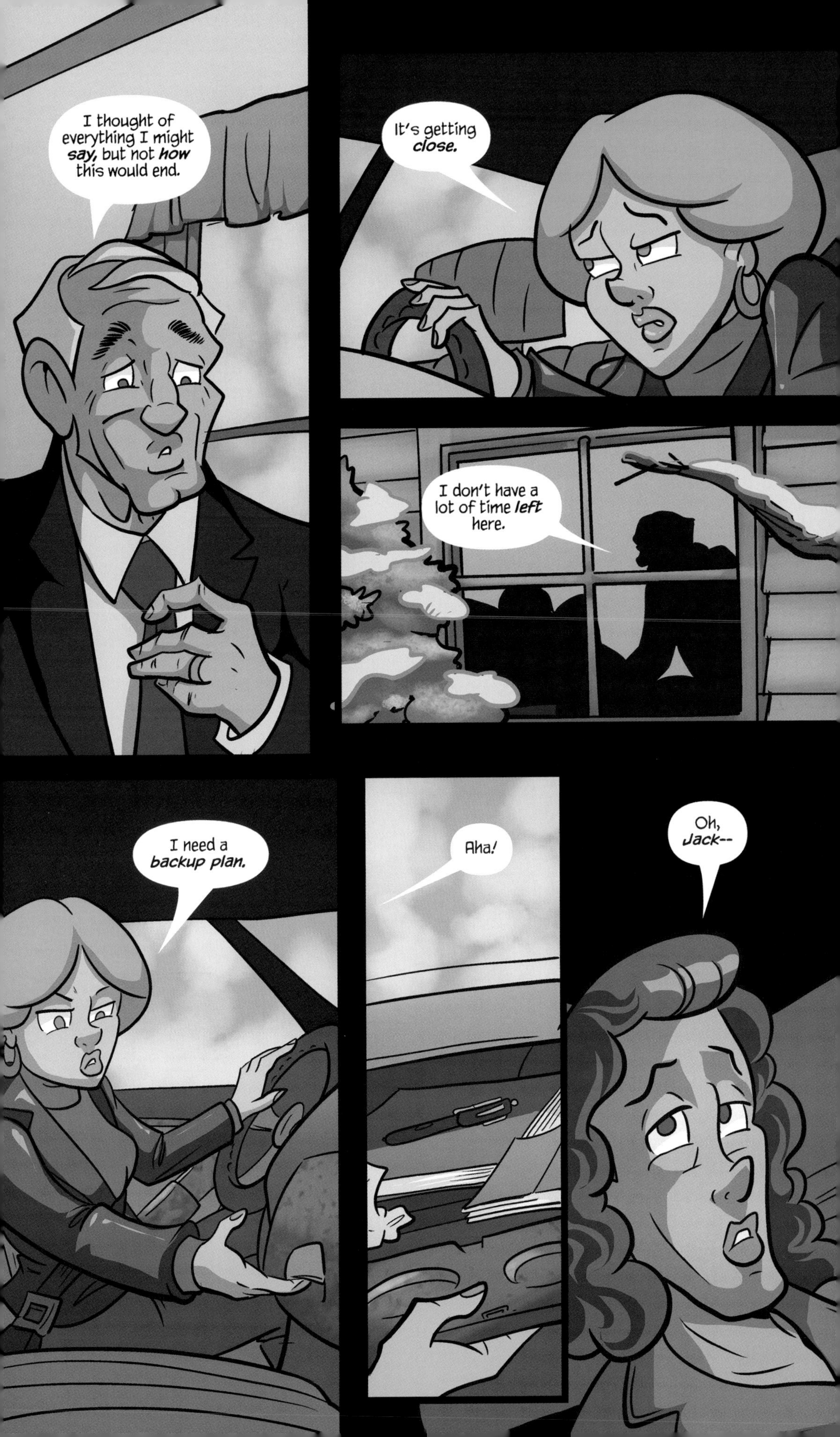
I thought of everything I might *say,* but not *how* this would end.
It's getting *close.*
I don't have a lot of time *left* here.
I need a *backup plan.*
Aha!
Oh, *Jack--*

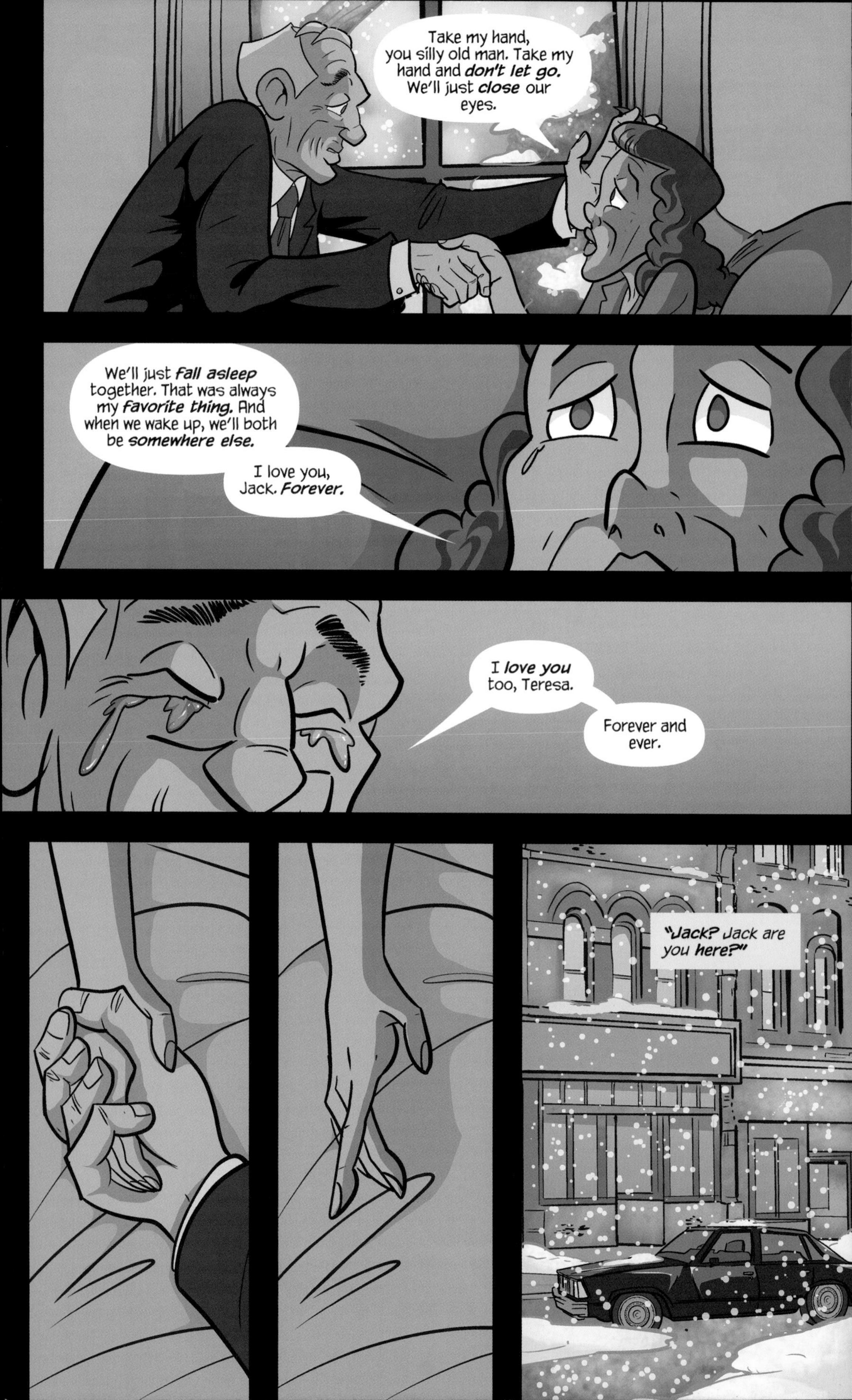
Take my hand, you silly old man. Take my hand and ***don't let go.*** We'll just ***close*** our eyes.
We'll just ***fall asleep*** together. That was always my ***favorite thing.*** And when we wake up, we'll both be ***somewhere else.***
I love you, Jack. ***Forever.***
I ***love you*** too, Teresa.
Forever and ever.
"Jack? Jack are you ***here?***"

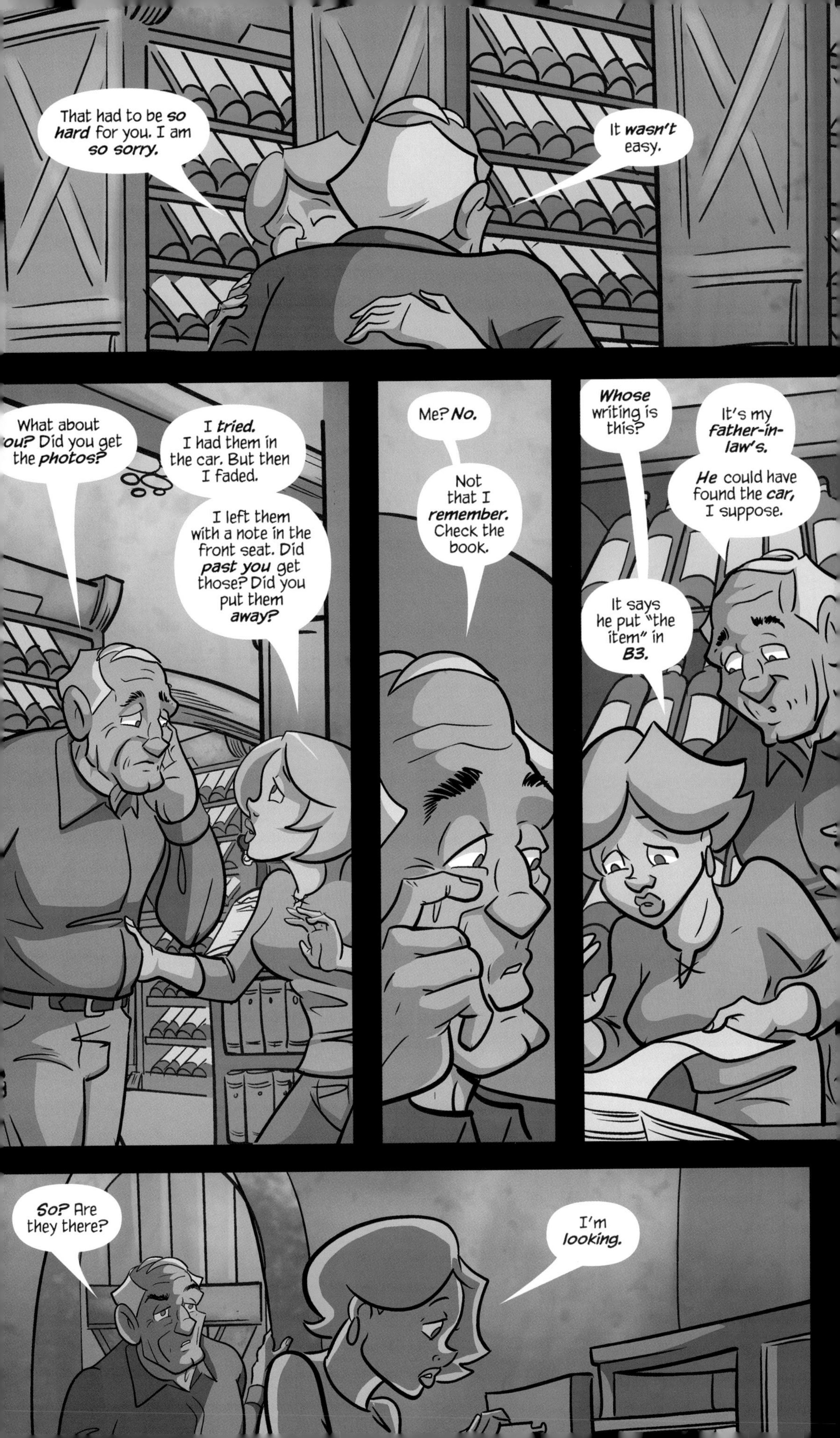
That had to be **so hard** for you. I am **so sorry.**
It **wasn't** easy.
What about ou? Did you get the **photos?**
I **tried.** I had them in the car. But then I faded.
I left them with a note in the front seat. Did **past you** get those? Did you put them **away?**
Me? **No.**
Not that I **remember.** Check the book.
**Whose** writing is this?
It's my **father-in-law's.**
**He** could have found the **car,** I suppose.
It says he put "the item" in **B3.**
**So?** Are they there?
I'm **looking.**

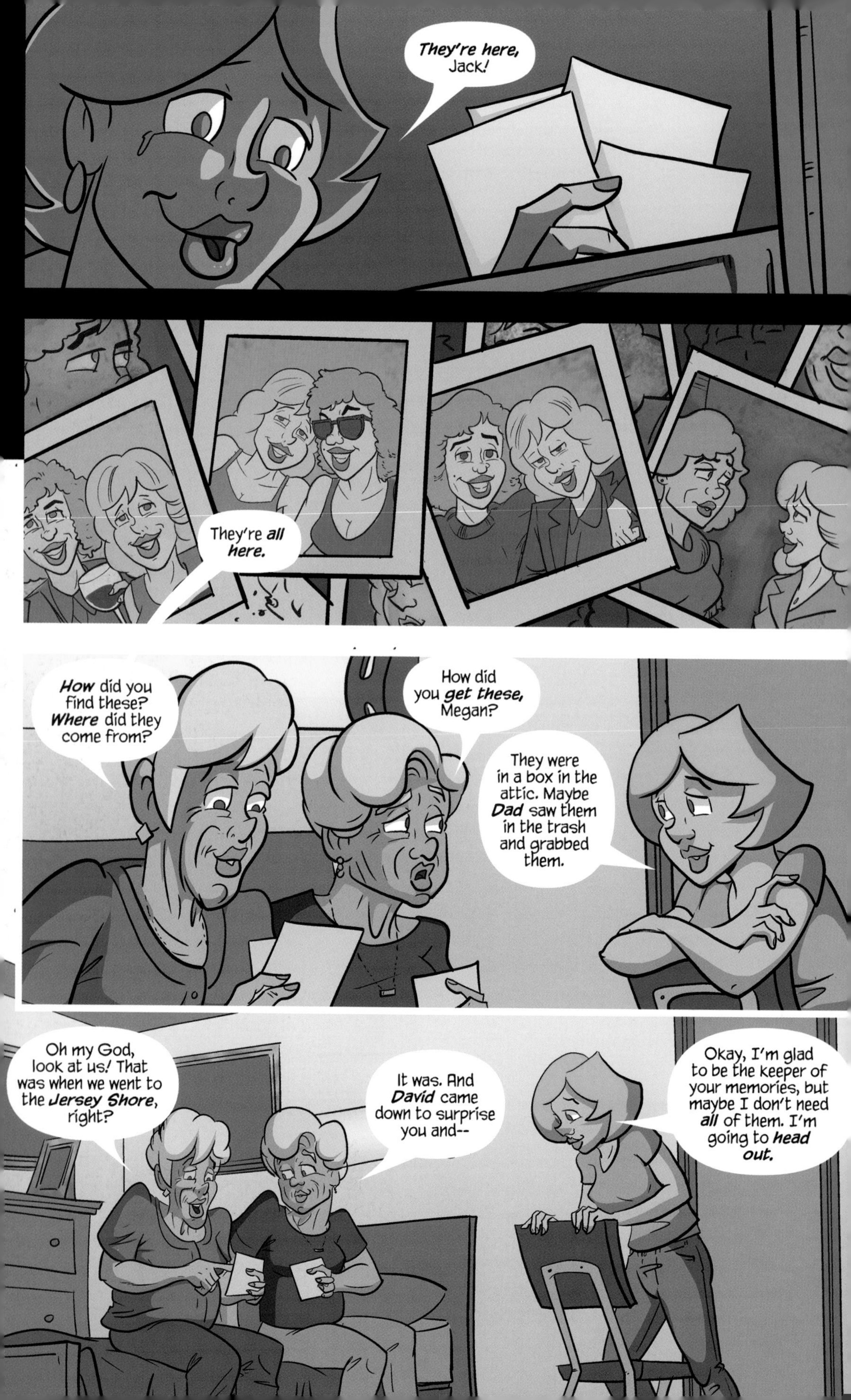

*They're here,* Jack!
They're *all here.*
*How* did you find these? *Where* did they come from?
How did you *get these,* Megan?
They were in a box in the attic. Maybe *Dad* saw them in the trash and grabbed them.
Oh my God, look at us! That was when we went to the *Jersey Shore,* right?
It was. And *David* came down to surprise you and--
Okay, I'm glad to be the keeper of your memories, but maybe I don't need *all* of them. I'm going to *head out.*

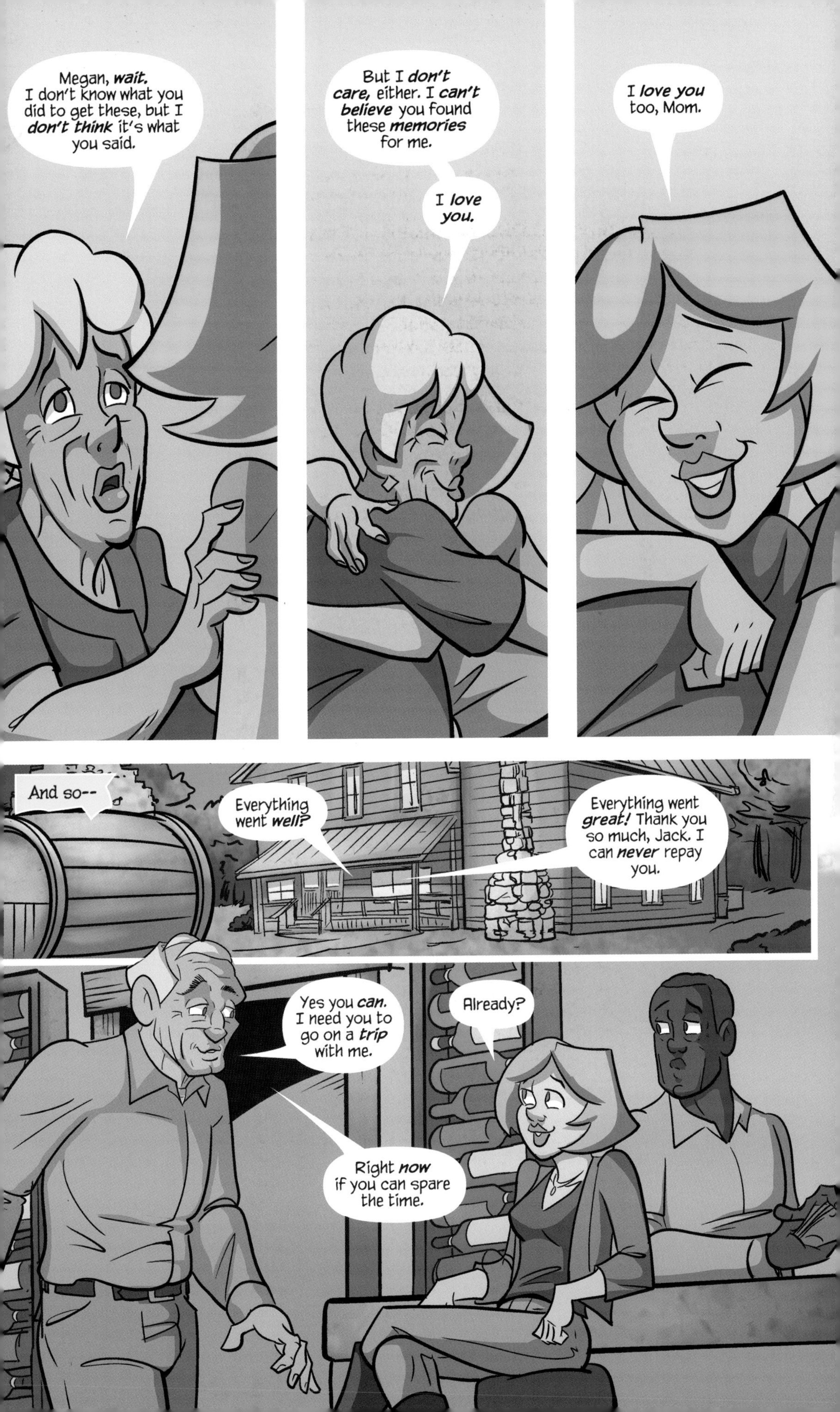
Megan, *wait.* I don't know what you did to get these, but I *don't think* it's what you said.
But I *don't care,* either. I *can't believe* you found these *memories* for me.
I *love you.*
I *love you* too, Mom.
And so--
Everything went *well?*
Everything went *great!* Thank you so much, Jack. I can *never* repay you.
Yes you *can.* I need you to go on a *trip* with me.
Right *now* if you can spare the time.
Already?

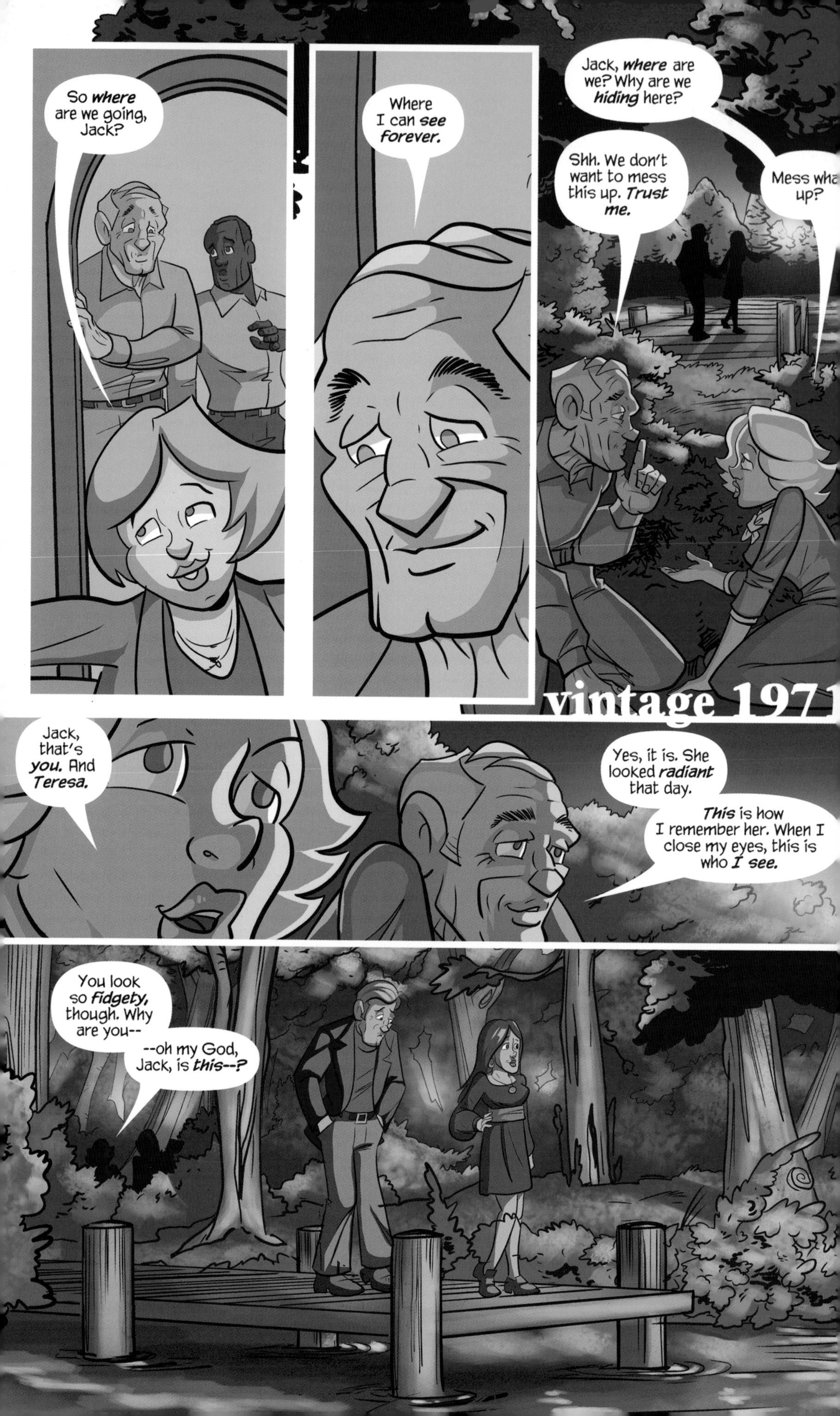

So *where* are we going, Jack?
Where I can *see forever.*
Jack, *where* are we? Why are we *hiding* here?
Shh. We don't want to mess this up. *Trust me.*
Mess wha up?
vintage 197
Jack, that's *you.* And *Teresa.*
Yes, it is. She looked *radiant* that day.
*This* is how I remember her. When I close my eyes, this is who *I see.*
You look so *fidgety,* though. Why are you--
--oh my God, Jack, is *this--?*

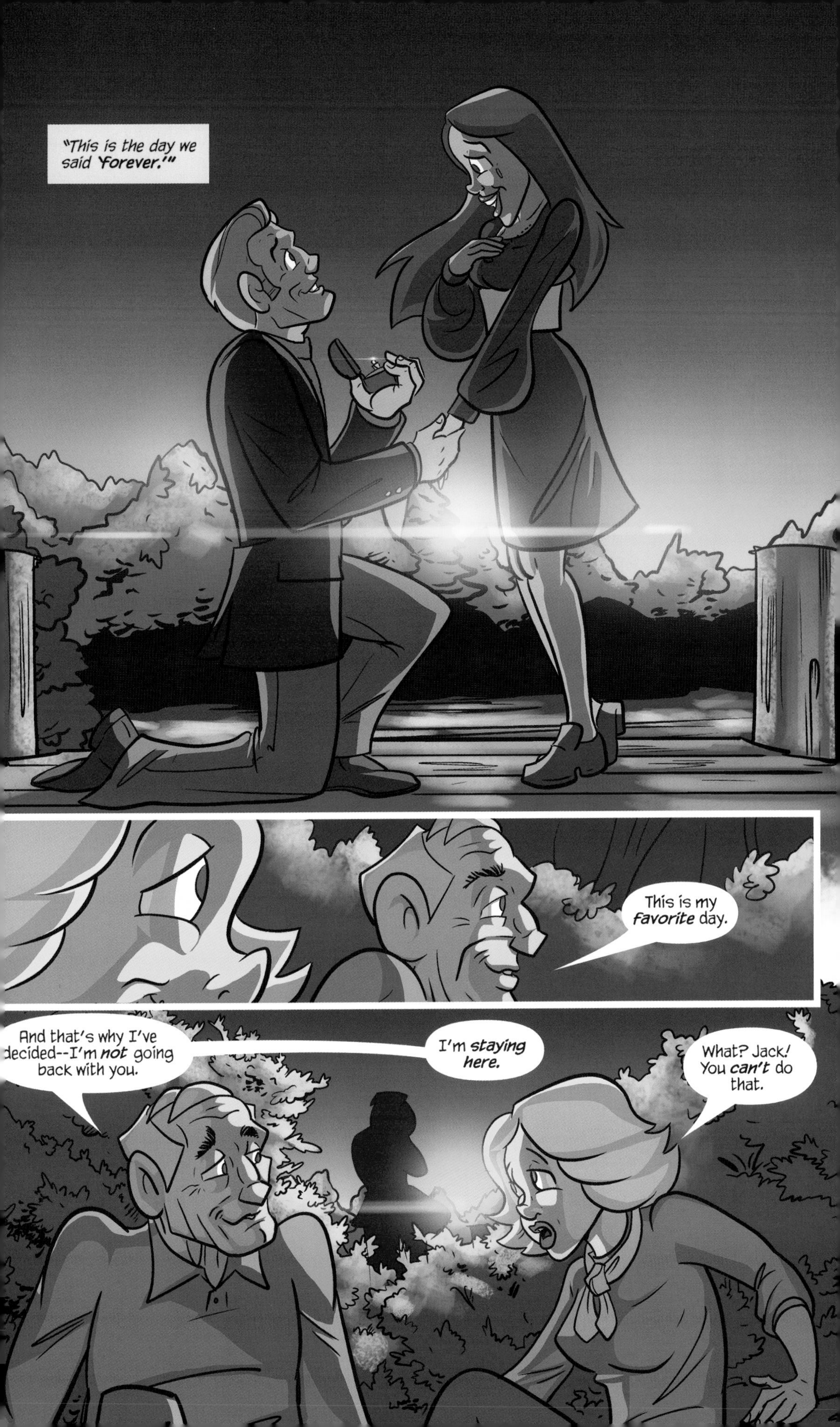
"This is the day we said *forever.*"
This is my *favorite* day.
And that's why I've decided--I'm *not* going back with you.
I'm *staying here.*
What? Jack! You *can't* do that.

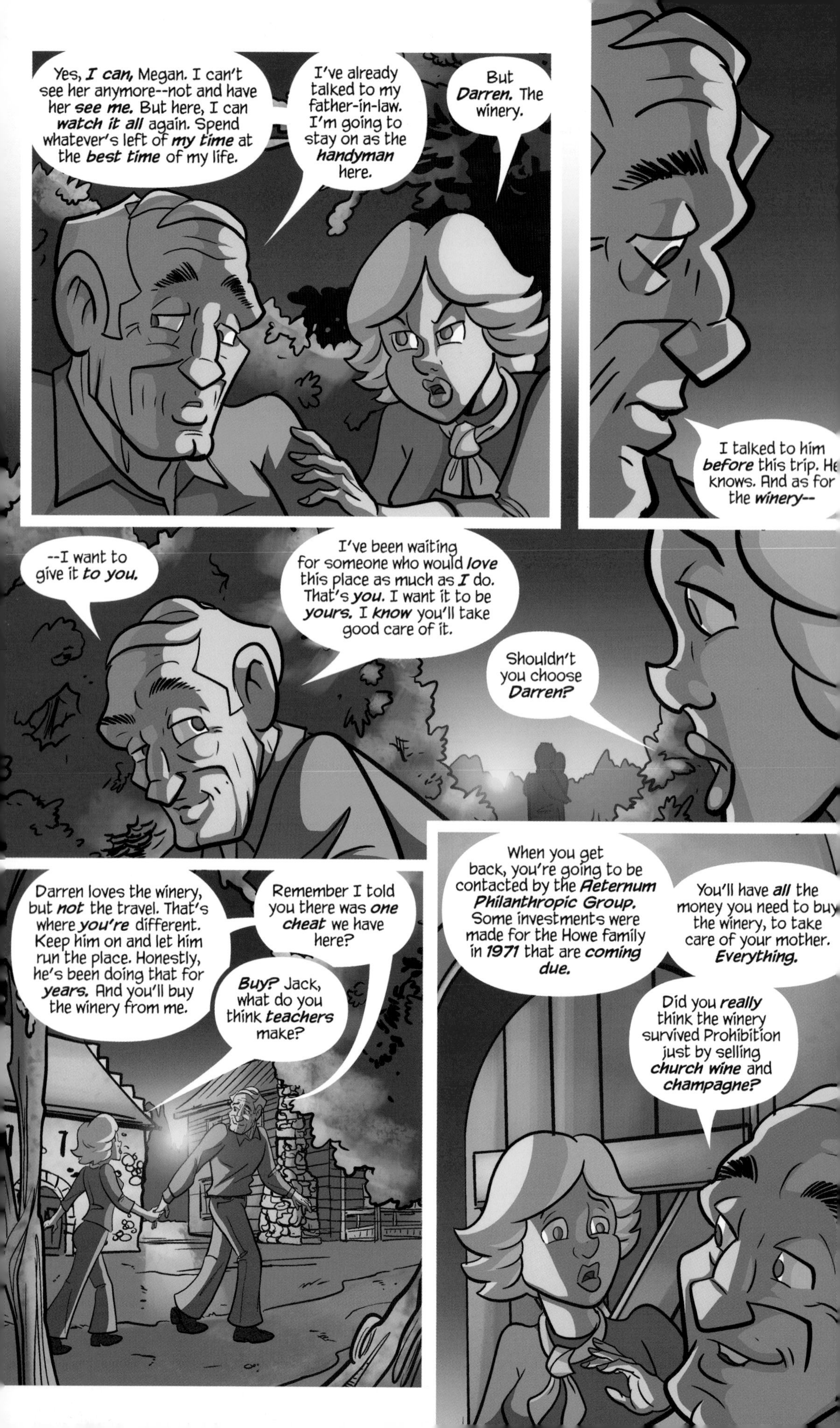
Yes, I can, Megan. I can't see her anymore--not and have her see me. But here, I can watch it all again. Spend whatever's left of my time at the best time of my life.
I've already talked to my father-in-law. I'm going to stay on as the handyman here.
But Darren. The winery.
I talked to him before this trip. He knows. And as for the winery--
--I want to give it to you.
I've been waiting for someone who would love this place as much as I do. That's you. I want it to be yours. I know you'll take good care of it.
Shouldn't you choose Darren?
Darren loves the winery, but not the travel. That's where you're different. Keep him on and let him run the place. Honestly, he's been doing that for years. And you'll buy the winery from me.
Buy? Jack, what do you think teachers make?
Remember I told you there was one cheat we have here?
When you get back, you're going to be contacted by the Aeternum Philanthropic Group. Some investments were made for the Howe family in 1971 that are coming due.
You'll have all the money you need to buy the winery, to take care of your mother. Everything.
Did you really think the winery survived Prohibition just by selling church wine and champagne?

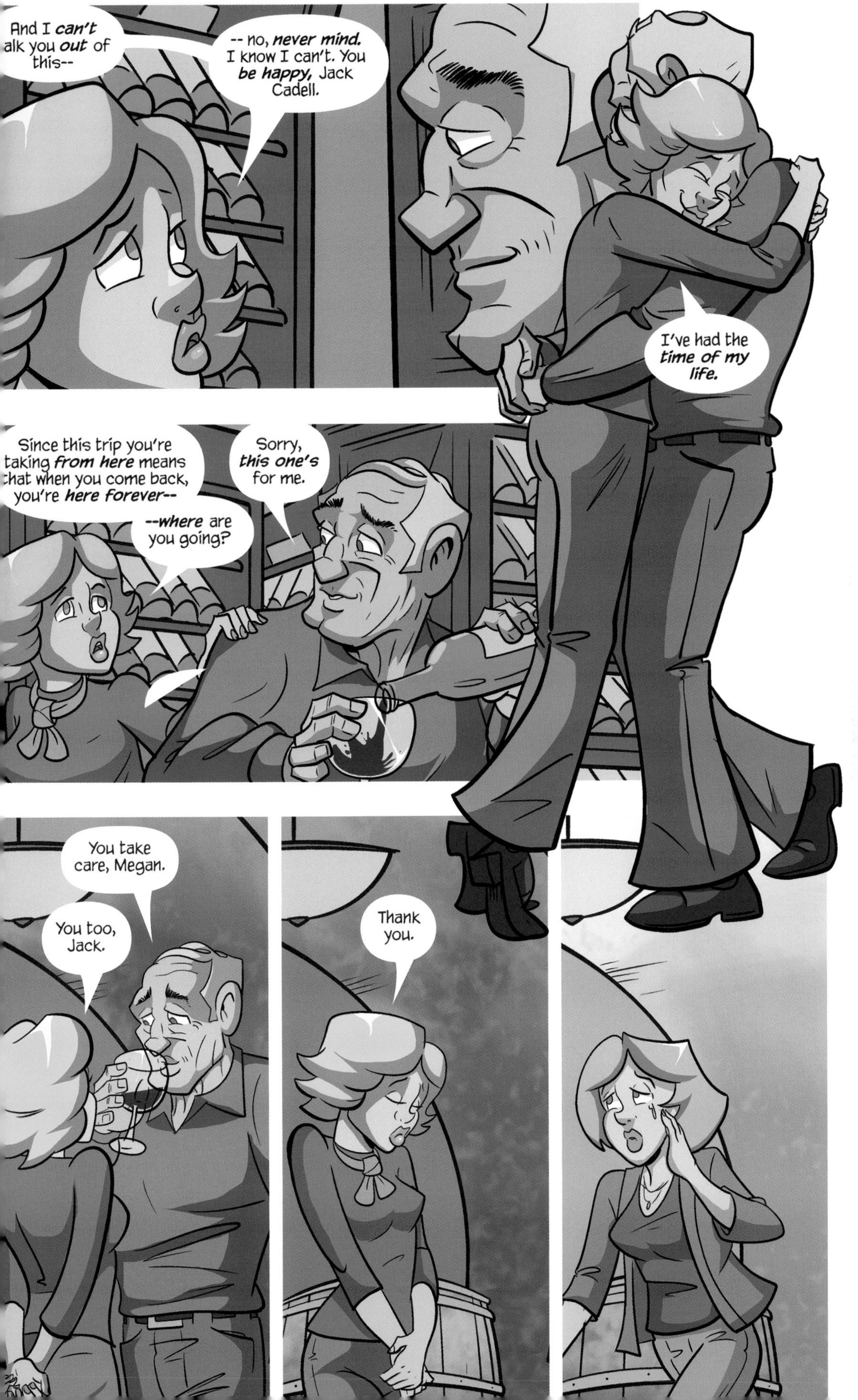
And I can't alk you out of this--
-- no, never mind. I know I can't. You be happy, Jack Cadell.
I've had the time of my life.
Since this trip you're taking from here means that when you come back, you're here forever--
--where are you going?
Sorry, this one's for me.
You take care, Megan.
You too, Jack.
Thank you.

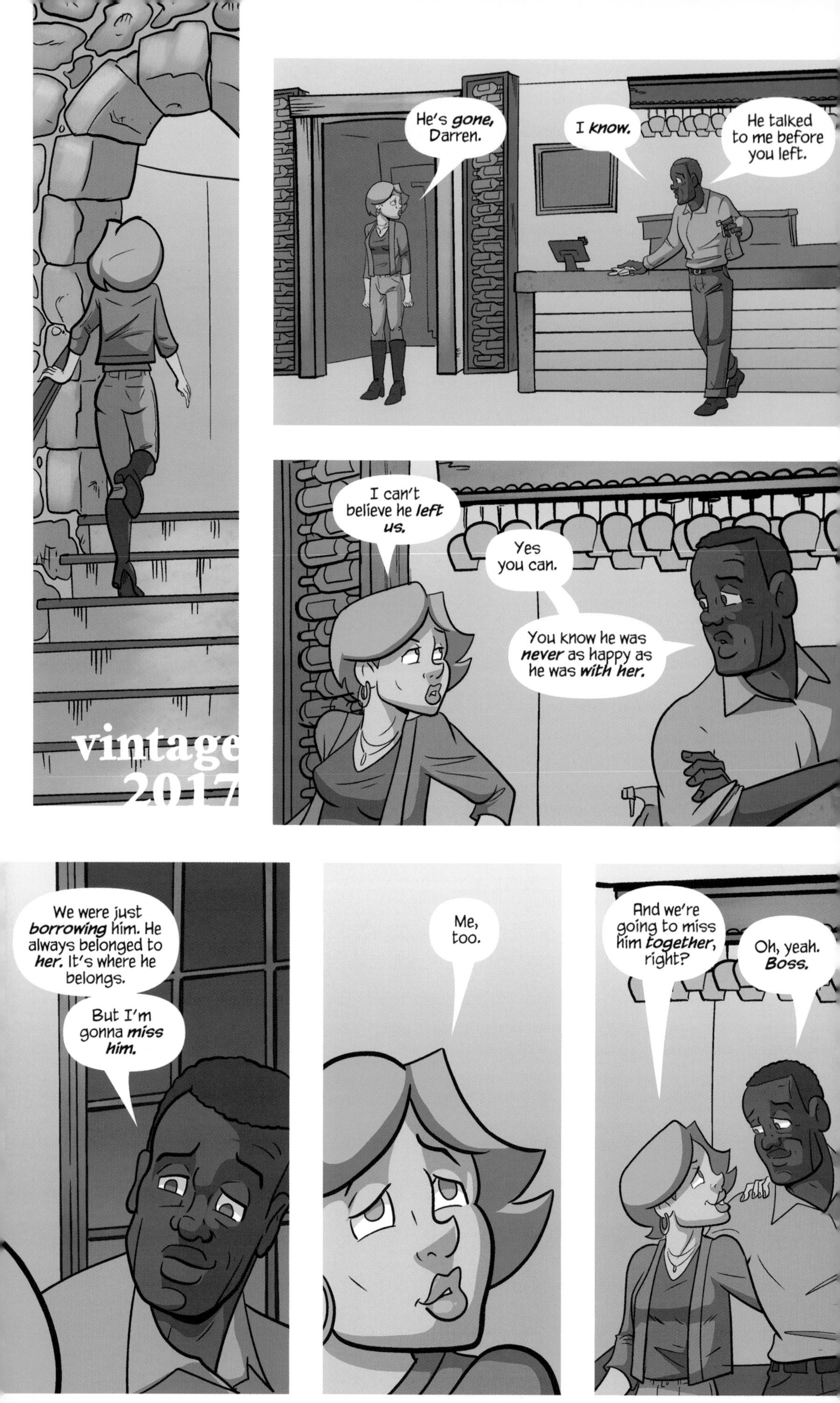
vintage
2017
He's gone, Darren.
I know.
He talked to me before you left.
I can't believe he left us.
Yes you can.
You know he was never as happy as he was with her.
We were just borrowing him. He always belonged to her. It's where he belongs.
But I'm gonna miss him.
Me, too.
And we're going to miss him together, right?
Oh, yeah. Boss.

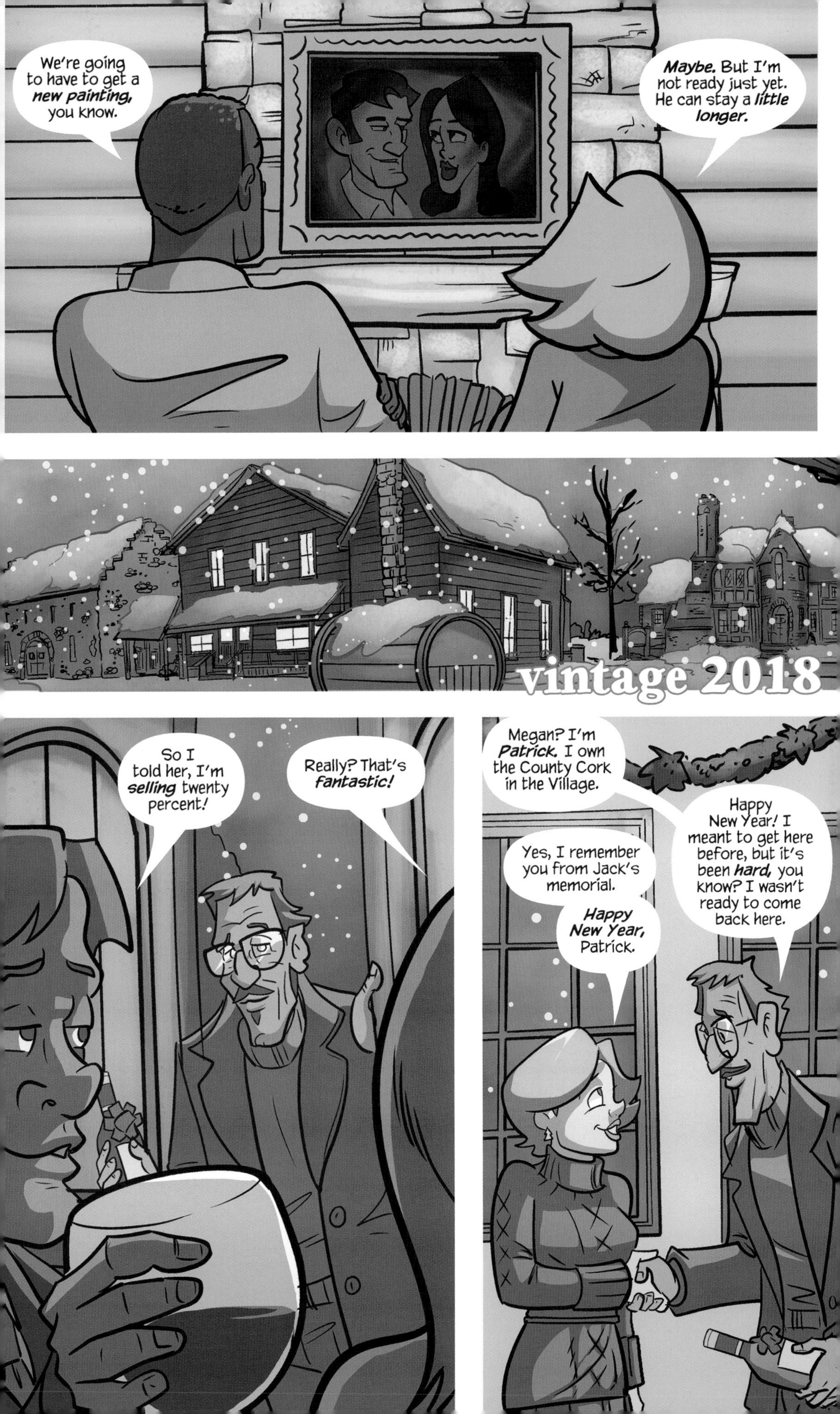

We're going to have to get a new painting, you know.
Maybe. But I'm not ready just yet. He can stay a little longer.
vintage 2018
So I told her, I'm selling twenty percent!
Really? That's fantastic!
Megan? I'm Patrick. I own the County Cork in the Village.
Happy New Year! I meant to get here before, but it's been hard, you know? I wasn't ready to come back here.
Yes, I remember you from Jack's memorial.
Happy New Year, Patrick.

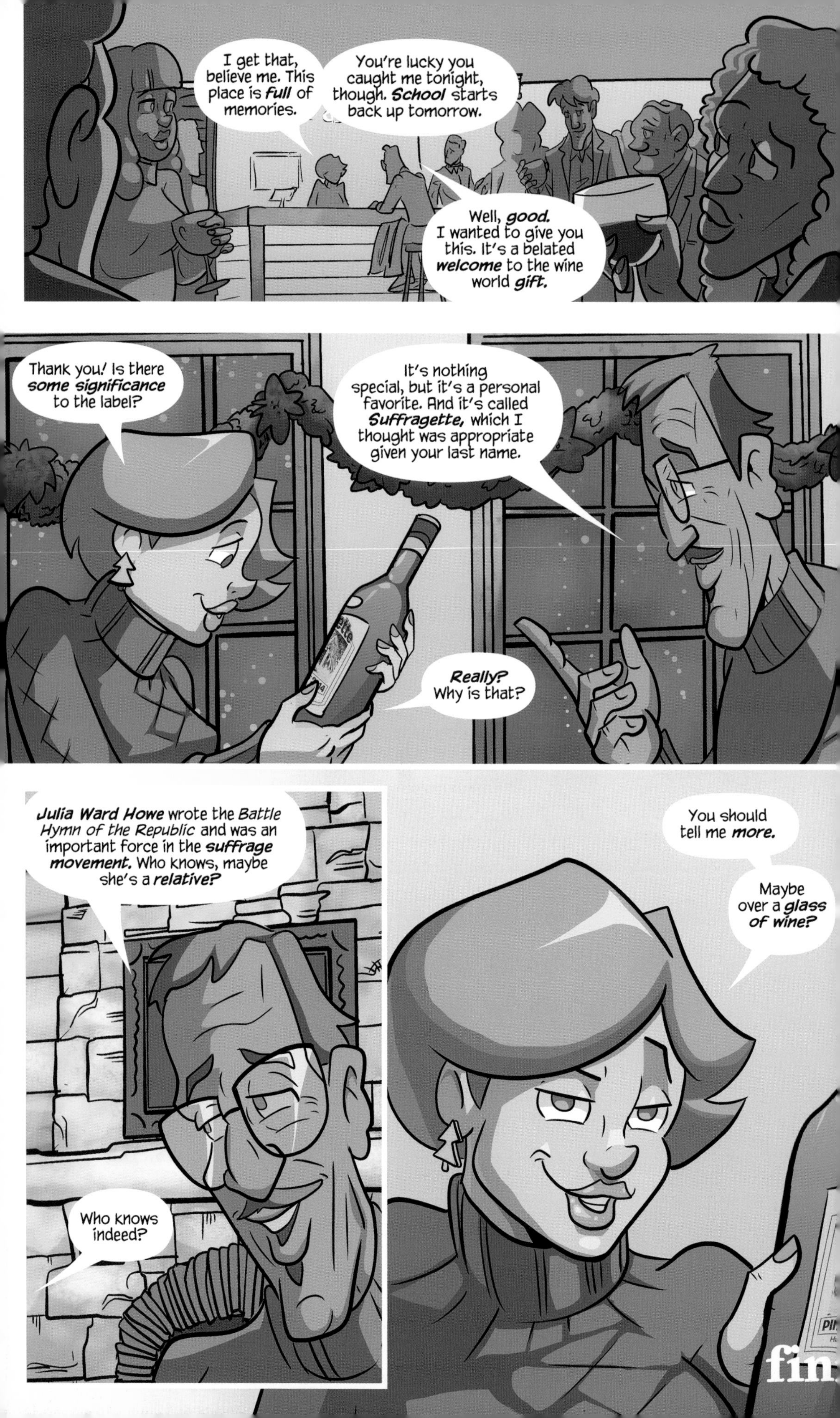

I get that, believe me. This place is *full* of memories.
You're lucky you caught me tonight, though. ***School*** starts back up tomorrow.
Well, ***good.*** I wanted to give you this. It's a belated ***welcome*** to the wine world ***gift.***
Thank you! Is there ***some significance*** to the label?
It's nothing special, but it's a personal favorite. And it's called ***Suffragette,*** which I thought was appropriate given your last name.
***Really?*** Why is that?
***Julia Ward Howe*** wrote the *Battle Hymn of the Republic* and was an important force in the ***suffrage movement.*** Who knows, maybe she's a ***relative?***
Who knows indeed?
You should tell me ***more.***
Maybe over a ***glass of wine?***
fin

# Uncorking the Story

Just like the Aeternum Winery, this book has some murky beginnings.

I remember Kurt Busiek tweeting something about daring someone to write a comic about a winery. And it just hit me. Or I remembered an idea. But suddenly there it was: A winery that, when you drink a bottle from 1912, you go back to 1912.

I feel like there was more. That there was some other story, that it was percolating in my brain. That it came about in some other way. But suddenly, this idea had always been there.

Just like Aeternum.

It was a good concept. But there was no story for it.

I was pretty fresh off of writing *Long Distance* and I was bound and determined not to let too much time go between projects like I had between that and *Love and Capes*. It had also been a rough summer, and I was spending a lot of time taking walks in my tree-filled neighborhood. It was turning to fall and I just started thinking about drawing trees and how cool it would be to show the changing of seasons and time.

And then everything clicked. (Or clinked.) Telling the love story of the this old man who owned the winery non-linearly by weaving trips back in time with his new friend, a young lady, with whom he's decided to share the secrets of the winery.

But this wasn't the story I was planning on telling next. I had some other ideas. Honestly, I can't remember what they were now. Maybe a spy story. Maybe one with angels. But, whatever, when *Time and Vine* hit, I didn't have any other choice. It just got its hooks in me.

This needed some research.

The first thing I did was Google "oldest winery in the United States."

# Brotherhood Winery

There's a winery in New York state called Brotherhood. It started in 1839, and it was perfect. It was the time period I wanted. It was the place I wanted. Sure, California is known for its wines, but the history in New York was too good. I initially wanted to go back to the American Revolution, but the Civil War would work just fine. That was almost two hundred years to play with.

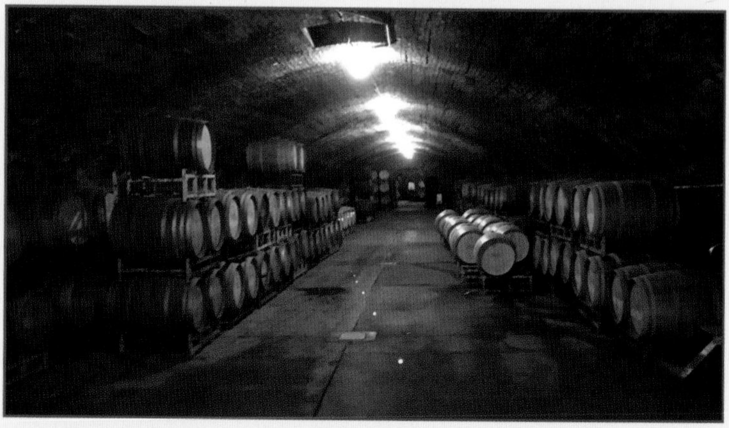

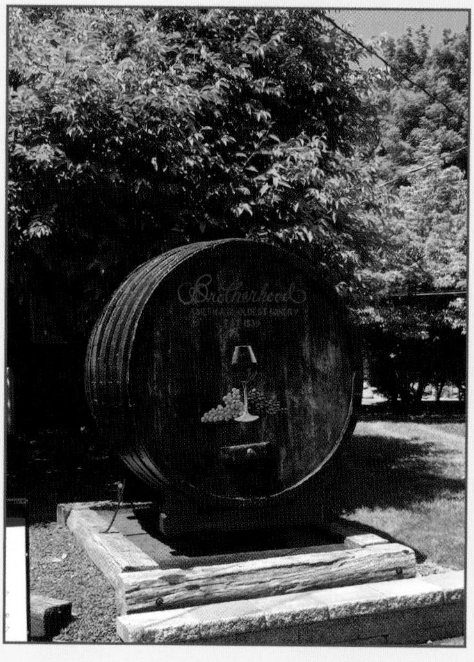
Brotherhood

They had a book, which I spent maybe fifteen minutes agonizing about buying before I ordered it. I read it the minute it came. The story of this winery became my road map for my story: surviving Prohibition, multiple owners and a storied history.

Still, this was going to require a field trip, of course. Fortunately friends of mine live in New Jersey and offered to go with me. It's so hard getting people to go to wineries. Except for the part where it isn't.

We took a trip and I learned so much. I learned about the champagne, the cider, the church wine. I walked the grounds and took the tour. I bought some wine, of course. And even drank some. You know. For science.

And, to flash ahead, Brotherhood was very kind when I called for research purposes. You know how Jack says you could call locally-made sparkling wine "champagne" in chapter one? They were my source on that.

But this is a tale of three wineries.

## Debonne Vineyards

Northeast Ohio, where I live, has some really amazing wineries in the

Grand River Valley. I've gone to more than a few of them. One of them, Debonne Vineyards, is one of the better known ones. And, at a wine festival I went to, I learned that the sommelier was someone that I went to grade school with. And their winemaker was someone I went to high school with.

That's some tight plotting.

So, I imposed upon my friend for a tour. One winter's morning, I went out there and got the full tour. Everything I know about making wine came from that trip. My friend spent way too much time answering all my questions.

Side note: One of the cool things Debonne has is "cask wine." They have a giant cask filled with two-thirds of the best wine they've ever made over the years. They pour in another third of the curent year's best. And then they let it

mix and draw out one third and sell it.

That sounded magical. But cask wines, they don't have vintages. So that wouldn't work for what I needed.

Because of that, I knew enough to write about making wine, I hoped.

## Hundley Cellars

But there's a third place, Hundley Cellars, that I really love. It's a fun, rustic building and it's just kind of perfect. And, if you ever go there, along with whatever wine you enjoy, get the brownie pretzel dessert. That thing haunts me.

Hundley had a fireplace, and I imagined the painting of Jack and his wife hanging over it. That was the feeling of the place I wanted to write about. That was the first visual in my head.

## Best Laid Plans

So I had it. Or so I thought. I worked out my story and David Hedgecock, my editor, approved it. I started going forward. As I usually did, I started straying from my plot. My original idea was that Megan would use the winery to get in touch with the mother she was losing.

But then I wrote issue two. And I had Megan go back to the

Eighties and run into her mother. I wanted her to see her mother doing something that she never imagined. Smoking? But that wasn't enough. I needed something bigger. Something that would change how she would see her mom.

And then something whispered in my ear "She has a sister."

That wasn't my plan. Megan didn't have an unknown aunt in my pitch. But then she did. And it made so much sense. That was my story, and I didn't even see it.

From there, everything just kind of happened. Megan's story became so much bigger and so much more important. Her story finally had the same heft as Jack's. And it was just so natural.

How natural? You would think that I'd planned to have Jack's wife's death coincide with Megan's birth.

Except I didn't. It was destiny.

## Above and Beyond

I haven't done this before, but I want to call some people out specifically:

*Mike Bokausek,* my first and most trusted reader, who didn't mind me leaving his family at Universal Studios so I could set up in Jake's Bar and script issue #3. Because of him, Jack and Megan's first meeting plays so well, and the time travel stuff sounds so clear.

*Kara Evans,* who named the winery and responded to all my "hey, what if I did this?" texts. As well as being moral support, and my chief wine consultant.

*Lora Innes,* who told me this story was as much Megan's story as Jack's. Also, for being my friend to whom I can text historical underwear questions.

And *Marc Nathan,* who said "and he's drunk all the wine" and believed in this story more than I did sometimes.

# Labeling the Past

**You might not notice, but the Aeternum Winery has had different labels throughout the years. They're barely seen, but I wanted to have labels that represented the graphic design of each period.**

AETERNUM WINERY
1866
PINOT NOIR
JEFFERSONVILLE • NY
JEFFERSONVILLE ⋆ NY
Aeternum Winery
1945
CABERNET SAUVIGNON
Aeternum Winery
19 cabernet sauvignon 87
JEFFERSONVILLE ⋆ NY
Aeternum WINERY
2016
MERLOT
JEFFERSONVILLE • NY

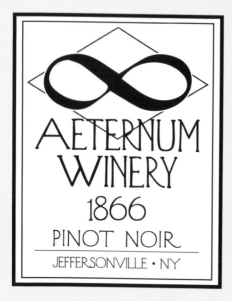

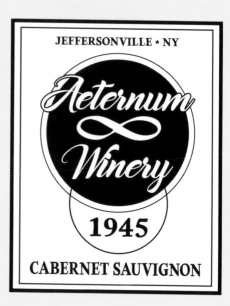

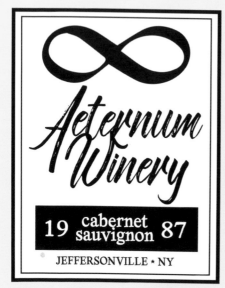

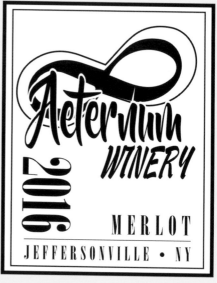

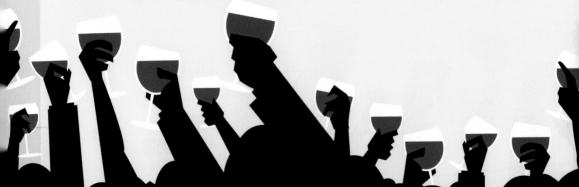

# Concept Art

To the right is the first real piece of concept art I did for *Time and Vine*. I was experimenting with styles and coloring techniques and everything in this piece. I remember giving Jack what I clearly thought was a Darwyn Cooke nose. Honestly, both he and Megan have distinctive noses to help the characters be recognizable as we see Jack at multiple ages and Megan with multiple hairstyles. I went back to this piece any time I felt lost.

I was extremely fortunate, too, that I found Luigi Anderson to color the book. He managed to bring a nuance to the book that I wouldn't have been able to (as evidenced by this sample page reproduced here). He brought a different feel to each time period that I would have been unable to. If I'd colored it, a lot of the romance would have been lost on the page.

## Zahler

Thom Zahler figured out how to write his wine bills off for a year. What else do you need to know about him?

He's a graduate of the Kubert School and has worked in comics for over fifteen years. He created the superhero romantic comedy *Love and Capes* published by IDW, and the magical romance *Warning Label* for Line Webtoons. He writes and draws covers for IDW's *My Little Pony* series, too, because he's versatile.

He has also written for the Disney XD series *Ultimate Spider-Man: Web Warriors* and the Netflix series *Knights of the Zodiac*.

He lives in northeast Ohio in an ice fortress with two cats, more action figures than he can count, and a constantly dwindling supply of wine. He has a goatee now, too. So he's evil.

Follow him on Twitter and Instagram @thomzahler.

## Luigi Anderson

David "Luigi" Anderson is a Texas-born, Atlanta-based artist who has been drawing ever since he could hold a pencil. It wasn't until he was almost out of college that he managed to put to good use all the hours spent with crayon in hand, filling page after page in his favorite coloring books, when Oni press gave him his first coloring job. The rest has been history; a great new career working with incredible talent on awesome books. People have said he's really good at this whole coloring business, but people say a lot of things that aren't true, so you may not want to believe them just yet.

## Special Thanks to

Chris "Doc" Wyatt ★ Bill Williams ★ Greg Weisman ★ Scott Weinstein
Brian Ward ★ Deitri Villarreal ★ Ed Trebets ★ Sean Tiffany
Paul Storrie ★ Eugene Son ★ Jill Smith ★ James Santangelo
Joel Sandrey ★ Chris Ryall ★ Roger Price ★ Marc Nathan ★ Chase Marotz
Jon Monson-Foon ★ David Kemp ★ Jesse Jackson
Tony Isabella ★ Lora Innes ★ Bob Ingersoll ★ Hundley Cellars
Bob Greenberger ★ Greg Goldstein ★ Tony Fleecs ★ Alan Evans
Kara Evans ★ Todd Dezago ★ Carmen DeLuccia ★ Debonne Vineyards
Kelly Dale ★ Luke Daab ★ Katie Cook ★ Steve Conley
Mike Collins ★ Kurt Busiek ★ Brotherhood Winery
Mike Bokausek ★ Christy Blanch

*Cover art photography by David Kemp*